I0634639

Mistake

LOST BOYS BOOK 1

EMILIA FINN

bee*lieve*
PUBLISHING, Pty Ltd.

Copyright © 2023 Emilia Finn

All rights reserved. No part of this publication may be reproduced, distributed, or transmitted in any form or by any means, including photocopying, recording, or other electronic or mechanical methods, without the prior written permission of the publisher, except in the case of brief quotations embodied in critical reviews and certain other noncommercial uses permitted by copyright law. For permission requests, write to the publisher, addressed "Attention: Permissions Coordinator," at the address below:

info@beelievepublishing.com

ISBN: 978 1 922623 25 6 (Paperback)

Any references to historical events, real people, or real places are used fictitiously. Names, characters, and places are products of the author's imagination.

Front cover photography by: Wander Aguilar

Front cover models: Cooper S

Cover design: Britt @ The Hatters

Editing: Bird's Eye Editing

First printing edition 2023.

Beelieve Publishing, Pty Ltd

PO Box 407,

Woy Woy, NSW, 2256

Australia

www.emiliafinn.com

EMILIA FINN, the ROLLERS logo, the CHECKMATE SECURITY logo, STACKED DECK logo, and INAMORATA are all trade marks of Beelieve Publishing, Pty Ltd

Also by Emilia Finn

Sinful Promise

Lost Boys

MISTAKE

REGRET

Rollin On Novellas

(Do not read before finishing the Rollin On Series)

Begin Again – A Short Story

Written in the Stars – A Short Story

Full Circle – A Short Story

Worth Fighting For – A Bobby & Kit Novella

Maya Blake

FIRST DAY JITTERS

"Ms. Blake?" A beautiful brunette woman who can't be a hell of a lot older than my twenty-five years steps out of a school administration office with a stomach stretching ahead of her, indicating at least eight months of hard pregnancy. She wears a youthful glow in her cheeks, carries a white folder under her left arm, and grips a juice smoothie in her right hand.

Stopping in front of me with a wide smile, she transfers her smoothie and offers her hand to me. "I'm Brittany Reilly. I'm helping you with orientation today."

"Oh." Nervously, I shoot to my feet and shake her hand. "Okay. Hi."

Releasing me, she glances down at the folder under her arm and works to read my name on the front. "May-uh or My-uh?"

"My-uh," I confirm with a shaky smile.

Anxiety swarms my stomach and makes my hands shake, but I hold my head high and pretend I have myself under control. Because this is the first day of the rest of my life.

Hopefully.

"It's Maya Blake," I repeat, surer this time. "Thanks for meeting with me, Ms. Reilly."

"You can call me Britt." She makes a wide turn, very semi-truck-esque, so her stomach leads the way, then she starts along the hall. "This is the junior side of our school..."

I dash in three-inch heels to catch up to the woman in skater shoes.

"I can show you the senior side, too, if you want, but as a kindergarten teacher, I doubt you'll be heading that way anytime soon. Plus," she stops at the double-wide front doors of the main building and exhales like our trek has been as taxing as climbing a mountain. "It's a long walk I don't want to make today."

A soft smile works its way free to replace my worry. "It's fine." Then I look down at her stomach. "Is that your first baby?"

She scoffs. "Not even close. I've lost count at this point. Junior playground is over that way." She gestures toward the left of the main building. "Swings and climbing frame and whatnot." Then she turns on her heels and almost hits me with her bulging belly. "It's too hot for an outside tour today, but that's where you'll take the kids for playtime. Kindergarten schedule is different than the older grades, which means they'll get time on the playground separate from the older kids for the first month of the school year. It helps them not be so overwhelmed by all the noise and moving bodies."

We continue through the air-conditioned halls of my new school.

My new job.

Using my new degree—I was a late starter, due to circumstances I wasn't allowed to control.

"We have a cafeteria on both sides of campus, though many of the littles pack a lunch." Bringing her smoothie up to sip, she continues our tour on surprisingly fast feet. "Teachers can eat in the cafeteria if they prefer, though most of us just inhale whatever we can find in our desks if we're not on playground duty."

She passes a colorful classroom and nods toward the door. "That's mine. I teach a mixed class of fourth and fifth grade, though I'm working on the handoff with my sub right now, since I'm taking maternity leave soon."

"Too bad you didn't get pregnant just a couple months earlier," I joke. A desperate laugh works its way along my throat, but turns to a pained gurgle when the woman looks across at me with a side-eye that promises pain.

"I mean..." I swallow my smile and stammer, "I-I just meant, if you'd had your baby at the start of summer, you could be back at work now and you wouldn't need to find a sub or do the handover."

"Solid plan," she simpers. Though, I swear, evil lingers in her stare. "But I did that last year."

"Oh!" A surprised squeak rolls through my lips. "Well... okay."

She flashes a sadistic grin and continues past her door. "As you know, the school year begins today, but kindergarten students start tomorrow. That gives the older kids time to settle in. For the first two weeks, start and stop time is staggered, so the kindies arrive half an hour after everyone else, and they'll leave half an hour earlier. That gets them through the school without the crazy crowd crushing them in the halls. That also means you can take the next few hours to prep your classroom and orient yourself. With you being new, and them being new, it might be a little messy as you all figure out your roles."

Moving into a new hallway and slowing her steps, she extends her arms—to-go cup in one hand and folder in the other—to show off what I suppose is my hall. "Kindergarten. There are five classes this year, sixteen students per class. All your other kindergarten teachers are pretty cool. Ms. Parker is in K1, she's Katie. Mrs. Alesi is K2, she's Laine, and she typically switches things up every couple of years. Sometimes she's kindergarten, other times, she's third or fourth grade. Mr. Robards is K3. His name is Alan. Mrs. Tanyan. Nicole. K4. Then there's you: K5. I'll bring you through and introduce you to each of them shortly, but first..." She stops in front of a bland, beige door and gestures inward. "Your classroom."

My very own classroom.

My heart skips in my chest, but my feet take me forward. Because this has been my dream, my every wish and want and fantasy: to work with children and break away from that high-flying, corporate career path my lawyer parents demanded of me.

What do you get when a criminal lawyer marries a corporate lawyer, and they make a baby?

You get me: Maya Blake, the nerdy math whiz who is *obviously* supposed to follow in her parents' footsteps and take over the firm.

Either of them.

"I love it." Awed, I make my way past desks pushed into square groupings.

Three pods of desks create the flow of the classroom. Six students per pod. String hangs from the ceiling, with tiny pegs on the ends to hang

3

artwork, and a rainbow mural takes up an entire wall, with the alphabet on the colors. Numbers sprawl across the bottom of the wall. In one corner, an entire case of books sits on display, while on the floor below, soft pillows wait for kids to snuggle in.

"Oh my gosh." I turn in a circle and try to see everything at once. "I love this so much."

A soft snicker works just under Britt's breath as she strolls toward a door. "You're still young." Opening it, she reveals a walk-in closet of sorts. "Lots of art supplies in here. The other kindergarten teachers chipped in to get you started, but next year, you'll have to raise a little cash on your own. The school district is pretty crappy with funding, so we do what we can to make it work."

"I'll buy everything," I chatter instantly. "Every single thing, I promise. And I'll pay back my colleagues."

"They don't need you to pay them back." She closes the door. "It was a gift. Also, some of these kids are super young. Some of them will want a nap, so you have crash pads in the closet. Pull them out if you need to, but eventually, you'll want to work on getting the children through their day without the rest. Can't be napping in sixth grade, so that's a job that falls on you. Also, pants-wetting..."

"Can't be wetting their pants in sixth grade," I pseudo-parrot with a smile. "I'll work on reminding them to use the bathroom."

"Great. In addition, administration will want to see the other stuff you're working on. They want your lesson plans."

She lifts her hands when my face twists in exasperation. "I don't like it either. And I don't always do as I'm told. I'm just letting you know what they'll expect. They tried to order six months in advance, but we thought that was ridiculous and said no."

She brings her juice to her lips and grins behind the straw. "Sometimes we get away with being disobedient. Sometimes we don't. Figure out which battles you'll give up and which you'll die for, then get on with things."

She turns toward the desk at the head of the room. "We've left a little gift in your top drawer. It's a *welcome to our school* thing." She sniggers. "It's not liquor. Though, sometimes we wish that was allowed." Perching her butt on the edge of my desk—*my* desk!—she sets her folder down and exhales an exhausted breath. "Questions so far?"

My head shakes side to side of its own volition. "I don't think so. Do we know who my students are this year?"

"We do." Opening her file, she tugs out a sheet of paper and offers it. "You have my son this year."

"Oh?" I scan the names—Tatum and Juniper, Emily and Summer. Quickly, I zero in on a Charlie Reilly and glance up, hoping to read her eyes. "Is this a good thing? A bad thing? Did you have a say in this? Because why the hell would you give your child to the new teacher if you have four others with experience?"

She snorts and reaches out to take back the list. "We all have to start somewhere, and none of us screw up the kids too permanently. Charlie's my oldest. He's a brute, but he's unapologetically a gentleman. You won't get too much trouble from him. I'm not so lucky." She takes out a second list, this one from her back pocket. "I have who this *whole* town knows as 'the Devil Twins'."

"Th-the Devil Twins?" I unfold the sheet she hands me and scan her roster. Only two children share a last name, so I take them to be the culprits. "Robert and Luke Hart?"

"Rob and Luke," she exhales. "It sure as hell sucks for my sub, because she'll get those boys during their 'coming down from summer' detox. Hopefully, by the time I'm back, they'll be settled in and not setting things on fire."

"Oh my gosh," I extend my hand and allow her to take back the sheet. "Is it really that bad? What do their parents say? Why haven't they been separated yet? Ya know, divide and conquer."

She sips her smoothie and giggles. "Full disclosure: they're my nephews, so I don't feel I have room to kick up a fuss. They're devils, but so are their parents. It was bound to go this way."

"Oh god." With a roll of my eyes, I turn away from the woman who was purposely setting me up. "I promise I'll do my very best this year with your son." I walk the perimeter of the room, trailing my fingers along the rainbow wall, and touching the textured brushstrokes beneath the alphabet. "I'll do what I can with the brutish gentleman named Charlie, and you'll do what you can with the Devil Twins."

"That's all anyone can ask of us."

With a grunt, she pushes off the desk, but leaves behind the folder. For my reading pleasure, I guess.

"Come on. I'll introduce you to your kindie colleagues, then I'm going back to save my sub from whatever those boys are doing to her."

She heads toward the doorway and peeks over her shoulder as I finish my tour.

It takes me a minute to stop and look up. Then another for my brain to focus on her, and not my plans for the year.

I want to teach. I want to be the very first memory these children ever have of school. I want to be remembered, even when these five and six-year-olds have graduated and are thinking back over their education.

I want to be a core memory that makes them smile.

I won't fail them.

"I know I sound kinda cranky and intolerant," Britt says. "But I swear," a glowing smile fills her face and sparkles in her eyes, "I *love* my job. And sparring with the crazy kids is ninety percent of why I enjoy it so much. Let's go." She brings her smoothie up once more and sips. "I'll take you to Laine first. Laine Alesi. More full disclosure: she's my best friend."

Cole Miller

A JOB WORTH DOING...

Darkness falls across my city, while the summer breeze moves through my inch-long hair. I sit back in my 2015 Ford Mustang, my fingers playing across the steering wheel, and my boot tapping the floor to the same beat as the tune coming through my speakers.

My car's an older model now compared to those currently on the market, but I'm a loyal man, and I never forget when my ass has been saved: whether it was by a friend, or a machine.

In the passenger seat, my brother from a different mother, Preston Danes, spies a brand-new luxury Mercedes that retails around a hundred and four grand off the showroom floor.

It should be criminal that the stupidly rich folks with more money than sense don't lock up their purchases at night. But the fact they don't... well, it pays my bills.

"Box ordered one in Snow, yeah?"

"Mmm." Pres's affirmation comes out on a slow grunt. "He would accept pearl too." Lowering his binoculars, he peers across at me with eyes that appear damn near black at night.

He's a foster kid, just like me. Bounced through the system till we became official runaways somewhere in our teens. Eventually, we ended up in the same circles. Same city. Same parties. We both found a way to make money, and that way just so happened to also be the same.

Except, where I drive, he's a fuckin' whiz with the electronics. Where I would slip a wedge in the door and pry my way in with brute strength, Pres makes the computers sing for him. Something to do with radiofrequencies and keyless entry.

I dunno.

Some would call us thieves. Others might consider we have the entrepreneurial spirit. I call it paying my fucking rent and not ending up on the street again.

"You wanna take it tonight?" he murmurs in the quiet.

My music is down low, and not even dogs bark in these rich-folks neighborhoods. They're too busy sleeping inside mansions on king-sized beds and chowing down on hundred-dollar steaks. They don't give a fuck who's outside looking to steal Mommy's new SUV.

When I say nothing, Pres lowers his hands and glances across to me. "Tonight? Or you wanna come back tomorrow and make sure this isn't a stitch-up?"

"Tonight'll do. I've got groceries to buy."

Reaching into my pocket and taking out my car keys, I slap them to Pres's palm, then I flip my hand over and wait for him to replace them with a different set.

"It's damn near two in the morning," I tell him. "Assholes are asleep. Even if the place is wired with alarms, I'm gonna be gone before they drag themselves outta bed and get downstairs. You take the Mustang, drive her out the way we came, and get gone. I'll do my thing and then meet you back at Box's. Radios?"

He drops a shiny new key fob in my palm, then follows it with a device that's kind of like a phone, but kind of like a walkie talkie, too.

Like the keyless entry shit, we're working with channels and frequencies, but in our case, we're the only two guys in the city who get to listen in.

"Stay in touch," he instructs seriously. "I don't wanna have to come find you again."

I scoff and place my fingers on the doorhandle to my left. "Straight back to Box's. I'll take a ten-minute detour to make sure cops aren't following me back, then I'll expect to find my baby already tucked in safe for the night."

He only closes his fingers around the Mustang's key and rolls his eyes.

"It's creepy how attached you are to your car, man. You'd fuck her if the tailpipe wasn't so hot."

I push the door open with a snort. "Cars've never let me down, Pres." I place my feet on the road and keep it all quiet. My voice, my steps—hell, my breathing... all silent. "I've never been cheated on by a car. I've never been lied to by a car. And never ever has my car told me I need more money to keep her satisfied."

Moving around the hood, I tap my palm to his when he climbs out, an almost silent, down-low five, then I continue to the door he left wide open and slowly close it so the catch snicks, but the sound doesn't carry along the quiet neighborhood.

Dogs might be asleep on their owner's faces right now, but that doesn't mean we come out here with pots and pans and start banging shit together.

"You clear out," I tell him across the roof of the Mustang. "I'll give you a five-minute lead, then I'll take a tour around the city. I won't be far behind you." I lift my hand and grit through tight lips, "Don't scratch her, don't grind her gears, don't speed, and don't get me a ticket. I wanna see her in the same condition I gave her to you."

Smiling, he ignores me and drops into the driver's seat. Closing the door with a quiet click, he turns over the engine and has me clenching my jaw when she roars in the dark.

On my left, the passenger side window slides open, then Pres leans across the seats and shakes his head when I lower down to catch his eyes. "Your codependence is concerning. But your lack of trust is worse."

"She's all I got," I hiss in response.

He only winks. "You got me, too, bitch. At least, till the zombies take over. Then I'mma eat your flesh and dance on your ashes."

A soft laugh rolls along my chest and escapes on an exhale of air. "Only one of us is a bitch, Pres. We both know it ain't me."

Tapping the roof, I take a step back and allow him room to leave, then as my taillights dim in the darkness and he rips the Mustang around a corner sharp enough to leave a little rubber on the road, I slip the key fob in my pocket and take out the radio to switch it on.

I wait for the usual muted beeps. The humming connection as his device and mine search for each other, then I get a final bleat to let me know we're on.

Bringing the device up, I hold the button on the side and snarl, "I smell burning rubber, fucker. What did I say?"

"Go get me a Mercedes, Miller. Then we'll discuss your tires. By the way, you probably need an alignment. She's pulling a little to the left. Did you know?"

"Fuck she is." I fade into the darkness and find a spot beneath a tree to hang out for my five minutes. To give Pres time to go, and the cops, less chance to put us together if this hits the news. "She never pulls any way except where I want her to go. Stop speeding."

"I'm not speeding!" he laughs. "I'm driving Miss Daisy over here." His tone turns serious. "You got a cruiser on West and Thirty-Fourth, checking for suspicious activity."

"Sitting or cruising?"

"Sitting. Sucking each other's dicks and having a good time. Don't come down West and you won't see 'em."

"Got it. But if the Benz is wired up and security comes for me, that means I've only got thirty seconds till the closest cop is on me. That's a tight window."

"Well..." I don't have to see him to know he's shrugging. "I already said we can come back tomorrow. No one said we have to do this shit on a Monday, ya know?"

"I have plans tomorrow."

When the neighborhood remains silent, and house lights remain off, I step out from beneath my tree and make my way toward the parked Mercedes. She lives about a hundred yards from where we stopped, which means I've gotta get from here to there without cops, dogs, or owners getting antsy.

"I'm walking now," I tell him. "Ninety feet. Where are you?"

"About a minute and a half away," he chuckles. "You said you'd give me five. Do you often jack too soon?" He pauses, and likely wrinkles his nose that way he does. "That's the real reason the ladies are mad at you, huh?"

"Shut the fuck up. Seventy yards, lights are still out."

"Keep your head down, bruh. Even if security cameras get you, all they're gonna get is a five-feet, six inches tall dude dressed all in black. A hundred pounds. No muscle mass to speak of. Does it suck to be you?"

"Five-six, my ass," I snicker.

He teases because he's smaller—and by smaller, I mean a hair off six feet. Chicks still dig it. But I'm six-two, so he's insecure because he's older and, in his mind at least, wiser. So for the little brother to not be *little* is... vexing to him.

"Forty feet out. You pass any more cops on your travels?"

"None yet, but I'm about to head across the bridge. You going over or under?"

"Depends, I guess." The closer I get, the quicker my feet move. My heart thuds just a little harder, and my left hand digs into my pocket in search of tools I don't need.

The problem with rich folks getting richer is their expensive luxury cars are getting easier to steal. We once needed to get through the door, break the steering lock, and yank out the right wires to get them started. Now, we just need the keyless entry, and we're off.

And if you know a guy like Preston Danes, then you have unfettered access to damn near every vehicle in the city—including those belonging to circuit judges and the chief of police.

Ya know, if you feel like tempting fate.

"I'm heading in," I announce when I'm just six feet away. "Putting you down. I'll pick you up in a few."

"Godspeed, little zombie. I'll see you soon."

Slipping the device into my back pocket and fishing out the key fob, I release the locks and grit my teeth when the car elicits two sharp beeps and the headlights flash.

From walking to sprinting, I yank the door open and dive in, then I jam my palm to the keyless start and swing my seatbelt on before the door even closes.

Too much noise. Too much attention.

Tearing the Benz out of the driveway, I regret the way the tires squeak on the newly poured pavement, but I've come too far to undo my work. Instead, I shove the car into drive and peel away from the house as lights flash on inside.

Maybe they're not so fat. Not so stupid.

Some oldies station plays quietly from the sound system, grating on my nerves and making my heart pound heavier, so as I tear the SUV around the curve at the end of the street—toward Thirty-Sixth, instead of Thirty-Fourth and the sitting cops—I lift my hip from the seat and take out Preston's radio. Switching it back on, I toss it to the passenger seat and check my rearview mirror for the inevitable flash of red and blue.

"I'm moving." I tap buttons on the steering wheel and change the radio station until finally, I stop on something a little less Mozart and a little more Foo Fighters. "Occupants woke," I tell my partner. "Lights were coming on inside."

"Which means you don't get to do your tour-de-city," Pres answers. "They're gonna have that make, model, and plate out to every cop car in the next thirty seconds. Means you gotta go A to B in one straight line."

Nodding, I reply, "I'm gonna go under."

I zip around a tight corner and make my way south through quiet residential streets. Soon, I'll cross into the business district, and after that, the industrial end of the city.

That's where I'm going. That's where Box's warehouse sits and accepts cars that simply... vanish.

"Pres?"

When he says nothing, I repeat, "I'm going under. You catch that? The tunnels are older, so less cameras, less cops, less traffic..."

"Yep. But the cops are waking up, Miller." I hear the Mustang's tires screech on a turn, and after that, the drone of police radio chatter as Pres tunes in. "They're coming for you."

"Do they know where I am yet?"

I'm hopeful they're looking the wrong way. Hopeful they're too slow to follow me toward the tunnels, when everyone else in the city uses the new bridge. But then blue and red light up my rearview mirror and answer my question.

"Fuck!"

Screw speeding laws, and screw road rules. I thank Mercedes Benz for giving their SUVs a banging engine, then I scream into the tunnels with flashing lights spinning a quarter of a mile behind me.

"They gotchu," Preston drones. "How you doing?"

"In the tunnel."

Then, because I know every inch of this place like the back of my hand, I switch off my lights and zip through blind.

"A tenth of the way in," I report. "No one's in here, and cops aren't close enough to see me yet. I'm moving stealth."

"Of course you are." I can *hear* him rolling his eyes. "Because nobody cares if you fold yourself over a median barrier. I don't care if you die, bitch. I'm not attached or anything."

"Uh-huh."

I drive deeper into the tunnel, further underground, and use only the narrow strips of light coming through the holes dug for air ventilation to guide me. It's lucky the moon's full tonight and leading me home.

"Halfway through." Then I look in the mirror. "I still see red and blue, but their headlights don't have me yet."

"They're whining," he snickers. "Radio's all abuzz about how the fuck you disappeared."

"It's a straight tunnel," I counter dryly. "They saw me come in. Common sense says I gotta come out again. Two thirds."

"Cut left and move down East Eighty-Sixth when you exit. They've got a structure fire there tonight, which means it'll be crawling with crew, but none of them are looking for you."

"Thanks."

The interior of the windshield fogs from my racing breath. The strobing lights of red and blue grow brighter, and the sirens are no longer a distant, tinny sound. The po-po are coming for me, and my car won't be faster than theirs.

"Preston, where are you?"

"Pulling into Box's now. How long until you exit the tunnel?"

"Ten," I breathe. "Nine." I press my foot to the floor and use up every horse Mercedes thought to sell their customer. "Eight. Seven."

"Six," he commands. "Five. Don't screw up."

I flip my lights back on and prepare to emerge into moonlight almost as bright as daylight, now that my vision has adjusted to pitch-black. "Three. Two."

A police cruiser screams into my lane and stops with a squeal of his tires.

"Fuck!" I slam my foot to the brake for just a beat of my heart, flip the car from automatic to manual, then I roll it back to third so the gearbox grinds, and drop the clutch to fang my way past the blockage and onto the street outside.

The SUV slides wide and takes up the wrong lanes, but it's two in the morning, so I use what I've got, and thank the universe for keeping most folks at home in their beds tonight.

"Get me outta here!" I shout to Pres. "Cops are gonna follow me to the warehouse otherwise."

"Take a left. Now."

I'd ask how he knows where I am at this exact moment, but chances are, he long ago fed me a GPS tracking dot so I'm always locatable on his laptop.

Now that he's back at Box's, he no longer requires verbal updates. And because he's the only dude on this planet I trust with my life, I do as I'm told and cut left.

"Good. Three streets in," he coaches, "switch it right and pull onto Eighty-Eighth. Get around that corner before the cops do, and you can pull her into the parking lot right there. Straight underground, zip it in, and shut her down. Box says he'll pick her up when the heat dies down in an hour."

"Alright."

I check my rearview mirror and note that two hundred and fifty yards still separate me and the cops, so I yank the SUV around the corner and hold my breath when she almost lifts to two wheels. Dropping to second gear, I slam my foot to the floor and find my speed again with a squeal of my tires.

"Heading in." I hit the driveway of the parking garage with a scrape to the bottom of the Mercedes.

Every scrape, every ding, is a dollar sign Box will deduct from what he pays me, but I'd rather give him back a thousand from the five he's paying me than see myself in prison orange and hoping to find a dollar or two in my commissary account.

Tearing the SUV down one level to avoid the cops on the street seeing me unless they come in here, I squeal into a space and cut the engine so all I hear is the click of the hot machinery taking a breath of relief. I snag the key fob and my radio, and in under a second, I'm out of the car with the door locked and my hands in my pockets. Shoulders down, head down.

Eyes on my feet, I cross the parking garage and step out on the next block to emerge in a kind of Chinatown. Restaurants are closed, and lights are out, but the lingering smell of delicious food swirls in my gut and reminds me I'm hungry.

"Where am I going, Pres?" I keep my words quiet, and when a trio of cop cars flies past at the end of the street, I press myself into the shadows and make sure my eyes stay down. "Pres? Where the fuck are you?"

"Here." My white Mustang pulls up with a screech, then the window slides down and my friend's goofy grin lifts a metric ton of stress from my shoulders. "Get in, bitch."

I cast a look along the street to make sure we're alone, then I skip across and yank the door open. Dropping into the passenger side and tossing the radio, I close the door, fix my seatbelt, and look across at Pres as he takes off again.

While the radio chatter mentions cops going east, Pres makes sure we drive west.

"Are you getting rusty," he asks, "or do you have a specific issue with driving soccer mom cars?"

"Shut the fuck up." I drop my head back and close my eyes, finally able to take a breath and know we're good.

We got through. A hundred-thousand-dollar car is as good as packaged up, and I have another four grand coming my way within the hour.

"I'd probably do better if I didn't have you bitching at me the entire drive."

"Uh-huh." Like he's driving Miss Daisy again, he keeps his speed down and his movements leisurely. "Wanna do McDonald's drive-thru?"

When I open my eyes, he tilts his chin toward the golden arches a block away. "I could do with some nugs, bruh. Stealing cars always makes me hungry."

I choke out a laugh and shake my head. "Yeah. Let's get the nugs. Sure."

"You seem tense." Giggling, riding high on the successful job we just pulled, he rips the Mustang into the McDonald's driveway so fast that the bottom of my bumper scrapes on the concrete.

Instantly, his humor makes way for a terrified gurgle, and his fear-filled eyes slide my way. "I didn't mean to do that."

"Get the fuck out of my seat!"

The second he pulls her into the drive-thru lane, I unbuckle my belt and shove out of the door.

The chick who works the night shift talks through the little box and asks us what we want, but I ignore her words and open the driver's side door. "Get. The. Fuck. Out."

"I said I was sorry!" But he laughs again, unconcerned that I might wring his neck if not for the thing we call loyalty. "Cole!" He extends his long limbs and slides out of the car, but instead of walking away, he wraps me up in a noisy hug that could have the cops thinking he's driving drunk. "Don't be mad at me, Cole Miller! You know I can't handle when you're cranky at me."

"Get out of my fucking way." I push him off and force my lips flat, even when he stumbles into the menu screen and tempts me to smile.

Sliding into my seat and exhaling at the feel of the leather under my ass, I grip the steering wheel in one hand and close the door with the other. When Pres jumps in on the passenger side and closes his own door, chittering laughter following every move he makes, I nudge the car forward and stop directly in front of the speaker box.

"Tell the chick what you want," I grit out. "Don't forget to ask for the kiddie toy. We both know you have the mental aptitude of a third-grader."

Snorting, he leans too far into my space. "Hey there, darling Miss Mac. Can I please have some nuggies?"

Maya

DON'T STARE SO MUCH, MAYA. IT'S CREEPY.

The school bell rings, and children scream across the playground. They carry backpacks larger than their bodies, and wear shoes still shiny from their moms back-to-school shopping frenzy. Pigtails bounce, and smiles fill two-thirds of the children's faces.

The other third appear to be half a second from peeing their pants in terror.

I watch as the first and second graders make their way off the playground and into the halls, shoving each other to be the first through the door, while third and fourth graders move a little slower. They've seen this show before, and they long ago decided school isn't all that much fun.

On the outskirts of the property, kindergarten families linger.

Like Britt said, the little ones start thirty minutes after the others; an attempt to separate them from the herd. But families are too keen, too nervous and unwilling to be late, so they're now too early, and the anxiety jumps from parent to child.

Mother to daughter.

Father to son.

"Take a seat and chill for your thirty minutes, if you want." Brittany comes out to stand beside me. Her stomach is somehow larger than it was yesterday, her eyes, more tired. She rubs a gentle hand along her swollen abdomen and watches a father and his son play on the swings.

The father is on the swing. The son is throwing bark chips at his back.

"You're gonna be exhausted if you work through all your adrenaline now and don't save any for when class starts."

"Don't you have to be in class?" Licking my dry lips, I glance away from the playing duo and look to Britt. "Your third graders have already gone in."

"I'm a kindie mom this year, remember?" Smiling, she gazes back across the playground. "My sub has my students for now, so I can send my kid off to his first ever school day."

"But..." I check to see if she's stuffed a five-year-old behind her pregnant frame. "You forgot your kid."

Snickering, she tips her chin toward the swings. "He's over there, with my husband... the eternal child. Come on." She pushes away from her spot by the school's front doors and heads onto the cushy grass. "I'll introduce you to them."

"Oh." *I'm meeting my first student!* I dash from my spot, only needing to go three steps before I'm caught up with my only friend in this small town.

Because she's so slow, and they're so far away, I take a moment to look the man up and down.

"*That's* your husband?" I gape. He's about three feet wide from shoulder to shoulder. And though he's sitting, I still see his long torso and even longer legs. "He's a fricken' giant."

"Giant pain in my ass," she grumbles with a smile. "And he's a pro fighter, so he—"

My heart skips in my chest. "Like... WWE pro?"

She scoffs. "Not like WWE. Hey, Reilly!"

Her bark has both males on the playground looking up.

They're mirrors of each other, with the attitude in their stares, the hardness in their features, and the black hair that dangles in front of their eyes. And in the way their lips curl up when they process who's calling them.

The little boy drops his handful of bark chips and wipes his hands on his jeans, while his father pushes off the swing and proves he's an easy six foot something... maybe six-four. He wears jeans too, and a button-up shirt, but the buttons remain undone to show off a tight black shirt that draws a woman's eyes to the broad pectoral muscles just beneath.

"He's, uh..." I swallow down my nerves and cough to make damn sure they stay there. "Somethin'."

She snickers. "You get to peek once, since I've learned I have to share him with the world. You're new, and you didn't grow up here, which means it's okay to stare... once."

"Okay."

So I do just that. Because maybe I'm intent on living my life for me right now. I'm in this new season of independence and career and freedom. And I'll be damned if I move to a new town and tie myself down with someone else's problems. But that doesn't mean I don't see what God did for Britt.

"I mean... *Wowza*."

"Annnnd you're done."

She steps into the man's waiting arms and side-hugs him, since she can't do it the traditional way, with a giant unborn baby separating them. I'm sure she intends for a quick hug and release, but her husband presses a kiss to her temple and renders her still for a beat. Then two. Three, while he breathes her in.

Watching on, the boy says nothing. He only waits with a sly grin, like this is a common occurrence in his home and he knows his place. Not that he's *less than* anyone else in his family. But that Mom deserves a big hug, and Dad's the one who'll give it to her first.

Finally, she pulls away, accepting her man's dinner-plate hand wrapped around hers, and turns to extend her other hand for the little boy to take. Together, they present a united family, and me, the intruder.

"Miss Blake, this is my son, Charlie Reilly." She smiles down at him. "Charlie, this is Miss Blake. She's your teacher this year. But she's kinda new, so I know you're gonna be on your best behavior, right?"

He nods eagerly. "Best."

He might be in kindergarten. He might be five freaking years old. But he's large for his age, and confident enough to drop his mom's hand and step forward.

He stops just a foot in front of me and raises his hand to shake, and when I stare in surprise for a moment too long, he takes the chance to reach up and push the black hair from his eyes. "It's nice to meet you, Miss Blake. I'm gonna be good this year, I promise."

"Oh, well..." I crouch and take his hand with mine. He has beautiful blue eyes and lashes longer than any I'll ever have—naturally or from a salon. "It's nice to meet you, Charlie. Is that what you'd like to be called? Charlie? Is there a nickname you prefer?"

"Charlie *is* my nickname." He pumps my hand with a strength that surprises me. "My real name is Charles Alexander. Charles for my grandpa, and Alexander for my Uncle Alex. Charlie is the name I use."

"Well, okay." I release his hand and study the cutie's smirk; it matches his father's. "You said you're gonna be good this year, huh? You promised."

He wraps his still-pudgy fingers around the straps of his backpack. "Yes, Miss Blake."

"Are you normally not good?"

Behind him, his father snorts.

"I sometimes get a little excited," the boy answers instead. "If I was in Miss Laine's class, I might get written up and sent to the principal's office 'cuz she thinks she can spar with me."

"S—" I glance up at his parents. "Spar?"

"He means sass versus sass," Britt says. "No hands are thrown."

My eyes drop back to Charlie's. "You won't spar with me?"

Slowly, slyly, his lips curl high on one side. "Maybe sometimes. When you're not new anymore. But if the other kids get in on it and make class crappy, I'll make them stop."

"C-crappy?"

"No cussing," Britt hisses. Then she smiles for me. "Don't judge me based on my firstborn. He was our tester kid. The next one is better behaved."

Again, her husband laughs. "That's not true either." Finally, he extends his hand. Bare forearm, bursting with muscle and tattoos and long veins that pulse with blood. "Jack Reilly."

Pushing up to stand, I take his hand and shake it just once. "Maya Blake. You're a fighter?"

He's arrogant. And proud. And not the least bit shy when he drops my hand and tilts his chin in the affirmative. "I am. But I still have brain cells left, so you don't have to worry about that."

"Daddy's the world champion," Charlie says seriously. Informatively.

My eyes widen and snap back to the man.

"Five times so far," the boy continues.

"World champion? Like... Rocky Balboa champion of the world? *Adriannnnn.*" My voice trails off to show just how lame I am. "Apollo Creed. *If he dies, he dies?*"

"Rocky was a boxer," Jack clarifies on a chuckle. "And fictional. But sure, similar."

"'Cept we roll," Charlie adds again. "We have two legs to use as well. No need to box with our hands and forget feet can knock a man out."

Britt reaches out and wraps her hand around Charlie's mouth. "He's getting excited."

"You f-fight with your feet?" I stare at Jack a little longer, but not because he's handsome. "Like... mixed martial arts?"

"Basically." He glances across the playground when more of my students and families wander closer. "Charlie won't roll with a single other kid while on school property or on school time. You have our word."

I look down at the child, wide eyed, and wonder if he's one of those crazy fit preschoolers with a six-pack hidden under his shirt. "You fight too, Charlie?"

"My whole family fights," he answers smugly. "My Uncle Bobby was the heavyweight world champion before Dad. And another one of my uncles was too." He stops and flashes a teasing grin. "It's in our blood. And plus, we have a gym across town where we train other fighters. We're probably looking for a new contender soon," he goes on, "'Cuz Dad's feeling old."

"I'm thirty-one," Jack grumbles. Peering down at his son, he purses his lips and shows off a dimple I'd not yet noticed. When Charlie looks up and grins, I find a matching mark on the five-year-old's cheek. "Thirty-one's not old, kid."

"It is for a fighter," he sniggers. Then he looks at me. "Maybe I'll be champion someday too, but that's still a long time away, and Daddy definitely can't last that long. He already got hurt too many times, so we're shopping around for new muscle."

"You don't have anyone else with your blood?" I tease. "I thought you had a whole gym of uncles."

"Dad is the youngest of all the parents," he giggles. "And I have cousins. Smalls is gonna be world champion eventually, but she's gotta graduate first. And Bean's gonna be champ too, but they're girls. Dad's a boy, so we need one of those."

21

Well, of course.

I straighten my back and study Britt as a curious thought hits me. "Do you fight too, when you're not pregnant?"

"God no. It's not my thing. But two of my sisters-in-law do. They kick ass. *Anyway*," she adds when Charlie's eager eyes shoot up—*because she cussed?* "I think it might be time for us to head in. My husband has to get to the gym, and I have to relieve my sub before she tears her hair out and the Devil Twins set the school on fire."

"Oh my gosh, the Devil Twins," I breathe. "I forgot you mentioned them yesterday." Then I look down at Charlie. "Your cousins?"

Nodding, he flashes a smug grin. "They fight too. And my Uncle Jon sometimes kicks Dad's butt for fun. Especially at Christmastime."

"And we're done." Britt swings her son around and starts walking. "Time for school, Terror." She glances over her shoulder to catch my eye. "The others are gonna start heading in when we do, so I suggest you get to your classroom."

"Right!"

I break away from where my feet seem stuck to the grass, ignoring Jack's humored chuckle, and walking beside Britt all the way to the double wide doors of the school, I find calm when the sound of my low heels click against hallway linoleum.

"Okay," I say and take a deep breath. Then again, "Okay."

"You're gonna be fine," Britt assures me.

She walks with her son by her side all the way back to our class, and when I peek over my shoulder, I find Jack strolling with a smirk playing on his lips, and behind him, a half dozen other new families.

"They're five-year-olds," she continues. Pushing through my door and into the brightly lit classroom, she releases her son and smiles when he automatically heads across the space to place his bag on one of the sixteen hooks I labeled yesterday.

"They don't know what school is like," she adds. "They have no expectations, which means you get to decide what this year will look like. Do you want them to come in and sit at their desks right away? Or will they sit on the floor? In a circle? In lines? Will they take out books? Do they even know how to read?"

With every word she speaks, my eyes grow wide with worry. But all she does is walk over to press a kiss to the top of her son's head.

"You're gonna be fine," she says to him. Then she pivots to me. "You're gonna be fine too." Finally, she turns to the door and makes her way to her husband while other children file in. "Take me out, Reilly. For the next hour, we can be child-free."

Jack takes Britt's hand in his and lifts the other in a peace sign. "We'll see you at two, Miss Blake. If you need help with a circuit breaker for the noisy students, ask Charlie. He's been raised with more cousins than kids in your class. He's got this."

"O-oh, okay."

I swallow my nerves and watch on as the bulky fighter—who *has* to be at least two hundred and fifty pounds of solid muscle—leads his wife away. And as though this entire town takes their cues from that couple, other families drop their children and turn too.

Kids filter in. Hooks are utilized, and desks are explored. I've added tags to every chair so children know where to sit. Though most of these kids won't know how to read yet, the majority will recognize their names.

"Miss Blake." A parent-set stops in front of me as their little girl—a pigtail-wearing cutie—offers me a flower plucked from somewhere between here and wherever they live. "This is Lily," the man says. "She's five, just like the others, but she's a little small for her age. So, ya know..."

I smile in return. "Take care of her."

I crouch low and look into the beauty's pretty eyes. Accepting the flower, I bring it to my nose to smell. "Hi, Lily. My name's Miss Blake. Are you excited for school today?"

"I'm a bit scared," she whispers, a stark contrast after I've just spent ten minutes talking to a boy too big for his age. "Because this is my first day."

"Well..." I consider her for a moment. "It's my first day too. How about we work together to make sure we both have the very best day?"

"Oh, hey, Squeak." Charlie saunters closer and yanks the girl from between me and her parents. Pulling her under his arm, he squeezes her close and meets my eyes. "She's my cousin too." Then he glances up at her parents. "I got this."

"I'm sure you do," the dad chuckles.

When I push up to stand tall, and Charlie steers the girl away, I clear my throat, which only makes the dad's smile grow more severe.

"It's gonna be a fun day," he murmurs. "You got a couple of our favorites in your class this year. That practically makes you family at this point."

"Are you enjoying our little town?" The mom offers her hand, and smiles when I take it. "I'm Sammy Turner." Then she peeks across at her husband. "That's Samuel Turner."

I look at him. Then back to her. "Are you..." Back to him. "Is she kidding?"

She releases my hand and chokes out a laugh. "Not even a little. Our parents liked the same name, we guess. It was an issue back in high school, and I worried others would tease us. But..." She lifts her shoulders in a shrug. "Bullies are irrelevant. Also, he answers to Scotch. Use whatever name you need, we'll answer."

"Samuel and Sammy." I study *Scotch* and accept his hand when he brings it up. "Makes it easier for me to remember. Is there anything I need to know about Lily before you leave?"

"Nah." He drops my hand and sets his on his hip. "She was a little sickly as a baby, but she's good now."

"Just small," I nod.

"Just small," he confirms with a kind smile. "Anything she needs, Charlie'll make sure she gets."

He pokes a thumb back over his shoulder to indicate toward the hall. "You met Britt? My little sister. She made a baby with the fighter, which is how we got that giant over there. But I'm cool with it, because he—"

"Because he protects your daughter," I finish for him. "I understand."

Knowing my students are getting a little antsy, a little louder—and that Charlie can only do so much before he's tempted to *get excited* with them—I take a step back. "I'll speak with you both this afternoon when you pick Lily up. You don't need to worry. Britt will be here all day too, plus..." I gesture toward the boy, "Charlie."

"And that's our cue to go." Wrapping her arm around Scotch's torso, Sammy snuggles in tight and allows him to lead her back into the hall.

"We'll see you this afternoon," Sammy calls back to me. Then she waves to the little girl to say her goodbyes.

Turning from the now-empty doorway, I study my students and do a fast head count. Fourteen. Fifteen. Sixteen five-year-olds zoom around and explore their new classroom. Charlie walks with Lily, while others walk alone. One or two hang in separate corners, their arms crossed and their heads down.

They're shy.

"Alright." *It's time to put your degree to work, Maya. Otherwise, what the hell was all the arguing for, anyway?* Clapping my hands loud enough to echo across the room, I draw fifteen sets of eyes my way; the sixteenth—Charlie's—watch Lily. "I want you all to place one finger," I lift one high so they see, "On your nose. Right now please."

Noise cuts away, and fidgeting hands come up to do as I ask. Some children's eyes cross as they stare at their finger, while others eagerly watch me for more instruction.

"My name is Miss Blake." Slowly lowering my finger, I make my way through the room and stop in front of my desk so I can lean on it. "I'm your new kindergarten teacher, and I would love to get to know you all. But to do that, we're going to have to play a game."

Eyes light up. Energy pulses, purely because of that one word.

"But for Miss Blake to explain the game to you all, I have to be able to talk while no one else talks." I lift a finger again. "If you can hear me and understand, I want you to place *two* fingers on the tip of your nose."

Like eager little soldiers, tiny hands snap up and follow my instructions.

"Wonderful!" I clap my hands together and make eye contact with every single set that gazes back at me. "So, I'm going to do my best to learn all of your names, and you have to do your best to learn mine." I point toward a little girl with white-blonde hair left to dangle loose. "What's your name?"

"Savanah," she answers oh-so-sweetly. *She's a people-pleaser*—an impression punctuated when she dips low into what can only be described as a curtsy. "Savanah Stevens."

"Hello, Savanah. It's so nice to meet you. Can you remember what my name is?"

"Uh..." A rosy blush fills her cheeks. "Miss Chick?"

A fast smile crosses my lips. I have no clue where she plucked *Chick* from. "It's Miss Blake. Can you come over here," I point at a colored dot on the floor between their desks and mine, "and sit down on the red spot for me? Then I need you to wait patiently while I meet everyone else."

"Okay!" She dashes closer and drops like a ton of bricks. Then she crosses her legs and snaps her spine straight. Finally, she eagerly glances around and searches for who I'll call upon next.

"You," I point toward our smallest, "are Lily. Do you remember my name?"

"Miss Blake," she responds shyly. And before I can ask, she slips away from Charlie and wanders to the colored dot on Savanah's left.

"I'm Charlie," the largest announces. Swaggering my way with broad shoulders and swinging hands, he drops beside his cousin. "You're Miss Blake. And you should come to our gym sometime so you can see the difference between WWE and MMA."

"Uh... thank you, Charlie."

No thanks.

I gesture toward another child. "What's your name?"

"J-June, Miss Blake."

"Thank you for calling Blake and Shannon Law, this is Theresa speaking. How may I direct you?"

"Hey." I wander out of the school at a little past four. My kids have gone home. My first day is complete, and though some of my colleagues are staying till five, I have nothing to do but go home and ruminate on Hurricane Charlie and his cute little classmates. "It's Maya," I tell my mom's receptionist. "I'd like to speak to her, please."

"Of course." Without saying goodbye, Theresa places me on hold so classical music pipes through the call and makes my jaw tense, purely because I've associated that music with frustrating conversations.

My mother is... good at arguing. And that might be the nicest thing I can say about the woman.

Her career as a high-flying corporate lawyer is a calling she felt from a young age. Where most little girls play with dolls and tour the Barbie Mansion, my mother sat her dolls down and reenacted legal scenarios. Where I married my Barbies, she divorced hers.

And when she went to law school and met Roderick Blake on her third day on campus, she laughed that meeting off and stayed single for an additional six years.

No way was she railroading her career for a man.

Paige Blake—Paige Keenan back then—was a shark, in and out of the classroom. Often the professor's favorite, her ability to argue numbers until her opponent would rather kill themselves than continue on meant she graduated with honors and waltzed her way into what was once Shannon and Shannon Law Firm.

She mediated that divorce too, until the male Shannon walked away with his hands in the air and a couple of kids to raise, since their mother didn't want to bother, while the female Shannon congratulated my mother with an offer for partner.

Eight years after meeting, Paige and Roderick married, she took his name, and somehow, Blake was placed first on the firm's stationery head, despite Shannon's seniority.

Seven years after that, I was born. An only child. The one and only disruption my mother would allow in her elite career.

Though, even then, legend has it that she worked until six in the evening the day I was born. I arrived at eleven that night. The next day was a Saturday, and by Monday, Paige was back at work, and I was being raised by my grandmother.

The sweetest, warmest, kindest person I've ever known, Lauralyn Keenan was a star in an otherwise dark, dark sky. And then she passed… four years, eight months, eleven days, and approximately thirty-six minutes ago.

I love my parents, of course. But I *loved* Grammy.

"Maya?" Mom's rushed tone catches me off guard as the line connects.

I step off the curb at the end of the school block, glance left and right to check for cars, then I continue on and move onto the curb on the other side.

"What is it, honey?"

"Hey, Mom." I note the way my molars grind at just those two words. The way my hands flex tight, and my shoulders come up high in defense.

It's an old coping mechanism. Being the daughter of a couple of lawyers meant learning to explain and state your case, or sitting down and shutting your mouth.

I have done both over the years.

"I was just calling to say hello." I force a smile and wander toward the center of town. "I just got off work, so I wanted to—"

"Work," she mutters, then talking away from the phone, "Have Roger set up a meeting for Thursday at four. He needs to get ahead of this thing before Frances neuters him." Then back to me. "You mean the job where you babysit thirty of someone else's kids for less than minimum wage?" She scoffs and sits back at her desk so I hear her chair squeak.

I know that, behind her, the city skyline stretches out as far as her eye can see, while in front of her is a law firm boasting more than a hundred and twenty staff, seventeen secretaries, and enough paralegals to choke a clown car.

"You're better than that, sweetheart. And we both know you have the credits to go back to law school."

"Mom!" This is why my teeth ache. This is why my hands hurt from being clenched too tight. "I don't want to go to law school. Why can't you respect my wishes?"

"So you've called to argue with me?" I don't have to see her face to know she rolls her eyes. "Why even call if you're only going to pick a fight?"

"I'm not picking a fight! I called to share with you how much fun I had today."

I step off the end of another block and cross the street with a fast glance to the almost nonexistent traffic, then I step up again and pass a diner that reads *Franky's* on the sign out front.

The scent of warm apple pie lingers in the air, tempting me to stop, but I refuse to go in there and occupy a booth so the world can listen in on my troubles.

"I called to celebrate with you, Mother. I called so we could share in something good that happened to me today."

"Something good," she scoffs. "You wiped a kid's butt and cleaned up his boogers, and you want to pretend you're more than a glorified babysitter."

"Mom—"

"I only push because I know you can do better," she reasons, so fucking calmly. "You've completed four years already, sweetheart. You've come so far. It would be such a waste to have spent those years in law school for nothing."

"Not for nothing," I grit out. "We had a deal, Mom. I would do pre-law. I would give it an entire four years, and if, at the end, it still wasn't for me, I could transfer out."

"You were supposed to like it. It would have grown on you, honey. You were at the top of your classes!"

"Just because I could be good at it doesn't mean I should do it. I could probably be good at taking speed too, Mother. Do you suggest I do it?"

"Don't try to be humorous, sweetheart. It creates wrinkles—and emphasizes how little you know about amphetamines. When are you coming home to visit? You know your father would like to see you."

My nostrils flare from the rage I feel in my blood. From the dismissal spoon-fed straight into my mouth every time I won't conform.

"Maybe next weekend," I grit out. "I'll have to see how my schedule and workload stand."

"Your workload," she guffaws. "Uh-huh. I'm certain grading pictures of rainbows will be a challenging task."

"Mom—"

"Listen, I have to go, sweetheart. I'm in court tomorrow at nine, and I need to discuss the file with my assistant. *This*," she adds, because she's so intent on always having the last word, "is what it is to have a workload that interferes with home life. Not rainbows." She *tut-tut-tut*s.

"I'd be happy to fund your time in school, honey," she presses. "You know I would, so long as your grades remain satisfactory and your professors report that you're applying yourself. Then the moment you graduate, I have an office waiting for you, right beside mine."

"Don't bother," I spit out. "I already finished my degree, Mother— and I don't even need you to pay for it. I'll do it myself."

"Yes," she scoffs as I turn a corner and slam face-first into a body that feels like a brick wall. "With your father's credit card!"

Hands reach out and grab my arms. The oxygen in my lungs bursts out on a grunted exhale, then cologne replaces it so all I smell is my wall.

Which is actually a man.

"Uh…"

"Watch where you're going," he murmurs. His lips move, but they're hard to see, as a dark cap shadows his face. His jaw is strong and broad, his hands gripping and tight.

My mother continues somewhere far away. "You break his heart with your decisions. Do you realize that?"

The strange man's hands release me so it's almost a shove as he pushes me back to the *actual* wall of the store on the corner. "You shouldn't walk around town yammering on the phone and not watching where you're going. It's not safe. And frankly," he adds as an aside, "it's rude."

"Are you even listening to me?" My mother's voice cuts through our exchange. "You interrupted my day with this, Maya! *You* called *me*. And now you won't even listen to what I've got to say!"

"Eyes up," the guy coaches. Then he's gone. His hands in his jean pockets, his long legs eating up the sidewalk till he's around the corner and gone from my sight.

I remain in place, breathing the scent of man out of my lungs, and replacing it with—I lean forward so I can look to the building at my back —*coffee*. Then I flop back until I hit the brick again.

It holds me up, when I'm not sure I'd stay vertical if not for the assist.

"I'm hanging up, Maya! The next time you deign to waste my time, expect to be billed. My clients *pay* me—"

"Mom?"

I'm breathless. *Why am I breathless?*

Bringing the phone to my ear, then pulling it back again so her shrieking voice doesn't make my eardrums bleed, I close my eyes and press my free palm to my chest. "Mom, I'm sorry. I dropped my phone. I didn't mean..." I allow my eyes to flutter open again and look to my left to make sure the stranger is gone. *Or to get another peek?* "I didn't mean to waste your time. I stumbled and dropped my phone, so..."

"Oh." With the wind taken from her sails—and maybe, just *maybe*, a sliver of maternal instinct working through her veins—Paige Blake clears her throat. "Well... okay. Did you hurt yourself, sweetheart? Is the sidewalk in that podunk town a hazard?"

"No, it's..." I shake my head. "Not a hazard. It was my clumsiness. And this isn't a podunk town, Mom. It's actually really pretty."

Standing on the corner outside of a coffee shop, I glance along Main Street toward a park a couple blocks down, a massive tree eating up the center, offering shade for families to picnic beneath on a warm spring day. I look the other way and find a cute ice cream parlor with the old-style booths and checkered flooring reminiscent of the nineteen-fifties.

"This town is beautiful, Mom. It's quaint. And I haven't met anyone yet that didn't go out of their way to be friendly."

Except one.

"It's a town of blue-collar steel factory workers," she sneers. "I swear to

30

you, Maya Elizabeth, if you dare bring a man home to meet your father and I, and he isn't college-educated…"

"Mom!" I let out a groan that goes all the way down to the soles of my feet. "I have no intention of ever bringing a man home to you. If at some point I find one I like, I certainly won't be subjecting him to the Blake family badgering. Besides…" Frowning, I look down at the sidewalk. "I'm not here to date. I'm here to work—in my *dream* job."

"Dream," she scoffs. "Because that's the only town where your so-called job will pay you enough to cover rent. Surely, you can dream bigger."

She exhales, clearly drained by having the same conversation over and over again. "What if you stay in that… *job*," she says the word like it comes with a layer of *ick*, "get it out of your system for a year, but still attend law school? You know you have the intellect to carry both. Especially when babysitting toddlers takes none at all."

"Mom!"

"Consider it," she snarls. "Think of your future, honey. Because I assure you, that's all I've done since the day of your conception."

My conception; not the day of my birth, or even the day they found out they were pregnant, but the day of *conception*. Because that process was as clinical as signing legal documents and my father depositing sperm into a cup. Turkey basters. Insemination. Because God forbid they just make a baby the traditional way.

"I have to go, Mom." A dejected sigh works along my throat, a stark acceptance that I am *other* compared to what they surely hoped to create in a test tube twenty-five years ago. "But before I do, and I know you're busy…." *Stroke the ego.* It's how we get her to do anything she doesn't like. "I had another reason for calling today."

"Of course you did." Her tone changes from nagging mother to the cold, calculated hunter who heads a law firm. "That's very Maya of you, to have an ulterior motive. Is it money?" Already, she counts zeroes in her head. "How much do you need?"

"Not money." Pushing away from the wall, I cross the three feet back to the corner and peek around for any sight of the man in all black. Black jeans, black shirt, black ballcap, and no tolerance for anyone getting in his way. "Um…" I drag my bottom lip between my teeth. "I was calling for Grammy's things."

"Oh for goodness sake, *this* again?" Paige Blake is nothing if not fed up with her daughter's pleas for what her daughter is entitled to—by law, and by the sealed will my grandmother had written up before she passed. "Are you serious, Maya?"

"Grammy promised me her diaries," I implore. "Her pictures. She promised me her memoirs and her locket. These things aren't valuable to you, Mother. But they're sentimental to me."

"And I, as her only child, am entitled to them first," she coldly responds. "Why must you make everything a fight, Maya? Why do you insist on painting me as the bad guy?"

"Because I just want her diaries!" I burst out. "This doesn't need to be a fight, Mom. It's an exchange of what is legally mine."

"Legally yours?" She coughs out a laugh. Then another. "*Legally* yours?" Then she does the Cruella, head-thrown-back cackle. "If you'd finished law school, you'd know how wrong you are."

"Mo—"

"Complete your education," she cuts in before I can go on. "Do a year with mine or your father's firm and prove to us you've moved past this ridiculous dream you carry to babysit children all day long, and I'll give you the diaries. In fact, I'll give them to you on your graduation day. A token of goodwill," she adds, like she actually thinks she'd be doing me a favor. "You're better than what you've chosen for yourself, Maya, and just like when you were a child, I forgive you for your inability to think ahead. It's the signature of an immature brain, after all. As your mother, it's my job to think for you."

"I'm not a child. I'm not fourteen years old and asking to go to Sarah Glasson's party, Mom. I'm a twenty-five-year-old woman who hasn't come home in five years because you refuse to treat me as an equal in your home."

"Because you are not our equal," she chitters. *Chitters.* "You will always remain our child, Maya. But someday, I hope we can all meet on the same intellectual level."

"So your answer is no to the diaries?" Pushing away from the corner and trudging along Main Street, I continue in the direction I've started. "Is that your official answer, Mother? You will not deliver to me the things Grammy made certain to itemize in her will?"

"Of course I'll give them to you." Her tone is too cheerful. Because she's about to drop the hammer. "Once you've *earned* them. I have to go now, okay, honey? I have work to do and a judge who thrills in speaking down to me in a courtroom."

Gee. I wonder why.

"Come home this weekend," she panders. "Your father would love a visit. He thinks you're upset with him."

*I **am** upset with him!*

But instead of saying that, I grumble, "I'll talk to you another day."

Pulling the phone away before either of us finds discomfort in the lack of *I love you*s that most mothers and daughters share at the conclusion of a discussion, I kill the call and slip the device into my back pocket. Then I stop where I am... and look up when I realize I have no clue where the hell I've walked to.

Obviously, I'm still on Main Street. *But where? Why here?*

I've stopped in front of a glass-fronted building with *Christina Cooper Studios* written in script on the window. Inside, framed photographs grace the walls—some in color, but most in black and white. Some portraits are small, while many others are fifty inches or more.

Catching my eye after my day with a little boy who dubbed himself a *Roller* is a canvas print of what appears to be a cage. Men fight inside. One is laid out on his back, while the other sits tall, his arm mid-swing and heading directly for his opponent's face.

Fighters.

On the ground.

Rollers?

I don't go in, and I make sure not to come too close to the window, even if the afternoon sun creates a glare and makes it difficult for me to see inside. But I stare for a moment.

I scan to the next portrait and find a young woman—*a young teen, maybe?*—with wild, curly hair, and her gloved hands held high in victory. Another girl, this one with long, mahogany locks, stands beside her, a gleeful smile wrapped around a pink mouth guard. On the curly one's other side, a man whose eyes radiate a level of pride I have *never* seen in my parents' gaze.

The image of the men brought me closer to the glass, but I stay for the girl. For her smug grin, and the spatter of blood on her cheek. The savagery of what she's just done, but the delight with which she did it.

The man—*her father? Her trainer?*—who holds her close. And the girl—*her opponent? Or maybe her friend?*—who finds complete pleasure in standing beside a champion.

"You look creepy staring in the window, ya know?"

"*Argh!*" I jump and spin, rapping my elbow against the glass, then gasp when I turn to find a woman with curls. *Wild* curls. A smug grin.

Thankfully, no blood on her cheek.

"Oh my gosh!" Humiliated, I study the teen and wonder if she'll wear my blood like warpaint next. "You're..." Speechless, I point back toward the studio. "She..."

She points at me. "Stalker?"

"What? No!" *Schoolteacher about to lose her job.* "Definitely n— No. I was just wandering by and got distracted."

"Maya?" The studio door opens on my left, scaring me forward another step, then I twist and find Britt standing in the doorway with a playful grin. On her left, Charlie smirks like he knows I'm an idiot. "Smalls? Are you being mean to Miss Blake?"

"Miss Blake?" *Smalls... the curls... the world champion 'after she graduates school'. Oh god.* "Teacher?"

My eyes are wide. My heart thundering. "Fighter?"

"She's my cousin too, Miss Blake." Charlie's entirely too pleased with himself. Too arrogant when he steps out of the studio and stops on my right.

He taps my hand and points to the girl. "Cousin." Then he points to the studio. "My aunty. She's not a Cooper anymore. But no one got fussy about her keeping the studio name." Then he looks up at me. "Whatcha doing down at this end of Main Street? You live down here?"

"Uh... No, I..." I shake my head. "I don't live down here. In fact, I—" I point over the girl's head. "I live that way, I think."

"You *think*?" Charlie laughs entirely too loudly. "You got lost on your first day, Miss Blake? That's silly."

Britt sniggers. "We'll help you get home. Do you have a car?"

"Oh, no, I'm not lost." I lick my dry bottom lip. "I've come for a walk," I tell them. "The sun is lovely, and it's still early enough in the afternoon, I don't have to rush home. I have a car," I add when Britt's brows shoot high. "I do, but I live close to the school, so I walked. And just now,

I had a phone call to make, so I did it while walking. That's..." *I'm rambling. I look stupid in front of my student.* "I'm not lost."

"Well..." Slowly, her brows settle back into place. "As long as you're sure." Then she glances to the studio. "Smalls had to come down here today for a promo shoot. I wanted to talk to Tina for a sec, and Charlie doesn't know what personal space is," she shoots a look down at him, "so he followed."

"It's because I love you," he says so sweetly... with a side of menace. "And Smalls."

"Wh-why..." I look at the girl. The massive hair. "Why do they call you Smalls?"

She snorts, not shy the way her little cousin Lily is. "Because my dad's name is Biggie. We can't be a matching pair if they called me Tupac. There's way too much baggage there."

"Her name is Evelyn. But her mother," Britt points back at the studio, "was a self-righteous *'you can't cuss in front of my kid'* mom. Then Aiden, Tina's husband, called Evie 'Smalls' one day when she was a toddler. Evie called him 'Biggie' back, and here we are. Rival wars always waging in the same home."

"And lots of cussing, I assume."

"Not by me, Miss Blake." Evie bats her lashes. "I'm the innocent kid in that mess."

"You should come to dinner tonight." With a simple change in subject, Britt brings my attention around like a whip. "We're setting the kids up with a movie and pizza, while the parents go out to dinner. Smalls is 'sitting, and Ben will be there too, to keep Smalls out of jail."

"Ben? " Too many names. Too much information. "I don't—"

"Ben's just a guy," Evie sniffs. Finally losing a little of that arrogance, she glances away. "He's kinda stupid, really. And annoying."

"And by *annoying*," Britt rolls her eyes, "she means he keeps her out of trouble and off the cops' radar."

"Difficult," Evie counters, "when his dad *is* the cops."

"Keep your enemies close, baby girl." Stepping around, Britt pulls her niece in for a side hug, but her eyes are for me. "Dinner?"

"Oh, no, I... I was just going to—"

"Go home," she cuts in. "Sit alone. Talk to your cat?"

"I—I don't have a cat." I look down at Charlie. "I don't think it would be smart for me to have a pet."

"I have a dog," Charlie inserts happily. "She's the smartest dog on the planet."

"You have no pets," Britt pushes back at me, "and you have no friends in town yet. Considering I know, am married to, or am related to about two-thirds of its residents, I think you coming to dinner might be a smart choice. You can meet everyone in one sweep, get to know a bunch of parents you'll probably run into at school...Plus, it's only dinner, which means early in, early out."

"Well... I..."

"Club 188." Reaching into the bag on her side and taking out a pen and an old, scrunched-up ball of paper, she scribbles. "It's within walking distance too. In fact," she glances up and wrinkles her nose, "there's not much in this town that isn't walking distance. 188 is just a couple of streets over. It's a nightclub for drinking and whatnot, but they do food before the drinking crowd arrives. It's two levels, so we'll take the top and stay away from most of the noise."

Finishing her note, she extends her hand and waits for me to take it. "Address," she explains, "time, and my cell number, in case you chicken out and want to make excuses."

"I can make excuses?" I ask. "You'll accept them?"

She laughs. "No. I'll talk you around, then I'll save you a seat with the family."

"I mean..." Each person in our group watches me. Smiling. Smug. "If it's dinner, my seat probably needed to be accounted for when your table was reserved. It's too late to—"

"Nice attempt," Britt taunts. "But not an issue. I know club management."

With a megawatt grin, Evie points two thumbs back at herself. "I'm management."

"E-excuse me..." I study her, then Britt. "What?"

"Technically, she owns the place," Britt says. "Like, in the most legal sense. But the family manages it for her till she's done with school. Her aunt works the bar, her mom keeps the books organized, and the rest of us take turns helping."

"But she's..." I look at her again. "You're a child."

"Hardly," she counters impatiently. "And I've owned the place since I was three. My dad was a crooked, *crooked* man," she adds with a taunting glint in her stare. "But he was also filthy rich."

"I don't..." My eyes widen, and my stomach hollows. "Biggie?"

"No. Biggie's my stepdad. My real father is pushing up daisies, I think." Then she shrugs. "I don't care what he's doing these days. But... 'management'? That's me. I'll get you a seat at the table tonight, so long as you talk to me about Charlie's classroom behavior. Is he a total jerk?"

"Hey!" Charlie slaps the side of Evie's leg. "I'm not a jerk."

She doesn't react to his five-year-old response—the first of those I've witnessed from him all day. She only stares into my eyes and waits. "So...? Did he pee his pants?"

"Smalls!"

"No..." I try to hold back my smile. "He did not wet his pants."

"I told you I wouldn't," Charlie grumbles. "Why are you trying to embarrass me?"

"He got a little girlfriend in class?" she asks instead. "He's real smooth with the ladies, so you've gotta be careful with him."

"Enough." Britt catches her son's second swing before it makes contact with Evie's thigh, then she opens the studio door and waits with a lifted brow for her niece to pass. "You go do the shoot so your mom can be done and go home. You," she speaks to Charlie. "We don't hit except at the gym." Then she catches my eye and transforms her grin. "See you at the club. Don't expect five-star food; it's a club owned by a toddler, after all. But it's decent enough, and the new friends you gain will make up for it."

Sliding her fingers between Charlie's so they're embracing, rather than her restraining him, she waddles out of the way and allows the studio door to close. "I'm going home, because I have a whole bunch of kids to shower and prepare for a quiet night. I have to pee more than you could ever know, and my son needs a lecture on physical violence in retaliation for hurt feelings." She sends a pointed look his way. "We don't do that."

"If we fight with emotion," he sighs, "we lose."

"There you go." Glancing back up at me, she waves goodbye and starts away. "If you get lost and can't find your home, call me and I'll help. My place is about ten minutes from here, so I can come back and get you."

"O-okay…" I look down at the note in my hand, then to Britt's tiny waist from my view of her back.

She's a trim, athletic woman, if not for the three basketballs stretching out ahead of her. Her hair is longer than mine, straighter and softer, so the locks almost touch her backside. Her shoulders are delicate in a tank top, but strong too, and an intricate tattoo takes up a portion of her right shoulder blade.

She holds her son's hand and waddles to the corner of the block, then, while I remain standing in front of Christina Cooper's studio, *not* staring at the canvas of the fighter girls, they turn the corner and disappear from my view.

Dinner? I think to myself.

Do I actually *want* to get dinner with a family I don't know, whose children continue to keep me on my back foot… all after a conversation with my dragon mother?

Maya

THERE ARE SO MANY OF THEM

Club 188 is as Britt explained: two stories tall, with music thumping on the ground floor, a band on a makeshift stage, and a bar that spans the entire back wall. Up the metal stairs that are a tripping hazard for any drunk woman in heels, I find a second, smaller bar, booths lining the wall, and tall tables littered throughout the rest of the space.

The area is packed, but every single body belongs to a cute woman in cut-off shorts and a top that accentuates every perfect dip and curve, or a man way too large, way too muscular, and far more tattooed than any other I know.

Almost any other I know.

In fact, they're all like Jack Reilly... fighters.

"Maya!" A blonde woman I've never met in my life breaks away from her date and rushes to the top of the stairs where I wait.

I wear a cute dress with a tight-ish torso, but with a floating skirt and heels. Britt said it's a club, after all, and my five feet, four and a half inches tends to always be in need of a little lift. But the woman who greets me with a large smile wears no heels at all.

Actually, she wears Converse high-tops and *still* towers over me.

"You're Maya Blake, right?" She pulls me in for a hug, entirely too comfortable with herself, then stepping back, she stares down at me with beautiful blue-green eyes that pop under blonde hair. "My name is Kit

Kincaid." She takes my hand in hers and turns to gesture toward the crowd. "Britt's my sister-in-law. You met my brother today."

"I did?" I study her. Her beautiful features, and her cunning grin. I stop on the single dimple in her cheek, and finally, familiarity clicks. "Jack Reilly's your brother?"

"He is," she beams. "I was Kit Reilly before marriage. And you teach Charlie, who was named for our dad."

"I do."

I let her tug me away so we pass tables of overly fit people. I don't mean to be intimidated, but these people... this family...

"You all work out?"

She snorts. "We own a gym, and most of the guys are pro fighters. It comes with the territory. Their sport is how we pay the bills."

Stopping by the bar, she raps her knuckles on the top and draws the eyes of a woman not a hell of a lot shorter than me.

Unlike Kit's long, blonde locks, or even Brittany's streaming mahogany, this woman wears hers in a pixie cut that frames her face and shows off a sly gleam in her eyes.

Wandering closer in a tight tank top and an array of necklaces that vary from silver that plunges and teases her cleavage, to others that are nothing more than chokers circling her slim neck, the woman stops in front of us and purses her smiling lips. "You must be Maya Blake."

"I don't..." I look from one woman to the other. "I don't know how everyone seems to know my name."

The bartender reaches down to pick up a glass. Without asking what I want, she begins making a cocktail that whets my appetite.

Tequila. Triple sec. Lime juice.

"Everyone in this town knows everyone else, Maya. Which means when someone new comes along, we know they're new, and we quickly find out who they are." She grabs a blender and fills it with ice. "Add in that you're teaching our children, and we're going to make sure you're cool."

The blender whirs loud enough to make her shout, but not so shocking that anyone looks our way.

"Britt already told us who you are, and seeing as how she's my neighbor, I asked her all the relevant questions this morning before she went to school. She vouches for you. Charlie thinks you're the shit. Smalls thinks you're a little shy, which means she'll test your boundaries. And I..." Finishing with the blender, she combines all her ingredients, and dips a fresh glass in salt to circle the rim, then slicing a wedge of lime and placing it on the rim as well, she presents to me her gift, "am Casey. My friends get to call me Tink, since apparently that name is never going away. And just so we can avoid later awkwardness, I'm aware that you're aware of the Devil Twins."

"The Devil—" I reach out for my drink, but stop before taking it in my fingers. "The Devil Twins?"

"Mine." She grins, as though proud to be the mother of arsonists. "They're really not as bad as rumors would have you believe. Mostly, they're everyone else's scapegoats, since they fit the profile of troublemakers."

"So..." I drag my bottom lip between my teeth. "They're innocent, but they take the blame?"

"They're not innocent." She laughs. "But I don't believe they light nearly as many fires as everyone claims."

Gesturing over my shoulder, she nods until I follow her gaze to a muscled man standing beside the one Kit left.

I study him for a moment; his short hair compared to the one beside him. They both wear ink the way I wear skin. They're well over six feet tall, and if I were inclined to measure, I'd bet their biceps were as big as my head.

Slowly, I bring my gaze back to Tink.

"Mine," she repeats with a smug grin. "Jon Hart. Another scapegoat. A lost-boy, if you will. But beneath that is a sweetheart who doesn't mind the rep he must carry."

She picks up my drink and offers it across the bar. "Welcome to town, Maya Blake. We're happy to have you. Honestly, I'm just happy I'm not the only woman suffering from height issues anymore." She wrinkles her nose. "They'll probably bring it up to tease you, but don't take it personally. People around here show love by mocking you. It's a thing."

"It's a thing," Kit confirms. Taking my arm, she turns me to the crowd once more and starts toward the group in the middle.

For just a moment, my nerves thunder in my blood and make it damn near impossible to hear anything but my heart. My stomach swirls, and the thought of adding tequila to the mix makes my palms sweat. But when the group of guys opens up with welcoming smiles to let us join, it's the gap between them that draws my attention.

Because in a booth lining the wall is a different guy. Dark clothes, dangerous stare.

"This is Maya Blake," Kit announces to her family.

Though, my interest remains on the stranger I bumped into earlier today. His glare, burning against my face, and his large hands, wrapped around a glass of what must surely be water.

Because if it's liquor, he's certain to end up in the hospital.

"It's nice to meet you, Maya." The guy Kit was cuddling takes my hand first, drawing my attention away from the stranger and sinking me instead into a chocolate gaze. "I'm Bobby."

"H-hi, Bobby."

Then the Devils' dad takes my hand. "And I'm Jon. Welcome to town, Maya. How are you enjoying it so far?"

"Uh..." I let him shake my hand. I let him hold it and look down at me. But my gaze slides through the space between men, to the guy who is yet to look away.

He sits in a booth with a few others—five of them, by my fast count—and though his face is turned toward his friend, his eyes are on me. His watch like a physical caress that makes me feel entirely too exposed in my tight dress.

"Maya?"

"It's good." I yank my focus back to Jon Hart and hate the way my cheeks fill with a blush. "I like it here. It's, uh... it's a pretty town, but somehow comes with a lot of personality."

"That's because of our kids," Bobby teases. His shoulders are broad and muscled, tattooed and somewhat... pretty. But in the two inches between him and Jon is a man whose eyes burn a mesmerizing hazel.

"We had too many of 'em," he adds with a chuckle. "Now they're coming of age and filling the school. We'd apologize, but..." He smirks when I peel my eyes back to his. "Well, we kinda like them, and we enjoy the idea of retiring on their riches someday. So we'll probably keep them."

"I heard you're renting an apartment two blocks from Main," Jon interjects. "That old-fashioned building with the concrete mailboxes out front?"

"I... uh..." I frown. "I am. How is that common knowledge?"

He scoffs. "Small town perks. Once you've been around a while, you learn who owns what and what's available. Bobby," he tilts his head to his friend, "actually lived in those apartments when he was small."

"You did?" I bring my gaze back to his chocolate eyes. "It really is a small town."

He smiles. "I was born in a different city, but my family moved back when I was a toddler. That's where we lived for a bit, my parents and I."

"Mac also lived there," another guy, similar to the first, steps forward and offers his hand. "Jimmy Kincaid." He tilts his head toward Bobby. "I'm the youngest. And the best fighter. Our buddy Mac and his mom lived in those apartments, too, a few years back. If you ever need help or a friend, they're pretty good people to know."

"Oh, well..." I bring my hand away when he releases me. "That's nice. Everyone seems so... friendly," I settle on.

"Most around here are," he says. "No one gives anyone trouble... unless it's trouble they're asking for."

"Like this crew," Jon acknowledges the elephant in my world and rolls his eyes to the side to indicate the group in the booth. "Don't know them," he continues, softer now. "They're not from around here. But they're looking to be noticed."

"They are?" I swallow down my nerves and bring my drink up to sip. "Why do you say that?"

"Because they don't live here," Bobby murmurs. "And there's a whole level of the club downstairs they could've sat in tonight. We don't mind sharing our space," he clarifies, "but it would appear they've gone out of their way to be where we can see. So..." He shrugs. "I'll watch them. If they wanna get noisy, we'll head over and introduce ourselves. If they just wanna drink and be chill, then that's cool too."

"Tink said," and like they don't know who Tink is—*I'm an idiot*—I nod toward the woman at the bar, "everyone knows everyone, and those they don't know, they figure it out fast. So why..." I spy the stranger between Bobby's and Jon's arms, "don't you know who they are?"

"Because they didn't think to introduce themselves yet, I suppose." Bobby grabs Kit's hand and pulls her into his side. "Maybe they're just here for a drink, and that's the end of it. In which case..."

"We'll accept their credit cards and bank their money." Jon finishes. "You hungry?"

"Yeah," I nod. "I am. But I'll pay. Ya know, with my credit card."

Jimmy chuckles. "This is family dinner, Maya. And you were invited by Britt. That means you don't pay."

"Are you sure?" I fumble the drink in my hand and quickly bring my purse up. "It's fine," I continue. "I—"

"We won't accept your money." Jon gently reaches out and pushes my hands back down. "You won't need that here."

At a signal I don't see, he takes a step back. Then another.

"I'll see you around, Miss Blake. It was nice meeting you."

"Yeah, you too." I lift my hand to wave. Because I'm a socially awkward porcupine. "Jesus." I lower my arm, then bring my drink closer, instead of risking soaking the cute, married fighter. "I'm so weird sometimes."

Bobby only sniggers. "You'll be okay before long. Food will be up soon. Find a seat and talk to whoever. Everyone knows who you are, so sit at any table, and you'll find conversation."

"And if I sit alone?" I ponder. "Because I'm awkward and weird."

"Then we'll bring our chairs to you," Jimmy says easily. "Talk to anyone in this club, Maya, and you'll find a friend."

Looking to Kit, he winks until her lips turn flat, then he turns away and sidles up behind a woman I surely hope is his wife, considering the way he grabs her.

"Meeting new people can be intimidating." Kit places a reassuring hand on my arm. Her eyes are so kind, and her expression shows empathy. "Meeting an entire family like ours can be... well, a thing of horror for an introvert. But Britt will be here in a minute, so you'll have that familiar face."

Kit looks over my shoulder to the bar, receiving the same non-vocal signal Jon did, then she brings her attention back to me. "I'll be back. I've just gotta take care of some stuff. Drink your margarita and have a good time."

Squeezing my arm, she smiles one last time before she and Bobby walk away and leave me all alone.

Horror, meet introvert.

"Oh god," I groan.

I want to go home.

Cole

DINNER AND A DATE

"Jack Reilly just walked in."

Preston sits across from me while music thumps and the Kincaid family, in all their fucking glory, move around and drink. Some joke. Most talk. Everyone spares a glance for the new girl, though she doesn't see any but those who directly step forward and speak to her.

She's oblivious; to her admirers, to her obliviousness. To the seductiveness of her innocence. She's shy and shaky, and now she's drinking tequila.

Tonight's gonna get messy if she consumes more than one.

"He owns the brand-new Mustang out front," Pres continues across from me. "Luxury model GT. Two-door. Five-liter, V8 engine. Active exhaust valves, six-speed short shifting gear box. Four hundred and fifty horses, eighty-three grand off the lot."

He leans onto the table between us while I watch her walk. While she peruses her seating options and, from the corner of her eyes, peeks back at me.

"Cole!" he hisses. "You listening to me?"

"Yeah." Dragging the corner of my lip between my teeth, I peel my eyes from Maya Blake's trim frame in a sexy dress and instead meet Pres' unkind stare. "I'm listening."

"That car's still in production," he grits between his teeth. "Which makes Reilly's a special batch only for rich boys. It makes the one out front worth a fuck heap more than the eighty-thousand-dollar tag."

"And Box wants it." I twist my head again to catch sight of *her*. The awkward woman who argues on the phone while she walks, and crashes into people because she's not watching where she goes. "I got it."

"Keyless entry," he pushes. "I already grabbed the VIN and had a new fob made up. We have the keys, Miller. You just have to stop staring at legs and pay a-fucking-tention to me."

"I'm listening." Scowling, I bring my eyes back around to him. "Why are you so fucking tense? That's usually my job."

"Because we're inside the lion's den," he growls. "Because our job is to steal from a world fucking champion fighter. And though I know you can slither and slide out of a man's grip, I don't particularly wanna be on the end of that motherfucker's fist if he catches us."

"Are we ever caught?" I bring my glass of water up and slide my free hand across the table to swipe the fob he discreetly sets down. Wrapping my fingers around the black plastic, I swallow a mouthful and bring my hand back. "Literally never, Pres. So you need to calm down."

"Literally never... *so far*," he grumbles.

Then, just as the man himself, Jack Reilly, wanders past our booth, Pres firms his lips and tries on his 'I'm just minding my business' face.

The moment Reilly is gone, Pres releases his breath and leans closer to me. "He's going to use our fuckin' heads for bowling balls if you screw up."

"So we make sure I don't screw up." Pushing up to stand, I drop the fob in my pocket and grab my water to keep my hands busy, then I wink for my best friend and turn away from the booth.

We're here to steal from the rich and sell it to someone else, but I walk through the crowd like I'm one of them. I smile for those who smile at me, and I nod my head when the wives watch me go. I mumble non-committal *hey*s when some of the fighters say it to me, then I come to a stop behind the only other person in this club who doesn't quite *fit*.

Maya Blake.

She smells of sex and roses, and her trim build draws a man's eyes down, begging his hands to touch.

"You look about as comfortable here as I am." I lean closer, grinning when she jumps at my voice.

Setting my water on the table beside her elbow, I slide onto the empty stool on her left and leave my legs wide, so I'm practically surrounding her without actually touching.

I wait patiently as she glances my way. As though too scared to confirm who sits with her. I wait as her soft green stare meets mine, then as her eyes drop and scan my body. My thighs, wrapped in jeans, and then my chest, covered with a white shirt, and a button-up over top. I smile when her study comes to my jaw, unshaven as it is, then I wink when our eyes meet once more.

Because winking isn't the most douchebag shit possible when meeting a new woman.

"Cole Miller." I place my hand between us and wait for her to take it. I've watched a dozen other men do the same tonight, and every single time, she's done as socially accepted and shook their hands. Now it's my turn. "And you're Maya Blake."

"I've been told that several times tonight." Finally, after making me wait a lifetime, she reaches across and shakes my hand. "No one here asks my name. They *tell* me."

Her eyes flicker down and watch my lips as they curl up to the side.

"Does it bother you that they do that?" Though I'd like to hold on longer, maybe pull our joined hands to my lap to see what she'd do, I release her when she pulls it free. "Does it bother you that no one asks?"

She shakes her head, an instant response, before shrugging. "It doesn't *bother* me, exactly. But it's kind of jarring. They're watching you, by the way."

"Hmm?" I grab my water, since I need something to fidget with before I'm tempted to reach out and brush the long hair off her shoulder. "Who?"

"All of them." She wears lipstick tonight, fire engine red and startling like a siren. "All the fighters. They're keeping an eye on you and your friends."

"They are?" I don't look around. I don't give up so much information so soon. "Why? What did I do?"

"Apparently, they know everyone in town. And it would seem you're a drive-by."

They're a perceptive bunch of bastards.

"Drive-by's are allowed, right?" I glance across the room to the top of the stairs and take care not to make eye contact with those who watch us. "There was no sign out there saying I had to be one of them to enter."

Again, she shrugs. "I'm new too. I only know they're watching you and your friends to make sure you're not causing trouble." Taking a sip of her margarita, she licks her lips and enjoys the salt that rests on the bottom. "Where are you from, and why are you here?"

I drag my gaze away from her plump bottom lip and instead down to the small slit in her dress. "Where are *you* from, and why are you here?"

"The city." Like it doesn't bother her to reveal her business, she brings her drink up for a second taste. "I grew up only an hour away. And I live here now because I graduated college and got a job at the school." Glancing across with beautiful eyes that stand out between dark, *dark* lashes and eyeliner, she purses her lips. "Now your turn. And why were you skulking around the streets earlier today?"

A slow grin tugs my lips across. "You're not as unobservant as you let people believe, Blake. And I grew up in the city, too. Guess that makes us both suspicious outsiders."

She stares ahead at a group of men who think each is funnier than the one before. "I was invited here. You... have eyes on you."

"As do you, beautiful. I feel like we didn't get to meet each other properly." With an odd staccato in my heart, I leave my water on the table and bring my hand up in the space between us. "Hi, I'm Cole Miller."

When her questioning eyes come around to study mine, I add, "And you are?"

She stares, confounded and confused. Then, hesitantly, as though she doesn't trust my motivation, she takes my hand a second time. "Maya Elizabeth Blake. I'm new to town. Moved here just a few days ago."

"It's a pleasure to meet you." I hold on for a beat too long. For a pause that brings a sweet blush to her cheeks and a slight panic to her perfect eyes. Then I release her hand and slide her margarita closer. "How'd you get a personal invitation to this shindig if you only just moved to town?"

"Because I teach one of their kids, down at the school. I suppose I looked lonely and nervous, which resulted in a dinner invitation tonight. So..." She runs a hand along her dress. Intended, I'm sure, to show off her presence, and not necessarily her curves... though it's the latter I focus on. "Here I am," she mouths after a long beat. "It pays to know people. And you?"

I bring my water up and choke out a soft laugh as I swallow. "Well... I know you now. So maybe I'll get an invitation next time and fewer glares of accusation. What grade do you teach?"

She runs the top of her finger along the rim of her glass. "Hmm?"

"You said you teach at the school. So what grade?"

"Oh." Color warms her cheeks. "Kindergarten. Today was my first official day."

"So you just graduated college in May?"

"Mmhm. Took me a little longer to get to the end, compared to the others in my classes. But... I got here."

"Slow learner?" I ask, genuinely curious. "Needed a little extra time?"

She scoffs. "I did pre-law for four years first, then transferred the credits I could and finished it out."

"Pre-law?" I bark out in surprise. "You're not slow at all. How the fuck did you go from lawyer to kindergarten teacher?"

"A step down?" She lifts a sharp brow and threatens my life with a look. "From corporate highflyer to snot wiper?"

"I didn't say that."

When a server wanders closer and lingers by our table, I smile and meet her eyes.

"Can we get a couple of sodas? Coke for me." Then, "Maya?"

"Coke's fine." She pushes her half-consumed alcohol away and reaches up to push hair behind her ear. "Thank you."

"My kindergarten teacher was the best fucking person I ever knew." I smile and wait for Maya's defensive glare to come back my way. "Mrs. Granger. She was old as God and so sweet to us all. She fed me more often than my parents did, and when I struggled with book work, she sat with me in the afternoons and helped me along. We're not talking algebra here, Maya. But counting to ten."

I look down and study the condensation ring my water leaves on the table. "I was slow as fuck and sometimes stupider than mud. But Mrs. Granger took pity on me when no one else did."

"That's..." I watch the wall she built slowly crumble. "Sweet. Do you still keep in contact with her?"

I shake my head and draw circles on the tabletop. "She died when I was in fifth grade. Took all my protections with her. I was hungry again, beaten up regularly, and the other teachers seemed to get off on treating me like shit. Like it somehow made them superior to kick me around."

"That's awful." Pouting in such a way that it doesn't look young and silly, but rather, delicious and kind, she reaches across and pats my forearm. It's quick, then it's gone. "Did you turn out alright in the end?" She looks me up and down, as though she can tell everything about my life with just a single study. "Did you catch up at school? Did you do alright in life?"

"Nope. I fell behind and dropped out of school long before my senior year." *Now I boost cars and piss off rich folks.* "I learned how to fight, though." Casting a glance back to the crowd surrounding us, I find Jack Reilly in the middle. He's the strongest of them all. The fastest. The best. "I'm no pro, but I learned how to not get my ass kicked."

"Well, that's all a little..." She pauses for a long, loaded beat. "Sad. The kid version of you deserved better."

"I know," I laugh. "I tried telling them that. But they said I was talking back, so they slapped me with more detention." I nod toward her. "Why'd you do an undergraduate in law, only to turn around to work with kids?"

"Because the first was expected of me. My parents offered to pay my way through school, intending for me to go into law. I thought they'd relax on the rules after I showed I could apply myself, so I accepted the deal and did my four years. Stayed on the Dean's list the whole way through. I thought that would be grounds to discuss a change in major. My parents disagreed and threatened to pull funding."

"So..."

"So I pulled funding on my own, even though I couldn't qualify for scholarships because they earned too much. I worked my way through as best I could, and came out the other side with a five-figure debt instead of six figures." She grabs her margarita and lifts it as though in cheers. "I got what I wanted in the end. Mostly," she adds as a bitter aside. "And now they're wondering why I won't go home to visit them."

"Because of money?" I ask. "You bailed because they wouldn't give you the money you asked for?"

"I bailed because I no longer wished to be controlled and manipulated. The money was just a tool in their arsenal. I took that tool away by no longer needing them to pay my way."

She looks up with a smile when our server comes back with our sodas. "Thank you."

She takes one for herself, then slowly pushes the other toward my hand. "I don't know who you are, Cole Miller. And that means I no longer wish to discuss my private life. What do you do for work?"

"Are we on a date?" I challenge. *Deflect, asshole.* "Is this tit for tat?"

"Well... no." Her cheeks warm with a tinge of embarrassment, but her eyes remain hard. Scalding.

Very *lawyerly* of her.

"You asked about mine, so I thought you were open to talking about yours." Grabbing her little purse and dropping cash down by my hand for her soda, she pushes up to stand. "However, if you're not open to *tit for tat*," she mocks my words, "then that probably concludes our time. I'm going home, climbing into fat pants, and watching something trashy and stupider than mud."

Tapping my shoulder with a gentle brush of her fingertips, she drags them away again, leaving behind an inferno beneath my skin and an odd pit in my stomach as I turn to watch her leave.

She goes to the group Jack Reilly hangs with, and pulls a different brunette in for a fast hug. Then she backs away, shaking her head.

Maybe they ask her to stay.

Perhaps they beg her to wait for the food.

It's possible they ask what the fuck I did to upset her, considering several sets of eyes come to me, but when I only watch her and she continues to shake her head, they bring their attention back to her.

Maya Blake is a beautiful woman who shivers under the stare of dozens of strangers. But she hardens under the stare of one. Her hands shake when she's to meet *the family*, but her words are firm when she speaks to me.

She's a contradiction of vulnerable and strong. Introvert. But assertive.

She's shy. But she has boundaries no man will dance upon without her permission.

As she says her goodbyes and makes her way to the stairs, I turn to look across at my booth, only to stop on Pres' hard glare. His curious gauging. His narrowed eyes, and his sidelong peeks.

When I remain seated and neither invite him closer nor tell him to stay away, he unfolds his legs and slips out of the booth.

Fighters' eyes follow his every step, but they remain passive.

As soon as Preston is within a foot, he claps my shoulders and drops down onto the stool Maya deserted. "What the fuck was that?" he grumbles. "You like drawing attention to yourself?"

"She's pretty." I turn my back on the fighters and take her soda for myself. "She's got spine, too."

"Yeah, and about a hundred people in this club who wanna protect her. You enjoy putting a target on your back?"

"No." I bring her Coke to my lips and chug an icy mouthful. "They're watching us, too."

"I know they're watching us! What the fuck do you think I was just saying?"

"No, I mean she told me they're watching us. Something about making sure we're not trouble."

"Shit," he hisses. He drops his head low and studies the top of the table like it holds a treasure trove of secrets. "We can't boost and not expect to be caught."

"Not tonight," I agree.

I don't reach down to the fob still in my pocket. I don't even look back at the guy whose car I intend to take. I simply drink my Coke and mind my business, and when a couple minutes have passed and Maya is no doubt out of the club, I set my glass down and push up to stand.

"I'm going home," I announce for Preston—and for anyone else thinking to listen in. "I'll catch you at work tomorrow." I clap Pres' hand and squeeze just long enough to make damn sure he doesn't get up to follow me. "I'll see you around, buddy."

Turning on my heels, I leave Maya's cash on the table, knowing it covers both of our drinks, then I cross the room and pass fighters who've earned their victories with formal training in a gym and years upon years of instruction from the professionals.

They're the type of fighters who get to step up on the world stage.

I'm just a scrapper who learned to fight because it meant the difference between a full stomach or not.

Passing the core group of guys and meeting the eyes of the one I know as Jon Hart, I nod. He nods. We don't know each other, but in this moment in time, we connect. Then it's gone, and my feet propel me faster.

Down the steel staircase and past the bar on the bottom level. I move through the dancers at a clipped pace, and past the band whose eyes remain mostly on the upstairs level of the club.

They play, they sing, they serenade their crowd. But their attention is for someone upstairs.

Shoving through the club doors and into the dusk light outside, I pass the shiny new GT and stop by mine. Older. Slower. But the love I have for her is enough to get us through the envy of wanting something shinier.

I unlock the car and open the door, but before I slide in, I peer to one end of the block in search of Maya Blake. Striking out, I look to the other end, and find the woman in heels, plodding her way along the street in a short dress.

It's not pitch-black outside yet, so chances are she'll be safe on her journey home. But that doesn't mean I'll leave her to chance.

Sliding into the driver's seat and turning over the engine, I grin when my measly three hundred and ten horses roar to life. She's loud enough to make people look, and smooth enough that all but car aficionados know she's a few years old. She's always washed and buffed, which means the paint is still as good as when she rolled off the manufacturing line, and she has no scars, but for the scrape my best fucking friend put on her last night in the McDonald's drive-thru.

Reversing away from the club and slipping the shift into first, I angle in the direction Maya left, and catch up after just a minute of slow rolling.

The sun sets in front of her, so she wears a slight halo as she walks, and though she clearly carries a dose of man-hater somewhere deep in her blood, she doesn't walk in a rage. She doesn't fix her skirt or stumble in her heels.

She's just a woman out for a stroll.

And I... am a man who wants more of what he experienced inside 188.

I roll my passenger window down and drive as slowly as she walks. "Maya? You want a ride?"

Stunned, though the noise of my engine really should've alerted her to my presence, she swings her gaze to me and scowls. "What?"

We're moving at about two miles an hour, which means I hardly have to look in front of me. "It's not safe walking at night. Boogeyman might jump out and get you. So…" I slow the car and stop, then I reach across to rest my hand on the doorhandle. "Get in. I'll take you home."

She laughs—like, head thrown back, barking in my face laughter. "I don't even know you, Cole! You're a guy I met for two seconds. You stare, and you refuse to speak about yourself." Shaking her head, she resumes walking. "I'd rather try my luck with the boogeyman, thanks."

"I can't let you walk home alone." I release the clutch and bring the car forward another few feet. "Maya, I don't have to know you to know I don't want you to get hurt walking home alone. That's just being a decent human."

"I don't need your protection." She shows off her cell in one hand, and her purse in the other. "I have a direct line with 9-1-1 if I need it, and a can of pepper spray for annoying guys who approach me in a club and expect to know all my private business within thirty-seconds of meeting one another." Dropping her hands again, she shakes her head, like I'm the stupid one. "You can go home, Cole. Your conscience needn't worry about me."

"My conscience won't ever heal again if I leave now and catch you on the news tomorrow. Some lowlife sees you walking, sun's going down, bushes are just," I nod over her shoulder, "over there. A dude can pull you across in half a second, and he can relieve you of your phone in the next. Then you're stuck, he's doing things you don't like, and I…" I glance along the road to make sure I won't crash, "never sleep again, because I left when I could've stopped it."

"There are nearly four billion other women on this planet, Cole Miller. Some of them are probably having a tough time right this second. Why don't you go worry about them instead?"

"Because I can't save them."

I smile when she looks across at me, when her stare registers something akin to surprise.

"I don't know them, I don't know where they are, and I don't have control over what's happening to those four billion. But I know you, Maya Elizabeth. I know where you are, and how vulnerable your situation is right now. And I *can* control that."

Her left brow comes up in challenge. "You wanna *control* me?"

I chuckle, knowing this woman has triggers that'll burn me if I touch too often. "Your situation," I repeat. "For as long as I stay right here and keep you in my sights, the situation is controlled and I know you're safe. The second I drive away and leave you alone, fuck knows what could happen. I don't wanna risk it, because I'd like to eventually sleep tonight. So... either you get in and I drive you home, or you stay out there, but I continue to follow you. One of those options ends with you getting blisters on your feet."

In that smooth, practiced way women are so good at, Maya walks out of her heels. One. She bends to collect it. Then two. She bends again. Then standing tall—or, tall for her—she meets my eyes with smugness glittering in hers. "I'm gonna be just fine. Thank you, though."

"Then I guess I'll drive in this direction of my own volition." I straighten in my seat and study the road ahead. The established trees, and the pretty sunset in front of her. "It just so happens we're heading the same way. What a fun coincidence, huh?"

"You're a stubborn mule." With an exasperated huff, she continues her trek and risks any number of diseases if she steps on glass or a used needle.

Which one of us is stubborn?

"Did you enjoy your night with the Kincaids?" I ask oh-so-casually. "Are they nice people?"

"Sure, they're nice. They went out of their way to be welcoming to the new chick in town, but I think I'm allergic to that many people unless they're five-year-olds." Bringing a hand up, she fake-sneezes. "Escape was my best course of action."

"Well, of course. Safety first. Are you an only child?"

She drops her playful smile and scowls instead. "Are you?"

"I am, actually." I rev my engine in apology for this Miss-Daisy-driving shit I'm forcing upon her. "Single mom who didn't much care. Absent dad who *definitely* didn't care. I probably have a dozen half-siblings scattered along Interstate 90, if we're being entirely honest, but I have no way of knowing for sure. You?"

Her scowl remains, marking her forehead and forcing a wrinkle she'll regret twenty years from now. "Only child. Test-tube baby." She peers across and fakes a smile. "I doubt my parents have ever actually touched each other."

Instead of commenting on her mother's sex life, I drill down on her *why*. "Test tube because your mom had trouble conceiving?"

"No. Test tube because my parents were busy living their lives and furthering their careers. Honestly, I'm surprised they didn't use a surrogate. It would've saved my mother the recovery time and the unsightly stretch marks."

"*Unsightly.*"

Bringing my hand away from the wheel, I brush fingers along my chin and chuckle at the pompous squeak in her voice. "You say fancy words when you're frustrated. What do your folks do for work?"

"They're lawyers, duh." She huffs them away so I might finally take a hint and stop asking. "What about your parents?"

"My mother was a professional seductress. She wanted to be taken care of, so she shopped for men far more often than she shopped for diapers or formula. I haven't heard from her in a while, but I assume she's still doing the same old shit. And legend has it my father drove trucks for a living, but I can't say for sure. If that's true, then he probably has a missus and kids in every major city—none of which he pays a dime to support. I left home a long time ago and never went back. How old are you?"

"Twenty-five. Are we playing Twenty Questions?"

"Sure, if that's what you want. And same."

"Same?" she parrots. "Same what?"

"I'm also twenty-five. But I'm a January baby, which means I'm almost certainly older than you."

"July," she grudgingly allows. "What do you do for work?"

"Why are you so fucking fixated with what I do for work? Jesus, Blake. Money-obsessed much?"

"Curious," she counters instead. "You know my job, so it's fair I know what you do."

"So we're back to tit for tat," I retort. "You don't give up shit unless you get the same back?"

"Oh please." She slows her walk and considers me with a roll of her eyes. "I know you're a twenty-five-year-old Capricorn high-school dropout. You know I'm a kindergarten teacher with a half a law degree and parents who never have sex. That's *obviously* not an even exchange of information. Are you embarrassed about your job? Is that why you won't tell me?"

"I'm not fucking embarrassed. I just don't like putting my business out there for strangers to know. Are you staying in town for long? Or is this a stopover for you for a year or two?"

"I'll probably stay." She shrugs, again allowing me to not answer her question.

How does *I do illegal shit and hope to not end up in prison* sound?

"It's a pretty town, and the school is lovely," she continues. "The people are nice, and the kids are sweet." Slowly, a genuine grin tips her lips to the side. "I've got this one kid who knows everyone, I swear. He's either related to them, or best friends with them." Peering my way, she adds, "he's a world champion fighter, apparently."

"World champion?" I frown. "In your class?"

"He's five," she snickers. "But his father is the actual champion, and nepotism is as good a reason as any when choosing future careers."

"Hence," I drawl, "your lawyer folks forcing you into a four-year undergraduate for something you don't even want."

"Mm," she growls. "That's about the gist of it."

When she starts around the corner, I follow her, only to feel my temper grow when parked cars block my view of her perfect legs in a sexy dress for a minute too long.

The sun is gone, and the sunset is barely a hint of orange on the horizon. Shrubs are everywhere, and the noise of my engine will mask any sound a fucking attacker might make if he wants to grab her quick-like.

Yanking the wheel to the side and switching the car off, I unsnap my seatbelt and push out of the car so the absence of my engine makes her startle and turn. Dropping the keys into my pocket beside Jack 'The Jackhammer' Reilly's duplicate, I stride and catch up to the beauty within seconds.

Slipping my hands in my pockets to keep them away from her body, I slow my walk and wait for her to start again. "So you got Reilly's kid in your class? Are they nice?"

"Jack and Britt?" She looks up at me, tilting her head back, now that she doesn't have heels to help with our height difference. Moving again, she turns and studies the sidewalk ahead. "They're really nice. Do you know them?"

"Never met 'em before in my life. The kid cool?"

"He's a smartass," she answers easily. "Too big for his age, but he's affectionate too, always hugging his little cousin or keeping an eye on her.

He loves his mother and idolizes his father, and I honestly think he's proud of how many people he's related to. Which is weird to me, considering I have no siblings at all."

"You have cousins?"

"On my father's side. But my entire family is a little stuffy. The money-obsessed, status-driven, social-climbing kind. They're more interested in how they appear to the outside world, than who they actually are on the inside. They don't care if they hurt others, and they don't seem to believe in karma."

"Karma?" I like how she smells. How her perfume plays on the warm, end-of-summer breeze, and how her hair feathers my arm as we walk. "How do you mean?"

"Well... I believe that what goes around comes around. If I'm bad to people, people will be bad to me. If I steal or harm or do bad in any way, then the universe will come around and do the same to me."

"So, if you lie, others will lie to you?"

"Right. And if I steal, things will be stolen from me."

Well... that's awkward for me. I glance back to make sure my Mustang remains exactly where I left her.

"So being a lawyer," I steer our conversation in a slightly different direction, "which is basically lying for a living, didn't feel good to you?"

"Not all lawyers lie," she exhales. "But my parents definitely do. Most of those I've met do. And none of those I've interacted with are truly happy beneath the wads of cash they have access to." Concertedly, she looks across and peeks up at me from beneath long lashes. "I'd rather be broke, happy, and on a baked bean diet, than rich but with no dignity."

"Spoken like a girl who's never gone hungry," I shake my head. "Things start to look a little less black and white when you're three days in and have no promise of a meal anytime soon. Karma seems less intimidating when you're at a crossroads, choosing between starvation or stealing an apple from the weekend markets." I lift my chin and wait for her eyes. "Are we nearly at your apartment?"

"I don't..." Startling back to reality, she stops in place and looks around. She glances to her left and frowns, then to our right so her frown turns to a wrinkling scowl. "Shit."

Taking out her phone, she unlocks the screen so it lights up her face, then she speaks her address in and groans when Siri tells her we've come too far.

"Back this way." She holds her heels under the crook of her left arm, and her purse under her right. Her hair swings as she spins, and her shoulders flex, proving she's no couch potato. She doesn't lift, but she sure as shit keeps active enough to fire up her muscles. "Sorry, I got turned around."

"Fine with me." I walk on her right side and match her speed as we stroll. "I've got all night, Maya Elizabeth. How does it feel to have told your parents to fuck themselves?"

"I never told them that. No contact is better than an emotional outburst. And only my mother calls me Maya Elizabeth." She glares up at me. "She doesn't mean it endearingly."

"Well..." My lips tug high into a grin. "I do. It's a pretty name, and I feel kinda tough saying it. *Maya Elizabeth*. You got a man?"

"What?" Her brows pinch into a severe frown. "One: I've lived here for a day. How on earth would you expect me to have a man? And two: my dating status has absolutely nothing to do with you. You're presumptive and rude."

"Fancy words," I snigger. "I was just checking. Have you finished unpacking since you moved?"

"No, I've been busy. Why are you here if you don't even live in this town?"

"I heard the club is a cool place to be. And I have business here with Jack Reilly."

"You do?" Like she thinks she's won a morsel of my truth, she tilts her head and meets my eyes. "What business?"

"*My* business." I grab her elbow and steer her off the sidewalk. "Siri says you're in here. Do you like your apartment?"

"S-sure." She studies the ugly brown brick building and shakes her arm free of my hold. "It's nice enough, and none of the neighbors bother me. Are you going back to the city now?"

"Uh-huh." I pull the glass front door open to allow her in first. "Unless you invite me up for a cup of tea and a banging good time."

Just as I expect, she swings around with a feral growl. "Are you insane!? Are you seriously so assuming and stupid?"

"Stupider than dirt." I catch her wrist when it looks like she might smack me with the pointed end of her heels. "You're twitchy, huh? I only asked for a cup of tea."

"You asked for a one-night stand," she sneers. "With a person you literally met an hour ago. Have you no shame?"

"I met you about five hours ago, actually, if you count that time you ran into me. People have done worse on less."

"You're a pig." Tucking her heels away and snatching her wrist from my grasp, she turns toward the stairs and glares down her nose at me. "I'm here to stay, Cole. For a positive change, a new career, a fresh start at a life where no one expects anything of me." Lifting her proud chin, she purses her lips. "I have no intention of letting you sabotage that for me. Thanks for walking me home, even when I told you not to."

"Lucky I did," I goad. "You might've stayed lost."

"I overran my destination because *you* were distracting me. Now that I'm home, you can leave again. I doubt we'll see each other in the future."

"Uh-huh." I drop my hands in my pockets and spin a Mustang key fob between my fingers. *Reilly's fob? Or mine?* I can't tell without looking. "Maybe," I concede. "Maybe not. But if I *do* see you... I think I'll say hello."

"Don't bother. I don't intend to remember you."

I laugh and watch her legs as she navigates the stairs. "You're so snooty when you're frustrated. You dislike the family you came from, Maya Elizabeth, but you're like them too. I don't even have to meet them to know where you get that fancy vocabulary and disdain from."

"Go away." She continues up the stairs and holds the bottom of her dress so I can't get a peek at what's underneath. "Have a nice life."

"It's nicer now that I know you!" I call out.

I can't walk away, even if I wanted to. So I watch her instead. The long, long lines of her legs, and the definition in her muscular calves. She has a perfect ass that comes from doing spin class and yoga, and thighs that promise she works them too. She's got a socialite's body: trim, fit, and sexy. But, I'm certain, no fucking clue how to use any of it to get herself out of trouble.

If she's ever pulled into the bushes against her will and held down to be taken advantage of, there's no way she's coming out again the same person.

She's snooty, because it's the only defense mechanism she has. But beneath that, she's naïve and sheltered. She's mad at the family who raised her within tight constraints, but she's never gone hungry a moment in her life.

She hates the leash they try to trap her with. But if she knew my world of neglect, she might reconsider what she thinks is freedom.

When she leaves my view and moves onto the next flight of stairs, I go to the first step and lean onto the handrail to look up. "It was lovely meeting you, Maya Elizabeth. I had a lovely date tonight."

"Not a date!" she snaps. "See you never, Cole Miller."

Chuckling under my breath, I wait for the sound of her keys in a lock, and then for the door to open and close. Once I know she's securely inside, I turn on my heels and waltz out of the building, heading in the direction of my car a block away, while in my pocket, my phone vibrates, and the counterfeit key fob warms my thigh.

I touch neither while I'm on the street.

No cops cruise by to check on the stranger wandering town, and no fighters come out to *watch* me. My eyes scan the dark street, and my instincts keep me on high alert, but the moment I slip into my car and close the door to secure me inside, I accept Pres's call and put him on speaker.

"I'm here." I toss the phone to the passenger seat and fix my seatbelt before starting the car. "I'm on my way back now."

"Where the fuck did you go?" he hisses beneath the sound of a live band. "Dude! *Everyone* was watching you. *Everyone* knows your name and face now."

"I walked that chick home." Pulling away from the curb, I head back in the club's direction. "She was gonna walk alone. It's dark out, and she's not nearly as badass as she thinks she is. If some random guy stepped in her way for a chat she didn't want, she would've been screwed."

"*You're* a random guy!" he barks out. "You don't know her."

"Of course I know her." A satisfied smile stretches along my lips. "She's Maya Blake."

Her parents are frigid and controlling, her upbringing was calculated and lonely, her education was top-notch but she didn't want it. And now... she smiles when she talks about five-year-olds.

"She's decent," I tell him. "What happened at the club after I left?"

He scoffs. "They've got someone like me here. A tech fucking genius with eyes all over this town. Jimmy Kincaid asked her to keep watch, so now the whole fucking club knows she's home and you're on the move. I sure as shit hope you didn't open your mouth about why we're here."

I roll my eyes and pull up to a stop outside the club. "Not my first day on the job, Pres. I'm here."

I grab my phone and kill our call, and just seconds later, the passenger door opens and my best friend slides in.

"We need to walk away from this one for now." He fixes his seatbelt and tosses his cell into the center console to join mine. "We're supposed to be invisible, Cole. Instead, you invited your ass to family dinner, walked their girl home, and now everyone knows your name."

He shakes his head and drops it back to close his eyes. "So fucking stupid, man. We need to disappear for a few months to make them forget who the fuck we are. And by then, Box probably won't want the Mustang anyway. Its current value lies in the fact it hasn't been released to the public yet, dickhead."

"You're too sensitive." Pulling away from the curb, I cut across town and hit the freeway within minutes. Normal folks worry about speed traps and highway patrol. But knowing Preston means we get a free run all the way back. "They associate me with her. Not with a car. I'd be far more concerned if something happened to *her* tonight."

"So you walked her home." He massages the pad of his thumbs over his closed eyes. "Redirection and association. When they think of you, they think of her. When the car is boosted, they're looking for a ghost."

"That's a smart boy." I reach across and shove the side of his face until he growls. "We'll be back in a few days to do the job. Tell Box tonight was recon. Next time is payday. Line up our next job, too, while you're at it. I've got bills to pay. And stop stressing so fucking much." I glance across at him. "It's bad for your health."

Maya

THAT WAY HE STARES

Life as a kindergarten teacher is about as predictable *and* unpredictable as one might expect.

As in, I was aware my job would include soothing scared children. School is a big step, and these kids were toddlers just a short while ago. This is probably the first time they've been away from their parents for more than a few minutes, and it's probably the first time they've had to eat on a schedule, instead of snacking all day long.

These children have to go to the bathroom on their own now, and fix buttons and zippers without help. Some of them lose a shoe—or both—during the course of their day, and many of them are transitioning from daytime naps to daytime *make Miss Blake pay*.

All of that, of course, is predictable.

What I never could have expected was to find my students beating on a sixth grader because he tripped sweet Lily Turner on the playground.

And by *my students*, I mean Charlie Reilly.

What I never could have predicted is the way a senior student—aka 'Bean' Kincaid—would need to cross the school and take control of her cousin's manic rage before he did too much damage. And then, how Britt would need to head off the Devil Twins, because sixth graders picked on Lily and they found out about it.

I never could've foreseen the parent-teacher interviews I would later conduct with Britt and her massively buff husband, or Tink and the handsome man she claimed as her own inside Club 188. Or Jimmy Kincaid and his fighter wife, who took my news of a family brawl with twitching lips and stoic nods of their heads.

And if I *could have* anticipated how awkward those conversations would be, it's possible I might've quit before I accepted my job in the first place.

I don't call my mother for advice, and I definitely don't visit home on the weekend to see my father. I have no friends to turn to in this town to blow off steam, and all my coworkers are already friends with Britt.

Which means my week remains unbearably quiet while I work through the mess all on my own.

"So I'm going to tell you all a story today." I sit on the floor in the center of my classroom, holding a book for my circle of students to see. "It's the story of an ant and a grasshopper." I study each set of eyes that watch me with eager anticipation. The glint in their stares, and the bottled energy they try so hard to keep in after already being cooped up inside for an hour. "Does everyone know what an ant is?"

"Little bugs!" One student raises their hand, but blurts their answer before I can call upon them. "They're black," he continues. "And they make houses in dirt."

"Good, thank you." Then I scan the rest of my class. "And do you all know what a grasshopper is?"

"Long legs!" Savanah announces, hers squirming as she talks. "And they have little wings they rub together."

"Excellent, thank you. But remember," I look around the circle. "You need to raise your hands and wait for Miss Blake to select you. Until then, I'd like for you not to shout."

Opening the book, I reveal a wintery picture, with ice and snow and Christmas decorations blurred in the background. In the foreground, a grasshopper stands on its back legs and holds a violin in its cartoony hands.

"This story is about being lazy. Does anyone know what lazy means?"

"Not doing what you're told!" Again, a little hand shoots up high as words explode free of a little mouth. "My mom says I'm lazy when I leave my trash on the counter instead of in the can," the boy tells me.

"Good example, thank you, Elias. But remember..." I raise my hand. "Wait until I call on you. Because look," I glance over at Savanah, who waits quietly with her hand raised. "Savanah's doing the right thing, but you didn't give her a chance to be selected."

Warmth floods Elias' cheeks while he *fidget, fidget, fidgets* with his fingers. "I'm sorry, Miss Blake."

I could keep going. Reprimanding. Teaching and reading. But there isn't a child in the room who doesn't squirm. Not even the sweet and softly spoken Lily. She waits, bathed in Charlie's shadow, tiny compared to her overly large cousin, but she sits on her hands and rocks side to side.

And so, I have a choice to make.

Do I want to be the boring and naggy kindergarten teacher these children remember as a pain in their asses? Or do I want to be more? Do I want to be better?

"Alright." Surprising them all, I push up to stand—and grin when their necks stretch back and their eyes widen with astonishment.

Placing the book under my arm, I move to my desk and grab a pair of sunglasses. Then I turn back and point to the ceiling. "Everyone up! We're going on an adventure."

Gasps and squeals of joy. Excitement and glee. Every one of my students shoots to their feet and chatters amongst themselves.

Where are we going?

What are we doing?

What kind of adventure?

"We have to be quiet." I move to the door to block their exit, then I place the tip of my finger on the end of my nose so, even without asking them, my students do the same.

"We're walking through the halls, and every single other class is working hard and learning. So this is a test for you all. If you can be quiet and sensible, Miss Blake will organize more adventures. But if you're noisy and disruptive, we'll never do it again."

I meet Charlie's eyes, knowing he could make or break any given situation. "Can I trust you?"

Beaming with confidence, he nods. "Promise."

I hold his stare for a beat longer. Penetrating and assertive so he knows I mean business. Then I nod and look down at sweet Savanah, the teacher's pet and people-pleaser. "Okay. I want you all in two lines. Savanah." I place her on the left, then I point to the floor beside her.

"Elias. Everyone else, choose a line. Make the numbers even. Then hands on the shoulder of the person in front of you."

Like I'm commanding an army regiment, I line them up and space them out. I place hands on shoulders and smile when the children vibrate with energy. Then, when Charlie takes his place at the end, and beside him, Lily rests her hands on the shoulders of the girl in front of her, I nod my approval and open the door. "Remember, Miss Blake needs you to be quiet."

"Okay!" they all whisper-hiss.

"Follow me."

Our book in my hand, I start into the hall. We walk the corridors and pass classroom doors where eyes follow us with avid attention. My students beam, smug with their thrilling journey, while others gaze our way in quiet envy.

I pass Britt's classroom and keep an eye on Charlie so he doesn't break away from our pack and crash her lesson. When we're clear, I lead them through the double front doors of the building and down the steps.

Cutting left, I head toward the play equipment, and smile as each kid's silent smirk turns to squeaks of joy.

"We have five minutes to explore," I tell them. "You can talk, but no shouting or squealing. Take turns on the swings, and be kind to your class-mates. After that, Miss Blake would like to read our story."

They sprint away with thrilling screams and leave me behind, shaking my head. They're five years old and outside on a school day. How could I possibly expect silent acceptance?

While my students play, some lining up to use a swing, I study the vast playground and watch as cars potter by on the street outside. I'm just one woman, watching over sixteen children. Being on school grounds makes us safe, in theory, but there's no security fence that'll keep anyone away if they choose to make trouble.

The sun beats down on us, still too hot as we approach the end of the summer, but the playground is rife with shady trees, and a gentle breeze cuts through them all to break up the heat.

"Four minutes," I announce after the first is up. Then I cast my gaze toward the eastern side of the school when I hear the disciplined, seem-ingly choreographed *thud-thud-thud* of footsteps hitting pavement.

Fighters jog around the corner. Three. Four. Five of them, sweating all over their tank tops. They wear shorts that go to their knees, with slits along the side to reveal a little thigh as they run, and tanks that are more skin than fabric. The sides are basically nonexistent, so I catch muscles flexing, and tattoos rippling with each pace. Arms bulge, and breath races as the lingering heat torments them more than it does me.

"That's my dad." Charlie stops beside me so his shoulder brushes my hip.

When I break away from the view of men with bodies not all that different from Cole Miller's, I look down at a beaming Charlie.

"My dad and my uncles," he continues proudly. "They run by here a couple times a day while they're working out. They say they just like to run this way, but I know they're making sure everything is safe and how it should be."

"They come by a *couple* times a day?" Stunned, I bring my gaze back to the group. "Every single day?"

"Five miles before breakfast," he giggles. "More in the middle of the day. And a few more in the afternoon—except when they're trying to bulk up."

He drops his hands in his pockets and rocks back on his heels as the men push on, and Lily contentedly swings.

"They only do the bulking as we head into a title fight. Build," he explains. "Then cardio. Then build more, then cardio, so they can move all that extra weight fast. No point having it if it's too heavy."

"Well... no, I suppose not." They're all larger than anyone I've ever known. Not just in height, but muscle. Width. "How big do you think they'd be if they didn't work in a gym?"

He considers my question for a long beat. "Still kinda big, I think. Their daddies were fighters, too. It's in our blood."

When Lily's swing slows and she wriggles closer to the edge to get down, Charlie breaks away, though he waves for his dad when their eyes meet.

The men don't come onto school property. And Charlie doesn't rush to the fence to say his hellos. They just wave and grin, then the men move along, and Charlie helps his cousin to her feet.

"I think I know who the lazy one is in your story, Miss Blake." He holds the swing in his hand and watches his cousin wander away. "It's the grasshopper, huh? The one with the violin."

I look down at the book and shrug. "I guess we'll find out when we read it. Why do you think it's the grasshopper?"

"Because it's snowy and cold in the story, but he's playing a violin." Then he points to an anthill Lily has discovered and, leading toward it, a line of its inhabitants working together to move crumbs as big as their bodies. "Ants work hard to gather food. Grasshoppers just make noise all summer and annoy the crap out of me."

"Alright." Quickly, I clap my hands and hope no one goes home to inform their parents of a colorful new word in their vocabulary. "Let's all come sit under this shady tree." I gesture the way I'd like my students to go, and as they wander over and create a circle, I lower myself onto an upraised root in front of them all.

"So, we have our ants, and we have our grasshopper." I glance around our circle, and grin when I find that the constant wriggling bodies have stilled, and now-smiling faces gleam with a rosy sheen of sweat after just a few minutes of running their energy out.

"Now remember, if you'd like to answer a question, raise your hand so Miss Blake can choose you. It's important we're respectful of our new classmates and friends."

~

"Hi, Reginald. Thanks for taking my call." When the line connects at the end of my workday, and the estate attorney I've been trying to reach for a week answers, I hold my cell between my shoulder and ear, and wander out of the ice cream parlor in the middle of Main Street.

The desserts in there are overpriced, and the woman who watches her teen staff with a sour-faced and cranky disposition seems to take pleasure in every trill of the cash register. But since it's hot, and I'm in need of something sweet, I catch the melting delicacy before it dribbles onto my wrist, and smile as I amble onto the sidewalk outside.

"It's Maya Blake," I continue into my phone. "I've been trying to reach you."

"I've been unwell," Reginald answers with a rasp in his voice. "I'm sorry, Miss Blake. Dorothy has been holding all but my most urgent messages while I get better."

"I'm glad you're back now." I study the street for a moment: left, then right. Since I already explored right and ended up in front of a photography studio, I turn left today and head toward the large copse of trees I spy a couple blocks over. "I was hoping to touch base with you about my grandmother's estate. She passed five years ago, Mr. Waysmith. Her will was up to date, and her wishes had been spelled out clearly. At the time the will was created, I was a minor. But when Grammy passed, I was twenty, which, by all laws and standards, made me an adult. The issue is that my parents have intercepted my inheritance and insist on holding it prisoner despite my requests for release. I've come to you for help understanding my rights in the matter."

"Is it money?" He flicks through sheets of paper, though I have no clue what they might say. "Are you after a cash sum, Miss Blake?"

"No, I..." I shake my head and cross the street in search of the shade provided from shop fronts. "My grandmother was independently wealthy, so there *is* money there for me. But that's not what I seek. She promised me diaries, Mr. Waysmith. Memoirs. She was a writer in her time."

"Published?" he asks.

"No. They were her scribbled thoughts, but they're special to me. They were something she and I shared when I was younger. We even wrote a few pages together over the years. Her will specifically points out that those diaries are to come to me, but my mother seized them. I was away at college at the time of the will-reading, so my mother assured me she'd collect what was mine and keep it safe until the next time I was home."

"And she hasn't given them to you?" he concludes as I make my way around the corner. "Is that what you're saying, Miss Blake?"

"That's what I'm saying. The documentation is there, so I assume I have grounds for a judge's ruling in my favor, but that'll come after extensive expenses, and even then, no one will hold her hand and *force* her to give them to me. Negotiations have been unsuccessful. Pointing out the section of Grammy's will that stipulates what I was to receive hasn't worked. And now, I just..." I slide my tongue along the melting ice cream and shake my head. "I don't know what to do, Mr. Waysmith. I simply have no clue how to rectify this situation and receive what was promised to me. But the diaries," I plead, "the locket... they're all so important to me. I don't even care if she keeps the money."

"Whose mother was your grandmother, Miss Blake? Paternal or maternal?"

"Maternal," I answer easily. "Though it hardly matters."

"She was your mother's mother, and it is your mother who is withholding your property. I think it matters greatly. Have you considered an enforcement order? The police could escort you into your mother's home to recover the diaries."

"I've thought about it, but I'd rather not escalate things with police involvement. I'm not interested in creating a war with my family. Besides," I chase another dribbling line of ice cream, "what's to stop her from moving the diaries somewhere else until the search is complete? We won't find them, she remains in charge and smug with her success, and I'm no better off. I've called you hoping for alternative advice."

"Well..." He thinks for a moment and flicks a pen against his desk. "Next step is court. The matter would go back to a judge, as you've already pointed out. The judge will likely rule in your favor, considering your grandmother's written wishes, and your mother would be handed orders stipulating a return of the property by a certain date."

"But like I said," frustration builds in my blood as I move from sidewalk to grass. As my view opens from the street to a glittering lake in the middle of town. Sunlight glares back into my eyes, but I continue closer anyway. The water is a promising nirvana in the middle of this putrid heat. "Even if a judge stamps an order and demands she deliver the diaries, no one will physically make her. All she has to do is stall, then stall some more. *She lost them. She forgot her deadline. She's unwell and needs more time.* She could drag this out for decades, Mr. Waysmith, and I'm left with no clear plan going forward. The trust Grammy intended for me is easy, considering a judge could order the transfer and a bank would simply do it. But the diaries and locket: those are priceless to me. They're irreplaceable. I was hoping you might've seen a case like this before and had a solution I'd not yet considered."

"If you want my brutal honesty, Miss Blake, these types of situations..." I don't have to see him to know he shakes his head. "They come across my desk on a regular basis. Cases are fought in a courtroom, and hundreds of thousands of dollars are spent on lawyers who fight amongst themselves and line their own pockets. Often, judges don't care one way or the other, and as you've already commented, no one can physically force someone to hand over such property. More than a few times in my fifty years practicing, these supposed items have *'gone missing'*. They've simply vanished, and no matter how much noise the intended party makes, the courts cannot physically make the exchange of items that supposedly cannot be found."

"So... I'm screwed?" I take a bite of my cone and come to a stop at the beginning of an aging wooden pier, toe my shoes off, and gingerly step on. "No one can enforce it, which means I'll never get my things?"

"Not without lengthy and expensive litigation," he counters. "Public shaming might help. I'd be willing to take your case on, Miss Blake. I like money as much as the next man, and I'm getting pretty close to my retirement. But knowing who your parents are, and being keenly aware they know their way around a court case, I don't fancy our chances of seeing your things ever again. Have you considered just... going there and taking them?"

"Like... breaking in?" I grumble. "Mr. Waysmith, what kind of advice is that?"

"Not advice," he chuckles. "I'm not your counsel. We have not exchanged contracts or finances. And of course I didn't mean break in. Surely, you could just go to visit someday. Liberate your possessions. Once you have them, your parents would fight a losing battle to get them back."

"So, steal? You're suggesting I rob my childhood home?" Lowering to sit on the splintering wood, I dip my toes in the water and exhale a cleansing breath that, I hope, will release the frustration from my blood. "I cannot steal, Mr. Waysmith. I refuse."

"But it's your property," he argues with a smile in his tone. "Do you still have a room in your parents' home, Miss Blake?"

"A room? Like, a—"

"A childhood bedroom," he presses. "Your old bed. Bookshelves. Maybe a desk and stuffed toys."

"Yes, I..." I look across the glistening water and set my unwanted ice cream on the pier beside my leg. It'll melt through the wooden slats within a minute, and the cone will become bird food soon after. "I still have my bedroom."

"And should you visit sometime and wish to bring your old favorite teddy away with you, would you consider it stealing? Or simply collecting your belongings?"

"Mr. Waysmith..."

"Not legal advice," he snickers. "I'm just a man who knows the realistic outcome of your situation, and I'm too old to not shoot straight these days. You could spend decades in court and dole out enough money to buy a house, you could destroy whatever relationship you want with your parents, win your case and get the orders you wish, and *still*, you may never again read your grandmother's scribbles. *Or...*" He pauses for a tense beat. "You could just take them. I know which I would choose."

"But—"

"I suggest you decide what these things are worth to you, then determine the lengths you'd go to get them back. I do *not* advise breaking the law, Miss Blake. And I insist you neither hurt yourself, nor anyone else in your pursuit of these things. I just... I know what I'd do."

"Fine." I draw a deep breath and stop only when my chest expands, then I release it on an exhale when I spy a man across the lake.

A shiny white Mustang, and broad shoulders encased in a tight black shirt.

It's ridiculous that my stomach dips at the sight of the guy who solicited me for a one-time fuck just a few nights ago. But that's what it does. It spins and swirls when his eyes stop on me and his lips curl into a devious smile.

Stunning my pulse into an erratic sprint, he starts across the grass and onto the rickety wooden pier.

"Miss Blake—"

"Thank you for your advice, Mr. Waysmith. I'll take it under consideration and think about my options."

"Alright. Well..." Surprised by my sudden change in tone, he searches for sense. "Good day to you, then."

"Yeah. Goodbye—"

"Well, hi there, Maya Elizabeth." Unafraid of the rickety dock, Cole comes to stand over me, his broad body and wide shoulders shielding me from the worst of the summer glare. When I glance up and find the sun at his back, all I see are his shadowed features, save for a smug grin. "Sunbathing is bad for you, did you know that? Never heard of melanoma?"

"I'm not sunbathing." Tugging my feet from the water and pushing up to stand, I hold my phone tight in one hand and grit my teeth when the failing wood groans beneath my weight. "I was taking a call and searching for privacy."

I move a half-step left to go around him. But Cole remains in place and allows his smirk to grow larger.

"Can you move, please? I was just leaving."

"Can't." He grabs my arms and twists our bodies, forcing us into an odd dance-shuffle so my heels hang over the edge of the dock, and his hands are the only reason I don't topple backward. "Not a lot of room to work here."

"No shit."

I don't push him away and risk losing my footing. Instead, I grab onto his forearms, muscular as they are, and refuse to let him know I'm thinking about them. About the ropey muscle beneath his skin, and the contrast of no tattoos at all, compared to the vast array on show every time I see a fighter in town.

"Don't let me go!" I snarl. "Don't you dare."

He's playful and arrogant, allowing me to lean back another inch or two. If he opens his fingers, I'll be choking beneath a rotting dock, and walking home in sopping wet clothes. "You have no reason not to trust me." He allows me to dip back another half a foot, so a squeal escapes my throat and an infuriating chuckle comes from his. "I've been good to you, Maya Elizabeth."

"You've been a pain in my ass!" I cling to his strength and propel myself around until my feet touch solid wood on his other side. My pulse hammers in my throat, and adrenaline fires through my blood.

It's not like falling into the lake will kill me. But my body reacts as though it would.

"Why are you even over here?" Brushing his hands away, I spin and stomp toward the end of the pier. "Why'd you come over if you were only gonna bother me?"

He follows in my peripherals, a slow swagger to contrast my plodding glide. "Because you looked lonely." His voice is unhurried. Easy, they say, *like a Sunday morning*. "That's twice I've found you on the phone, Maya Elizabeth. Twice, you've looked really fucking sad afterward. I saw you, and we're friends now, so I did what friends do and came over to check on you."

"We're not friends! We're not even acquaintances." I bend to collect my shoes. "We're just two people who crossed paths one time."

"Well... three times." He lifts his hand and raises a single digit. "When you ran into me on Main Street last week." A second finger. "Then again that night when we ended up in the same club. I could say the walk home was another path crossed, but I literally followed you out, so I'll merge that with the previous path." Then a third finger. "And now... at the lake. That's three, Maya Elizabeth."

"Stop calling me Maya Elizabeth!" I hug my shoes close, just like the last time I saw him, and charge onto the grass with my eyes and attention straight ahead. I refuse to look back, though I know he follows. "I'm not sad, by the way. I'm busy."

"Looked sad to me," he singsongs. "Did someone die? Or is the pout your normal facial expression?"

"You're a jackass." I glare over my shoulder—exactly like I said I wouldn't—and loathe how the sun shines on his face and shows off a cute smile under five o'clock stubble.

I'd be lying if I said he didn't look good. I'd be fooling myself if I didn't accept that his strong body, his long legs encased in jeans, and his wide shoulders don't intrigue me.

Where I come from, guys don't look like him. In my world, men spend eons in law libraries, hunched over thick books, too busy to be anything but scrawny. Too involved in their academics to bother looking at a woman the way Cole looks at me.

There were different guys in the classes I took to become a teacher, but still, they never looked like Cole. They tended to be softer. Gentler. And none, in all the time I attended, followed me home or offered a fast bang. None *ever* looked into my eyes and saw the grief I felt when my grandma passed, or the anger I experienced when my mother nagged me to transfer back to law.

If I'm being entirely honest with myself, I'm not sure any of them saw me... period.

"Stop walking away from me all the time, Maya."

"Why are you always following me?" I stop under a massive weeping tree and use its shade for respite, then I drop my shoes to the grass and sit so I can pull them on. "We don't know each other, Cole. You're just... a dude I met for a minute."

"But we *met*." He comes to a stop in front of me, kneeling so his massive shoulders block out my entire view of the lake.

Though it hardly matters, because now I see the bridge of his nose, and the slight flare of his nostrils. I see the pores on his cheeks, and the lashes that flutter down and kiss when he blinks. I get an up-close view of the sinewy muscle in his pecs, and the way he rests his forearm on his knee so his hand and fingers dangle beside it.

"We met," he breathes. "And considering the four billion chicks and four billion dudes who all walk this planet, me and you meeting, even for a minute, has to mean something, no?"

My eyes narrow to suspicious slits.

Maybe it's the lawyer in me. Or maybe it's just my twenty-five-year-old spinster heart, but his sweet words elicit a response entirely different than he expects.

"What do you want, Cole?"

"Huh?"

"What. Do. You. Want?" I slow my words and enunciate every syllable. "We're not friends. We're not even neighbors. We don't live in the same town, and I have no desire to return to the city. Maybe you just want a bed buddy, or maybe you're looking for someone to torment. But I'm not that person for you, so..." I shove my shoe on and leave the laces untied.

I'd rather risk falling on my face than sit here and stare at him for longer than necessary.

"I'm not a one-night stand kind of girl. I have no hate for those who are, I carry no judgment. But she's not me. I'm not looking for a friend, and I have no desire to get chatty with a guy who this whole town watches suspiciously, since you're not from here, you associate with no one except me, and you don't seem to understand the word *no*."

"The whole town?" He skips everything else I said and focuses on that one detail. "The *whole* town thinks I'm sus? Geez." He reaches up and wipes a hand across his stubbled jaw. "Tough crowd, huh? I just got here, and already, I'm their most wanted?"

"It's because no one knows who you are." I pull my second shoe on and push up to stand so I tower over him. I hate how his face is still as high as my breasts. How his shoulders are broader than my body by a long shot, and how, even while I insult him, he smiles. "It's because you're pushy and abrupt. I don't see you making friends with the locals, just the new chick —which could be construed as a red flag. Also, you solicit women for sex within an hour of knowing them."

Slowly, as though weighing his response, he straightens his legs and takes back his position of power. "I solicited *you* for sex..." he ponders. "Correct. But it was, like, thirty percent a joke. I figured you needed a distraction, so I gave it to you."

"Only thirty percent?" I lift my chin and look anywhere but into his eyes. "What of the other seventy?"

He shrugs. "I would absolutely fuck you if you gave me the come-hither eyes. I'm a man, not a eunuch."

"Disgusting." I turn on my heels and accept the stinging slap of my shoelaces on my skin as I stride away. "You're such a pig."

"I haven't been introduced to other people in town yet!" He breaks away from the shade of the tree and jogs to catch up. "I met you because we ran into each other. Everyone else... I mean, would you walk into a club and go up to a group of folks you don't know, folks you never *need* to know, and just introduce yourself?"

He grabs my wrist with a quick snatch so my body teeters forward, but his hold slings me around with a fast swoop. "People don't meet new friends that way, Maya."

My breath races, and my chest thrums with adrenaline.

"That's just weird," he continues. "But if it's what would remove those red flags from above my head, then tell me whose group to crash." He darts his tongue out to wet his bottom lip, setting a trap for me and winning his little game when my eyes predictably drop. "Tell me who to become best friends with."

"You're still pushy," I murmur, my voice nowhere near as strong as it was a moment ago. "And abrupt."

"Your need to beat around the bush and throw flowery words into a sentence is *your* red flag. I prefer direct communication." Leaning closer, closer, so his breath flavors my tongue, he grins when my own breath cuts off on a gasp. "Are you still mad at me?"

"I don't..." I swallow to lubricate my parched throat. "I don't know."

He chuckles and releases my arm so I stumble back a step. But then he lowers to one knee and begins tying my laces. "I'd feel pretty bad if you fell over and hurt yourself because of these." His hands move quickly, but his gaze slides along my body and up to my eyes. "Wanna tell me why you were sad on the phone?"

I press my lips tight and shake my head. "I wasn't sad."

"You were feeling somethin', babe." He knows when I lie, and unapologetically calls me out for it. "Frustrated?" he wonders. "Angry? Exhausted? It was a big emotion, Maya Elizabeth. And since we're both new to town, and neither of us have friends," finishing my laces, he reaches up and taps his muscular shoulder, "I insist you lean on your best buddy Cole and tell me your secrets."

"You're not my best buddy." I roll my eyes and turn away, but I'm damn well aware that I keep him in my peripherals as he pushes up to stand. "And I was feeling private feelings. About my private business."

"And I'm your private friend." He falls into step on my left so his shoulder brushes mine. "And since I don't know anyone else in town, it's not likely I'll spill your secrets."

He's intense. Arrogant. Insistent. And convincing, when no one else could possibly be.

"I did four years in law school," I start with an exhale. "Top of my classes. So although I didn't sit the bar or become a practicing lawyer, I still consider myself somewhat knowledgeable in some areas of the law."

He considers my words for a long beat. "Okay... Are you having legal trouble?"

"I'm having family trouble." And once again, I find myself spilling my guts, when Cole has never told me a damn thing about himself. "My grandmother died several years ago. She was my best friend. She was more my mother than my mother ever was."

"That's tough." For the first time maybe *ever*, his voice turns serious. "It would suck to lose someone you're that close with."

"It did. But as typically happens in high-conflict families when people pass, Grammy's will was read, and certain things were allocated to certain people."

"Ah..." He drops his hands in his pockets and wanders with me across the grass. "I see. Where there's a will, there's some asshole fighting for their piece of the pie."

Grinning, he glances down at me. "Am I to assume your grandmother was filthy rich, and now someone's cousin's mother's pet sitter's sister has come looking for her share?"

He's ridiculous and presumptive; qualities that, I'm coming to find, make him oddly charming.

"Sort of," I admit softly. "My grandmother had built reasonable wealth. Nothing people would kill over, but enough to keep a recipient comfortable."

He snorts. "Where I come from, dudes will kill one another over ten bucks and a Big Mac. But alright. So someone wants their share of Grammy's money?"

"It's me," I confess. "I'm the recipient."

When his brows come up in judgment, I add, "It's not money I'm after, Cole—though, by law, I'm entitled to a little. It's her diaries I need."

"Her diaries?" He considers that and brings a hand up to rub along his jaw. "Is she secretly Emily Bronte, and the diaries are worth billions?"

"No. They're worth nothing, as far as money goes. But to me, they're worth—"

"The world," he concludes with a nod. "They hold sentimental value."

"Yes. They hold our memories and our dreams. Our plans and promises and cute little stories, and special dates we celebrated, and jokes we'd written, and secrets we couldn't say out loud to anyone else."

Emotion backs up in my throat as I remember the woman who tolerated so much, purely so she could stay in my life. She was treated terribly by my parents, by her own daughter, knowing that if she pushed back, they'd simply remove her from our home.

From my life.

So she ate crow and played the submissive, all to maintain access to me.

"Those diaries are all I want, but my mother, who is also a lawyer, is refusing to hand them over."

"But..." A thick line creases his forehead and shows where he keeps his anger. "The will said they're for you?"

"Yes. The will clearly states who gets what."

"So the diaries are your property?"

"Yes," I answer again. "But my mother has possession of them."

"Can you not just... ya know, demand them? They're yours."

"Well..." I draw a deep breath and step up onto the sidewalk that leads us back to Main Street. "I've tried demanding them. I've tried negotiating for them. I tried arguing with my mother. And lately, I've gone mostly non-contact, in hopes of deescalating all the emotion bouncing between us."

"And still no dice?"

"No dice," I exhale. "So then I called a lawyer." I point my thumb over my shoulder, to indicate the lake we just left. "I called an estate attorney to get his advice."

"Which obviously didn't pan out. Hence," he softly chuckles, "the sad face I noticed when I got there."

"Pretty much." I stop on a street corner and consider which direction to walk. *Home? School? The park at the end?* "It's been a few years already, and my mother is holding those books hostage to hurt me. She claims she'll return them if I go back to law school and eventually take a position in her or my father's firm."

"Of course they each have a firm," he grumbles, unimpressed. "Because... rich people." Rolling his eyes, he grabs my hand and pulls me toward the park. "But you definitely don't want to go back to being a lawyer?"

"No." I shake my hand free and clasp it with my other one to discourage him from reaching out a second time. "And even if I did, I don't enjoy the idea of my own family using blackmail to conduct business or control my entire life plan. I'm happy as a teacher, Cole. I'm content here, and I don't want to change what I've worked so hard to achieve."

"That's fair..." he murmurs. "Only the truly lucky people get to work a job they love." Glancing down at me, he asks, "Where are the diaries?"

My brain moves too slow. It's too bogged down in the details of everything I've experienced this week: my new job, my new town, my mother, and then, this guy. "Huh?"

"The diaries," he chuckles. "Where are they?"

"Uh... at my parents' home."

"Right," he grins so it taunts. "But where?"

"Oh! Likely in the safe in my mother's office. It's where she keeps the things she wants control over most. And before you suggest I go there and steal," I purse my lips when he dares to act offended, like he wasn't thinking it, "I don't know the code to get in, nor do I intend to try. I believe in karma, remember? I refuse to tip the scales of the universe in any way that'll hurt me."

"I hardly consider it stealing." He glances away to study the street around us. "They're your diaries. If *anyone* is stealing," his tone firmer now, he brings his eyes back to me, "it's your mom. She's being a bitch."

I laugh. It's loud and bordering on hysterical. But Cole might be the first person I've ever met who called my mother what she is. "Wow." Still giggling, I cover my mouth and shake my head. "You just put it out there, huh?"

"Direct communication."

He grabs my arm when I step off the curb to cross over and a car turns the corner too fast. It would have plowed me down if not for his interference.

He yanks me back, seemingly angry at my obliviousness, and when the car continues on, leaving us behind, he releases me with a huff of impatience. "You need to watch where you're going, Maya Elizabeth. I can't follow you everywhere you go every single day of your life."

"And yet..." With the street clear, I cross over and leave him behind as embarrassment and anger course through my blood. "I've survived twenty-five years without you."

"Fuck knows how." He moves faster to keep up. "Walking home at night. Short dress. High heels. A neon *'come get me'* sign on your back."

"Only to men like you, evidently."

Instead of heading to the park, I turn at the end of the next block and move toward home. I don't even have to worry about showing the stranger where I live: *he already knows.*

"If you consider a woman alone at night fair play to do what you want, then that's an issue you might like to discuss with a therapist. Or a judge. But it's not for you to put on me."

"Men think it," he grits out. "Not all men. But some. And it's the *some* who don't give a fuck what you want, or what a judge is gonna say. The cops and the courts aren't gonna get involved till after he's already hurt you. And by then...?" He takes my wrist and spins me back till our chests clash. "By then, you've already been violated.

"I won't say I'm sorry for knowing and understanding the realities of what you face, Maya Elizabeth. But your parents sure as shit should apologize for allowing you to be a grown-ass woman and still this fucking naïve."

"I have no clue why we continue to bicker." I pull my arm from his grasp and take a giant step back. "You act and speak like we've been friends our whole lives and I owe you some kind of behavior *you* deem acceptable, when in reality, you're a stranger to me. You're no one!"

My words make his eyes darken. My dismissal makes his chest broaden.

"You're just a guy who won't leave me alone. But I assure you, I'll be fine without your *guiding* hand." I take another step back. Then a third. "Go back to the city. Go on with your life. I hardly see how ours need to intersect anymore."

And with that pithy—*I wish*—goodbye, I turn on my heels and start toward my apartment.

I leave the overprotective, overly large, entirely too-direct Cole Miller in my past, and I work hard not to focus on how my stomach rolls with nausea.

Why does it hurt to walk, when I swear, I neither know nor care about the stranger who pushes his opinions on me? Why do my hands shake? And why the hell does adrenaline surge in my blood?

Why does this feel so big?

"Maya?" Cole remains in place, his feet shoulder-width apart and his countenance neither angry, nor sad. He's just... there.

I turn fifteen yards from where he stands and squint at the sun attempting to blind me. Bringing a hand up, I shade my eyes and study the man who, for some unknown reason, makes me look twice. Three times. Four and five and maybe six dozen more.

Walk away, Maya. Turn around and move on with your life. "What?"

"Come to dinner with me tonight." His intense stare sends a bolt of electricity burning through my veins. "I don't want to just be a stranger. And I'd like to level up from 'not an acquaintance' to something a little better."

"Bed buddy?" I call back. "That's what you want?"

"Friend." He doesn't care that our conversation is loud enough for anyone to listen in. He doesn't even care that people stick their heads out of stores to see what all the commotion is about. "I'd like to start by being your friend. Besides, you said the fact I have none in town is a red flag. So..."

He flashes a smug grin he's surely used on a million women before me.

This is a mistake, Maya. A giant, flashing, stupid, ridiculous, preventable mistake.

And yet, the single word leaves my lips before my brain has time to stop it.

"Okay."

"Yeah?" With long, meaty strides along the sidewalk, he closes the space between us in just a single beat of my heart, not stopping until the toes of his boots touch mine, and his breath feathers along my lips. "Dinner? Tonight?"

Oxygen clogs in my lungs, and nerves skitter in my veins.

Someday, I might look back on this and know I should've walked away. Turn and run and stayed far, far from the devilishly handsome town grifter. But for today, my brain is still on vacation, and my head tips forward on my neck. "Dinner. Tonight."

"Excellent." Surprising me, and maybe even himself, Cole cups my face in his hands and presses a fast kiss to my cheek. It's decent. It's quick. It flirts with the corner of my lips. But then it's gone.

He backs away, the eclipse to my sun and the shade I hide behind in this stifling heat. "I'll come get you at eight." He stops at the edge of the sidewalk without looking, somehow knowing it's there without a stumble. "I already know your address, so you don't have to fret. I'll organize everything. You just be ready."

He's bossy. And demanding. And he takes advantage of the fact I say nothing at all, since my body rides on shock and stunned mutism.

With one last smirk of victory, he turns on his heels and skips across the street. Probably back to the lake to collect his car. Likely on his way to harass some other poor woman in the four hours between now and the date he somehow finagled from me.

"What the hell did you do?" I chide myself. Dropping my head and turning toward home, I breathe through my stupidest decision yet.

I want to spin back and shout that I've changed my mind. I want to demand release from this commitment I made, and instead stay home to watch another episode of whatever the hell is on Netflix.

But I don't. For some ridiculous reason, I continue walking until I find myself in my building, climbing the stairs and walking through my front door. Then I end up in my bedroom, perusing my closet of outfits, and agonizing over the exact right one that might result in Cole Miller looking at me *that way* he does.

Because my desire for his approving stare somehow supersedes my need for common sense and sensibility.

Dammit.

Cole

EVERYTHING... AND THEN NOTHING

"**F**inally!" Pres has set up office on Main Street and works his laptop inside a diner named Franky's. He takes up an entire booth and bops under headphones covering his ears while some weird code plays across his screen. Whatever it is he does, it's done in privacy, and though he glares as I cross the restaurant and slide into the booth opposite him, he doesn't say anything that might land us in trouble. "Where the hell have you been?"

"Hanging with a friend." I flash a playful grin and turn to my right when a beautiful server with wide hips and bright red lipstick ambles closer with a coffee pot.

She's probably not a hell of a lot older than me, but she's got a shiny rock on her left hand and a smile that says she's friendly but not to be trifled with.

She's pretty. But she doesn't call to me the way the stuffy Maya Elizabeth Blake does.

"Coffee?" She flips over the mug in front of me and starts pouring. "Are you boys hungry?"

"I actually kinda am." I lean back to check the display fridge across the way, and spying a cherry pie that glistens under the overhead lights, I come back to sit tall and meet the server's eyes. "A slice of the cherry pie, please. I've got a date tonight, so I don't wanna fill up too early."

"You got a date?" Preston drags his attention away from his computer screen and scowls as the server heads away to plate up my pie. "Are you fucking with me right now, Cole? *A date?*"

"A date." I spin my coffee mug to make circles on the table, but I don't rush to drink. It's hot as Hades outside, and I have no desire to boil my insides more than necessary. "Maya Blake. She's my age, she's beautiful, she's got sass enough to make me wanna test her, and she's agreed to dinner." Leaning closer, I add, "I'm gonna take her to 188."

With that, his eyes widen. "You're taking her to dinner," he repeats, slower this time, "at Club 188. Tonight."

"I sure am. Because going places in this town alone is apparently weird and attention-grabbing. So I got me a date."

"You got you a date," he mouths. Then, finding the brilliance in my plan, his lips slide up on one side. "Fuckin' A. Smart move."

He glances out the window when one of the town's fighters wanders past with his arm wrapped over a girl's shoulders—not a dude and his wife, but rather, a grown-ass man and his teenage daughter.

"Aiden Kincaid," Pres murmurs so quietly I barely hear him. Then he drops his eyes to his computer as the duo comes through the diner door amid laughter and chatty conversation.

"He sucked, Biggie! You asked for my opinion on the guy's ground game, and I'm telling you, he's better off sitting on a cactus. It'll hurt less than if we drop him in a cage with other, better fighters."

The girl with wild, curly hair and a smile too big to be real—or at least, *I* sure as shit never smiled like that as a teen—wanders to the counter and steps under my server's arm for a fast side hug. "Miss Katrina, tell Biggie I know what I'm talking about."

"What are you talking about?" Katrina releases the girl and steps back to continue plating my order. "And why do I have to convince him of anything?"

"Because she's saying no to my fighter," the guy grumbles. "She's not even giving him a chance."

"Because he sucks!" she exclaims. "He's big, but big doesn't win fights if he doesn't know his head from his ass. He's tall, he's long, he's got muscle, and Biggie's desperate for a fighter to focus on, so he's ignoring the single, glaring fact that the guy has watermelon for brains and remains entirely unteachable."

"Unteachable?" Katrina strolls across the diner and sets my pie down on the table. She's blind to me now, working on instinct. "How is someone unteachable? Why?"

"Because he thinks he's the shit," she responds. "He thinks he's better than he actually is, and though he *pretends* to listen to Biggie, the second he's out of the octagon and it's just me watching him, he drops the act. He doesn't respect that I'm better than him, and he sure as hell doesn't take instruction."

Frowning, Katrina turns her back on me and folds her arms. "You call this grown man out for being arrogant. But have you considered you're just not as good as you think?"

"Ha!" The girl barks out the first guffaw. Then a second. A third. "Hahaha. You're so cute when you talk like this, Miss Katrina."

"And your ego will be the reason you get your ass handed to you," *Biggie* responds seriously. He grabs the girl and pulls her back under his arm. "You're good, Smalls. But you become unteachable, too, if you always think you're the best."

"I *am* the best," she presses, "because I'm teachable, and my daddy is the teacher." She snuggles in for a side hug and exhales what could only be a sigh of contentment. "You asked for my opinion, and I'm giving it to you. Save your time and energy and keep looking. We're in no real rush for a contender anyway. Uncle Jack's doing fine. He's still fit, and his arm is holding up. We need a heavyweight, but we don't want dead weight."

Stepping out from under his arm, she finally studies the rest of the diner, and grins when she catches me watching them.

In a panic, I drop my eyes and pick up my fork to shovel pie into my mouth.

"You have a fighter's body."

"Smalls!" In my peripherals, *Biggie* reaches out to stop his daughter.

But she brushes his hands off and steamrolls my way. "Do you fight?"

"Hm?" I keep my head down. My attention on my pie. "I don't..." I shake my head, then I look to Preston. "How was your day?"

"Um..." He's as stuck as I am. Speechless. Useless.

"You." The curly-haired teen stops beside our table so her hip almost touches my elbow. "My name's Evelyn Kincaid, and you're new to town."

Shut my mouth. Say nothing.

"I know you're new to town, because I heard my uncles talking about you at breakfast this morning."

Eyes down. Do not engage.

"My Uncle Jack, who is the world freakin' champion right now, was bitchin' about how he's tired, and my Uncle Bobby, who *was* the world champion before Jack, was saying how he, Jack, needs to stop whining. Beneath all that, they were saying it seems like they can't find a decent fighter anymore."

"Smalls," Aiden Kincaid's rumbling voice carries across the diner. "Leave him alone and come back over here."

"This is a small town," she continues, "which is nice and all, but eventually, we learn who can fight and who is just a big mouth with no talent." She glances back at her father and pops her hip. "Our current guy is the second." Then she brings her attention back to me. "He's young enough, and he's heavy enough. But his mouth is bigger than his brain, and the second he's in the cage with me, his true character comes out. He's sexist, he's patronizing, he's dumber than dirt, and he's a douchebag."

I don't mean to laugh. I don't mean to enter this conversation at all. But a soft chuckle escapes my chest and comes out so my shoulders bounce. "Someone once said I was dumber than dirt."

Her lips curl up, her entire personality void of shyness. "Someone said that about you?"

"A few someones," I admit. "Maybe I'm like your other guy: big enough, but too stupid to learn."

"Nah." Dropping a hand on her hip, she looks me up and down. "Only the truly dumb are dumb. The self-aware are teachable." Bringing her eyes back to mine, she asks, "You fight?"

"To survive," Pres inserts unhelpfully. "Sometimes folks like to pick on him because he's big. So they step up and shove. Then he's forced to look after himself."

"Best fight is the fight you walk away from," she says, as though reciting a lesson that's been drilled into her head since conception. Then, "Second best fight is one you didn't start, but that you definitely finished."

"I get a few of the latter," I concede. She's a kid, but she's a fighter in her heart and soul. She's wise beyond her years, even if she's a little arrogant around the edges. "I don't start fights, since chances are I'm the idiot the cops will arrest and prosecute. I don't have a fancy name or money to buy my way out of trouble. That means I do what I've gotta do to shut it down. Then I walk away and hope the police don't follow me home."

"You should drop by the gym." She twists back to her dad and purses her lips. "Invite him to the gym, Biggie."

"Smalls," he starts again, exhausted by her antics. "I can't just—"

She twirls back and pins me with a look. Then, offering her hand, bruised knuckles and muscular forearms, she grins when our gazes meet. "My name is Evelyn Kincaid, of *the* Kincaids. I have a fancy name, I have a gym, and I'm formally inviting you to come show us what you got. If you're good, we might pay your way to going pro."

"Uh..." I stare at her hand. At her expectation. I lean forward and look past her to her father for a beat. Then I bring my eyes back to Evelyn and smirk. "You're a kid. But thanks."

"You're a fighter," she counters, "whether you identify as one or not. And though my daddy says I have to work on my arrogance, I guarantee every fighter, even one like you, knows who the Kincaids are. You know what we represent, and you know who the hell I am. So..." She flashes a smug grin. "Come down to the gym. If you suck, we move on, and I go back to my life tomorrow. No skin off my back. But if you're good, maybe Biggie will move on from his dying dreams of that other guy, and stop wasting our money."

"And we're done." Aiden crosses the diner and tugs the girl under his arm, half hug, half restraint. Taking out a twenty and dropping it on the table by my hand, he tells me, "I'll pay for your pie, since my daughter interrupted your meal." Then he hugs Evelyn close and glances to an entertained server as she wanders back to the counter. "I'm taking her outta here before she starts a brawl."

"Alright." Katrina fusses with her display fridge and snickers. "Where's Ben? He's usually here to chill her out."

"Ben doesn't control me!" Smalls squirms in her dad's grip. "Ben's a dummy who doesn't know his head from his ass. And your fighter sucks, Biggie. That's all I'm saying." She slams a fist against his ribs as he drags her out the door.

"She's sassy." Pres taps away at his computer and chuckles behind the screen.

"She's always been sassy," Katrina volunteers, though Preston wasn't talking directly to her. "She's the daughter of a Roller, niece to a few too many champions, and though she doesn't know it yet—or at least, she won't admit it—she's the future wife of another champion."

"Ben?" I bring another bite of pie to my lips. "That her boyfriend?"

"Her best friend," she corrects with a smile. "He's a fighter, and he'll go pro soon enough. But in the meantime, she's still wrestling between the '*boys have cooties*' and the '*I love him so much*' phase of adolescence. I've got a hundred bucks on their future nuptials. They're still babies, and no one is interested in making them grow up too soon. But there isn't a soul around here betting against their happily ever after."

Closing the dessert fridge and wiping her hands on a towel, Katrina circles the counter and smiles as a new face walks through the door.

It doesn't take a genius to understand he's responsible for the rock she wears on her finger.

On the way to him, Katrina swings by my table, though she doesn't stop. "If Evie says she wants you to come by the gym, I suggest you head on over and introduce yourself. They've already got a contender in Ben, but they've got a year or two between now and when he's ready for the world title. Which means if you're interested, this might be a good time to take her up on her offer."

I frown in response. "But... she's a kid."

Katrina laughs at my words and turns to stroll backwards. "She knows a champion when she sees one." Finally, she winks and backs straight into her man's arms.

"Hey there, Cap." She twists and reaches up to wrap her hands over his shoulders. "How's it going?"

Grinning, he presses a kiss to the tip of her nose. "What are the specials today?"

~

I roll to a stop outside Maya's apartment at eight on the dot, with music whispering through my speakers, and my engine rumbling with a satisfied growl. My stomach dips with nerves, and my knees bounce so the toe of my shoe taps the floor.

Because beneath the odd excitement I carry for a night with the beautiful socialite, disgust roils in my belly for what I'm about to do to her.

I should drive away. Pull away from the curb, take my ass home. Refuse to use her as cover so I can walk back into Club 188 and not stand out the way I do when I'm alone.

She speaks of diaries, when money was taken from her.

She speaks of karma, when it was she who was stolen from.

She's got a spine and an attitude that keeps me on my toes, but just beneath the surface, a sensitivity that makes her feel too much too easily. She's vulnerable and sweet. Too trusting, and far too innocent for me to tarnish with my very existence.

She didn't even want to see me again.

And yet, she said yes to dinner.

Cutting the engine and bringing my hands up to scrub my face, I consider my options and search desperately for one that gets me what I need—Jack Reilly's ride, parked inside Box's garage—without Maya's feelings being hurt.

Because they will be. Her heart will break when she realizes my invitation was nothing more than a cover for walking back inside a club crawling with folks related to, or fond of, the champion with a car someone else wants.

She doesn't have to be emotionally invested for her feelings to get hurt. She simply has to experience the sting of rejection that my bait and switch will create.

Even if I do like her, even if I think she's the prettiest thing I've ever had the pleasure of seeing up close. Even if her brains and defiance intrigue the fuck out of me.

If I could have a do-over, I might wish to meet her inside a different club. In a different town. I'd ask her out for real, and soak up the sight of whatever beautiful dress she wore to impress me. I'd study her long legs, and I'd squirrel away the memory of her *high* high heels, because without them, she feels a little too on the short side.

Just drive away, Cole.

I drop my hands and keep my eyes on the road in front of me, instead of on the light emanating from the apartments on my right. But I wrap my palms around the steering wheel, and picture how she'll look at me in just a few hours, when she realizes my ulterior motives for tonight... the pain I'll inflict, and the heartache she'll experience because of me.

Abruptly, I make up my mind and reach down to start the engine again.

It's better to be stood up than used.

Taking the car out of park and sliding my foot onto the clutch, I prepare to slip into first and get the hell out of this neighborhood, but a *tap-tap-tap* on the side window makes me jump so hard, the entire car rocks on its chassis.

Adrenaline surges in my blood, and my fight or flight prepares to go to war. But as I swing my gaze around, I lock onto Maya's stunning smile and playful eyes.

Busted.

Surely, she knows I intended to leave. Certainly, she felt the change in the air as I slipped the Mustang into gear. She *must* know I was readying to stand her up. But instead of anger, she opens the car door and drops into the passenger seat.

"Hey."

She smells of sex, flowers, and something sweet I wouldn't mind sampling with my tongue to make sure I've deciphered every exotic flavor.

Closing the door and twisting to grab her seatbelt, she inadvertently shows off entirely too much thigh, and scrambles those thoughts I had about getting out of town.

"I'm kinda starving," she chatters, turning back to fix her belt and fuss with the fabric of her dress. "I didn't have dinner yet, since you said we were—ya know. But I had a protein water thingy, because my blood sugar was dropping."

Finally done fussing, she looks across and shoots me a radiant smile that arrows straight to my fucking heart and leaves me breathless. "Lucky I saw you drive up, because I realized I hadn't given you my phone number. And you didn't know which apartment I was in, so you couldn't come in and greet me at my door."

Anger.

Nerves.

Anxiety.

Frustration.

Loneliness.

Contentment.

All these emotions batter my system as I take my foot off the clutch and pull away from the curb. Contentment, because she's right here with me, but the rest because I neither earned her nor do I intend to follow through on what she deserves.

"It's still kinda warm out, huh?" Settling in, she exhales a sweet breath so I taste her toothpaste in the air. "I always feel kinda bad for guys who wear jeans all year long. You don't know what it's like to wear a skirt and feel the breeze on your legs the way we do."

"You shouldn't have to come down to a date's car." Of all the things I could say, of all the tones I could use, I growl and take my bad mood out on her.

Turning out of her street and toward the club, I glance across and meet her curious stare.

"What?"

"A man asks you out to dinner," I grit out. "Means he acts like a fucking gentleman and comes to your door. At the absolute *least*, he gets out of his damn car to greet you. He opens your door and helps you in. You don't do all that shit on your own."

"Uh..." Her soft green eyes are rimmed with black, a cat-eye look that is as seductive as it is innocent, because it only illustrates just how fucking naïve her worldview is. "I'm sorry, what?"

"Lift your fucking standards, Maya! Maybe your shitty parents warped your sense of value, and maybe the only person who treated you well has passed now, but I swear to God, you date a man who doesn't do better than that shit I just pulled, and I'm gonna come back to this tiny-ass town and beat him stupid till he begs for your forgiveness."

I turn at the next corner and spy the club further along the street. I see the parking lot out front, and the lights on eaves of the building. I see the line of cars parked in a row, and right beside a-not-yet-released Mustang GT worth more than all the money I've ever earned *collectively*, is an empty space, as though the universe wants to invite me right in.

"You'll *come back* to this town?" Maya's voice is softer than expected as I flick my indicator on and roll into the club parking lot. "Are you leaving?"

"Eventually." I pull into the space beside Reilly's and loathe the warmth of the dupe fob in my pocket.

If not for Maya, I could get out now, unlock his car, and complete the job Box is nagging me for. I'm already late for delivery. Already pissing off a customer who wants, not only an unreleased car, but a car that belongs to a champion fighter.

"I don't live here, Maya Elizabeth. I'm just visiting. And you're

93

entirely too casual about a guy who didn't even get out of the fucking car to help you in. That was shitty of me."

"But..." She turns in her seat, unsnapping her belt and resting her back on the door as I kill the engine. "You asked me out so we could become *friends*. Friends don't expect friends to hold doors and kiss cheeks every time they see each other."

"I asked you out because you're beautiful and mouthy and refuse to back down in an argument. So where the fuck is your spine when it comes to self-worth?"

"Excuse me?" What *were* smiling eyes are now dangerous daggers. "My self-worth? What the hell is that supposed to mean?"

"It means you demand so much in every other facet of your life. You want the job *you* want. You want your grandma's diaries. You created boundaries between you and your toxic-ass parents. You stand up for yourself always... but you don't expect a man to come to your fucking door?"

"I have hands too," she snarls in response. "I can open a door just fine on my own."

"But you shouldn't have to! You should demand better. Because the idea of me going home after this and never seeing you again, and you allowing a man to treat you like shit..."

"Like shit?"

"It pisses me off!" I snap so loud, she jumps in her seat. "It pisses me off you would let a man into your life and find absolutely no issue with him being a lazy, inconsiderate prick."

"You?" She points my way, still confused. "You're the inconsiderate prick?"

"Well, obviously! I didn't even get out of my fucking car. I didn't say sorry. And you didn't even get mad about it."

"I'm getting pretty mad about you shouting at me," she grits through tight teeth. "You wanna follow me home, you wanna save me. You want to protect me from every other bad guy on the planet. But when *you're* the bad guy, it's *my* fault?"

"Yes!"

I drop my head back and close my eyes, if only to cut off the venom she sees in them. The venom I hold for myself.

"No," I try again, gentler this time. "It's not your fault I'm a dick. But it is your responsibility to not accept dick behavior. Say no, Maya." Opening my eyes and catching sight of the Mustang on my right, I shake my head. "Demand better. From me, and from every other asshole you meet. Because you deserve better than deep-fried, shit food inside a noisy club, and a guy who won't even get out of his car to meet you at your door."

Turning to her, I hate how beautiful she is, and how compassionate her eyes are. How she remains in this car with a guy who treats her poorly, and how, instead of getting angry, she searches for a way to understand.

"I'm sorry I invited you here tonight." Darting my tongue forward, I wet my dry lips. "I'm sorry I did this to you."

"You're sorry you met me?" she ponders. "Or you're just sorry about the dickish, prickish stuff?"

"The dick, prick stuff." I study her beautiful eyes in the dark. "I'm definitely not sorry I met you."

"So let's keep what's working. Toss away what's not. You don't want deep-fried food in a noisy club?" She twists in her seat and refastens her belt. "Take me somewhere else. You don't like that you didn't open the door?" She opens hers and pushes it wide enough to make me frown. "Get out and fix it for me."

"What?" I study her profile, and the soft tremor in her lips as she tries not to laugh. "What are you doing with your door?"

"I'm demanding better. So get out and close my door, Cole Miller. Then drive us away from here. It's the gentlemanly thing to do."

"Drive us a—Where? Where the fuck do you want me to take you?"

"Anywhere! I don't care. Just drive and stop being a dickish prick."

"Maya—"

"Close my door, Cole Miller!"

I unsnap my seatbelt with a fast flourish and shove out of my side to rush to hers. Grabbing her doorhandle, I lean into the gap instead of closing it, then looking down at her playful expression, I study her dancing eyes, and her thighs, bare because her dress shifts each time she moves.

She wears red heels tonight, to match the red on her lips, and her hair dangles loose, as though to prove she's not always rigid and uptight. Her dress, like last time, is tight around the torso, and flares from her hips.

She knows what style complements her body, and I suppose she went and bought in bulk.

Rich people solutions.

"You look so beautiful, Maya Elizabeth." Leaning in, I love and hate how she freezes, waiting for me to make my move.

She won't initiate contact, and yet, she doesn't say no.

Because she wants it? Or because she was never taught that she controls who touches?

Before I can mull it over too long, my lips press to her cheek, and a warm blush fills it until my stomach turns in response.

She's too sweet. Too innocent. Too fucking perfect.

And I... am a broke car thief.

Awesome.

Pulling away and slowly closing her door, I push up straight and circle my car once more. I watch the newer Mustang in my peripherals. The glistening, unmarked paint, and the wide racer wheels Reilly somehow conned the manufacturer into putting on for him.

Eighty thousand dollars retail. But this one, worth so much more because of its unreleased status.

Peeling my eyes away and ignoring the burn of the fob against my thigh, I slide into mine and close the door to lock myself and Maya inside. Just the two of us, the darkness, and the intoxicating scent of her perfume playing through my every inhalation.

"So..." I start the car and say goodbye to Reilly's Mustang—for now. Even knowing Box wants it tonight. Even brutally aware that my next injection of cash depends on the delivery of that one specific vehicle, I back out of my parking spot and head toward the street with nerves bubbling in my stomach. "Where would you like to go?"

She settles into her seat, almost melting into the shape of the leather, then turning just her head to show off a seductive smile beneath street-lights, she lifts her shoulder in a dainty shrug. "Let's just drive."

My palms sweat, because I have a job to do and a product to deliver. But the thought of hitting the highway with this woman is my kind of heaven. Music. Moonlight. And her. "Are you hungry?"

"Starving." The word comes out on a rumble, but she crosses her left leg over the right and shows off more of her tantalizing thigh. "I'm not fancy, Cole. Drive-thru would keep me happy."

"I don't see why it should," I grumble.

But I pull off the street just as soon as I come upon the right driveway, and rolling closer to the speaker boxes, I order us a little bit of everything. Sliders. Onion rings. Fries. Chicken tenders.

Finger foods, so we can nibble what we want and not need two hands to work a giant-ass burger.

As soon as we have our food, and the scent of fried oil replaces the sexy scent of Maya's perfume, I wind the windows down and cross the railroad tracks heading out of town.

"Let's finish our game of Twenty Questions." I recline back in my seat and grin as the warm summer breeze whips through the car. The only light we see comes from my very own headlights, and the only people in the world, on this stretch of highway, at this point in time, is us. "First kiss?"

"Oh geez." She digs into the paper bag on her lap and takes out a carton of fries. She holds them between us so I can reach, but selects her own to eat too. "Mathew Eastlin, eighth grade. He kissed me under the bleachers, and an hour later, received something akin to a cease and desist from my parents." She takes a long fry and bites the end off with a smile. "He never kissed me again after that."

"Mathew..." I play the name through my mouth and take a handful of fries. "Did he kiss you with tongue?"

"You're such a pig." Pulling back her offering, she eats the fries on her own and lifts her shoulder to keep me away when I reach for more. "Why does our game have to include tongue?"

"It doesn't." I snatch the bag from between her legs and chuckle when the sharp *snap* of paper makes her gasp. "My tongue is safely over here in my mouth. First time having sex?"

"Is none of your business. Who was your first kiss?"

I consider for a moment. "I was pretty drunk. We were at some frat party and getting noisy, so I don't really remember. But my buddy Preston assures me it was with a beautiful blonde bikini model."

"Uh-huh." She rolls her eyes. "And a frat party? You didn't even kiss a girl till college?"

I choke out a laugh. "I was fourteen, *crashing* a frat party. And before you ask, I'm led to believe that was my first time having sex, too."

"When you were fourteen?" She casts a side glance my way and fails to conceal the scowl marring her face. "You had sex when you were fourteen? While you were drunk?"

"Fourteen-year-old me thought he was hot shit, and all grown up." I reach into the takeout bag and select a package of chicken tenders. *Protein, baby.* "I was glad to have gotten through that step without remembering too much. I doubt I was all that impressive."

She snorts. "You were fourteen! And if you were at a college party, chances are you slept with someone much older than you. Do you realize, if caught, she would have ended up on a sex offender's list?"

"Lucky she didn't get caught then." I set my meal on the center console near the gearshift, *because I'm a nice guy who shares,* unlike Maya and her fries. "I never saw her again. Copped no heat from it. Didn't cry when she didn't stay to cuddle, because I was a big boy now. So... all's well that ends well." I toss half a tender into my mouth and chew around the steaming chicken. "Your turn, Maya Elizabeth."

"It annoys me when you call me that." Exhaling a frustrated breath, she turns back my way and drops the three-quarters-full fries back in the bag and takes a tender instead. "I was eighteen. There was no statutory rape involved. He didn't stay to cuddle, but I was okay with it, since I'm not really all that interested in the awkward chat *after*. It was just..." she shrugs. "Sex."

"Did you come?"

"No. And your line of questioning remains inappropriate."

"And yet," I point a tender her way. "You continue to answer. Have you come with a different dude? Has anyone on this planet found your G spot?"

"*I've* found it." Pursing her lips, she looks across at me and smirks, knowing she fucks with me. "They say if you want a job done well..."

"Do it yourself." My cock stirs in my jeans and sends a pleasurable shot of electricity through my veins. "Noted. But you didn't answer the original question."

"Hmm?" She reaches for her Coke in the cup holders and brings the straw to her lips. "What didn't I answer?"

"Has a man made you come? Not you, not your fingers, and not a little vibrating toy. But a man?"

She sips slowly, torturously, in the dark.

She thinks she's in control, but I still see the blush in her cheeks.

"No. I can't say a man has ever gotten me over the line. And before you go bragging about your conquests," she sets her drink down and takes the chicken from my grasp, "I told those men they did fine. And my friends say the same, even if the guy sucks. It was long ago drilled into our DNA; please men, stroke their egos. So even if we didn't come, we say we did. Because, hell, we'd feel bad making them feel inferior."

"Are you implying the women I've been with have lied to me?" I press a palm to my chest and glare. "Are you saying those whose worlds I've rocked... *lied* about said world-rocking?"

"You wouldn't be the first to hear it. You won't be the last."

"I take offense to this line of discussion. For myself, and all of mankind."

"Then maybe you and your people should try harder." She squeezes a little further away on her seat, as though afraid of retaliation. Not the way battered women twitch in fear of a backhand, but perhaps, afraid of me reaching across and tickling. "Stop taking a woman's word for it. Start doing the actual work to get the job done. I assure you, when I pleasure myself, I'm not talking at the end."

"You're saucy on date night." I study the open highway and the mile line markers we pass every minute or so. "Touch yourself now and show me what needs to be done. Ya know, research, for me and my fellow man." I peek across to catch her sly smirk. "If you refuse, then I can only conclude your claims that women don't come are simply attention-seeking on your part."

"Or..." she sniggers. "You can do your own research without me, since I'm not interested in being dictated to." Reaching into the greasy paper bag, she takes out onion rings and bites one in half. "My turn to ask questions."

"Oh yay." I roll my eyes and look straight ahead. "I'll touch my cock if you want. Happily. I've never had a serious girlfriend. In fact, this is my first ever actual date where I pick a woman up and take her somewhere. Which," I add with a tap of my hand to the steering wheel, "I clearly suck at, since I didn't get your door, I shouted at you, and our plans to eat somewhere morphed into shitty drive-thru food in the car."

"And yet, I'm enjoying myself. Why no girlfriends?"

"Because women are fucking drama!" I look her way as though to ask *are you serious*? "Women are fuckin' crazy, Maya. Tell me I'm wrong."

"Well..." She considers for a moment. Then shrugs. "I guess. I'd like to say *I'm* not drama, since I don't cause it and I never dwell in it. But my very existence is drama; as in, my parents and their overbearing ways, my grandmother's estate and the trouble I'm having with that, plus, there's that thing about men being unable to truly satisfy a woman."

"The last isn't true," I counter. "You just haven't met the right man yet."

Silence hangs for a beat, deafening and loaded as she studies the side of my face. I feel her stare, and grin the longer she remains stuck. Then she clears her throat, eliciting a chuckle from deep inside my chest.

"Anyway..."

"Mmm..." I scoff. "*Anyway.* Are you done with the question game? I already told you about my sex life."

"What do you do for work?" She asks so innocently, but when I look across, I see the determination in her stare. "You still haven't answered that question, and I've gotta say, the secrecy makes it all the more intriguing."

"It's not a secret." *It fucking is.* "I just don't have anything interesting to say. It's a job. I earn money. I pay rent and buy food with that money. End of story."

"But what *work* do you do?" Done with her meal, she drops the package of onion rings back into the larger paper bag and takes out a handful of napkins to wipe her fingers. "What exactly does your job entail, and why the hell do you continue to run circles around it instead of giving a straight answer?"

"You sound like a fucking lawyer, do you realize that?" With a shake of my head, I nudge the wheel just a fraction of an inch and follow the highway around a gentle bend. "You don't get the answer you want, so you push, push, push to satisfy your own curiosity."

"So... answer," she taunts. "Then you'll know you satisfied a woman —in one way, at least."

My eyes narrow to slits at her not-at-all veiled insult, which only makes her burst out laughing and huddle into the corner between her seat and the door. "You get so cranky," she howls. "So ridiculously angry when I call your manhood into question."

"My manhood needn't be called into question!" I bark out. "It did nothing to you."

"I mean, your insecurity leads me to wonder if it did anything to anyone... ever."

"You're a pain in my ass." I straighten out the car and reach across to press my fingers to her ribs. Not a tickle, and not a caress.

Still, she squeals and jumps from my touch. "Stop!" She bats my hand away and shows off entirely too much leg when she squirms. "Cole! No tickling."

"Stop talking about my cock, unless you're discussing how you'll take it." Pulling my hand back, I purse my lips and *know* all this is just a distraction. A shiny diversion in hopes she'll get the hell off the topic of my job.

But she's a lawyer, whether she likes it or not. She's the daughter of a couple of sharks. And she's a teacher, who tolerates a bunch of five-year-olds all day long. She's nothing if not patient and persistent.

"I... work with cars," I hedge. "With the engines and the computers and whatnot."

"So you're a mechanic?" Her breath still races, her smile too big. But she calms herself and straightens her dress. "Why was that so difficult to answer?" Then as though a thought hits her, she reaches across and grabs my hand. Opening my fingers and turning it palm-side up, I know she searches for the black stains every mechanic on the planet possesses. "Work with gloves?" she asks.

I should panic under the grand inquisition of the Honorable Maya Blake. But my brain concentrates on her soft touch, and her gentle fingertips searching my palm. I feel her breath on my skin, and her warm thighs beneath my hand.

"I also like to fight sometimes," I admit quietly. Timidly. "Not, like, brawling in the street. But when I have spare cash lying around, I like to visit this gym a couple blocks over from my apartment. They don't do much with me, since those places focus on their contenders and leave the rest of us to work out on our own. But they have all the equipment, and their competition fighters can always do with a sparring partner. So when the timing is right and I'm in the mood, I like to climb into the ring and go a round."

"And...?" She doesn't let my hand go, though she has no true excuse to continue holding on. "Do you win?"

I snort. "Sometimes. Those sessions aren't there for us to whale on each other. It's more of a practice. But, sure..." I shrug. "I don't get my ass beat."

"Ya know, I have that kid in my class. Charlie." Glancing up, she waits for me to look across and meet her eyes. "He says he's gonna be the next world champion."

The Rollers. Jack Reilly. My entire fucking reason for being here.

"One of his cousins—a teenager—came up to me today in the diner. Told me she was looking for a contender, since Jack's getting old." Scoffing, I look down at my *fighter body*. "She picked me outta nowhere, could tell just by looking that I fight sometimes. I brushed her off and went on with my day, but she's got an eye."

I flatten my lips and wonder, for just a minute, what that life could be like. "She was saying I should come down to the gym and show them what I've got."

Maya plays with my hand, rolling my fingers closed, then opening them again to trace the long digits. "Are you?"

"Am I what?"

"Gonna go down to the gym. Show them what you can do?"

I cough out an incredulous laugh. "Fuck no. I'm not what they're looking for, Maya. I don't have formal training. I don't have the right family or the right name. I don't have any of that shit. I just have the shoulders that most fighters have, and a face someone might find pleasure in rearranging."

Her brows pull close in a frown. "I don't think I'd be happy if someone rearranged your face." Setting my hand in her lap, she leans back against the door and studies my profile. "If nothing mattered in the world, not money or families or expectations of upbringings or jobs," she waits for me to peer across, "what would you do for a living? What is your dream?"

"I don't have a dream." I go back to studying the freeway. The mile markers. The reflection of the signs when my headlights bounce off of them. "Guys like me can't afford to do anything except sleep, so that we can be rested when we wake the next day, so we can get on with the job that pays our bills."

I look across and pause dangerously long when she lifts her legs and folds them on the seat. Her dress falls into the gap between to cover her panties, and my hand just kind of... floats, with no clue where to go that won't land me with a restraining order.

Thankfully—or horribly, maybe—she takes it again and draws circles in the center of my palm. "I'd like for you to consider a dream," she murmurs. "I know it's hard sometimes for someone who hasn't been allowed to do that in the past. But try really hard. This is our first date, this is *your* first proper date ever, so set reality aside and just *think*. If nothing else mattered and the world was fair, would you work with cars? Or would you become a world champion fighter? Or," she adds before I can argue, "would you do something else entirely? The sky's the limit."

"Well..." Dreaming, *wondering*, are cruel exercises for a man like me. They highlight what I'll never have, and leave me feeling all sorts of fucking disappointed when I go to bed later tonight, alone, and think over what I'll never achieve.

But Maya is a woman who, I've learned, doesn't take no for an answer. She's a woman who, I've discovered, I don't like saying no to. So I try. For just a few minutes, while we drive and the wind is warm and fried food sits in my belly, I consider what life could be like if money was never an issue.

"Cole?"

"I'd fight." I whisper the words, as though speaking them too loudly would bring bad luck raining down on my head. "I'm good at it. I like it. I like the competition, and I enjoy the sport. Plus, those champions make buckets of money and never have to worry about paying their bills again. So..." I nod when that dream comes clear in my mind. "I wouldn't mind a taste of that."

"And money is important to you?" she asks. "Above all else, that's your primary focus?"

I snort. "It's *everyone's* primary focus, Maya Elizabeth. Maybe they don't say it out loud, but I assure you, money is where it starts and ends. Every single time."

"Not for me. Money isn't—"

"That's because you've never had to be hungry," I cut in. "You were raised rich, so you never had to think about what it's like being broke. It was easy for you to dump law school and try out teaching, because you've never had to sleep cold before. And no matter how controlling and shitty your parents are, all you need to do, if the teaching thing doesn't work out, is call them up, eat a little humble pie, and *voila*, you're not hungry anymore. But guys like me," I slowly drag my hand from her grasp and place it on the steering wheel. "We don't have a safety net. We have no one to catch us. So fuck yes, money is important to me. I'd like to someday reach a point where I'm not counting pennies."

"I wouldn't call my parents if teaching didn't work out." Pouting, she turns in her seat and faces the front again. "If I was fired and the world was falling down, I wouldn't call them to save me."

"You say that now," I argue. "While your belly is full and life is chugging along nicely. But if you were legitimately starving and all you had to do was make that call." I scoff under my breath. "You'd be swiping that phone unlocked so fast, your head would spin."

"But I wouldn't." She's stubborn and persistent. Pouty and beautiful. "I would call you."

"Me?"

"For a meal." She clarifies. "If the world was being cruel, and I was down to my last penny and so hungry I'd be tempted to call my parents," her lips curl into a sweet grin, "well, I have this friend named Cole Miller. We talked once about how there are four billion women on the planet, but he didn't know or care about them. But he knew me, and since saving me was within his control…"

"You'd call me for a meal," I chuckle. "Awesome. We live in different towns. Our lives will never intersect again, since our meeting last week was freak at best. I'm broke more often than I'm lush. But sure, you call me up, Maya Elizabeth, and I'll get you a meal and a bed." I meet her eyes and smirk. "A meal for an orgasm."

"Sure," she rolls her eyes. "Because I value sex at two-ninety-nine and a cheeseburger." She purses her lips. "Why don't you go to the gym and show them what you've got?"

"What?"

"The fighters," she exhales, like my confusion is exhausting to her. "They gave you an opening. You could live your dreams. Why the hell wouldn't you take them up on that? At best, you've walked toward a massive opportunity, which just so happens to align with the sport you love. And at worst, you've spent a day with a world champion fighter. What've you got to lose?"

"Actually." I'm done with my food, and I'm done with it sitting between us, so I scrunch the top of the bag closed and set it on the floor of the back seat, then I wind my windows up so it's just me and Maya again.

Her perfume. Her intoxicating scent. Her sass, and her bare legs, sexy and long and just for my eyes.

"I wasn't invited down there by the world champion. A teenage girl with a big mouth invited me. So I'm thinking, at best, I'll get laughed out of the gym if I turn up. At worst, the cops will be called when I ask to speak to the kid. So no," I chuckle. "I don't think I will."

"You're looking for an excuse not to hope."

Glancing up as we approach the city and the skyline glows ahead of us, she furrows her brows. "Where are we going?"

"Just driving." Casual, I laze back in my seat. Because driving is what I do for fun. It's how I relax. And sure, gas costs an arm and a kidney these days, but hell, taking Maya to dinner at the club would've cost just as much as onion rings and a tank of gas, anyway. "We can turn around anytime you want. I'll take you back home and make sure you get inside in one piece."

Setting my elbow on the middle console and draping my hand near the gear shift, I act like fire doesn't burn beneath my skin when she reaches across and takes it again.

Not to hold my hand. But to study it. To trace designs and torment me without truly trying.

"You grew up here?" she ponders. She speaks of the city, but her eyes remain focused on my fingers. "Born here?"

"Mm. Every day of my life." I nod toward the western side of the city and grunt, "Over that way. I was raised in a piece of shit hovel with no heating, rats for pets, and neighbors who liked to look at little kids. I was faster than the others who lived nearby," I explain. "Stronger. More street-smart. Which meant I lived, when some of them didn't."

"That's awful." Frowning, she lifts her chin straight ahead. "I was raised in the northern suburbs. No rats for pets. We always had heating and cooling, and more often than not, everyone I knew had an in-ground pool and brand-new cars. If I ever gave in and became a lawyer, I think I'd drive myself over to the west side and help the kids who deserved better. No one should go through winter without heating. Rats aren't *supposed* to be pets, unless they're actually wanted and clean and kept. Perverts aren't supposed to look at children. And you shouldn't have had to be the strongest and fastest one to survive."

"All very martyrish of you, Maya Elizabeth. But that's reality for a massive number of kids, then and now. Besides," I add as an afterthought. "I think you'd be too soft to make change for the better."

"Excuse me?" Her hands grow tighter around mine. "What the hell does that mean?"

"I mean... you wouldn't be able to handle it. You couldn't cope with the nasty shit that happens."

I cross the city limits and slow the car to match crawling traffic. Drive-thrus on every block, and women walking most corners. Neon lights draw drinkers into bars, and apartment lights glimmer from television sets playing the evening news.

"You expect the world to be rainbows and unicorns," I explain, "and you think the worst a parent can do to their child is not deliver the inheritance their grandma intended for them. But in the real world," I cut in when she opens her mouth to argue, "some kids starve, and others freeze to death in the winter. To be too soft for that world isn't a character flaw on your part, Maya. I'm not saying it's bad that you couldn't hack it. I'm just saying... you wouldn't last. And I wouldn't like to know you're experiencing that shit on a daily basis. You'd internalize those kids' struggles, you'd feel it all way too much, and eventually, before your first year was up, you'd explode and quit, because it'd be too much for you, to know those babies live in filth and go to bed hungry."

"So you're not insulting me," she bites out angrily. "But you think I'm weak. And that's okay, because you're sexually attracted to me, which means I fulfill my role as something tasty to look at, but I needn't bother aiming higher?"

"You're projecting." Turning my hand in hers, I lay my palm flat on her thigh. To touch. To hold. Because she's about to flip her shit and toss me out of my own car. "I didn't say you're weak. I said you feel. And fuck, but I think that's beautiful. I think you chose teaching over legal for good reason, and I'm really fucking proud of you for knowing your limits and working within them."

"I'm not a teacher because it's *easy* or within my limits!" she snarls, shoving my hand off her lap. "I do it because that's what my heart wants.

Jesus, Cole. You are the single most offensive person I've ever met in my entire life. And I know my mother!"

"Fancy words," I tease with a laugh.

Her anger should concern me, but she does that frustrated growl of hers, which only makes my stomach tingle and my cock twitch.

Driving with no true thought for where we're going, I head toward my neighborhood; not just the one I grew up in, but the one I still live in. Taking another left a block before my apartment, I come to a stop outside a massive brick warehouse that I think was once a munition factory.

Back in the war, when the men fought, and the women joined the workforce, because someone had to make the explosives.

"Come on." I pull up in front of enormous hangar doors that were chained shut eons ago and have been graffitied a million times over the past eighty years.

Snagging my car keys and pushing my door open, I shake my head when Maya only sits back in her chair and folds her arms.

She's cranky, and she has her pout on lock.

So I circle the car and come around to her door. Opening it, I rest my elbow on the roof and lean closer so that, if she just turned her face, we'd be damn near nose to nose. "Come for a walk with me, Maya Elizabeth."

"No." She purses her lips and harrumphs when I reach in and unsnap her seatbelt. "If this were a movie, the audience would be shouting at me not to go inside the dilapidated building. It's obviously where I die."

"Well…" I push her seatbelt away and wrap my hand around her bicep. Gently, I tug her out so she has no choice but to follow or fall to the dirt outside the car. "I promise not to let you die. In fact, I swear for the rest of time to stand between you and danger, no matter the threat, no matter the time or place."

"All the more opportunity for you to control this one woman out of four billion?" She's petulant and grumpy, but she steps out of the car and straightens her spine so the tip of her nose almost brushes my chin. Bright red heels match bright red lips, but onion rings stole some of the perfect lines she drew in before leaving her apartment. "You're seriously the strangest man I've ever met, Cole." Inhaling, she slowly brings her eyes up to meet mine. "We don't even know each other, but you're so demanding and bossy and weird."

"All part of my charm." I loop her arm around mine, then I lean in and press a kiss to the center of her forehead.

Why? *I have no fucking clue.*

The consequences? *Still to be determined.*

Alarms sound somewhere in the back of my brain and send adrenaline pulsing through my veins, but I keep my panic on mute and turn away to lead my date around the side of the building.

"This is basically where I grew up," I tell her in the dark.

The streetlights surrounding us long ago blacked out, and the city has no desire to spend money where it doesn't bring a return. But I learned a lifetime ago how many steps it takes to get from one place to the next.

"Not literally," I assure her when her eyes widen. "Like I said, I lived in a shitty apartment. But when you don't like where you're forced to sleep at night, you tend to go out and explore."

I bring us to a stop by a low window and know, though it's easy access for anyone to come and go, this entire building will be empty. Because I claimed it, and from the moment I was able, I defended it from intruders.

"Watch your head." I unravel our arms and step through the empty window first, dropping to my feet inside the cold building, then I turn back and look up as she anxiously glances around.

"Sit on the ledge," I tell her. "Legs in first. I'll lower you down."

"To my death?" She brings a shaking hand up and presses a perfect nail between her teeth. "Are you trying to kill me, Cole?"

"Nope. I made a promise." Stepping to the wall and reaching through the window, I take her hands and gently tug her closer. She has to crouch, and then she has to sit, and because the floor of the warehouse is lower than the ground level outside, she has to be lowered in and set on her feet. "Stop freaking out. Have I let you down yet?"

"Well..." She lowers to her ass and flashes a little panty. Though I doubt she realizes it. "There was the time you followed me home when I asked you not to." Settled on the lip of the window, she looks down and exhales when I set my hands on her hips and lift. "There was the time you asked me out on a date, didn't come to my door, and subsequently shouted at me."

I set her on her feet and hold on a minute longer. Because her chest presses to mine, and her breath bathes my tongue.

"There was the time you altered our date plans, only to bring me to an abandoned warehouse and have me killed."

"Except," I counter, "you got home safe that time I followed you, you shouted back at me earlier, and," I release her and grin when she stumbles back a step, "you're still alive. So, have I failed you? Or are you searching for a reason to be cranky?"

"A little bit like how you search for reasons not to reach for your dreams."

She glances around the dark warehouse, the entire space one massive room with one-ton machinery interspersed in even rows. The air in here is chilly, despite the warmth outside, so when she brings her hands up to rub the goosebumps from her skin, I step closer again and wrap her up against my side.

Then we walk. And explore. And pass pockets of this warehouse that, to her eye, are just part of the scenery. But to me, I see the pile of car magazines I read over the years, and in another area, the wrappers from snacks I stole, traded, or, on my lush days, bought.

"I think you should go to the gym." She runs the tips of her fingers across a colossal steel press as we pass. "That girl you said asked you... the one you think might get the cops called on you?"

"Evelyn Kincaid." I picture her in my mind. The teen with wild hair and an arrogant smirk. Biceps that prove she's no slouch, and a gait that promises she's confident in who she is. But then I think of cops slapping a pair of cuffs on my wrists, because I'm a grown-ass man who steals for a living... asking for a private meeting with a child. "She's a kid."

"She has sway in that gym." Walking, Maya glances up, and her eyes, green in the sun, appear black in here. "I've only lived in town for a couple of weeks, and already, I've heard how she's going pro just as soon as she's finished with school. And when she does, she's taking a team with her. Her father is arguably the best grappler in the country, and he taught her how to fight from the moment she was an able toddler. Word is, if she says she wants a fighter, her family listens and makes it happen."

Forcing a chuckle, I pull Maya's lithe body in tighter.

She can't possibly know it, but we pass a shadowed pocket of the building where I've curled up more than a couple of times to sleep through the worst nights. When my mom was fucking her newest Mr. Right and I needed safe haven somewhere else.

I wasn't beaten too often as a child. I wasn't starved to death, or mentally screwed over. So really, I had it better than others. I was just... ignored, mostly. Forgotten. Until eventually, she emptied our apartment and ditched town without me.

"I think I'll continue on with the life I have. It's comfortable. I know what I'm doing, and I know my place in this world."

Coming to a stop in front of a press that packed bullets for the MG-42, a machine gun the Nazis particularly liked—though we don't talk about why we made them here, too—I bring Maya around so her back presses to the cold steel, and her chest pauses, filled with air. I continue forward to take up her space, stopping only when her legs twine with mine and her hands lift to my shoulders.

She's stunned to silence, and scared, if only long enough for her heart to thud and the beat to become visible in her throat. And I... well, I guess I'm all about breaking the rules I long ago set out for myself. Starting with the fact I asked her out on a date, and not just a fast fuck in the back of my car. Second, that I brought her here, a place I've *never* brought a woman before. And third, that I bring a hand up and finger soft tendrils of her hair back behind her ear while my eyes, my entire heart and soul and focus, search her lips.

"Would it be ridiculous if I asked to kiss you?" I come closer. Closer. So I taste her on my tongue. But I don't close the gap and steal from her.

I'll steal anything from anyone, any time.

But not from Maya. I refuse to become another person in her life who takes without her permission.

Instead, I study her terrified eyes and slide my free hand down to stroke her thigh. "Maya?" I breathe. "Can I—"

"Yes." She pushes to her toes and presses her lips to mine, destroying whatever semblance of self-control I thought I possessed when she wraps her arms around my neck and opens her lips for me to dive in.

She tastes of sin and sex and something I could never afford. But she also tastes of drive-thru fountain Coke.

I can afford that.

Her legs already twine with mine, her hips moving, searching for somewhere to rest. So when I reach down and cup her thighs beneath the fabric of her dress, she goes all-in, lifting off her feet and forcing me to catch and press her against the steel at her back.

"Fuck." I groan when her legs come around my hips and her warm core presses to my cock. She's sweet and innocent in the real world. But in the dark, in my warehouse, she's forward and demanding and wet. "Maya—"

"You can touch me."

Cinching her arms tight, she holds most of her weight up and grinds when I crush her against the press. Her breath comes out on a moan, sizzling my throat on the way down and filling my lungs so I become intoxicated on the very air she exhales. My fingertips explore her creamy thighs and her firm ass. My palms hold, and my shoulders burn with the best kind of exhilaration as her tongue performs magic with mine.

For a shy, submissive woman in the daylight, she knows what she wants when it comes to this. She knows how to achieve her end goal.

Fuck, but she knows how to set me on fire and refuse me water to put it out.

Though, her eagerness is a balm that makes the fire enjoyable.

"This is crazy," she exhales in the single second I take to catch my breath. "I don't even know you, Cole. But now we're... and you're... and I'm..."

"Delicious."

Hitching her higher, I groan when she bounces off the steel press, and her pussy warms my cock in the best way. My jeans grind across her clit, eliciting a moan from somewhere deep in her chest. But she doesn't push me away. She doesn't panic and ask me to stop.

Moving my hands from her thighs and around to her ass, I slide my fingertips beneath the fabric of her underwear. I grip her tight, squeezing so she'll bruise tomorrow. Then I dive forward and press my lips to her neck. Biting. Nipping. Marking her fair skin and taking pleasure in knowing that once this night has passed, I'll have left something behind for her to remember me by.

We might never see each other again—chances are, we won't. And hell, eventually she'll find a man who will open doors and greet her with flowers. She'll move on and forget the thief.

But until that day comes, she'll remember Cole Miller.

"You taste so fuckin' good." Her shampoo fills my lungs, and the soft feather of her hair makes my skin hypersensitive. Best of all, her hands explore my body too. My shoulders and back. Her fingers dive into my hair, and her lips and teeth cruise along the shell of my ear. "Fuckkkkk."

"I'm aware what I'm about to say next is, ya know, cliché and used. But..."

"But what?" I break the seal of my lips on her neck and pull back to catch Maya's wild eyes. Her jittery stare. "What?"

"I don't normally do this." A hot blush fills her cheeks and works its way down to her chest. But she snickers. "I swear, I'm not typically this person."

"I don't think you give this to other men." Realizing she doesn't want me to think her a slut, I dive back in and taste her neck. Her scented skin, and the warm patch behind her ear. "I don't think that stuff about any woman, Maya." *Well, except my mother, I suppose.* But that's not something I want to think about while I hold *this* woman in my arms. "We're all adults, free to do what we want with our bodies."

"But I don't..." She shakes her head. "I don't do *this* with my body, usually."

"So, it's just for me." I glide my hand along her thigh and hitch her close. And though I don't mean to, my hips jerk forward in search of more. In search of *home.* "Fuck, Maya. I want you so bad."

"I want you too." She threads her fingers into my hair and yanks my head back with a jerk, breaking my kiss and rendering me searching and wild.

"Cole, I want..." She draws a deep breath; bracing herself, maybe, for words that scare her. "I want this... with you. Because I don't normally do this kind of stuff, but I want to know what it's like with you."

"You wanna fuck?" Pleasure and heat zing through my veins, zapping my fingertips like I've touched a live wire, while in my jeans, my cock grows until it hurts. "Maya, you wanna..."

"Have sex," she counters on an exhale. "Yeah, I want... Yes please."

"*Please.*" I choke out a laugh and hold her with just one arm, while reaching back, I snatch my wallet and open it in desperate search for a condom. "I mean, shit, Maya Elizabeth, you don't have to beg. I'm here for you."

"You don't have to be a dick about it."

She steals the wallet from my hand and checks each section. Cash—decent tonight, since I'm still cruising on last week's Mercedes haul. She finds my driver's license, and flicks it to the side with barely more than a glance. Finally, she finds my cache of condoms and purses her lips, since she has to know, somewhere in her lust-fogged brain, I keep those for... whenever. Not her, specifically.

Taking one out and tossing everything else to the dirt, she inspects the foil packet, searching for defects and an expiration date, by my best guess. When she's satisfied, she tears the foil open with her teeth and spits the trash away.

"Charming," I take her pebbled nipple between my lips.

While she plays with the rubber, I'll play with her tits, because fuck, it's not like I haven't been curious since we met.

"You want me to lay you out on the floor?" I ask breathlessly. "Make it kinda romantic?"

"I want you to make it real," she moans when I bite. "Don't put on a show, Cole. Don't pretend it's something it's not."

"Okay."

Breaking away from her breast, I snatch the rubber from between her fingers and reach down to unzip my jeans. I work one-handed to free my cock while she grinds. While her hormones overpower her brain, and her hips circle in search of purchase.

She wants a dirty fuck with the guy she hardly knows. She wants a fantasy fulfilled, and I'm the dude who gets to do it for her. Hell, I'm here for it. Because when she goes on and forgets me later in life, I'll still have the memory. I'll still get to revisit this place and time and, for just a little while, know I got to touch the sun and didn't get burned.

Placing the rubber over my cock and sliding it all the way to the base, I groan in anticipation of what's coming. I salivate at the thought of being so close to heaven. I whimper at the promise of pleasure her body will bring.

And because I know we're on the clock, I finish with my condom and reach between her legs to tear aside the flimsy underwear she chose for the night.

Fabric rips, and stitches snap. My aggressive yank brings Maya's breath out on a gasp, but she doesn't ask me to stop. She doesn't panic or push me away. So I shove her destroyed panties into my pocket and loathe when my hand brushes over Reilly's key fob.

It's a reminder of who I am.

It's a promise of the future I'll go back to after this.

Freeing my hand and slipping it between her legs, I'm tempted to touch. To slide my fingers between her wet folds and explore what she's promised.

But I don't.

For some insane reason I'll never truly understand, I forfeit that pleasure and circle my cock instead. Once. Twice. I feel the fire in my blood, and my release taunting in the depths of my nuts.

Then, without warning, I surge forward and seat myself deep inside her fiery pussy.

Maya cries out at my intrusion, a keening squeal that is both pleasure and pain. She drops her face to my shoulder and bites down hard enough to make me growl, but her walls flutter around my dick. Grasping. Begging for more. So I pull back to the tip, then glide in a second time and feel the spit in my throat turn to dust.

Parched.

Dry.

She's an unassuming succubus. She doesn't mean to be, and she sure as shit doesn't realize, but she takes from me and absorbs it within herself.

She becomes more beautiful, while my heart aches.

She becomes more amazing, while my brain searches for sense.

I slam her supple body against the steel press and enjoy the *thud, thud, thud* of the tempo I set for us. But like a bucket of water tossed down over my head, my phone chirps loud enough to echo through the warehouse.

I try to ignore it. I squeeze my eyes shut and focus only on how Maya feels wrapped around my cock. How her hands feel in my hair, and her legs feel cinched around my hips. But with every bleat of my phone, the pleasure rocketing through my veins dissipates. The hunger that controlled me only a moment ago tapers.

And then Maya's punishing teeth stop. Her cries. Her rippling pussy.

"What is that?" She's panting, but the sound no longer feels good. "Cole. Your phone is ringing."

Maya

A CLEAN BREAK IS BEST

In the single beat of my heart, everything changes.

Cole's impassioned movements slow.

His fevered hands no longer demand.

His tasting lips curl down in a frown.

What was the constant *thump, thump, thump* of his body taking mine is now just... an intrusion.

"Cole?"

Biting off a curse, he holds me up, pinioned on his dick, and carries my weight with just one arm. Then reaching into his pocket, he grabs his phone and groans after just a single glance at the screen.

"Fuck," he hisses.

Then, worst of all, perhaps worse than anything he's done since we met, he sets me back on my feet—carefully, of course, but cold. Indifferent. He steps back so his dick slides free, and the moisture between my legs is no longer a wet heat, but instead, a chilling reminder of what was taken from us.

Answering his call and turning away to fix his jeans, Cole leaves me standing against an unrelenting hunk of steel with my skirt askew and my heart thundering with nerves.

"Yeah?" His voice is mean, cutting... the way it was that first time we ran into each other.

I guess I'd forgotten that guy. The angry man in black. The intimidating one.

"I know I'm not there! I'm somewhere else."

He pauses for a minute to listen.

"Yeah. I know," he grits out. Then, "I fuckin' got it. I'll be back soon."

Shaking his head, he yanks the phone from his ear and kills the call, then dropping the device into his pocket, he slowly turns to me with detached pity in his eyes.

The worst of all looks. The coldest and most brutal, because in this moment, it's as though he simply... doesn't give a shit about me.

"Let's go." He steps toward me and fixes the skirt of my dress so I'm no longer exposed. He pats the fabric down and growls under his breath over things playing through his mind. Then snagging my hand, he spins away and starts walking. "We're going home."

"H-home?" I stumble in my heels and step in a divot in the hard-packed dirt, so the jolt shakes me to my very core. "Cole, what are you—"

"This was a mistake." He leads me back the way we came, past the machines and away from a stack of magazines I'm not sure he knows sit in a corner. His hand on mine is no longer a caress, but rather, a controlling guide.

He speed-walks toward the window we came in through, and though at this point, I expect him to climb out and leave me behind, he gentles himself enough to turn and lift me from the hips. He sets me on the sill and doesn't let go until I'm steady on my feet, but as soon as I'm standing on my own, he reverts to his emotionless self.

He presses his fists to the windowsill and lifts himself out with blood surging through his shoulders, then popping to his feet, he pushes up straight and snatches my hand much the same way my mother would before we crossed a street.

It's not a loving hold, but a *'you'll do as I say, and you'll walk where I tell you to'* grip that requires minimal care. As in, if she got me across the street without me being mown down by a bus, then her job as my mother and caretaker was done.

It makes my heart ache that, just a moment ago, we were one. Joined. Passionate and giving. And now... his touch reminds me of her.

Cole's lips remain pressed in a tight line. His entire frame, hard with anger and secrets he's yet to share.

Wordlessly, he drags me to his car, opens the door, and guides me in, stopping just short of shoving me down. Then he slams it shut so the car rocks, and my shoulders twitch high in response.

Tears burn my eyes, humiliating, but fortunately for me, hidden in the dark as Cole circles the back of the car and drops in on his side.

He starts the engine and presses his foot to the clutch so he can shift the gear into reverse, then he glances over his shoulder, straight past me, as he makes sure he won't run anyone over.

"What happened?" My voice is softer than I want. Shakier than acceptable. I turn my face toward my window so he doesn't get to see the tears in my eyes as streetlights flash closer. "Cole?" I clear my throat and work to ignore the slick between my legs. The feeling of being incomplete. The harsh reality that he took something from me so easily. "I don't understand what I did wrong."

"You didn't do anything wrong." Anger throbs through the car and stabs at my skin in waves. "Stop internalizing everyone else's shit and thinking you're the one who screwed something up."

"Well..." Frustrated, I glance to him. "We were fine. We were doing *that*, and then we weren't. So forgive me for being a little friggin' lost in the details."

"You didn't do anything wrong." He sits back now, casual, much like he was on the way into the city, but just beneath the surface of his relaxed look is an anger that pulses. Burns. "I have responsibilities, Maya. I have a life that honestly has nothing to do with your little town, or the people in it, or—"

"Or me?" I ask, my voice soft again as hurt sprints in my blood. "You have a life that has nothing to do with me?"

"Sounds meaner than I intend," he clarifies. "But yeah. Basically."

"So... you're done? You're sending me home and walking away?"

"That's the way it's got to be. It's the way it was always supposed to be."

"And the sex," I snarl. "Didn't think to finish first?"

"Would you be happier if I did?" He barks out a dangerous laugh that feels like splinters in my veins. "Would you feel more content if I came?"

"Maybe! At least then I might've gotten something from you. Who the hell called you, Cole? Because you're two different men, depending on which side of the call you're on."

He scoffs. "I'm the same man always, Maya Elizabeth. Don't ever forget that. I'm not the type you should spend time with. I'm not the one you should be intimate with. And you're sure as fuck better than a fast bang inside an abandoned warehouse."

"And yet," I sneer. "I was there. I was present, and I hold myself accountable for my choices. Do you?" I stare at the side of his face and try, as hard as I can, to burn him with my glare. "Do you accept responsibility for the things you do? Or was tonight just one of those things that happened and we move on from?"

"Tonight was something. Fuck if I know what it was, but it happened. Now it's done. You go home safe and sound, just like I promised. And I go on with my life and get back to work. Because that's how I pay my fucking bills."

"Your work? With cars?"

"Yep." He brushes his free hand over his face and exhales a frustrated breath. "With cars."

"And your work with cars needed to interrupt what we were just doing? What kind of bullshit excuse is that? Who the hell was on the other side of that phone call, Cole?"

"My world," he grumbles. Dropping his hand to the steering wheel and staring straight ahead, he shows me nothing but a hard jaw and unwavering resolve. "My reality called me, and it reminded me who the fuck I am and what I'm supposed to be doing."

"Which is what? What are you supposed to be doing?"

"Not being on a fucking date with a pretty girl! Not fucking her inside that warehouse. *That* warehouse! Jesus."

"Cole—"

"Just stop!" He cuts me off with a fast snap of his tongue. He leaves me no room to argue, and less room to bring us back to where we were just five minutes ago. "Maya, you need to let it go."

"Let *what* go? I have no clue what even happened back there!"

"Let this go. Let us go. Let whatever the fuck you think this could be, go. I'm gonna drop you off at your apartment, and I'm gonna drive away. I won't look back, and you won't come looking. Fuck, Maya. You're naïve and innocent and a little too fucking street stupid to survive this shitty world, but I'm leaving. And that means I don't get to protect you anymore."

"Stupid…" I breathe through the word that sticks like a thorn in my mind. "You think I'm stupid?"

"I think you're too trusting of everyone else, and not trusting enough of yourself. I think you think the world is unicorns and brunch and rich people and fancy cars and no college debts. I think you'll never get your grandma's diaries back, because you're not strong enough to take control of a situation that isn't really a situation at all, and I think eventually, you'll go home to your parents and become the good little lemming they want, because they're security, and someone like you needs a guard at the door."

"Wow…" I exhale past his blows. One, then another, then another. "You think so little of me?"

"I see you for exactly who you are, Maya. And what I see is fucking perfect. You're smart and sassy and beautiful and passionate. But you need someone to be hard. You need someone to enforce your boundaries, someone who won't take advantage of the fact you trust too fucking easily. I can't be that person for you, and I don't think you can grow to become the guard at your own door. Fact is, you'll either get married, or you'll go home—and I'll burn the fucking world down if you end up with a prick who *pretends* to guard your heart when really, he takes and takes and takes from you until there's nothing left."

"So that's it's, huh? I'm just a poor, little, defenseless woman, destined for a controlled and mediocre life under someone else's reign?"

"Pretty much." He exits the city limits and heads onto the freeway, toward home. "I don't have to like it to know it's how things will be. If this were a different life, and I was a different person, maybe I could be the guard. I could keep the assholes away, and help you speak up for yourself."

"Well, of course," I counter dryly. "Because I *need* you. I'm incapable of doing things for myself."

"Just stop." He doesn't shout this time. He merely exhales a gust of exhaustion and shakes his head. "We have an hour left, Maya. One single hour. Then I'm dropping you at your door and walking away."

Boldly, considering how much hate for him I hold in my heart at the moment, he reaches across and sets his hand on my thigh. He places it palm side up and waits, as though I could stomach the thought of holding it for the drive home. "Can we just listen to music and not argue?"

"Absolutely not." I pick his hand up and drop it inches from my lap, then I turn toward the door and stare out at the moonlight illuminating the sky.

He doesn't get to treat me like shit and expect comfort. He doesn't get to dump me as coldly as he has tonight, and still expect to touch.

"No?" Sighing, he grabs the steering wheel with both hands and grips tight so his knuckles turn white. "Probably best," he finally admits. "Clean break is always best."

Cole

THE BEGINNING OF THE END

It was such a pleasurable drive into the city. And so fucking icy on the way back.

We bickered at the beginning of our night, but it turns out the glacial silence upon our return is a thousand times worse.

I thought our constant arguing was a bad sign we would never truly get along. But in just an hour, I've discovered to argue means we're passionate. And to spit words at each other was a good sign, since it meant we were still talking.

Now... the quiet must surely be classified a war crime. It's as brutal as forcing a man to freeze. Or starve. Or peel back his own fucking skin.

I cross over the train tracks leading into the little fighter town and cut straight across to Maya's apartment. There's no need to wander anymore. No point in taking things slow and dragging out the trip so I can milk every last second with this beautiful woman.

I fractured whatever we had. Now I need to send her home and complete the break, cleanly, so she can heal.

It's time to put her on a shelf. Because guys like me don't get to keep nice things.

Soft music plays through my speakers, barely discernable under the sound of my own intruding thoughts. But as I pull onto Maya's street and come to a stop outside her apartment, I keep my lips shut. My apologies to myself.

Telling her that I'm sorry for being a prick won't help her. It'll only help me. And really, I don't deserve that shit.

"So I guess we're done then." Maya unsnaps her belt and flings it aside so hard, the metal clip hits the passenger side window. It doesn't smash the glass, and even if it did, I doubt she'd feel bad about it. "You got your date. And bad food. You even got laid... for a minute, anyway."

"Just go." I reach across, loathing how her perfume invades my lungs and holds me captive. Opening her door, I shove it wide and let her scent escape. "It was nice knowing you, Maya Elizabeth. But now you have to go."

"So easy," she seethes. Shaking her head, she lifts one foot and sets it on the road outside. Then the second. But before she stands, she turns back and pins me with a glare. "You deserve better than whatever happened tonight. Whoever called you, whatever they said... you deserve better."

"No." I set my hands on the wheel and force myself not to reach out. Not to pull her back in and spend another few hours breaking my own heart. For the first time in my life, I got to experience something good. Something pure and sweet and *way* out of my league. "*You* deserve better, Maya. And that's why I have to go."

"Sounds like a bullshit excuse to me." She pushes up to stand and leaves without giving me more. Not a single backward glance or a wave goodbye.

Though, I imagine if she did, it would be less of a wave and more of a middle finger.

She slams my door with enough strength to push home the point that she's done with me, with my world, and with my damned car. Then she saunters away. Her short dress a tantalizing tease, and her high heels, a seductive call for a man like me.

She still wears my marks on her neck, and I wear her lipstick on mine.

Like he somehow knows she's gone, my phone trills for the second time tonight and hardens my heart. Preston's name flashes with demand, so accepting the call and sending it through the speakers inside my car, I pull away from the curb and drive away.

From Maya.

From her purity.

From her kindness, and the passion in her eyes.

I drive away from the woman with brains enough to be a lawyer, but with the compassion and love to choose a small child's education instead. I drive away from the very best part of me, and leave her to live a life that doesn't survive on the losses that others must endure.

"I'm coming," I snarl for my friend. "I just dropped her off."

"You've nearly blown our whole fucking job," he growls in response. "It's nearly ten o'clock, Miller! Box is gonna come for us if we don't deliver, and Reilly's got a wife and kid at home, so how the fuck could you assume he'd still be at the club at this hour? You *know* once he drives it onto his property, you aren't getting anywhere near that damn car. His security is tighter than a nun's asshole, stupid."

"Is he still at the club?" I exit Maya's street and try so very hard to ignore the loss I feel in my soul. "Did he leave, Pres?"

"Well, no, he—"

"Exactly! He's there. So stop with the doomsday bullshit and shut the fuck up. I'm on my way. I'll pull up at the club, you take my car, I'll give you a five-minute lead, then I'll boost his. We'll get the job done, deliver to Box, he'll be happy, we'll live, and you'll stop whining like a little fucking bitch. Jesus." I smack the wheel and try so fucking hard to breathe through the rage in my blood. "Why are you so needy tonight?"

"Because it's like this job is jinxed," he growls. "Like, there's some serious retribution coming our way when the world fucking champion busts us boosting his car and smashes our faces in. It feels off, but we don't get a choice. We deliver, or we go hungry. And if we let Box down, not only don't we get the next contract, but he might take our heads, too."

"I'm a minute out," I sigh. "Not even a minute. So calm the fuck down. You won't get caught stealing shit, since you leave with my car before I touch anyone else's. And you don't have to worry about your face, since it's mine Reilly'll plant his fist in if he catches me."

Seeing my friend's telltale shadow in the dark a block from Club 188, I pull in and park beneath the shadow of a massive fir tree.

I kill the engine and wait for him to slide into the passenger side, but I keep my eyes on the road in front of me. On the parked cars lining the street, and those sitting in a line outside the club.

Reilly's Mustang sits exactly where it was last time I was in town, but beside it now sits a Humvee with massive black wheels and tinted windows no man gets to look through from the outside.

The club bounces. Music thumps. Drinkers drink, and Jack Reilly... fuck knows what he does. I guess he enjoys a late-night tipple of whiskey and a card game with his family while his wife and babies stay home.

"I've got the fob," I tell Pres. "We get in, we take it, and we haul ass to the gas station outside of town. He'll have reported it stolen before we get back to Box's, which means we can't drive it all the way home. So we load it up on the truck, then the truck gets it the rest of the way."

"I'll meet you at the gas station," he grumbles. "I'll be sitting on the north side waiting for you. Don't be late, and don't get caught."

I roll my eyes. "You know I won't."

I dig a hand into my pocket and take out both key fobs. One for my car, which I slap into Pres' waiting palm. The other, a dupe that'll get me time in jail simply for possessing it.

Knowing we risk being caught the longer we wait, I open my door and slide out. But I don't bother closing it, since Pres gets out on his side and jogs around to the driver's door. We switch places, he slaps a radio in my hand and starts my Mustang, then he leaves, zipping around the corner at the end of the block so my taillights disappear into the darkness and I'm left with nothing but time.

Five minutes to kill.

My heart in my throat, and a clock ticking in my mind.

The radio in my hand crackles to life as a car cruises past on the street. They drive slowly, carefully, but they don't see me because of the shadows I hide in.

"You got me?" Preston asks. "Copy?"

"I hear you, but I want radio silence," I tell him. "No distractions tonight."

"Jinxed," his voice shivers. "This shit is second nature to you, so the fact you need no distractions says we're fucked."

"No," I snarl. "It means I want you to shut the fuck up."

Making my way to the base of the large tree I stand beneath, I lean against the smooth wood and kick one foot over the other. Then I wait.

I count it down.

And think of Maya.

Of what it felt like to be inside her. Of what it was like to taste her. And to have her taste me. I think of the pleasure I felt, knowing she wanted me, and the thrill of us both knowing she was slumming, but for tonight, she wanted it. She was willing to stoop and find out what it is to be with someone like me.

And hell, I was excited to get a taste of something not destined for me. I wasn't even taking advantage; we both knew what we would each get out of the arrangement. Her, to try something daring and bold. And me... to touch the stars and hold one in my hand for a minute.

"Four minutes," Pres' voice comes through the radio. "I'm on Main Street now, heading toward the train tracks. No cops between you and here, but don't forget the station is just a street over from the club. Don't drive that way once you pick the car up."

Frustrated, I shake my head and bring the radio to my lips. "I know where the cop shop is, Pres. And I know how to get out of town. Now, I want *silence*."

I release my finger, only to press it down once more. "I don't wanna hear from you again till I've got the car and I'm heading your way. *I'll* break radio silence. Until then, shut the fuck up."

"You're cranky." I don't have to see him to know he rolls his eyes and drives my car one-handed.

In my mind, I see him flinging her across the tracks and risking bottoming out. More incentive, I suppose, for me to swipe Reilly's ride and haul ass to the gas station to switch out again.

"Why are you always so fucking angry these days, Miller? I never did anything to hurt your feelings."

His bullshit doesn't warrant a response, so I turn the radio all the way down, then I drop my hand by my side and go back to watching the club.

We could have minutes, or we could have hours. Maybe Reilly will smash my face in and prove why he's the current world champion. Or maybe the cops will nab me on my way out of town.

If they do, I get state-provided coveralls and a number sewn across my chest. The upside would be the fact I wouldn't have to worry about paying my bills for the next five to seven years.

There's always a silver lining, if you're desperate enough to find one.

With my heart in my throat and adrenaline building in my blood as each minute ticks by, I drop my hand into my pocket and take out my cell for one last peek.

No point, really. It's not like Maya has my number.

When I find the screen filled with missed calls from Box and his crew, I slip the device back into my pocket and push away from the tree.

It's time to get the job done.

I bring the radio to my lips, breaking my own instructions, and murmur, "I'm heading across now."

Moonlight illuminates my way, and the traffic in the street is all but nonexistent. This town is simply too small for consistent flow, which means if the cops get word of what I'm doing, I'll have only two cruisers to outrun, and not two dozen.

I take out Reilly's dupe fob, then quickening my steps, I cross the street and move from the tarred road to loose gravel.

The bouncer on the club door pays no attention to me, and a stumbling couple touch and tease. They make out and lose themselves in each other. They sure as shit don't see the ghost rushing through the parking lot.

I make my way between a Subaru SUV, and an F150 that takes up a space and a half. I hit the lock button on the fob and watch as the yet-to-be-released Mustang beeps to life. The headlights flicker on, and the interior lights brighten.

My palms sweat, and I swear, somehow, the music from inside the club grows louder. "Shittttt."

I duck away from the Subaru and dip between the Mustang and the Hummer while the groping couple gets noisy. Synced groans, fevered touches. If I had the time to stop and watch, I might think of Maya and me. Of what I almost had, and what I gave up all for the sake of a car I don't even want, and a payday I'll forever regret.

Wasn't worth it.

A rusting old truck rumbles into the parking lot as I open Reilly's door, and for reasons I'll never know, the Mustang throws up alarms so the bouncer springs away from the club door.

Headlights flash, and security systems wail. My heart thunders in my chest, and my instincts war: *Get in and go, or bolt and leave the car behind?*

I don't get time to truly consider, because the bouncer barrels my way and winds his fist back in preparation.

"Shit." I slam the car door shut and dart from between it and the Humvee.

Only an idiot would remain boxed in when a larger dude stalks his way.

"That was my bad, man." I throw my hands up in faux surrender. "I mistook this for my car. I also drive a—"

I don't get to finish my sentence, because the motherfucker wraps his meaty palm around my wrist and tries to turn me, but muscle memory has me ducking. I yank my arm away and spin with a back elbow that clips his jaw and steals his senses. But before I can sprint, I'm faced with another giant.

Fire zings in my veins, and freedom dangles in front of me, a carrot to a donkey. So I charge forward.

One jab, then a second. I catch him on the chin and snap his head around, but he's not as soft as the first. He comes back to face me and lifts his hands to go toe to toe.

"Stop." He wipes a line of blood from his lip. "You can stop all this right now, Cole. You don't have to f—"

"How the fuck do you know my name?"

My heart seizes when a pair of arms circle my neck from behind. They attempt to lock in and drag me unconscious, but I drop and roll, taking my captor with me and slamming him to his back. Adrenaline helps me surge to my feet and twist back to my growing crowd. I bounce on my toes and ball my fists for the next.

I have nowhere to run, and no way to get there, so I stand and prepare to fight.

But then Jack fucking Reilly himself steps through the tightening mob. His eyes burn with rage and his jaw ticks with anger. He glances to the gravel six feet from where I stand, and when I follow his gaze, I find the key fob Pres had made for the job.

"You tried to steal my fuckin' car? From outside my club?"

"Well, well, well…" Wild hair, crazy smile, and a phone held in front of her face to record everything, Evelyn 'Smalls' Kincaid jumps out of a rusting old truck and skips to her uncle's side. "It's actually *my* club, Unca Jack. And you," she peeks around her phone and meets my gaze. "Just became my next contender."

"What?" I glance around again, shaking from the dump of energy in my veins, and searching for my out. I take entirely too long to realize I've lost my radio and my escape plan—Pres—who was instructed not to call me. "I don't know what you mean." *Play dumb, dickhead. Then get outta town.* "I was attacked," I tell them all. Then I look into Reilly's eyes and know, no matter how much shit I talk, he doesn't believe a word I say. "I also drive a Mustang, so I went to get into the wrong one. Then I was attacked, and now I—"

"And now you're coming to my gym tomorrow," the girl presses arrogantly. "I'm leaving for college really soon, which means I have to make sure you're good before I go. If you suck, you can leave, but I already saw you fight, so..." She looks across and smiles for a brown-skinned dude who wears jeans and a button-up shirt with a cop badge pinned to the breast. "This is Oz. He's local PD. He also saw you fight."

"Officer." I turn to him and plead my innocence. "I didn't—"

"Try to steal?" he coughs out a taunting laugh. "Or attack, like, four guys in the space of thirty seconds?"

"They attacked me! They came at me."

"Because you tried to steal my uncle's car," Evie snickers. She lowers her phone—done filming, I suppose—and grins when a younger dude stops on her other side. *The Ben she supposedly loves and hates?* "You'll fight for me," she continues, "or you'll fight for flip flops and the good bunk in prison. Your call."

"Smalls." Officer Oz turns and scowls at the girl. "That's called blackmail. Which is also a crime."

"Good thing no one has video proof of that," she quips. Then she brings bright blue eyes back my way. "Also, I'm a minor. So no one will punish me."

Breaking formation and slipping her phone into her pocket, she comes out again with a business card. "My name. My number. My family's gym. We have, like, six days till I go to college, and I have a shitload of stuff to do between now and then, which means I wanna see you at the gym tomorrow at six."

"Or what?" I snatch the card and try to breathe through the fight still in my blood. I look over the girl's curls to Reilly, who remains pretty fucking pissed. "What if I get in my car and disappear?"

"Then Smalls hands her footage to the cops." The woman from the groping and kissing couple steps away from her tatted man and breaks through the tight circle surrounding me. She stops beside Evie and smirks in that 'gotcha' way. "Also, your boy Preston, he's decent with his tech, but you should know his lines aren't secure. We've been waiting all week for you to make your move and come for the car."

"Which is why he's still here," I breathe. I meet Reilly's icy stare and understand the reason he's not at home with his wife and kid. He was part of a bigger plan.

Angry, I bring my eyes back to the teen and snarl, "You knew I was coming here tonight. You fucking trapped me?"

"Hey!" Reilly storms forward and grabs his niece. He yanks her back and doesn't stop until his toes damn near touch mine. "You don't speak to her like that." Then he slams his fist to my chest and knocks me back a step. "And you don't act like life is unfair all because you got caught stealing."

"She's trying to blackmail me! She wants a fighter, and I want nothing to do with this fucking town."

"Shoulda thought of that before you tried to boost a car," Evie singsongs. She doesn't care that she's surrounded by men twice her size. And she sure as shit doesn't give a crap about the way I glare. "You know where to find me, and you know when I expect to see you. If you're late, the cops get their footage. If you're lazy, the cops get their footage."

"And if you run," the other woman adds, "we know where to find you."

"Cole?"

Maya's aching voice splinters my heart and brings me around with a skid. Gravel crunches under my feet and my pulse thunders in my head so I can hardly hear anything else. I find her wringing her hands between the men who tried to subdue me. A deep well of emotion makes her eyes glitter. Rage. Hurt. Despair. Disgust.

"You're stealing his car?"

"Uh oh," Jack's taunting voice batters at my back. "Now you're in trouble."

"I'll see you in the morning," Evie finishes smugly. Then, "I have to get home before I break curfew."

She has a curfew.
She's a fucking child.
But she holds my future in her hands and smiles while doing it.

"Stop!" I spin and charge forward.

It's not like I'm gonna hurt her, but Reilly, Oz the cop, and Ben—the dude who probably loves her back—create a wall I can't break through.

"Evie!" I bark out. "Stop!"

"I can't." She turns at the front of the rattling old truck parked in the middle of the driveway, and meets my eyes. "I'm on a deadline, Miller. And I know a fighter when I see one. You're better than a car thief, and your crew isn't even that good at what they do, considering our ballerina called you on your scheme a week ago."

"Well," the other woman ponders. "His crew is pretty good, actually. I absolutely wanna see him work some more."

"Your ballerin—" I search our growing crowd and plead for sense. "I don't... so your people saw me in the club, and they knew? And *you* saw me in the diner today, and you knew?"

"We knew you were using Maya as a cover, too," Reilly snarls. He crosses the crowd and stands in front of her so I'm robbed of seeing her. "We knew every fucking step you were taking, because you're not actually that good at this shit."

"Fuck I'm not," I grit out. It's ridiculous, really, that I should boast in front of these people. In front of Maya. In front of a cop! "I'm the smoothest around."

"You might've been," he counters. "But your tech let you down. Now Miss Blake knows you're a piece of shit, I know you can't be trusted, and though Smalls thinks you can fight, don't forget that bit about how she's leaving town in a week." A slow grin rolls along his lips till a single dimple pops in his cheek. "Believe it or not, she's been your security guard up till now. But your time's running out."

"I don't want this." I turn back and head toward Evie. "I don't want to fight for you. And I don't want to be in this fucking town for a second longer than I have to be."

"Liar," Maya's sweet voice stabs my heart: death by a thousand cuts. "You said your dream is to fight. You said—"

"I say a lot of shit." I don't take my eyes from Evie's. I don't give in and turn back to Maya. "I'm walking away. I'm never coming back. And I want you all to acknowledge that Maya was nothing but an innocent bystander in all this. She had no clue why I was here. She shouldn't be pu—"

Evie laughs. "No one thinks she did. Poor Miss Blake got taken advantage of. And now," she goes to the passenger door of the old truck and swings it wide so the hinges shriek, "she knows you're a jerk. I'll see you at six."

"I won't be there," I tell her. "I'm disappearing."

"Then you can expect the cops to come find you. With video proof."

Anxiety and fear roll in my belly. "Why are you doing this to me?"

"Because I know you have what it takes to be something more. Something better. Stealing cars for money is kinda tacky."

"This is blackmail," I bite out. "And you're still a kid."

"And this kid is going off to college." She shrugs. "I do what needs to be done, when it needs doing. Especially when it comes to fighters. I know them best of all. Sasquatch," she tilts her chin for the boy and lifts her hand to wave him closer. "My mom will kill me if we're home late again."

"Yeah." Captive to her every whim, he leaves the wall he and the cop created. "Like we're not already dead," he grumbles. "And Jack's gonna snitch, anyway."

"He's not gonna snitch," she snickers. "I'll see you on the mats, Miller. Don't look so worried. This is gonna be awesome."

"Alright." One of the crowd, a seven foot tall massive motherfucker I don't recognize, claps his hands together and walks to the middle of our grouping. "We're done now. Clear out, go home." Then he chuckles and meet's Jack's angry stare. "Take your car home and put it in the garage. I'll call Riggs and make sure he puts the Charger away for safekeeping. We got a car thief in our midst now till Smalls gets bored."

"I'll make sure you get home." The dude whose face felt the full force of my elbow moves to Maya and takes her arm in his hand. "It's getting late, Ms. Blake. You don't need to be out here in this mess."

"Maya?" Just saying her name empties the breath from my lungs. My knees knock together with nerves, and my chest feels hollow. "Wait, I—"

"I don't need an escort." She gently tugs her arm free and glances my way, just long enough to make it feel like a silver stake to my heart.

Her eyes hold contempt. Disgust. Hurt, too, but mostly hate.

Finally, with a shake of her head, she turns on her heels and walks away in the dress she wore on our date tonight.

I still have her panties in my pocket. I still feel her wrapped around my cock. But before, where she begged for answers, now she leaves me behind so I'm the only man left standing.

Bouncers wander away to do their jobs, and Reilly sweeps up my counterfeit fob before slipping into his car and backing out of the parking space. Evie and her friend ramble away in the squeaky truck, and the woman, the techy one, snatches my radio as she leaves, and studies it as her tattooed mate steers her away.

The Humvee leaves, and the Subaru after that.

They were all literally laying in wait for me. They positioned themselves, knowing I would be by to steal a fucking car tonight. And they all did it for... what? The wishes of a teen with too much hair?

Now it's just me... alone. No car, no ride, and no fucking clue what I'm supposed to do with the ultimatum of a lifetime.

In my pocket, my cell chirps to life and competes to be heard over the music inside the club.

Defeated, I scrub a hand over my face and walk back toward the shadows. To my tree, because it's my only refuge in this town.

Once I'm hidden beneath its canopy, I take out my phone and answer the call before it rings out. "Pres—"

"Where the fuck are you?" he booms. "Radio chatter says they got you."

"Yep." I close my eyes and rub my temple. "We're never getting the Mustang, Pres. You're gonna have to tell Box it's over."

Cole

ROUND ONE

Ethan 'Box' Bannin could be mistaken for a small-time car flipper. He doesn't even do the hard work of stealing them himself; he pays idiots like me and Pres to do it. Then, once we deliver, he takes possession of the vehicle, and nine times out of ten, he's already got a buyer lined up and money transfers in place.

Not all cars have to come with a six-figure price tag to get Box's attention. Some just carry nostalgic value that a buyer will spend oodles to claim. Others are rarer—or in Reilly's case, not yet released.

Regardless, these people who deal in stolen vehicles for a high price tend to get pissy when their goods aren't provided. And when they go to Box to complain, he typically comes looking for me.

I pull up outside the Rollin On Gym at a few minutes till six the next morning and slide out of my car with nothing: no bag, no gloves, no water. Evie wants a fighter, but if I'm the one she demands, then she can provide everything I need.

If I make this difficult enough, maybe she'll brush me aside as too much work and let me get on with my life without the threat of a cop coming for me.

Turning back to close my door, I hear footsteps on the gravel. Much too late, I spin, expecting to find Evie, or maybe even Jack Reilly ready to kick my ass, but it's the shiny end of a handgun I see, and at the other end, Box's thick hand wrapped around steel.

"You don't get to not deliver a product," he snarls, his voice dangerous enough to make my insides liquify. His finger presses to the trigger, and his eyes bubble with a manic rage that assures me, he won't hesitate to end my life. "You don't pick and choose which customers we please."

"I didn't... I—" My throat burns dry, while in my head, my pulse booms. *Thud. Thud. Thud.* "I got caught, Box. I didn't choose to—"

"You fucked up!" he spits out. "Now you need to fix it. You have two days to come up with a solution to our little fucking problem."

"I *can't* fix it." Bringing my hand up—in bravery, or stupidity, I'll never know—I brush the gun two inches to the right so I'll lose an ear instead of my life. "They know you want the car. They've known from the moment you put in your order. I *can't* take it."

"So find me something else," he growls. "Something better. And bring it to me before I have to come looking."

"Hey!" Reilly steps through the front door of the gym and stops on a skid when his eyes pause on Box's gun. His instincts war; turn the fuck around and beat it, or stand his ground and protect his property. "What the fuck are you doing?"

"Uncle Jack? What's—"

Evie tries to wander through the door in search of what all the fuss is about, but her uncle stuffs her behind his back, holding her there when she tries to fight him.

"Leave!" He stares Box down and points into the distance. "Don't ever step foot here again."

"You don't have to worry about me." Box lifts his hands and backs away with a taunting smile. "I was just talking to my friend."

"He's not your friend when he's in my gym." Jack's hands work to keep Evie hidden at his back, his eyes fiery and ready to kill—though, whether his ire is for me or Box, I don't entirely know. "Don't come back here again. In fact, take your gun and get the fuck out of my town. You have no business here."

"Like I said..." Box holsters his weapon and turns when a car screeches to a stop at the curb. "I was just visiting my friend." He gazes my way and winks. "I'll talk to you soon, Miller."

The silence is deafening while he climbs into his ride and closes the door, then as tires squeal and the car disappears around the corner.

The end of summer means the sun has already fought with the

horizon and won, which means sunlight burns my eyes and almost makes them water. But I don't look away from the corner for a whole minute. I watch, and I make sure he's not coming back here with his friends and bigger guns.

Finally, when I know he's gone, I allow myself to take a breath.

"That was creepy." Like she floats instead of walks, Evie pops up on my left, and smirks when I jump.

Box and guns and threats have got me a little fuckin' twitchy. *So what?*

"You have crappy friends," she murmurs. "And poor decision-making skills."

I try to make sense of the words she speaks. Of the discussion she has without me. Slowly, I peel my eyes away from the corner and stop on the girl. "What?"

"You're a grown-ass man," she inserts, "and you think stealing other people's things is a solid career choice?" She rolls her eyes skyward and turns on her bare feet, back toward the gym. "Let's go. I'm in a rush, and you piss my family off every time you're near."

"So let me go." I leave my car in the parking lot and drop my hands into my pockets—jeans, the worst choice for a day in the gym. Following the girl who wears shorts, a sports bra, and a wrap on just one hand, I find the second length of material hanging from the back of her waistband, since she has no pocket. "My presence here upsets people, so it's best if I just go."

"Not till I decide you can go."

She heads through what I suppose is the reception area of the gym, past her uncle who watches me like a hawk, then into a hall until a doorway reveals a regulation-size octagon and a half-dozen fighters who've already warmed their bodies.

Sweat dribbles on the infamous Bobby Kincaid's chest, and fire burns in Aiden Kincaid's eyes.

Aiden, as in Evie's murderous father who probably doesn't much like me after last night.

"Did you bring a pair of shorts to change into?" Evie snags her second wrap and pivots to walk backwards. "You need a minute to switch?"

I shake my head and study every face that watches me. Every impatient stare from every dude related to this girl whose opinion somehow rules an entire family.

135

They don't want me here. And I don't want to be here.

"No shorts," I grit out when Evie continues to wait for my response. "I don't have any gear with me."

Flattening her lips for a moment, she settles on a nod. "You'll regret that by the time you get home tonight. Denim will feel like razor blades on your skin after eight hours. But no gloves is fine. No point training with them, when you don't get them in competition."

She points a thumb over her shoulder. "Aiden *'Biggie'* Kincaid. Probably don't call him Biggie, though. That'll just feel weird. He's your contact once I leave town. You're expected to be here seven days a week, and for six of 'em, he'll work your ground game, since you had none of that when you were brawling in a parking lot last night."

Then she points to Bobby. "He'll work your stand up. He's got legs and a killer mawashi, which means he can knock a man's head off and make sure his descendants feel it."

Finally, she nods over my shoulder. "You'll be sparring with Jack. He's the youngest, the fittest, and the current world champion. If you can't beat him, there's no point in us putting your name forward to compete elsewhere."

"So if I lose to him," I peek over my shoulder and find his feral glare, "you'll let me get back to my life?"

Evie laughs, drawing my eyes back to her. "If you lose to him, you'll go home sore, which'll make tomorrow's training that much worse. But you'll keep coming back until I say you're done."

"What the fuck, kid?" Exhausted from a long night of no sleep, my temper finally snaps. Box's demands. Unstealable Mustangs. Hurting Maya. Even Preston's absence, since he's gone back to the city until I figure out what the fuck I'm supposed to do with this new twist in my life. Everything keeps swinging at me, and the universe refuses to cut me a break. "What makes you think you get to run this show, huh? You shouldn't get to dictate people's lives like this."

"And you shouldn't steal people's cars," she counters easily. Finishing her second wrap, she secures the fabric and flexes her hands to make sure they're comfortable. "You owe us your very best. Show me what you've got, earn your freedom. Eventually, we'll make you a champion or you'll go home a nobody, with nothing to look forward to except a stint in prison."

"Because you'll turn your footage over to the cops?"

Pursing her lips, she lifts her shoulders in a shrug. "Undecided. Give me all you've got, and I'll go easier on you with the authorities."

"Extortion."

She snickers. "We established last night that it was. You won't shame me into changing my mind." Turning, she looks to her father and accepts a stereo remote. "I wanna see him spar first. No warmup. No laps. No training."

"So you throw me to the wolves?" I snap. "Just like that?"

"You held your own last night just fine. No warmup, no running, no training. And," she twists to look down at my jeans, "you wore denim then, too. I figure you're gonna be okay. Uncle Jack," she waves him closer and points her remote at the stereo fixed to the wall. "Two-minute rounds. Look for submission, or knock each other the hell out."

She finds a fast-rapping Eminem song and turns it up loud enough, surely the neighbors complain about the noise. "Into the cage," she instructs with a pointed finger. "Use the fence to your advantage."

"Let's go." Aiden comes up behind me and claps my shoulder. It could almost look like he's my buddy, if not for the force of his hit and the low growl on his breath. "You're dangerous," he breathes so only I can hear him, "but she's focused on you. So ship up, or disappear for good. I'm not risking my baby for you."

"I'm *trying* to disappear," I sneer in response.

I stumble up the first step leading into the octagon and grab on to the cage so I don't fall on my face. Everyone else has bare feet and, all but Evie, bare chests. Knowing I have no choice but to do as I'm told, I head into the cage and work quickly on my shoes. I flip one boot off and tuck my sock inside, then I work on the next as Jack skips into the octagon and jumps around to warm himself up.

They don't want me to be warm. But they sure as shit give the champion time to be.

"It's bad business if he tears a hamstring on this." Evie stops outside the cage and grins when I look across. Somehow, she reads my mind. "I wanna see what you can do, Cole. I already know what he's capable of."

"There are probably a thousand fighters across the country who would kill to be your newest pet." Reaching back, I grab my shirt and pull it over my head until I'm in just my jeans.

I feel like a fuckin' creep standing shirtless in front of a teen, so I toss the fabric and turn back to face Jack. "They would die for this chance," I call back. "Why not pick one of them?"

"Because I have a soft spot for the down-on-his-luck type. I don't want someone who can afford to quit work and travel across the country to our tiny-ass town, just so they can plop themselves in our way and talk themselves into getting a chance. I want someone who *needs* to win just so he can eat."

"You exploit." I duck when Jack charges forward, and pivot away when he spins. "You take advantage of a guy who only wants to survive."

"I take a man who is hungry," she counters, "and I give him a chance to earn his meal. I make him work for it, so when he gets to feast, he knows he deserves every damn morsel. Watch that left jab."

I parry Reilly's left arm when it's just an inch from my chin, and circle so he has to chase.

It would be naïve of me to think he's really trying. Foolish of me to think I actually stand a chance.

But with every strike he sends my way, the sport warms my blood.

"Where are your legs?" Bobby comes to the octagon door and closes it so neither fighter falls out. "You've got two of 'em, but you use neither."

"I'm using them!" I drop my weight and slam a hook into Reilly's floating ribs. Then I quick-step out of reach before he turns. "I'm using them to run the fuck away."

Bobby smirks. "I want you to use them to *kick*. That's why we've got them. They're longer than your arms, and they hurt like a motherfucker when they hit."

"So why isn't the champion using them?"

Arrogance—that's my only excuse for mouthing off. Because before I even finish my sentence, Jack slams a kick just above my left knee and buckles my entire frame till I drop.

I fall to the canvas and clutch at my deadened leg, while the champion stands over me and stares with a look that demands I *stay down, asshole.*

"You've got a big mouth on you, Miller. And no fucking talent." He glances to his niece. "Remind me why we've pulled him out of the trash?"

"Ouch." Bobby grips the cage between his fingers and watches me with a sympathetic stare. "You're being mean, Jack. Give the kid a chance."

"He's hardly a fuckin' kid. He's a grown-ass dude who wanted to touch something that didn't belong to him. Those are choices made by a man."

"You're just salty about your car," Bobby laughs.

When I roll my head back and our eyes meet, he adds with a grin, "Jackhammer's a car fiend, so you've offended him on a personal level."

"Don't touch my fuckin' car." Jack grabs my hand, though I don't offer it, and yanks me to my feet so I stumble forward and search for balance on my dead leg. "And my wife is friendly with Maya Blake. So don't touch my wife's friends, either."

Balling his fist and telegraphing my upcoming sleep, he swings out fast and slams lethal knuckles against my jaw until my head snaps around, and my life flashes before my eyes.

My vision flickers, and my bad leg fails, so I slam to my knees and stay down, my head drooping on my shoulders, and my lungs clamoring to refill.

I've hardly moved, yet it feels like I've run a marathon.

"I love my car." Lowering to a crouch and meeting me on my level, Jack waits for my eyes. "I earned that fucker, just like Smalls wants you to earn your meal. But I love my wife more, and I think what you did to Maya was really fucking shitty."

He presses his palm to the side of my face and shoves until I fall to my side. "Using people is low, Miller. But using a woman as your shield? Toying with her emotions when she's already vulnerable in a new town?" He pushes up to stand and circles toward the cage door. "I'll never get on board with that. And as far as I'm concerned," he moves through the gate and past Bobby, "you'll never be good enough to compete on my level. Throw him out, Smalls. You chose wrong this time."

I lie on the canvas, my lungs screaming for air, and my body aching all over. My knee throbs with a lava-like intensity, and my brain rattles around inside my skull.

I'm damn near dead, but I force my eyes open. I command my consciousness to stay in my body, and not float off somewhere to avoid reality.

I'm a shitty person. I'm a thief. I'm a poor boy with a crappy bloodline, and to eat each night, I steal from others.

There's no redemption for me. There's no way to spin my story and make me the good guy. There are just men like Jack Reilly, the *real deal,* who has busted his ass for years to become the best.

And on a lazy weekday morning, at his niece's request, he came to the gym and laid a car thief out. He stepped in here today to appease Evie. And now he's done, his point proven. Now he gets to go home and spend time with the family he works so hard for.

Letting my head fall to the side, I search for Evie, my only fucking ally in a sea of enemies. Our eyes meet through the cage as she rests her forehead on the fence. The crisscross marks her face, and her fingertips turn white because of how she uses them to support her weight.

She's not mad as she watches me. She's not even petulant about her hunch gone wrong. She only studies me the way one might study a dog in the pound.

She knows I'm heading for slaughter, and though she thought to give me a home, we both know it's not happening.

My fate was sealed long ago.

Closing my eyes, I shake my head and turn away to escape her pity, but when I open them again and look through the other side of the cage, I find Maya staring back.

Her gaze burns with something I'm not sure I could label. Anger. And frustration. Maybe compassion, too. My heart knocks in my chest, and though I search for the strength to sit up, to call for her to come closer, I'm too slow, and she spins on her heels and leaves.

She wears tight jeans today, and sneakers so I see her ankles in the gaps between. She wears a concert shirt tied at the side to make it more form-fitting, and her hair in a high ponytail so the long strands hang loose and frame her face.

She's *here,* at six in the fucking morning. She came purely to watch me get my ass handed to me, and now she's leaving.

I'm sick to fucking death of watching her walk away. And yet, I'm the one who told her to go.

"Don't look at her." Aiden opens the cage gate and wanders in to stand over me.

As I roll my head back and meet his eyes, he reaches down to take my hand. "You fucked up with her, Miller. And chances are, you won't fix it."

He yanks me to my feet and holds on until I get myself steady. Then he peeks across at his daughter and murmurs just for me, "But *she* believes in you. *She* wants you to win. So harden the fuck up, shake off the pain, and reset yourself. We'll roll instead, and give your leg a rest."

My eyes go to the door, to the direction Maya left. Then they move to Evie, who stands her ground and waits for me to gather myself.

She stares like I'm still that pathetic dog. But at least she's here.

It should be sad, really, that she's the first and only person to ever believe in me. She's a fucking child. But she's consistent, and she insists.

Finding a small bit of comfort in that, I swallow and bring my gaze back to Aiden. "Okay, Coach." Drawing a deep breath, I nod again and turn away from the girl. "We can roll."

"To win?" he asks. "Or so you get a hug?"

I choke out a desperate laugh that borders on complete emotional breakdown. "To show her what I've got, I guess. She'll realize I wasn't worth her time, but at least she'll go to college knowing."

"Works for me."

He moves to the gate and accepts a bottle of water when Bobby offers, then he tosses it into my hands and tilts his chin as I break the seal and twist the cap off. "You're gonna regret your jeans by the end of the day."

"Yup." I bring the bottle up and chug half of it in one heaping gulp. "I know."

It's time to go to war.

Maya
YOUR MOVE

The world's worst date turned into the world's best sex... for a minute. Then it transformed *back* into the world's worst date, which ended in me being dropped at my door and told to skedaddle.

That turned into me getting into my car and following that asshole to find out why all the secrecy. Which turned into finding out his *'I work with cars'*... wasn't quite as expected.

"How are you doing, Miss Blake?"

Britt pokes her head into my classroom just a minute after the lunch bell sounds and students storm the halls in search of food. I remain at my desk, the call of lunch not nearly as enticing as it should be. Because for some ridiculous reason, I feel as though I weigh a ton, and my energy level is set at... *bleh*.

I glance across when the halls fall quiet and Britt says nothing more. Maybe I hope she's left, sparing me the sympathetic gaze of someone who knows what happened last night. But when I twist her way and find her stroking her stomach and watching me with a lifted brow, I exhale a deep sigh.

"Don't look at me like that." I drop my chin into my hand and use the other to forage in my desk drawer for cheap sugar. "It feels gross that you're tiptoeing around me." I find a candy bar and lethargically open the wrapper. "It's embarrassing."

"What's embarrassing?" She waddles into my classroom and leans on Charlie's desk near the front of the class. He needs to be near me; I've discovered that in my time here. When he's not being checked on constantly, his sillies take over and he leads my class in a rebellion. "I have no clue what you're embarrassed about."

"Oh please." I take a bite of my candy and chew like an unsophisticated cow out to pasture. "*Everyone* knows I was stupid and went out on a date with Cole. *Everyone* thinks I'm an idiot for giving him a chance."

She rubs a hand over her distended stomach and scoffs. "Literally no one thinks you're stupid. We know you went out on a date, but *hello*," she lifts her hand and shows off her wedding band, "I clearly accepted a date once too. It happens. It's not something to be ashamed of."

"With *him*?" I point toward my door, though Cole is nowhere near here. "I was in town for all of three seconds. I specifically said I would date no one, because I was happily finding myself after college. But oops, there he is, and he asked me out, so of course I said yes."

"So? Are you mad you went out with a guy? Because it's a thing. Single women do it every single day."

"I'm mad I went out with *that* guy! I'm mad I look stupid and vapid and silly to everyone I've met, because I accepted *his* date. It's embarrassing and dumb."

"Or," she cuts in quickly, "he's a guy who means something, and that's why you accepted his date. And maybe, although you're mad right now, you'll eventually discover he's important to your overall existence. I don't know if he will be," she adds when I open my mouth to argue, "he might just be some guy you met one time, or he might be *everything*. Neither of us know, and you sure as hell shouldn't be embarrassed about any of it. It's not a bad thing to give spontaneity a try, Maya. You're young, and it's fun to get a little wild. Particularly with a handsome stranger who pushes your buttons."

"He used me." I hate, hate, *hate* how my eyes burn with tears of rage. "He humiliated me in front of everyone."

"Girl," she actually throws her head back and laughs, "My husband, that beloved and gentle champion everyone fawns over, *publicly* told me to beat it after we slept together."

Leaning forward, she glances to my classroom door to make sure it remains void of little ears. "Except he didn't say *beat it*." She brings her

144

gaze back to me. "He told me to fuck off, and he might've called me a name that rhymes with *bore*. He was brutal," she adds as my mouth drops open.

Jack Reilly, the champion, the sweetheart, the doting dad and besotted husband, called her a whore.

Publicly?

"He did it in front of *all* those same people you think are judging you. The Kincaids are no strangers to men acting bad and women copping the brunt of their bullshit."

Finally, a slow grin crosses her lips. "I might've also mentioned wanting to bang Aiden Kincaid in that same conversation. So... you've always got that up your sleeve, if you want to explore."

My eyes widen with surprise. "You slept with your brother-in-law?"

"No," she snickers. "But I crushed on him pretty hard before he was my brother-in-law. Back then, he was just that hot fighter who *adored* the ground his wife walked on. I loved the way he watched her, and I was teaching Evie back then, so I got to watch her parents interact on a semi-regular basis. Then I slept with Jack," she adds with a sigh, like the act exhausts her, "and he publicly dissed me because the Jackhammer can be a jackass sometimes. You think I wasn't humiliated? You think I didn't wanna crawl into a candy bar and never come out again? *Especially* when I had to speak with Aiden and Tina about Evie's education?"

"I mean..." I take another bite of my lunch, but the sugar high I came searching for doesn't materialize. Instead, I pull back with a frown and drop the remaining half in the trash. "I guess you kinda know how I feel. He made me look stupid, Britt. And I don't like it."

"Jack made me look cheap," she counters with a shrug. "Sometimes, boys are dumb. But in the end, he was my everything, and he earned back my trust. You can't know if Cole is everything for you, or just a speed bump. But you don't get to the end until you've gone through the steps. So..." She pushes up to stand and groans when her baby visibly rolls in her stomach. "Enjoy the ride in the meantime, Maya. While you figure out whatever this is."

"So what are the steps?" I grumble. "What do you expect of me?"

"I don't know!" She throws her hands up and laughs. "I'm just saying you don't have to be embarrassed. No one is thinking about this nearly as much as you think they are."

I drag my bottom lip between my teeth, fidgeting and nervous. "I went to the gym this morning."

I didn't intend to tell her that, to divulge my newest secret, lest I stack more humiliation atop the pile I already carry. But here I go anyway, spilling to the only friend I have in this town.

"Jack was fighting with Cole," I explain. "And when Jack knocked him down, he said something about how Cole used me and should feel bad about it."

Britt's eyes soften. "He means it. Cole *should* feel bad. But don't assume that, while he was railing on Cole, he wasn't remembering his own flaws and bad behavior. People make mistakes, and as the years pass and they become better people, they hold regret for the shitty things they did to others. Do you wanna know what I think?" She wanders closer to my desk, closer, until the front of her thigh touches the hard wood, and the sweet smell of perfume and baby powder flitters into my lungs. "I think Jack's *especially* cranky because Cole reminds him of him."

"He..." Stunned, I shake my head. "Cole reminds Jack of Jack?"

"Mmm." She rubs gentle circles against her stomach. "The fighter with raw talent but a bad attitude. The dude destined for so much more, but unable to see past the drama right in front of him. Jack wasn't always the champion," she presses. "Before that, he was just the orphaned kid whose big sister took him in when he needed a home. He was the teen who got his ass kicked, because he kept getting in trouble with the cops. And later, once he'd straightened himself out and found the girl he wanted to grow old with..."

She pauses for a long beat, staring into my eyes until my stomach dips with nerves. "That girl died. Gone," she adds softly. "And suddenly, all that good behavior was for nothing, and he spiraled into the jerk I eventually met. The one who would publicly humiliate a woman when she'd done nothing to deserve it.

"He's an addict, Maya. These days, he won't risk even a sip of beer, because he's terrified of old behaviors resurfacing. He's an imperfect soul." She sighs happily. "But he's perfect in my eyes, and he tries every single day to be the best man he can be. If he was tough on Cole this morning, it's because he knows Cole can do better."

Rapping her knuckles on my desk, she winks and turns toward the door. "Regardless, whatever he said, none of it was to add to your embarrassment. It's Cole who should be ashamed, because you deserve better."

She pauses at my classroom door and peers back. "Eat something with protein for lunch before my son gets back and runs you ragged. He'll smell your weakness, and then make you wish you were dead."

"He's such a charming little boy." With a soft snigger, I sit back at my desk and take a deep breath as she walks away.

Am I overthinking all this?

I sure as hell don't feel like I am. I can't even look at a Kincaid without a crimson blush rushing to my cheeks, and I can't think about Cole without feeling that wash of resentment blister in my blood.

It's time to move on, Maya.

I glance across to the clock on the wall and push up to stand. I have ten minutes left until the lunch bell rings and the kids flood back in. Which means I have nine minutes to forage for protein and eat it in the sun.

Days pass. I keep to myself and stay under everyone's radar. I work. I teach. I *don't* go back to the gym to inquire if Cole is still in town, no matter how tempting the idea is, and I stay away from Main Street except for when I *must* be there, considering every time I wandered last week, Cole would find me and convince me to do stupid things.

Like go out on a date.

I sit in my apartment each night, preparing lesson plans and getting to know my students through the work they submit to me each day: their strengths, their weaknesses. I read their workbooks and learn who has grasped the alphabet, and who's not even close. I consider the next steps in our curriculum, so those who are advanced remain engaged, and those who need more time aren't left behind. And when I'm not doing that, I create seating charts that allow each student to get to know their peers.

Even Charlie, the outspoken and too-large little boy who insists on chaperoning his cousin's every move.

He has to move where I tell him, but I allow him, at least, to always have Lily within his sights.

His protective streak is adorable, if not a little exasperating.

147

Outside of teaching and planning, I spend an hour every afternoon down at the lake in the middle of town. The water is icy cold, the perfect balm as the summer heat holds on, and the crowds are non-existent, considering this town's population is laughably small.

Compared to the city, anyway.

I dive in for a few laps around sunset, when the sun is still bright, but the sting has passed, and while I swim, I switch off the world.

Grammy. My parents. My students.

Hell, I even turn off thoughts of Cole Miller... *sometimes.*

As I cut through the cold water and approach the man-made wall at one end of the lake, warmth pulses in my muscles, along with the languid flexibility that only comes for me when I swim. I resurface to take a deep breath, only to choke when I find a man's broad form sitting on the concrete.

His jeans, rolled up to his knees, and his bare feet, dipped in the water.

My body spasms from panic, because the sun is going down and I expect privacy out here in the evenings, but then my focus zooms in on Cole's tired face. The single, deeply etched wrinkle in the middle of his forehead, and his eyes, dark in the low light as he stares down at me.

"What the hell?" I tread water and stop barely short of throwing a handful in his face for scaring me. "What are you doing creeping up on a woman at night, Cole? Jesus!"

"I didn't mean to scare you." He rests his hands on the concrete on each side of his muscular thighs, so his shoulders droop, and with them, his head. "I was driving by and saw you, so I—"

"You can't see who is in the lake when you're driving." I paddle backwards to place space between us. Because he's still so handsome, and the pain he carries in his eyes makes me stupid. "You're lying."

"Okay..." He glances down at his lap, but grins. "I came looking for you. I saw you walk this way, but I didn't see you come out again."

"So you followed me?" I challenge. "Thief." I lift a hand to count labels on my fingers. "Liar. Stalker. Anything else?"

He brings his eyes up, but leaves his head down, holding my words in silence for an entire, loaded minute. "Fair. I was worried about you being in the water by yourself this late, so I came over to check on you."

"To control," I accuse, remembering one of our first conversations.

"You like to control situations, and you especially like to control the people in them."

"I just wanted to know you were okay. Fuck, Maya." With a shake of his head, he pushes up to stand and sets his dripping feet on the concrete. "You're fine," he declares. "You're alive. So I guess we're good and I can go."

"Guess so, *thief*. See you next time you try to control me."

He barks out a humorless laugh. "We're calling names today? That's cool."

"Just calling it as I see it." I'm a bitch, and I'm still reeling from the half-sex he gave and took away. "You're not apt to be upfront about things, so I figure labels will help us both understand what's real and what's fucking in an old derelict building."

"Sure, *coward*." He bends at the hips and snatches up his boots. "Tit for tat, yeah? You call me a thief, I'll call you a coward."

"Why am I a coward?" I swim toward the edge of the lake and hoist myself out of the water with a fast shove.

The evening breeze is cool, and my two-piece bathing suit leaves far too much for Cole to study. To stare at.

"Hey!" I clap my hands the way I do in class, and draw his eyes away from my boobs. "Why the hell am I a coward? Are you mixing me up with some other chick you've screwed over recently?"

He scoffs. "Got your diaries back yet, Maya Elizabeth?" Unashamed, his hungry eyes slide along my body so it almost feels like a physical caress. "You got a legal opinion. You got *my* opinion. You know the law isn't gonna help you get your shit back." His eyes snap back to mine, stealing my breath and robbing me of a chance to voice a witty comeback. "What have *you* done to get *your* shit back?"

"I'm not going to my parents' home and *stealing*." I say the word like it tastes disgusting. "Though it doesn't surprise me that you're a staunch advocate of taking things without permission."

He only flattens his lips and glares deep into my eyes. "Good for you, Maya, you've got a catchphrase to sling my way whenever you're mad. I steal cars. It's what I do. It's how I survive, and sure, I have to carry the karma that comes with that. But at least I can choose to stop stealing." With a filthy smirk, he turns away. "Seems you can't choose to stop being a coward."

"It's not cowardly to not want to steal!" I shout at his back, hating how he came here uninvited, purely to spew his unwanted opinions at me, then he gets to walk away again, having stolen my peace, and leaving me to think of him. "It's not cowardly to not want to be like you!"

"Uh-huh." He turns to walk backwards and takes his car keys from his pocket to bounce them in his palm. "But they're your diaries, Maya. So it's not really stealing, is it?"

"Your opinion is invalid."

"And you're nearly naked, frustrated, and using your fancy words." He winks, which only sends my anger surging hotter. "I'm sorry I was a dick to you last week, Maya Elizabeth. But in my defense, I tried *several* times to tell you to go away. I said you deserved better, and in response, you forced your way into our date."

"So I'm a desperate loser who *made* you take me out?"

Chuckling, he shakes his head so inch-long hair flickers across his brow. "I didn't say that. You can be mad at me, and you can think I'm a no-good thief—it's the truth, after all. But don't forget to look inside yourself when you're laying blame about what went down. I tried to warn you away." Dropping his boots on the grass and bending to slip them on, he glances my way and grins when I wrap my arms across my torso to cover up. "I tried to warn you a bunch of fuckin' times, but you wouldn't listen."

"Instead of warning me," I snarl in response, "you could've used that time to *not* steal things. Obviously, I liked you, Cole. It's clear I saw something worthy to warrant my time. So maybe you could have seen that as an opportunity to do better."

"I was in this town for *that* job!" he barks out. "Literally the only reason I ever met you was for that car." Finishing with his second shoe, he stands tall and pins me with a glare. "If I'd never come here for that stupid Mustang, I'd have never met you."

"And I wouldn't have been the town idiot!" Twisting, I snatch my towel and wrap it around my body. The relaxing swim I came here in search of floats away like a feather on the breeze. "You made me a laughingstock, Cole! Now everyone thinks I'm stupid."

"You put a whole lot of importance on what everyone else thinks," he mocks. Pursing his lips, he shakes his keys in his palm again. "First of all, fuck everyone else. They're not you, and their opinions shouldn't dictate how you feel about yourself. And second, I promise they don't think you're stupid. That family whose approval you seek? The fighters? They think you're sweeter than cherry fuckin' pie, and they punish me every single day for what I did."

He lifts his hands and shows off heavily bruised arms. Then he looks down at his legs. "Every fucking day, Maya, they beat my ass until I can barely stand on my own. I don't know why they think you're so sweet, when I know better. But that's the impression they have of you: innocent little Maya Elizabeth Blake. The kindergarten teacher who breathes in sugar and exhales sunshine. You're a hero in their eyes, because you teach their evil spawn and survive, and big bad Cole Miller hurt your feelings."

He turns on his heels and makes his way back to his car. "You're not innocent, Maya, and there's no one on this planet who could convince me you need special treatment. But you're still a coward."

His voice grows louder, to cover the distance between us. "Grow a pair, go to your parents', and take back what's yours." He beeps his car unlocked and swings the door open. "If you don't, you'll never get those diaries... and there has to come a point in your life when you accept that it's your own damn fault."

Lifting one foot into his car, he stops before he slides in. "And stop swimming in the damn lake at night. It's not safe, and I can't always save you."

"Screw you!"

I don't know what comes over me; I have no clue where my immaturity comes from. But I flip the jerk off and growl when he only slips into his car and laughs.

His headlights flash on when he starts the engine, blinding me as I hold my stance, raised finger and all. But I remain where I am as he backs away from the curb and turns toward Main Street.

I'm supposed to be a grown woman, a professional. A teacher of small, impressionable minds! But instead of taking the high road and shrugging off unimportant opinions, I busy myself with a useless sparring of words and rude finger gestures against a man I have no intention of associating with again.

"You're a jerk!" I don't exactly shout, but I don't keep my voice down, either.

It's time to go home. It's time to find another way to relax. If I'm lucky, now that Cole no longer needs to steal Jack Reilly's car, maybe he'll go back to the city and never bother me again.

"Yeah, right." I secure the towel around my body and tuck it in at my breasts, then I snag my things. Shirt and shorts. Car keys. Phone.

When I glance at the screen and spy a missed call from my mother, I want to scream. But I don't. I bottle it up and swallow it down, then I leave her call unanswered and make my way back to my car.

I drop things as I walk... a shoe that I have to stop and grab, then my keys, so I have to circle back and sweep them up. Cussing under my breath, I make a job that shouldn't really be a job at all so much harder because of my bad mood.

Unlocking my door and tossing my stuff into the passenger seat, I flop in next and know I wet the seat with the water soaking through my towel. Tomorrow, when I get in and head to school, chances are I'll get out again with a wet butt. The children will laugh, and my colleagues will have another reason to look at me strangely.

But this is what happens when parents neglect to teach a child how to regulate their emotions healthily. This is the result of growing up like me, in an environment where the only acceptable emotion was the fake crap that looked good for outsiders.

Shaking my head, I start my car and drive just a couple streets over until I get to my building. Reversing my steps of my departure from the lake and grabbing my things, I stomp up the stairwell and onto my floor, only to skid to a stop when I find a folded piece of paper taped to my door.

I remain frozen in place about ten feet away, hugging my clothes to my chest while my heart pounds with adrenaline.

I glance left, to the apartment beside mine, then right, to the stairwell leading up.

Finding myself alone, I hold my breath and tiptoe forward, though I can't honestly explain why I do either.

Plucking the note from my door and carefully unfolding it, I narrow my eyes and read each word with deliberation.

Maya Elizabeth.

I've gone looking for you. Because I feel like an asshole about everything that went down, and I miss your face more than I can reasonably explain. Chances are I found you, since this town is smaller than my city block and your energy draws me in like a fuckin' mosquito to a bug zapper.

And since you enrage me just as often as you make me happy, I probably didn't apologize the way I'd intended.

If at all.

So, to cover all my bases, I wrote this letter too.

I'm sorry for what I did to you, Maya. I'm sorry I hurt you, and I'm especially sorry I ever considered using you. Even if, in the end, I tried to set you free and scare you away. The fact I considered it in the first place makes me a prick.

If I found you tonight before you've read this and I said <u>more</u> hurtful things, I'm sorry for those too.

And if you bit back, since we both know you've got a temper and a scrappy side beneath the shine, I forgive you.

I don't know if you know, or if you even care, but I kinda got an offer from the Kincaids. They bust my ass every day, and they listen to that fire-cracker Evie more than they probably should. More than I do, that's for sure. This offer doesn't mean I'm good at fighting, and it sure as shit doesn't mean I've got a future in their gym. But for this week, they want me to stick around. They want me to try my hardest and see where we end up.

So... that's where I'm spending my time.

If you wanna come say hi, I promise to bite my tongue and not mention how I think you should confront your shitty parents and get your things back. And if I did see you in town, and I brought it up and called you a coward, I'm sorry. I probably meant what I said, but I'm sure I could've said it nicer.

I just know how much those diaries mean to you, and it pisses me off that those assholes won't let you have them back.

Or, well... you know what I mean.

I also wanted to tell you... I have this thing next week. It's just a little fight. Nothing crazy, and there are no trophies or titles or anything given to the winner. Just bragging rights. But Aiden Kincaid says I have to start there and work my way up if I wanna be taken seriously. Soooo, I guess I have my first fight next week.

And it's not a brawl in a dark parking lot.

It feels kinda big, even though Kincaid says it's not.

By then, Evie will be gone to college, and since she's basically my only fan in this town... I could do with a friend on my side of the octagon. If I found you before you're reading this, and I <u>didn't</u> mention the fight, it's probably because we bickered instead.

Not a great sign, I know. But still, I'm kinda hoping you might be interested in coming down to watch. I want you to see me do something good. Something worthy. Something not illegal.

I'm gonna drop my number at the end of this letter, since writing on paper feels weird as fuck.

I hope you come. But if you don't, I hope my apology is enough to make better the shit I did to you. Just know my behavior was about me, and not a reflection of you. It was about my life choices, and about my need to deliver after I made a promise; even if the promise was a smidge on the illegal side.

This is me, Maya. A car thief. And though it's not something I'm entirely proud of, I'm man enough to admit it's what I need to do to make ends meet.

But who knows, maybe if I win my fight, I'll get another. And eventually, maybe that'll pay my bills instead.

If you see me in town over the next week, but you don't want to say hey, I guess I understand. I'll try to respect your wishes. Though I think we both know I'm prickish enough to poke at you and try to elicit a response.

I'm a thief, remember? So if the only way I can see you is to steal and cheat for a scrap of your attention...

Anyway.

Stay strong and keep ignoring me. That's gonna be on you, since I clearly can't be trusted to keep my hands to myself.

I'm sorry for what happened the night of our date. Not just the end, but the part in the factory, too. The part where I touched and tasted what wasn't mine to touch or taste.

But also, the part where I stopped.

Because that might be my biggest regret ever.

I'll see you around, Maya Elizabeth.

Your move.

xx

Cole

Cole

I WANT A CLEAN FIGHT

"Circle around!" Aiden Kincaid clings to the cage inside his family's gym, shouting at me as one of their junior fighters sizes me up and jabs with a fast right hook.

The dude is about my age. Similar body. Similar skill set.

But for reasons unknown, Aiden wants *me* to win.

"Cole!" he booms when I take another fist to my chin. "Circle! Fuck."

"Atta boy." Jimmy, the youngest of the Kincaid brothers, stands on the other side of the cage and laughs when I see stars.

He's coaching my opponent, and he spares no one's feelings when knuckles meet bone.

"He drops that left," he instructs his fighter.

So I lift my left and circle.

"Keep at him and smack his jaw. He'll fall soon enough."

"Stop listening to him." Aiden rattles the cage and demands my attention.

But when I look to him, my opponent slams his fist against the side of my face so I turn a full three-sixty.

"Dammit, Cole! Watch *him*, stupid. But listen to me. Slip in. Knee to the canvas. Wrap him up and slam him to the floor. He's Jimmy's, which means his grapple is fucking weak."

"Hey!" Jimmy cackles when his fighter jabs and misses. "My ground and pound rocks, bitch!"

155

"Those who are good," Aiden says evenly, "never have to announce they're good. He's got legs," he speaks of my opposition, "but he doesn't use them. Swoop, wrap, throw him to the fucking canvas."

"Don't use my legs," the guy grits around a blood-red mouth guard. As though he has a point to prove, he lifts his knee and swings around to drive his shin against the side of my thigh.

But Aiden is always more action than he is words. He taught me how to counter that shit, so I charge forward and catch his leg against my side. Then I keep running, shoving my opponent backwards until we both slam to the canvas, and the whole floor shakes.

"No!" Entirely entertained, Jimmy hollers his disapproval. "Find mount!" he calls to his guy. "Find mount, or you say goodnight."

"Twist," Aiden instructs calmly. "He's got that chicken wing just hanging out there. Grab it, Cole."

My heart thunders in my chest and thuds in my ears. Adrenaline keeps me moving, spinning, climbing, although I've been at this for hours already. I spring over the top of my opponent and grab his flailing arm, then I hug it to my chest and fling myself backwards until I slam to the floor, and I tighten my legs. My foot touches his face, and my sweaty thighs hug his bicep, but I position his thumb to point back toward my chest, and I bridge.

"Lift your hips," Aiden coaches. "Tighten your legs and lift your hips."

"Scramble out!" Jimmy counter-coaches. "Scramble, dummy, or he's got you."

"Calm." Aiden is like a lighthouse in a stormy sea. Where his brothers are loud and showy, he's always solid, always relaxed. Where they shout, he speaks, and where they demand something fancy, he wants basics: take them to the ground, end it. *A quiet win is still a win.* "Bridge higher," he says. "Breathe properly."

I release my trapped breath on a wild gust that has my hips dropping, but I lift again before my captive can roll away.

He searches for freedom and uses my inexperience of formal training to his advantage. Because there's a difference between a guy who learned to fight for food, and a guy who fights for a trophy. The latter possesses finesse that the scrapper could never hope to achieve.

"Tell your boy to tap," Aiden says to his brother. "Cole will snap his arm if that's what needs to be done. It's dog eat dog, and the winner discusses a contract in our gym. Cole's hungrier."

"Don't tap!" Jimmy shouts. "If you tap, you lose. And if you lose, you've lost to a street urchin."

"Wow." I close my eyes and grit my teeth around the mouth guard Aiden had me mold my first day here. He didn't want me to lose my teeth, and I didn't relish the idea of a dentist's bill on top of the hot mess my life is. "Street urchin?" I murmur. "We're getting personal now?"

"You don't listen to the smack," Aiden coaches. "You never listen. You zen the fuck out and lift your damn hips."

I lift them, not realizing I was allowing them to lower.

"Don't tap!" Jimmy's voice turns frantic as I tuck my feet in and tighten my legs. "Don't do—"

Tap. Tap. Tap.

Shock makes me freeze. Hell, it makes me yank on the guy's arm that much harder. But then my eyes snap open and my arms swing wide to release my opponent. I desperately search for Aiden, for the truth, so when our gazes lock and his lips are curled into a rare grin, I ask, "I won?"

He chuckles and nods.

"I won?" I flip to my feet, only to almost sprawl again when blood rushes to my head and makes me dizzy. Then I spin in search of the other guy, only to find him lying flat on his back. I stand over him with a goofy grin and speak around my mouth guard. "Did I win?"

He nods, but closes his eyes and swallows. "I tapped."

"I won!" Like a cat high on catnip, I zoom across the canvas and climb the cage where Jimmy stands. "I won, bitch!" Then I bound off again and run to Aiden's side. "The street urchin won! I fuckin' won!"

"You won." Circling the octagon and grabbing a bottle of water as he goes, he opens the cage door and tosses the plastic so I have to catch it with my hands... or my face. "Not bad, considering you were a street thief just a few days ago." He tips his chin for his brother, a respectful *fuck you* in anyone's eyes, then he claps my shoulder and leads me out of the octagon. "You don't know it yet, but your strength will come in your grapple. Too many on the circuits these days prefer the stand up. And the fault in *that* lands squarely on our shoulders. Bobby, the fuckin' peacock, was the champ for too long, and he likes to stand. Now Jack is just as bad. Every up-and-coming fighter emulates what their heroes are doing, so if the champ isn't focusing on the ground game, then why the fuck should they?"

"Well... standing is more fun," I pant past the lip of my water bottle. "Being on the ground sucks."

"It sucks more for the other guy when you're a pro and he has no idea how to find the submission. Every fighter and his mother can throw a jab, but not all of them know how to roll. You'll find your titles in the grappling every single time, I promise you."

"No one finishes a fight standing up anymore?" I tip my water back and fill the void in my chest that feels like the Sahara Desert. Bringing a hand up while I swallow, I try to wipe dribbling sweat from my forehead. But my arm is sweaty too, so all I manage is to smoosh moisture around. "No one does that?"

"A guy'll get a stand up knock out because he got lucky. But only idiots rely on luck. My daughter chose you, Cole, even before she saw you fight. That means, to make her proud, we don't rely on luck. It means we train like champions, and you listen to the shit I have to say."

He shoves my shoulder forward and leads me into the gym kitchen with picnic benches down the center of the room and fridges at one end. "Grab something to eat. Lean protein, and lots of water. You get half an hour to do that and take a piss, then we're going for our five miles."

"Just you and me?" I stumble toward the sink and flip the tap on to refill my water. "Or is everyone going?"

"Just us today. Jack's working with Ben, Bobby's hanging with Jon, and Jimmy won't wanna run now that his fighter lost." He moves to the fridge and swings the door open, then reaching in blindly, he comes back out again with a shaker cup already prefilled with water.

He goes to the cupboard by my right and takes out a jumbo tub of whey protein, then scooping heaped servings into the water, he recaps his cup and looks to me. "I'll see you in twenty minutes."

He doesn't wait for my response, nor does he stick around to chat. He just circles out of the room and heads into the hall.

~

"Did I do something to piss you off?" I step out of the gym doors exactly on time and start jogging, not in the least bit surprised that Aiden takes off without pleasantries.

The September sun burns, and my stomach sloshes from my lunch, but I keep up, and silently thank the Kincaids for hooking me up with grappling shorts that don't chafe my legs.

"We were doing okay." I squint under the sun and regret not bringing my hat to stop the glare coming off the road. "I won, and you even smiled, but now you're cranky again."

"I'm not cranky," he grunts. "I'm just doing my job. Which is to train you up to be at least half the fighter we have in Ben."

"And am I?" I have to push harder to keep up—not because I'm lazy or slow, but because Kincaid moves faster as we cut around the corner and head through town. "Ben's a kid. Evie said he's got a couple years till he goes pro."

"He's eighteen," Aiden bites out. "He's plenty old enough, and he'll get his first pro fight soon." The guy with a square jaw and silver-gray eyes glances across to me. "She didn't need you, Cole. But she wanted you anyway."

"Evie?" Frowning, I pump my arms harder. "She... what?"

"We already have contenders. Plenty of them, and a champion. We're doing just fine, but she didn't wanna go to college, and she was looking for any reason to stay."

"So... me? She wanted me to be her excuse to stay?"

"She'd have taken anything. But I had to send her away, because I'm her father, and sometimes, we have to do what we think is best for those we love, even if it feels like we're tearing our own fucking arms off."

Shaking his head, he draws a heaving breath and lets it out on a noisy exhale. "It doesn't matter. She wanted you, she got you, and now she's passed you over to me. I'll train you to become a champion, because she hasn't been wrong yet, and when you win like you did today, I'll have made her proud."

"So..." My mind races from one thought to another. "I don't understand my place in all this. Does it make you angry if I win? Or is it worse if I lose? Would it be better if I just went away?"

"No." Rolling his eyes, he turns at the end of the next block, measuring his steps so our feet hit the asphalt at the same time and we create a constant *thump, thump, thump* that others will hear. "I'm just in a weird space today because my daughter is gone. And I'm feeling weirder yet, because I'm pretty fucking sure she's dating Ben, and that gives me the heebie-jeebies."

"Because he's a fighter?"

"Because he's a man!" he barks out. "Because he's the next world fucking champion, and shit, I knew this was coming. But that doesn't make it easier to accept. Evie's still a kid in my eyes. She's still three years old and snuggling on my lap during fight night, because she didn't want to share it with anyone but me. But now she shares this world with him—"

"And you're a jealous shrew," I tease. "Your baby grew up, and now she's got a new man in her life. You don't get to be number one anymore, and she's too big to curl up on your lap on fight night."

"First of all," he slows his steps and glares my way, "she's never too big. And we still watch the fights together. Second, she's a minor. Ben knows where the line is, so if he crosses it, he's dead, and I'll happily do my time."

"Uh-huh." For the first time in a long while, my problems slide away and allow me a reprieve to focus on someone else's. "If she likes him *like that*, and he likes her back, I doubt either of them will tell you when lines are crossed. That's not something a daddy is supposed to know."

"I'll know. And then I'll kill our contender." Then he laughs, a craziness in his tone that makes my blood run temporarily cold. "Maybe that's why she asked for you. She knew Ben would die soon. She's planning ahead and ensuring the gym keeps running."

"Or maybe she's planning on running away with him and never seeing you again. Either way, you need a new fighter."

Aiden's vicious stare swings around to threaten my life. "Say it again, Miller. See what happens."

"Hey, Uncle Aiden!" Charlie Reilly, the current champion's kid, jogs along the inside of the school fence and waves when we glance across.

I didn't realize we'd come this far across town already, but of course, now that I know, my eyes sweep the playground in search of Maya.

My heart trips in anticipation, and nerves slide through my veins until they materialize as sweaty palms. Anxious, I search, search, search, until finally, I find her and Britt standing by the playground.

Both women watch us, though only one of them narrows her eyes and folds her arms.

"Don't talk to me about my daughter when you've got your own troubles," Aiden growls so only I can hear. Then he pastes on a fake smile and waves for Charlie. "Hey, bud. How's school today?"

"Pretty fun!" The boy's moppy black hair flops into his eyes as he runs. "Miss Blake taught us about heat using Whoppers. We used our hot breath to melt the chocolate, then we got to eat it at the end."

"You got to eat chocolate in class?" Slowing his steps until he's merely walking, Aiden approaches the fence and rests his hands on his knees to catch his breath. "Chocolate? In class?"

"Yep!" Charlie wraps his fingers around the chain link much the same way the guys do outside the octagon. "I got six of them, because I told fibs and said I lost my Whopper."

"That's called lying," Aiden admonishes. Then he casts a sly side glance my way. "Miss Blake *hates* liars."

"Yup," I mutter. Setting my hands on my hips, I pace along the fence line and concentrate on slowing my breath. "She doesn't much like 'em at all." Then I meet the boy's cute stare. "Did you enjoy the chocolate? Even the ones you lied for?"

He runs a slobbery tongue around his lips. "Yup! Except I only ate four of them. I saved one for Squeak, because she would never tell fibs to get more. I figured I should give her an extra."

"And the other?" I come to a stop in front of a patch of wildflowers growing on this side of the school fence. They're a rainbow of colors and thrive in this summer heat only because a massive shady tree protects them from direct glare. "Who ate the sixth one, Charlie?"

"Duh." He flashes a wicked grin. "I gave it to Miss Blake and told her I was sorry for telling fibs."

The kid is only five, and probably heading to be the world champion in a decade. But for right now, he's a fuckin' genius when it comes to his kindergarten teacher.

Studying the bunch of flowers with renewed energy in my own troubled heart, I bend and select the prettiest one. A soft, baby pink with bright green leaves that match Maya's eyes when she's in the sun. Snapping it free and flicking a small ant from a petal, I approach the fence and get down on Charlie's level.

He watches me with a funny mixture of suspicion and pleasure.

"Can you give this to Miss Blake for me? Tell her Cole said he's sorry for telling fibs."

"Oh crap!" His hand comes through the fence like a whip and snatches the posy from my fingers. "You told fibs? That's no good, Miller." Knowing my luck, he'll take it to her and claim it as his own. Or worse, if he's anything like his father, he'll deliver it and say I told her to go fuck herself. "What did you tell fibs about?"

"Just grown-up stuff." *Definitely not that I tried to steal your daddy's car.* "Can you tell her what I said? That Cole is sorry."

"Sure." He takes a step back and smiles at the flower. "But my mom is gonna belt your butt for making me the messenger boy. She says grown-up things are for grown-ups, and using kids to pass messages is mootcher and not allowed."

"*Immature.*" Aiden chuckles so his shoulders bounce. "It's *immature,* kid. And yeah," he glances my way. "Britt has a thing about this. She's gonna whip your ass. Then Jack's gonna whip it right after."

"And you didn't think to tell me that before I gave him the flower?" I push up to stand with a huff and back away as Charlie sprints toward Miss Blake.

I'm tempted to stay and watch. Curious to see Maya's reaction, and hopeful enough that it'll make her smile. But the reality is, she'll probably add this to her long list of reasons I'm a piece of shit.

"Let's go." I turn and start jogging before Charlie reaches his destination.

Maya has my number now, but my inbox is void of anything from her. *Message received, loud and clear.*

Involving her student in my bullshit will just be another nail in the coffin she so lovingly built for me.

"Talk to me about Evie's love life," I taunt my coach. "I'd rather focus on that shit right now."

"Hey!" he booms. "Not fuckin' funny!"

Time passes, Pres calls me daily, Box stays away, though he fills my voicemail with demands to get back to work, and Jack spares me an hour a day to slam me against the canvas and move on with his life.

Evie wanted a contender, but the bar has been set: until I can stand up to the Jackhammer and at least hold my own, I'm not shit, and I'm in town on borrowed time.

Still, my fight approaches, and Aiden works with me every single day. He throws me into the octagon with his youngest brother more often than not, since Jimmy's fast, skilled, and young enough to still want to get sweaty. And when Jimmy's done belting me into submission, Aiden declares it's time to roll.

Because according to him, he doesn't want me to learn when I'm fresh and eager. He wants it drilled into my subconsciousness when I'm exhausted and on the brink of death. Something about forging a sword in fire. Muscle memory. Training my body to save my life when I'm down, and not just when I'm energetic.

Fuck knows if it'll work, but he's the boss, and Evie's on the other side of the country.

"Alright. Keep your hands up." Aiden winds a wrap around my knuckles in a locker room on the south side of the building that my fight is being held in. There are no crowds today except for the family and friends of the other guys. There are other competitors, since I'm not the only one fighting today, and there's Aiden and Jimmy Kincaid, since they're all I've got on this planet right now.

Preston isn't here, but that's because I didn't tell him about today.

And Maya's yet to make my phone light up. Not even after my *sorry-for-fibbing* flower.

Probably best that way.

"Your opponent's name is Matteo Tilly," Jimmy rumbles low enough to not be overhead by the other guys in here. "He's about twenty pounds heavier than you, but it's not muscle, and he's about two inches shorter."

"Which probably means his arms aren't as long," Aiden adds. "And his weight will make him slow."

"Chances are, he's gonna run at you with fists. So," Jimmy slaps mine, "hands up. Don't worry about his feet. He won't get them anywhere near your head till you're on the ground."

"Circle," Aiden coaches. "Tire him out. Make him chase you. It won't take long before he gasses, then you charge forward and take him to the mats. We've trained for that."

"Don't get fancy."

It's crazy that this should feel like a world championship. That my heart races and my forehead beads with sweat. This is a friendly competition between gyms, and there's nothing on the line but a clap on the shoulder and an 'atta boy' if I win.

But to me, the guy who never had much of anything, it feels like the stakes are so much higher.

This is the first time in my life I've been given the chance to do something *right*. Something kinda important. And it's all on the back of a mouthy teen stomping her feet and demanding her own way on something.

"I don't need a guillotine," I recite the things Aiden has pounded into my head this past week. "I just need the tap."

"Go for the arm," he agrees. "It's easy, he won't expect it, and you're fast enough to get the lock before his brain has even processed he's fucked."

"Don't worry about who's in the crowd." Jimmy bounces on his toes, a competitor at heart who can't help but feel the adrenaline in the air. "You don't pay attention to them. You watch Matteo, and you listen to us. Those are your only jobs out there, you got it?"

"How many times have you done this?" I accept my mouth guard from Aiden, but I don't slip it between my teeth just yet. "How many pep talks have you given before one of these fights?"

"An interclub fight?" Aiden's lips curl into a small grin as he finishes my second wrap. "A million times. I walked Bobby's wife out for hers."

"And I walked with my wife for hers," Jimmy adds. Then, "And she walked with me for mine."

"I've done this for many other kids, too," Aiden continues. "And I'll be Smalls' cornerman when she goes pro. I can tell you, it doesn't matter if we're prepping for one of these, or if we're getting ready for the world stage, the locker room pep talk is the same. Hands up." He swings his palm out and claps the side of my face. "Always, because if you get clipped, the fight's over, and we go home."

"Check the kicks," Jimmy inserts. "Leg up, take the hit on your shin and not your thigh."

"Both hurt," I grumble.

"Only one of them will end a fight. If you're lucky, he snaps his leg on your shin and we go home with the win."

"Brutal," I murmur under my breath.

"Check every strike," Aiden says. "Watch Tilly's chest. You don't need to look into his eyes or at his hands. You watch his collarbones: they'll tell you everything you need to know, because he doesn't move a single fucking limb without first moving his collarbones. By the time his fist is coming, you've already tagged it. That puts you ahead of him and shuts down his every move."

"Okay." Unable to help myself, I bounce on the balls of my feet and work to loosen my muscles. "I'll do it right, I promise."

"Cole Miller."

I turn at my name and find a dude in a bow tie holding a clipboard.

"Two-minute call," he announces. "You're up next."

"Okay." My lungs empty and my heart thuds in my chest. But I bounce back around to face Aiden. "Holy shit, Coach. I'm wiggin' out."

Chuckling, he claps a hand to my shoulder. Without the win. Without the work that goes in first, he gives me the payoff and settles my nerves. "You're gonna be fine. Aside from everything I've taught you, remember you're a street scrapper. Matteo has nothing but his once a week, *'my mom drove me here'* kiddie lessons. You didn't have that kinda life. Your mom didn't fold and iron a Gi for you every week."

"No fuckin' shit she didn't."

"So stop wiggin' and remember who the fuck you are. Get in, take him down, get the tap. Then you walk away a champion, and we advance you up the ladder."

"And if I lose?"

He snorts. "Then you get in your car and go back to your life. I'll turn around so you don't see me in your rearview mirror, laughing at you for being a pussy."

"Wow." I slip my mouth guard in and clap my hands together. "Harsh. Is that what you said to Bobby Kincaid's wife her first time?"

"Nope." He steps around and pushes me to walk in front. "I slapped her ass and told her to win."

He turns silent as I peek back and meet his eyes.

"Want me to slap your ass, Miller?"

"Fuck no."

Straightening out, I strut like this is the world fucking title and I've got a belt to win. Like this is a multi-million-dollar payday, and I have hundreds of thousands of fans in the stands just waiting to see me win.

I bounce my way through an empty hall, and I allow adrenaline to flood my veins. Not too much, since I want to save some for my fight. But enough to keep me warm. Enough to keep me moving.

"Three three-minute rounds," Jimmy says over the noise of the fight before ours. "If you can't get the knockout or the tap, then you better be standing at the end with the most points. There's no advancement, so win or lose, you only have one fight today. If it's all over in ten seconds because you forgot to keep your hands up, then there are no do-overs. We're just done. We go home, and you neck yourself for being so stupid."

"Jesus fuckin' Christ," I hiss. "Kincaids don't mince words on fight day, do you?"

"We're champions," Aiden explains. "We train champions. Smalls chose you, so if you don't win, she's gonna have to accept the fact she backed a dud."

"And no one has time for that pity party," Jimmy concludes.

He wears jeans today. Boots. A Rollin On Gym shirt the same as mine and Aiden's.

We're a team. We're a family, and for just a second, my heart and brain process that fact.

They didn't want me here, but they've pulled me in and made me one of them anyway.

"Smalls has classes today," Jimmy speaks louder to combat the shouting crowd. "But she's waiting for my text to let her know the outcome."

"Did she send any words of wisdom?" I ask. "Anything from the teen with a big mouth?"

"Yeah." He comes to a stop at the mouth of the big room and pats my shoulder. "She said don't fuck it up."

"Cole!"

Voices, shouts, so much fucking noise pull my attention to the seating on the far side of the room, where I find my own mini crowd. Women—Kincaid wives—and children—so fucking many of them. Even Charlie and his dad stand on the end, though they don't carry sparkly signs that hold my name like the ladies do.

"Go, Cole!" they shout. "You've got this!"

"Whattttt the fuck?" I cast a glance to Jimmy, considering his beautiful wife is one of the sign-swingers. "What are they doing?"

"You're repping our gym." He winks for his family and blows a kiss to his wife. "That means they come out and rep for you."

"Woooo!" the kids shriek. "Rollers in the house!"

Aiden chuckles on my right. "That's just mean."

When I look his way, he tilts his chin and nods to a guy I take to be Matteo Tilly. "They're psyching the poor dude out."

"Rollers are title-holders," Jimmy explains. "They're fucking with his head before he even steps into the cage."

"So if I win, it's probably only because he's already mentally flung himself off a fucking cliff?"

"A win is a win," he says. "Don't think for a second Jack doesn't hotdog around the octagon before his fights. Don't pretend like they don't all prance around and act a fool before gloves touch."

"*Ahem.*" A soft cough. A feminine throat-clearing invades my senses. Then, "E-excuse me?"

I spin at her voice and almost choke on my heart when I stop on Maya's beautiful green eyes.

Her hair is down today. Loose and floating around her shoulders, while her trim body is wrapped in a navy sundress with tiny little flowers spotted all over.

"Maya?"

My brain can't quite focus. Or process. Or hell, accept that she's here.

I look to her left, then to her right. I peek over her shoulders, then for the hell of it, I look over mine too. "What are you d—"

"You have one minute," Jimmy rumbles. Shaking his head, he steps a few feet to the left and leans in to chat to his brother.

"Cole," Maya starts again. "I—"

"You came to my fight?" I grab her hands. I shouldn't. I sure as fuck have no right. But I take them in mine and shuffle closer so her knuckles touch my stomach. "You're really here?"

A warm blush fills her cheeks, and her teeth come out to abuse her bottom lip. "I couldn't ignore this. Even if," slowly, she peels her fingers from my grasp, "we argue every time we're in the same space."

"That's just a tic we have," I rush out. "It's because we're both opinionated. But that's why I wrote you a letter. So you could see..." My pounding heart makes my chest ache. "Did you get my letter?"

"The one you taped to my front door?" Her eyes scour my face. My sweaty brow, and the mouth guard I lisp around. "I got it."

"So you know I'm sorry for being a jerk?" I don't know where to put my hands. I have no fucking clue what to do with them that doesn't include touching her, so I set them on my hips and hold onto those instead. "You know I have a big mouth and a trigger-happy temper. But under that, I'm sorry for being a dick."

"I mean... I know." She twitches when, behind me, the thud of a fighter slamming their opponent to the canvas makes the floor tremble. "I know you're sorry. And I got the flower too."

"Did you forgive Charlie for lying about his candy?"

Her eyes narrow until her brows almost touch. "What are you—"

"The whoppers," I push. "Did you forgive him?"

"Of course I—He's a child, and it was candy."

"So you can forgive me too. I know what I did wasn't candy, and I know my lies were bigger. I know it'll take longer. But forgiving him means you have the ability, at least, to consider eventually forgiving me too."

"Cole..." Her chest shrinks when she exhales. "I didn't come here to—"

"I'm sorry for what I did." I jump in before she can run away, and I take, take, take more than I deserve. Pressing a fast, dry kiss to the corner of her lips, I swallow down her gasp when she can't keep it in.

"I'm sorry. That's all I wanted to say. What I did was really fucking shitty, and you deserve better. I'm not saying we have to go out again or anything like that. I'm just saying... I want you to know I'm sorry."

"Are you still stealing cars?"

The fight behind me comes to an end, punctuated by the crowd shoving to their feet amid loud roars. But my attention is solely on the sun-kissed marks on Maya's cheeks. On her long lashes, and her firmed lips that scream disapproval.

"Are you still doing that stuff, Cole?"

I shake my head, an instant response, even if not a hundred percent accurate. "I haven't since that night. I haven't even left town. I've been inside the gym every day."

"And your life in the city?" she asks. "It just... stops? You've cut ties with them all that easily?"

Knowing I have to tell her the truth, I shake my head again. "No. The guy I..."

"Steal for. You can say it, Cole. Taking responsibility is the first step to me *not* wanting to hurt you for your lies."

Slowly, a playful grin crosses my lips, because her temper makes me happy. It's her cold indifference that breaks my aching heart. "The guy I *steal* for has been calling. He came out and saw me that next morning, but he hasn't been back since."

"He calls because he wants you to get back to work?"

"Shirt off." Jimmy moves closer and lifts the fabric of my shirt to reveal my chest. "Finish up," he adds. "You should be discussing fight plans, not dinner plans."

"Yes." I ignore him and answer Maya instead. "He wants me to get back to work, because I'm good at it, and he makes less money when I'm not around."

"And will you?" Her eyes slide across my chest; unintentional, I'm sure, but unable to stop. "When you finish here today and he calls you up for a job, will you go?"

"Maya..."

"Will you go?" she snaps. "Will you nod your head and run back like his little servant boy to do the crime?"

"It's how I pay my bills," I groan. "It's not a job you like, but it's my job, regardless. A man has to eat."

"So get a different job!" she snarls, her fiery eyes flickering back to mine. "Find a *new* way to eat."

"What do you think I'm doing?" I thrust my arm out and point toward the boxing ring. "I don't get to go directly to the top and have someone bankroll me just because I say so, Maya Elizabeth. But I've got a chance, okay? A teenager saw something in me no one else ever has, and she gave me a chance to make it something that could eventually, *maybe*, buy my groceries. What the fuck do you think we're doing here today?"

"Arguing." Her stare continues to burn. But her lips slip into a ghost of a smirk. "We're arguing like we always do."

"It's called foreplay."

I rush in and wrap my arm around her hips. Breaking the rules.

169

Destroying whatever scrap of trust she might've thought to give me. I yank her close and slam my lips against hers, groaning when her mouth opens and her breath races into my lungs. I slide my tongue against her top lip to ask for permission, then in when hers comes out to reciprocate.

Our tongues clash, and our teeth nip. I feel someone's hand on my shoulder. I hear someone's voice telling me to cut my shit and step up for my fight. But my entire heart and soul are invested in *her*.

"Cole!"

I splay my fingers across her back and enjoy the feel of her breasts pressed to my chest.

"Cole Miller!" Aiden's voice booms somewhere in the recesses of my mind.

I slide my tongue across Maya's and thrill in my victory when her arms come up and wrap around my neck.

"Dude!" Jimmy yanks me back a step, breaking our connection, and spinning me around until I see his face and not the one I want.

I have tunnel vision. His face at the end, and darkness around the sides.

My eyes wheel around wildly, searching, hunting, and my heart thunders against my diaphragm until it becomes almost impossible to catch my breath.

"That was a show my kids didn't need to see," the youngest Kincaid brother guffaws. "Now I gotta have the birds and the bees talk with my teens, and nobody wants that shit." Shaking his head, he claps my shoulder and turns me toward the ring.

Where the fuck is Maya?

He keeps hold of my shoulder and marches on. "Stand up," he instructs over the noise of the crowd. "Hands up. Tire him out, then take him to the mats. Try and get it all done in your first three minutes. If you do, I'll put in a good word at the gym so we can discuss that payday you want."

"Really?" What do I want more than I want Maya? A chance to survive without having to steal cars. "You'd discuss putting me on the payroll and making me pro?"

"Gotta win first." He shoves me when I reach the ring, so I stumble up the steps and slip through the ropes. "Win this fight, and we'll talk about the rest. If you lose," like he somehow senses where she is, he glances to my right and stops on Maya's heated stare, "you go back to the you she can't be with. She wants you, Miller. She wants it so fuckin' bad. But she can't be who she is and still date a car thief. Your worlds are too different, and she can't get behind the illegality of all your shit."

"I win," I bounce on the balls of my feet, "I get a paycheck. If I get a paycheck, I'm no longer breaking the law."

"Don't break the law, and you might get to date the cute kindergarten teacher again."

"Alright, fighters!"

Another voice. A referee in black pants and a blue button-up shirt moves between me and Matteo, though I can't honestly say I saw either of them step into the ring.

"I want a clean fight, and I want you to listen to my instructions. Protect yourselves at all times. If at any point I think you're done, I'm calling it, so keep moving, stay alert, and keep your hands up."

He looks to Matteo and waits for his nod. Then to me, so I do the same.

"Go back to your corners and wait for my *Go.*"

Maya

THE THINGS WE DO IN SECRET

"Oh my god." I sit in a chair all on my own, on the opposite side of the ring as the rest of the gym family and Cole's cheer squad. I bounce my knee and rest my elbows on my thighs, my chin in my hands.

I focus on Cole's muscular back, knowing, though I didn't actually see this much of his body when we were together, that he's grown larger in the last week.

His muscles stand out, and his shoulders sit taller. His abdomen sports a proudly defined six-pack, and his shorts rest tantalizingly—and dangerously—low on his hips.

He looks like every single boy I dreamed about as a teen, and he's standing right in front of me.

Wanting me.

"Let's fight!" The referee jumps out from between the two men, and spins when Cole's opponent rushes forward with a wildly swinging fist.

"Oh god." I cover my eyes and breathe through the panic in my blood.

Still, I'm a sucker, because I split my fingers and peek through the gaps as Cole skips around the ring and lands a hard jab to the other guy's chin.

"Well, that was a public display of almost-banging if I ever saw one." Britt and *all* of her pregnant stomach lower onto the chair beside mine. She grunts when she touches down, and opens her legs wide to find comfort. Thankfully, she wears denim shorts to make her pose reasonably family-friendly. "I got a little turned on by that, ya know? I miss having my man fuck me with his eyes just before he fights."

"God." I close my fingers and revel in the darkness. "He didn't f—do that with his eyes." Then I drop my hand and look her way. "And why do you miss it? Trouble in your marriage?"

She scoffs. "I don't remember the last time I wasn't pregnant, Maya. We're doing just fine. I just meant I miss those early days, when I was new to the fighting world and the crowd was cheering him on, but instead of looking at them, he saw only me. The stakes were higher, and the repercussions of failure seemed so much heavier. I mean, he still only sees me." She places a hand on her stomach and rubs gentle circles. "Me and our babies. But watching you and Cole..." Her grin notches higher. "Reminded me of times gone by."

"Catch his leg!" Aiden stands on the corner of the boxing ring and shouts his instructions. "He keeps giving it to you, Cole! Catch the damn thing and throw him to the ground."

"He'll learn," Britt sniggers.

When she glances my way, a fresh new blush stains my cheeks.

"So I guess you decided to forgive him. It was the flower, wasn't it?"

A desperate giggle rolls along my chest. "I don't..." I shake my head. "I have no clue what I'm doing. But I promise it wasn't the flower."

"Oh please." She turns back to watch the fight. "You act all pissy and mean, but I saw you dancing around that day. I saw you smile at the damn flower every chance you got."

"You're making things up in your mind."

No. She's really not.

"You're scared," she reasons. "Terrified of being hurt. And he's a bigger risk than regular guys, because he's super intense and kinda dark and dangerous. He already hurt you once, so you're freaking out that next time, *if* there's a next time, it will hurt a thousand times worse because you'll have risked your heart."

"Sure." I grit my teeth when Cole's opponent slams a fist against his jaw and snaps Cole's head around. "Thanks, Dr. Phil. Ouch." In sympathy, I reach up and touch my own jaw. "Doesn't that sting?"

"Yep," she grins. "And you keep brushing my words off, but you forget I already went through all this. The fear. The anxiety. The *what if he leaves and breaks my freakin' heart?*" Lifting her hand from her stomach, she drops it on my arm instead. "I wasn't born yesterday, Maya, and you're not the first woman in the world to feel the things you're feeling. Ah, shit." She wrinkles her nose when Cole's opponent swings around and wraps his arms around Cole's neck. "That's not great."

"He's going to lose?"

I can't watch. And yet, I can't look away. Being here is the worst kind of torture, because I want to support him, but I also have a driving urge to run the hell away and hide somewhere no one will ever find me again.

"Britt." I cling to her hand and watch every single move Cole makes. "What if he loses?"

"Then you take him somewhere private and kiss *all* his booboos better."

"Britt!" I cry out. "I'm being serious."

Cackling, she pries my fingers from hers and sets my hand back in my own lap. "If he loses, the Rollers kick his ass and train him to do better. Evie vouched for him, and what Smalls wants, she usually gets. That means Biggie isn't gonna dump Cole over one lost fight."

"And if he wins?"

I hold my breath and watch in abject horror as Cole cuts his losses and leans in to the fact that Matteo is basically monkey-back riding him. Instead of fighting it, he simply... slams them both to the canvas until the ground shakes.

"Britt! What if he wins?"

"Then you take him somewhere private," she giggles. "And kiss all his booboos better."

"Oh for God's sake." I shove up from my chair so the legs scrape against the floor, and rush to stand beside the Kincaid brothers at the side of the ring.

"You shouldn't be here." Calm, prepared, Aiden steps down from his platform to stand beside me, while his younger brother rides the boxing ring ropes and shouts his orders. "Folks have been thrown from the ring in the past, Miss Blake. And poor bystanders have been squished on the outside."

"I'll take the risk," I tell him.

My eyes follow Cole's face. The trickle of blood on his lip, and the second line coming from his nose. The rubber mouth guard makes his lips puff wider, and the blood pumping through his body makes veins stand tall in his forehead.

"Is he doing okay?" I ask. "Like, I know he's on the bottom and all that, but is he—"

"He's doing just fine." Aiden folds his arms across his chest and tilts his chin toward the center of the ring. "We talked all this through. His opponent is a little heavier, which makes getting mount trickier, but..." His smile notches high when Cole scrambles from beneath and spins back fast enough to sit on the guy's hips.

It could almost be erotic, if not for the savagery of his fists flying down to bruise Matteo's face.

"He'll come over to the left in a sec," Aiden murmurs, nodding when Cole does exactly that. "He'll grab his arm, and—"

Thud!

Cole's back hits the canvas and his hips jut high.

Definitely erotic, if I were inclined to think of his hips elsewhere.

"Bridge!" Aiden loses his composure and takes a step closer to the ring. "Cole! Bridge higher."

My heart gallops in my chest, and my hands come up to cover my mouth. Not my eyes, though I know there's a genuine possibility I'll regret watching. I study the side of Cole's face, the blood that makes it red, and his chest that pumps larger, larger from the fight. I take in the way he grits his teeth, and the muscles that stand out in his thighs as he squeezes them tighter.

I watch the referee move to his stomach to get down on their level. Then I release a gushing breath when he waves his hands.

"It's over!" He throws Cole to the side and yanks Matteo the other way.

Behind me, the crowd springs to their feet and roars.

Cole rolls backward, flipping over until he ends up in a crouch, and though his body heaves in search of fresh oxygen, his smile, bloodied and devious, makes my heart skip when our eyes meet.

"Winner!" The referee pushes to his feet and waits as Cole drops his head.

He shakes it side to side, so one could almost think he's sad about something. But his smile, so beautiful, so proud, contradicts that.

"In his debut fight," the referee pushes on, since the next fighters already wait a couple of feet from where I stand. "Cole Miller, from the Rollin On Gym, wins by tap out." He grabs Cole's arm and lifts it to the sky. "Well done, boys."

"Come back this way." Aiden slips his hand around my elbow and gently tugs me away from the ring as Matteo's friends flood forward to help him out, and Jimmy does the same for Cole. "His legs are gonna be rubbery, and his voice is gonna be loud," he warns. "The high from a win is next-level. So if you don't want that kinda heat, I suggest you leave now."

Stay, he's saying, and expect another public display of... whatever it was we did a few minutes ago. Or go, and avoid the show in front of the family I was so sure was judging me.

"Maya?" Cole's voice carries over the noise of everyone else inside this building. But about thirty people stand between us, making it impossible for me to see him.

"Maya!" he calls again.

Nervous—honestly, terrified—I meet Aiden's eyes and nod. "I think I'll stay."

"Good." He winks and releases my arm. "He'll like that. And he worked hard enough to deserve it. Over here!" He raises a hand, and with it, his voice. "Come find me, Miller."

"Have fun." Britt sidles up on my left and grins as the crowd slowly thins. "I'll see you when I see you."

"Maya!" The moment our eyes lock, Cole charges across the space between us. He must've collected his shirt from Jimmy in the last ten seconds, because he holds it in his blood-stained hand. When he's close enough, he grabs my arm and keeps on walking.

"Cole!" I stumble on my feet and leave my stomach somewhere back near the boxing ring. But I let him pull me along. I let his extraordinary strength impress me, and when I'm certain I won't trip, I allow my eyes to scour his muscular back.

"Cole Miller!" When the excitement and ridiculousness of this moment gets to me, a laugh rolls free of my chest. "Where the hell are you taking me?"

"In here."

He yanks me into the hall, then swings the first available door open. He looks inside for just a beat and discovers nothing but a broom closet,

177

but he deems it useful for whatever his intentions, and shoves me in so fast, I squeal and reach out for something to hold on to.

He follows me in and shuts the door so darkness swallows us both. Then the telltale *snick* of a lock makes my heart thud to a stop.

Blood pounds in my ears, and my stomach whooshes with nerves. But when I feel his chest press to my back, and his bruising hand grip my thigh, I'm not sure I could say no to any of this, even if I still had my wits about me.

It's like that night we went to the abandoned factory. My common sense leaves me stranded, and my hormones toss all caution to the wind.

I know better. I'm a smart, collected, free-thinking woman. But when Cole has that look in his eyes, nothing on planet Earth makes sense anymore.

"I wanted privacy." His body emanates enough heat to turn this small room into a sauna within a minute. His hot breath on my neck, and his sweating chest on my back. "I didn't want to share that with anyone else. Not even for a minute."

Slowly, carefully, I turn in his arms and use my hands to determine exactly where he stands. Not even a sliver of light comes through the doorway, which means we're blind. Both of us. But the loss of one sense only makes the remaining four work harder.

I feel him under my hands, and I *feel him* pressed to my hip.

I smell his sweat in the air, a delicious concoction of cologne and Cole.

I taste his breath on my tongue, and I hear his racing heart as he works to calm from his bout in a boxing ring.

"You won, Cole." My grin is giddy, though I know he can't see. Wrapping my arms over his shoulders and whimpering when his hands drop to knead my thighs, I slide my fingers through his sweaty hair and hold on. "I'm really, really proud of you."

He buries his face against my neck and bites. Tastes. Taunts. "It could be like this if I work hard enough." He lifts me, so ridiculously easily, the fast swoop of his hands stealing my breath away. "If I bust my ass and train how Kincaid wants me to, I could win again. And if I win enough times, eventually they'll start paying me."

"Cole—"

"And if they pay me, maybe you'll stay. You'll give me a chance to get it right, and I'll rent a cute house somewhere in town so we can get to know each other. Like, *really* get to know each other." He bites down on my neck and pulls my skin until it hurts. "We don't have to rush, Maya Elizabeth. But maybe we could... start."

"You tried to send me away." *Damn common sense. Damn, damn, damn you!* "Cole, you told me a bunch of times to go away."

"That's because you deserved better than a car thief." Pulling back, he swaps sides and buzzes his stubbled jaw along my flesh. "I was nothing but a fuckin' street urchin, and you were way too fancy for that."

"Cole—"

"I'm still a nobody," he pushes. "But I'm a nobody who just won his debut fight and is on a first-name basis with champions who could really turn that into something."

He holds me up with just one hand, while the other slips between my legs and torments me with a magical touch.

"I'm still a nobody," he adds breathlessly, "but I'm a nobody who'll work until he drops to become a somebody. And if you'd just let me be near you..." He comes back and takes my lips with his. Adrenaline pushes him on, and the high after his win, as Aiden said, makes him give so much more. "You don't even have to date me. Not yet, anyway. We definitely don't have to have sex or anything. Just let me be near you."

"Cole..." That's all I can say. It's all I've got, as his tongue and teeth and hands control my body.

I drop my head back and smack it on a shelf, but I don't feel the pain. I don't feel anything except what he wants me to feel.

"Give us time," he hurries on, as though afraid of my rejection. "Let me get a written reference from Kincaid. He'll vouch for how fucking hard I worked this week. And I'll keep doing it. I'll make all this worth their time. I'll do it for me."

"For you?" My brain focuses on those two words. My eyes snap open, though I still don't see him. My heart gallops, and my back arches from the shelves he contorts me around. "You'll do that for you?"

"And for you." Diving in, he presses a fast kiss to my lips. "I'll do anything you want me to, so long as you give me a chance to make things right."

"No, don't change..." I shake my head. "I like that you'll do it for you. You said it right the first time."

"I did?" His breathing remains erratic, his chest crushing mine, and his fingers working closer, closer to my apex. "That's what you want?"

"Yes. Because you deserve better too." I open my legs wider, knowing we're fighting a losing battle. Then I slip my hand into the waistband of his shorts, and whimper when I find him rock-hard and waiting.

"Fuck!" Something crashes to the floor on my left, and Cole's grunt is a gust of wind that hits me like a wall. "Fuck, Maya. Yes?"

"Yes?"

"You wanna?" He moves his fingers beneath my panties and deep inside my pussy.

Like last time, he doesn't wait, and he doesn't ask permission. He doesn't start slow, doesn't prime me. He just takes, takes, takes. But when he takes, he also gives so deliciously.

"Maya, do you wanna?"

"Have sex?" I pant through the release he already teases closer. "Yes. But quick," I giggle. "People will know what we're doing in here."

"Fuck everyone else."

He sets me on my feet and whips my panties along my legs so the fabric almost burns on the way down. Then he lifts me again, rough hands and quick movements. He holds me with one arm and works the front of his shorts down until I feel his fiery length touch my thigh.

For just a moment, I think back to last week. To the last time we did this, and the cold dismissal he handed over when it suited him.

My blood runs cooler and my heart thumps painfully. But then his lips crash over mine and steal away the doubts creeping into my mind.

"I don't have a condom."

"What?" My brain is too fogged with lust. And worry. And love.

Well, not love.

But anxiety. And desire. And want.

"Cole, what?"

"I don't have a condom. Do you?"

"No, I..." My heart aches as I process his words. "Shit, no, I don't—"

He sets me on my feet. The action cold and jarring enough to make all my insecurities come racing back. But before I can completely lose my shit and give up on men altogether, he drops to his knees and buries his mouth against my dripping pussy.

Lifting my leg and placing it on his shoulder to open me wide, he digs his tongue deep inside my body and leaves me gasping for air.

"Then you come on my face," he growls against my clit.

He laps me up and makes a feast of his work, following his tongue with two thick fingers, so I feel the coarse cotton of his hand wraps against my thigh.

"Fuck," he groans so the vibrations reverberate through my body. "Fuck, Maya."

I clap a hand over my mouth and hold in the cry of pleasure that so desperately wants freedom.

I'm a schoolteacher. I have students in the next room. But in here, in the dark and steamy warmth, I'm Cole's plaything, and there isn't a temptation in the world that could convince me to be somewhere else.

"Oh god," I whimper as my release rockets me to the edge of oblivion.

My fingertips burn, and my core roils with lava. My orgasm teeters on a tightrope, and Cole makes everything a thousand times better when he lifts my second leg and bruises my thighs with his tight grip.

"Cole!" I squeak out. "Oh god. Oh shit."

He chuckles, but that only vibrates against my clit and brings me closer to the edge. "You taste so good. So fucking delicious."

"I'm going to come." *Am I whispering?* I think I am. But I can't be entirely sure. "Cole," I pull his hair, and whimper when that only results in a pleasurable growl from his throat. "I'm gonna come."

"Let it happen." He reaches up and smacks my ass.

His hand on my skin feels like fire. I've never been hit by a man before, not in anger, and never in pleasure. But a new reality dawns on me when he does it a second time, and my release gushes free.

I cry out, too loud, too frenzied, and inflict pain on myself when I slap my hand over my mouth to capture the sound. Tears burn my eyes, my lungs clamor for air, and still, my orgasm floods between us.

I know I make a mess. And yet, Cole laps it up and demands more.

"Oh god." My lungs fill to bursting. *Too much. Not enough.* My head spins, and sweat beads on my brow because I'm stuck inside a broom closet with a man who is basically a furnace after his fight. "Shit, Cole."

Sniggering, he continues to taste. To sample. To stroke my most sensitive areas.

He wraps his lips around my engorged clit, making me twitch from the hypersensitivity, and he holds me close, waiting. Soon, there's nothing left for me to give, and I'm merely... wrung out.

"You were all wound up," he murmurs.

My heart thunders at a deafening pace as, gently, he lowers one of my legs so my foot touches the concrete floor.

He doesn't rush me. Doesn't push me away. He only peppers kisses to my thigh, nips my skin, appreciates my body, until even my moans are just soft exhalations of air.

"You needed that more than you'll ever admit." I can hear the teasing in his voice.

So I retort, "Probably because the last time I had sex, the guy left me hanging before I could come."

Slowly, he lowers my second leg and holds my hips so I don't drop to the floor. Finally, when my knees stop knocking and my legs seem steady, he pushes up to stand, running his chest along my body so I feel him everywhere.

So I know exactly who I'm standing with in the dark.

"I deserve that." He presses a gentle kiss to my cheek. A second to the corner of my lips. "I was a dick, and you deserved to come."

"Yes I did." I swallow to lubricate my dry throat and wrap my arms around his neck. "Which is why I don't feel guilty that I came just now and you didn't."

He chokes out a desperate laugh and leans against me heavily enough to make it almost impossible for me to breathe. *Almost.* "Fair play, Maya Elizabeth. Next time, we both cross the finish line."

"Next time?" I wonder if the post-orgasmic high is like the post-*won-a-fight* high. "You just assume there'll be a next time. I don't recall agreeing to anything except this time."

"Mmm." His voice rumbles so I feel it in the air surrounding us. "I'll keep working on earning a commitment from you. And you keep on being you, annoying tendencies and all."

Snorting, I try to ignore the way my head swims from the lack of fresh air and the heat that Cole's body emits. "I have to get out of this closet. I think I'm gonna pass out."

"Okay." He bends again—for his shirt, perhaps—and makes quick work of shrugging it on. Then his hand wraps around mine in the dark, and tugs me closer until our lips clash and his tongue dances with mine.

I taste myself on his lips, but I don't feel the disgust I thought I would. It's not awful. It's just... different.

"I can't see you, Maya Elizabeth. But you'd be doing yourself a favor if you stopped blushing. Otherwise, everyone out there is gonna know what you did in here."

"What *I* did?" I rasp. "*I* didn't do anything."

"Except ride my face and come in my mouth." Pulling away, he cracks the door open and peeks into the hall outside.

The single line of light that crosses his face draws my eyes to his gritted jaw. To the muscle he holds even there, and then down to his wrapped hand circling mine.

"By the way," he looks back my way, "I'm not mad I didn't come this time."

"You're not?"

"Nah." His smile grows larger, sending bolts of electricity to my stomach. "I came about twenty times in the last week, and every single time, I thought about you."

"Pig." I spit the word and push into the hall, which is thankfully, all but empty. Those who linger pay us no attention, and those who would be apt to care what we're doing are nowhere in sight.

I shake my hand free of his and glance over my shoulder to meet his eyes. "Good fight, Cole. Now I'm going home."

"Sweet." He walks with a skip to catch up. "I'll come with you."

"Uh, no." I spin and press my hand to the middle of his too-large chest. Exhilaration rockets in my veins, because he's so large, so strong, but he looks down at me with deep adoration in his stare. "I'm going home *alone*, because that's what single women do. And you..."

He points back at himself, as though to confirm who '*you*' is.

"Are probably looking for a cute little place to rent in town. Ya know, since you won your fight and promised to give the Rollin On Gym a real go."

"I mean..." He drops his hands and sets them on his hips. "I did say that."

"And you're a man of your word, aren't you, Cole Miller? No lies?"

He nods. Then shakes his head. Then laughs. "No lies."

"Then I guess I'll see you around." I offer my hand and wait as he looks down at it. "Friend."

He drops his head and chuckles low on his breath. "Fuckin' cold, Maya Elizabeth." But he takes my hand and shakes it. "Oh, one thing before you go? *Friend*."

I peek up at him and drag my bottom lip between my teeth. "Mm?"

"Did you get your diaries back yet?"

"You're an ass!"

Cole

TIME TO SLEEP

I see her every day, down at the lake where she swims her laps, or in the school playground, since the Rollers somehow always time their five-mile run for the lunch school bell.

I see her in the grocery store in the afternoons, picking out fancy little dinners for one, or walking Main Street and bickering with someone—probably her mother—over the phone.

I see her so often, I'm almost absolutely positive she hasn't left town once, which means she hasn't gone to the city to have dinner with her folks, and she sure as hell hasn't taken the time to steal back her grandmother's possessions.

But with every arguing phone call, her eyes grow darker. Sadder, as she processes her loss and the very real chance she may never get what was supposed to be coming her way.

"Cole!"

Aiden's booming voice brings me around with a sharp twist so the bag I was working on swings wide and smacks the backs of my legs.

"I wanna see you in the octagon in five." Then he lifts his hand in a '*come here*' motion when Jack wanders into the room. "You too."

"What?" Always cranky, especially when I'm within sight, Reilly slides his eyes to me, then back to Aiden. "What do you want?"

"Octagon in five. We're working on submissions, and Cole needs someone his size."

185

"So *you* do it." Jack turns on his heels and walks back the way he came. "I've got shit to do."

"Octagon!" Aiden shouts louder. "Five fuckin' minutes, Jack."

"He doesn't have to—"

"He *does* have to," he cuts in before I can finish. "He needs to do it for himself—and you're the poor fucker who'll feel the pain. Get a drink." He claps my sweaty shoulder and turns away. "Take five. Then you come back ready to beat the world champion."

"B-beat?" For the first time in my life, I stutter. "Are you insane? I can't beat him!"

"Maybe not today," he calls back over his shoulder. "But you gotta beat him eventually, and this is a good day to get started. You'll never become a champion if you don't train with the best, and you can't train with the best if you and Jack keep ignoring each other. So I'm gonna put you both in the cage and lock the door. I suggest you take a minute to breathe." He stops at the doorway and glances back. "Get your affairs in order."

"Fuck, dude." My heart races as I hurriedly tear my gloves off and reveal sweaty wraps beneath. "You make it sound like he's gonna kill me."

"You'll live." He raps his knuckles against the doorframe before turning away. "But it's gonna be a painful lesson for you both. You've got three and a half minutes."

"Shit!" I toss my gloves to the mats and spin in a fucking circle as my brain frantically searches for how it'll spend its final three minutes.

My phone vibrates against the floor, a constant buzz that never stops, but when I snatch it up and read the screen to find Pres's name flashing back at me, I decline the call and instead make another.

To a number I stole... because I'm a good fucking thief.

I scoop up my water bottle and press the phone to my ear, then I uncap the lid and walk toward the gym's front door.

If I decide to bail on this and move to Tijuana, it's best I'm already near my car.

"Hello?" The line clicks, and her sweet voice attempts to soothe the frayed nerves in my body. "This is Maya speaking."

"It's me." I make my way to my car, squinting under the harsh sunlight, and rest my sweaty ass against the hood. "I know it's a school day and you're probably busy, but I just needed to talk to you for a sec."

"Cole?" Maya's tone turns a little sharper with worry. "What's wrong?"

"Kincaid's putting me in the cage with Reilly, so I was told to get my affairs in order."

"What does..." Children play on her end of the call. Small voices. Cries of delight, followed by cries of dissatisfaction. "Start again. And how'd you get my number? I never gave it to you."

"I stole it." There's no need to sugarcoat shit when I'm walking the Green Mile. "Couple of days ago, so the fact I haven't blown up your phone or texted you in the middle of the night asking for a picture of your ass should speak volumes about how much I respect you. But I'm gonna fight Reilly in a sec."

"You stole," she huffs. "Of *course* you stole, because that's what you do. Why are you fighting Jack?"

"Because Kincaid said I have to! He said I'm not worth shit if I can't stand up with Reilly, so it's time to shit or get off the pot."

"He said that?" She calls me out on my lies, every single fucking time. "He actually said those words?"

"No, but they were implied! I have two minutes before I lose my head and die, Maya, so I called you. Like, you're my one call. My lawyer and my family all wrapped up in one. I wanted to hear your voice before I bite the dust."

"You're being entirely too dramatic." I don't have to see her face to know she rolls her eyes. Then her breathing changes, so in my mind, I see her pushing up to stand, and perhaps moving around her classroom. "If Aiden wants you to *practice* with Jack, then I'm sure it's for a good reason, and that the situation is controlled and you're not in danger."

"Massive assumption for you to base our final words on, Maya. Don't you care about me at all? Is there no way my existence has penetrated your cold, hard heart?"

"Oh geez." She fucking laughs in my face—or, well, my ear. "You've gone full diva, Cole. What happened to that guy I first met? The dark, dangerous, kinda scary one who stared a lot and didn't speak much?"

"He's the me you get when I don't fucking know you. This is the me you get when Jack Reilly's about to smash my brain in."

"One minute!" Aiden's voice makes the entire gym shudder on its foundations. "Wrap it up."

"Oh lord," Maya sniggers. "It's like you're a gladiator, huh? Heading toward certain death. How did you expect me to help? I'm working, Cole, and you're... on borrowed time," she giggles.

"You're mocking me!" Another call beeps in my ear. "Maya! I called you for comfort, but all I get is ridicule."

"Because you're acting like a baby. It's a sanctioned, controlled, *careful* practice session inside a family gym whose reputation ensures they keep everything safe and secure." I *know* she shakes her head. "I'm certain you're safer there with grown-up-Reilly than I am here with his five-year-old kid who thinks that to terrorize is a form of flattery."

"Maya!"

"I have to go," she pushes on. "My students will rebel if I stay on the phone any longer. But call me this afternoon, okay? We'll chat."

"Assuming I'm alive!"

"I'm sure you will be," she teases. "And if you're not, I'll go through your belongings and take what I want before I let your friends have your stuff back. I have to go."

"Maya Elizabeth! Don't you hang up on me, woman."

"I'll talk to you later," she rushes out. "Love you."

"L—" My heart stops for a beat so drawn out, it stings. "What?"

"I mean, no! I..." Now it's her turn to panic. She moves around her classroom and, in my mind at least, flaps her arms in a frenzy. "It was a turn of phrase, Cole. I didn't mean it like—"

"You said *love you*." It should make me spin out. Freak out. Run the hell away from her, faster than I ever intended to run from Reilly. But in reality... her words settle in my stomach like warm cocoa on a winter morning. "You said you love me, Maya."

"I have to go. Don't read so much into standard, everyday phrases that friends say to other friends. You risk making it weird."

"Friends?" My eyes narrow to slits, while the call trying to interrupt us drops away. "Love, like, between friends?" I clarify. "That's what that was?"

"It was a phrase!"

Instead of continuing to argue, Maya kills our call and leaves me sitting on the hood of my Mustang... parked right next to a much prettier, much shinier Mustang. But before I get to dwell, or even jump back to panic about Jack smashing my face in, my phone trills again.

"Pres?"

I answer in a daze and try, in some faraway corner of my mind, to listen to my friend. But in the forefront of my consciousness, I filter through how I feel after hearing Maya say *love* and *you* in the same sentence. *Love you.*

Fuck, but I think that might be the very first time in my entire existence anyone has said those words to me.

"I've been trying to contact you," Preston's harsh words steal the warm, gooey wave I ride. "Box is tearing his place up, Cole. You've gone and pissed him right off."

"What?" It's like Maya is the tide, and Preston is the moon dragging her out so I can no longer touch. So I can't hold or appreciate or study or *feel*.

"Box! He had a couple of big jobs lined up for us, but you're not taking his calls, man. He's pissed."

"I'm busy." Goodbye Maya and *love you*; hello drama. "I'm not boosting cars right now, Pres. I told you."

"You can't just walk away," he growls. "Some of us rely on the paycheck Box sends our way, but for as long as you're not here, all he's sending me are assholes with guns and threats to kill us both. *My* job is to get you back in, or take a boot in my ribs for my troubles."

I push up to stand when Aiden appears in the gym's doorway. His face expectant, his feet ready to chase my cowardly ass down if I cut and run.

"Just ignore them," I tell Pres. "They'll want the money to keep rolling in, so for as long as I'm away, they'll find a new driver. If I come back, we'll pick up where we left off."

"If you come back? *If?*" he snarls. "What the fuck is going on with you, huh? This is your home!"

"I have other things happening for me right now. Better things." *The-world-champion-smashing-my-face-in things.* "Boosting cars is what we do to make ends meet when we have no other options. But this..." I look up at the signage of the gym and smile. "This is real. And it could be huge."

And then there's Maya...

I don't get to choose Box *and* keep her. It's one or the other, and there's no overlap in the middle. Not for us, and not in this lifetime.

"You should come over," I tell him, while impatiently, Aiden waves me inside. "Come visit me. See what's happening."

"And I *juuuust...*" He lets the word play out. "Ignore Box?"

"Wrap it up," Aiden grumbles. "Let's go."

"Just ignore him," I tell Pres. "He's a businessman riding a bad mood this week. But he'll find another driver easily enough. Listen, I have to go." I raise a single digit, risking my life, and tell Aiden to hold on for a minute. "I'm busy right now, Pres. But I want you to come out and see me. You're my best friend. Always. We don't need Box in our lives to facilitate that."

"Cole—"

"Love you."

"L—" He spasms, much the same way I'm sure Maya did when those words slipped past her lips. "What the fuck is wrong with you, dude?"

"You're right." A wild grin crosses my lips. "Friends don't say that."

"Who are you?" he breathes. "What did you do to my best friend?"

"I'm still me. But I'm the me who sometimes has good things happen. I've gotta go. I'll check in with you later."

"Cole!"

"See ya." I pull the phone from my ear and kill the call, then I look to Aiden, grinning although I'm walking toward death. "She said she loves me."

"She?" His eyes flicker with distrust. "I thought you were talking to a dude."

"Oh, I was. But before that, I was talking to Maya. And when we were saying goodbye, she said, and I quote," with a skip in my step, "*love you.*" I stare at him, walking blindly and not giving a single fuck if I crash. "That was a declaration of love, Kincaid."

"Sounds like it." He sets his hand on my shoulder and stops me just a hair's breadth before I walk straight into a steel beam. "Everything's coming up Millhouse for you, kid. And you didn't even have to shout at her to hear the words. But now you gotta fight."

He shoves me through the doorway so I stumble and catch sight of Reilly prowling the inside of the cage.

He's like a captured tiger. Enraged and ready for freedom. He's hungry, and angry, and I'm the lamb being sent to slaughter.

"Fuck." I spin back to Aiden and shake my head. "Actually, I'm not feeling well today, so I think I'm gonna head out and—"

"Turn." He steers me with a firm hand on my shoulder and leads me toward the cage door. "You survived the first time. You'll survive today.

You've been working on your grapple, so I wanna see you get him to the ground and find the submission."

"I can't—"

"Stop being a pussy. He's just a man. And before that, he was the annoying teen up in our space for a long fucking time, which means he's not infallible. He's just a fighter who put in the hours I'm trying to get from you."

"I was never the annoying teen in your life," Jack barks from the octagon. "I was always the fuckin' best."

Stalking toward the fence, he links his fingers in the gaps and glares into my eyes. "I want this more than you do, Miller. That's the difference between us. I earned it. I fucking bled and spewed and slayed my demons to be here. And you?" He laughs, but it's very *evil villain* and less humor. "You steal for gain. You take what you never earned. We're not the same."

"And now he's in your head." Rolling his eyes, Aiden marches me toward the gate and jogs to the bag I was working with ten minutes ago. Grabbing my mouth guard, he tosses it so I have no choice but to catch or let it roll to the filthy, sweaty floor. "He's fucking with you on purpose, Miller. And he's winning. You haven't even tapped gloves, and he's already kicking your ass, because you let him scare you."

"Or because he knows he can't beat me." Jack skips backwards, giving me space to enter the octagon. "Twenty-five years old?" He looks me up and down, knowing my damn age despite me never telling him. "I was already the fucking champion. I was the *returning* champion, and everyone knew my name."

He doesn't wait for Aiden to lock the gate. He doesn't even wait for him to announce the start of the end for me; he steps in quickly and makes contact with his knuckles against my jaw. "By twenty-five, I had it all, and I was in a position to retire at the top."

"But you didn't." I circle around and avoid a second swipe. "You nearly threw it all away and let your demons win." *Yeah, bitch.* I charge forward when he pauses in shock, and sink my fist into his ribs. *I did my research too.* "You started drinking and smoking and fucking anyone with two legs, right?" I weave when he turns with anger. "At twenty-five, you blew through millions of dollars, totaled cars, sent yourself broke, and moved back in with your mommy."

"Fuckkkkk." Aiden clings to the cage and watches us with wide eyes. "You guys are getting nasty."

"You don't know my shit!" Jack slips forward and slams a right hook under my ribs. "You don't know me at all. And I moved in with my sister. Not my mom."

I bark out a laugh and land a soft jab to his cheekbone. I didn't expect in a million years for it to get through, so I didn't bother putting my hips into it. "That's way better, then. Maybe I'm a thief in your eyes, and maybe that's all I'll ever be, but I take responsibility for my life. I have no one to catch me when I fail. So if that means I gotta steal to make rent, then that's what I'm gonna do. I don't have a rich sister to take me in."

"Whatever her financial status," he slams a heavy fist to the center of my chest, knocking the breath from my lungs, "she's got it because she worked for it. No stealing, and no handouts."

"And here I am, a fucking newb, going toe to toe with the champ."

I drop my head low and go for it, charging forward so my shoulder crashes to the middle of his torso, then I throw us both forward until he lands on his back and I scramble to take mount.

"Kinda says I'm working for it." I battle to grab his arm, but stay busy blocking his jabs. I'm on top, but he controls our fight with his legs wrapped around my hips. "I'm working my ass off to be worthy, Reilly. So you need to get the fuck over the car thing already."

"I'll never get over the car thing." He flips us, though I have no fucking clue how. But slamming me to my back and knocking the wind from my lungs, he wraps me up so I'm choking myself. "Cars are special to me. You'd have been better off trying to steal my son."

Outside the octagon, Aiden cackles with an uncharacteristically guffawing laugh.

"Instead, you tried to take something *I* earned. And then you botched it anyway. Like a little bitch."

"I was set up!" I fight his machine-like hold. The very least I can do is *not* be the one to choke myself out. "You had a tech chick lay a fucking trap. That's illegal, ain't it? Entrapment?"

He shrugs just a half a beat before sinking his elbow against the side of my face. "Why don't you go to the cops and complain about it? See what happens."

"Fuck you!" My vision turns darker, and a long line of blood dribbles into my eye. But I'm not out till I'm out. And hell, I've already lasted a minute or two in this cage with the champ, and I'm still awake. "I was set up by a fucking teenager who thought I had something special. She's your niece, no?" I grin and roll out from beneath him.

Momentary elation floods my veins, only to turn to dread when he takes my back and wraps his arm around my neck.

"Your niece thought I was special."

"*My* daughter," Aiden growls. "You keep your smack talk focused on Jack's failings. You don't bring my baby into this."

"I don't have failings!" Jack snaps. Tilting to the side, he lands on his back with a thud and pulls me over so I look up at the ceiling. He gets his hooks in, wrapping his feet around my thighs and locking them in so I'm stuck. "I busted my ass to overcome the shit life threw at me." He tightens his arm and cuts off my air. "I was thrown against the fucking wall a thousand times. But I got up again a thousand and one."

"Oh, boohoo." I work to bridge high, to break his hold, but he's like a boa constrictor and tightens his grip every time I move. "Life was hard for the millionaire golden child. The fuckin' tragedy."

"I've got money now, bitch. But that's because I earned it." He squeezes tighter. Tighter. So my vision turns spotty. "But my wife and family, Miller... they're safe and happy. And that's worth so much more."

"My girl said she loves me today." I'm going to sleep, but I float there with a giddy smile. "We're just friends," I slur. I *think* I slur. "But she said she loves me."

"He's going to sleep." Aiden's voice is like a whisper down a faraway tunnel. "Tap, Miller. You're not supposed to sleep."

"Don't wanna tap to the champ," I mumble.

Darkness takes over, but I dream of Maya. Of her *love you*.

"Not gonna tap..."

"And you're done." Aiden slaps my cheek and stands over me as my eyes flicker open.

Jack's boa-like hold is gone, his fighter body no longer beneath mine. Instead, I lie draped across the canvas with my arms and legs starfish-wide, my head drooping to the side so I catch sight of Aiden's legs, and behind him, the brunette Jimmy married.

She's a fighter too, fierce in her stance, but curious as she tilts her head and watches me.

"You in there?" Crouching, Aiden grabs my face and forces me to look his way. "You awake yet?"

"I slept?"

"Like a fuckin' baby," Jack's taunting snigger comes from somewhere behind me. Somewhere I can't be bothered to turn and see. "You talk a lot of shit for a guy who wanted to be swaddled and hugged to sleep."

"Shut the fuck up." Groaning, I sling my arm across my body and work my way to my side. Then to my stomach. Dragging my knees beneath me, then my elbows, I push up so I'm basically in the right position to be fucked. "I seriously slept?"

"You did pretty decent." In my peripherals, Jack makes his way to his feet and runs a hand along his lip to collect a line of blood. "You made me sweat," he rumbles. "And you lasted longer than I expected." Stepping closer, so I almost think he might help me up, I close my eyes again when he sets his foot against my ribs and knocks me back to the canvas. "I'll roll with you again tomorrow." Chuckling, he makes his way to the cage door and out. "As long as you don't steal anything between now and then."

"Yep." I'm tempted to take a nap, since I'm already down. Tempted to call it a day and simply... dream of Maya and her accidental *love you*. "I'll be ready then. Won't steal."

"Good. Keep putting in the hours, and you might fit in after all."

I open my eyes in time to catch him accepting a towel from the chick fighter. He wipes his face and mops up the crimson I made him bleed. Then he winks for his sister-in-law and walks toward the exit.

"I'm going to call Smalls." I don't know if he speaks to me or Aiden. "Gonna update her on her acquisition. Probably also check in to see if she's ready to come home."

"Don't ask her that!" Aiden stomps out of the cage and follows Jack across the room. "You know she's struggling, asshole! We all are. Don't make it worse for her."

"You have his respect, ya know?" The woman, Izzy, saunters toward the cage and stops with her fingers linked around the fence. She's a mom to teens, a wife and businesswoman, but beneath all that, she's a fighter with toned abs and more skill in the cage than I'll probably ever possess. "Jack," she clarifies. "He's actually one of our more chill fighters. He'll make friends with anyone, so it's just bad luck you put him off when you got to town."

"Can it be fixed?" I flop to my back and let my arms and legs drop wide. "Will he come around in the end?"

She nods. Not even a second of hesitation in her response. "Yeah. He's already getting there. But he wants you to earn it so he knows he's not wasting his time." Tapping the fence, she grins and takes a step back. "Good fight."

"I lost."

"You held your own against the current world champion, and in the end, he took you out with a choke, not a knockout. That's no small feat, Cole."

She steps away when Jimmy stops in the doorway. He doesn't even have to speak to summon his beautiful wife. He doesn't have to do shit except look at her, and instantly, she responds.

"He's gonna make damn sure you're worthy," she murmurs before she goes. "Then he'll hand you his title, just like Bobby gave it to him. He'll be your cornerman when it's time to go pro, I guarantee it."

"I've just gotta earn it." I look up at the ceiling and swallow to lubricate my dry throat.

I've gotta earn everything I get in this town, starting with a chance to fight professionally, and ending with Maya.

Because everything always ends with her.

Maya

I'VE GOT YOU, AND YOU'VE GOT ME

I hear the roar of an engine. The rumble of a fast car as it comes to a stop outside my apartment. While I fold my laundry and something banal plays on the television, I'm pulled from my almost-meditative state at the sound of a car door creaking open.

Then an obnoxious, "Maya Elizabeth!" shouted from the parking lot below.

Inside my chest, my heart skips with exhilaration, while in my hands, I fold a bra so the cups sit together.

"I said...!" he shouts again. "Maya. Elizabeth!"

With nerves in my belly and elation in my blood, I toss my underwear to the couch and bound to the window that overlooks my street. I shove the sash high so the iron weights crash inside the frame, then I poke my head outside and laugh at the image in front of me.

"Cole?" My voice shakes, but not in fear. Mostly, it's excitement. "Why are you standing on your car?"

"Because I like that thing you said about love!" he calls back. Then he looks down at his feet and grits his teeth. "If I dent my baby for this, I'm gonna be hella pissed."

"So get off your car!"

"Can't." He looks up again and lifts his arms to the sky. "Come out with me? Let's get a meal somewhere."

"It's not even five o'clock!" Then because I doubt myself, despite

197

knowing I checked the time only a few minutes ago, I pull back and study the clock to confirm. "Cole, it's too late for lunch, and too early for dinner."

"So?" He jumps off his hood and turns back to rub *her* all better. "Since when does a clock get to tell us what to do?" Peeking up at me, he flashes a devilish grin. "Come out with me, Maya. And maybe say that thing about love again. I wanna try it on for size."

"Oh god." An anxious groan works its way along my chest and out past my lips. "Cole, I told you that was—"

"A friend thing," he cuts in. "Yeah, I heard you. But I tested your hypothesis on my other friend, and he said that shit isn't right. So..." He throws his hands up. "I'm thinking you're full of shit."

"Hello?" My neighbor, a middle-aged woman in the apartment beside mine, pokes her head out and scowls. "I'm trying to watch *Jeopardy*. Shut up out here!"

Cole giggles. Like the child I'm not sure he ever truly got to be, he covers his mouth and sniggers. "Maya!" he whisper-shouts. "Let's go before she calls the cops on us!"

"I'm calling them in two seconds." She disappears back inside her window. "I'm getting my phone."

"Maya!"

"Fine!" With my heart in my throat and adrenaline zinging in my veins, I pull my head back inside and shut the window with a crash that rattles the glass pane. Then I look down at myself to consider my outfit.

I wasn't planning on company. Or going out in public. Which means I wear denim cutoffs and a tank with a skeletal hand holding a rose.

It's not at all appropriate for Miss Blake, Kindergarten Teacher to be walking around in. But school's out, and Britt's family beat people up for a living.

This shirt is fine, right?

"Maya!"

"I'm coming!"

I sprint through my living room and dash to slip my flip-flops on. Then grabbing my keys and phone from the kitchen counter, I swing my front door wide, and squeal when I find Cole standing on my doorstep, his smile giddy, and his hands hungry.

Somewhere along the way, we've moved from *creepy-dude-following-*

me-home, to *the-guy-who-treated-me-badly,* to this guy, the one who wants to hear the L word and who grabs me in public.

His hand goes to my hip, and his arm violently yanks me in until I crash against his chest, then he slams his lips over mine and swallows down the gasp of air I so desperately need.

His tongue dashes out and duels with mine. Vicious, but gentle. Passionate, but sweet. The kiss is over quickly, but pulling away, he continues to hold me tight. "You look beautiful." With his free hand, he reaches up and taps my messy bun so it flops to the other side. "Put on a pair of glasses, and we'll have this sexy librarian biker chick thing going on."

I step back, my heart thundering a dangerous beat, and laugh. "A librarian biker chick? That's an especially *niche* request. Do you wish I rode a motorcycle?"

"Fuck no." He wraps his hand around mine and pulls me into the hall. Grabbing the door, he slams it shut and slings his arm over my shoulder so our fingers remain linked and our ribs brush as we walk. "Motorcycles are crazy dangerous, Maya Elizabeth."

"Sure, but stealing cars and speeding across the city is fine," I counter seriously.

When he looks down in question, I flash a smile to let him know I'm kidding... sort of. "Why are you so loud this afternoon?"

"Loud?" He leads me down the stairs and out the front door of my building, then across the asphalt until he stops beside the passenger door of his car. Opening it wide and pressing a noisy kiss to my temple, he pushes me in and runs around to his side. "I'm not loud. I'm happy."

"So why are you happy?" I fix my seatbelt and warily watch on as he dances through doing the same. "What happened?"

"Why do I need a reason to be happy?" He starts his car and, I swear, groans a little when the engine roars. "Can't I just be a happy person?"

"Well... normal people could," I tease. "But you're you, and Cole Miller doesn't typically *jitterbug* his way through life."

"Yeah, well, I kinda have a hankering to jitterbug my way into your pants. Ya know," he drives out of my parking lot, "In a totally *friendly* way."

"You're such a pig." I roll my eyes and look out my window, Avoidance 101, as he cruises along my street. "What happened today specifically?" Then I twist back to study his eyes. "Are you high? Because you can't be a pro athlete but smoke drugs at the same time."

"Smoke drugs," he chuckles. "You sound like a genuine thug, Maya Elizabeth. And no." Settling back for the drive, he sets his free hand on my thigh at an entirely *unfriendly* distance from my vagina. "I'm not high. In fact, I've never been high in my life, because that shit not only affects your brain, but it costs money. I've never had either to spare. You look pretty, by the way."

"Thanks. Why are you so happy, if not because of marijuana?"

"I had a good day. This chick I'm kinda into is riding in my car wearing shorts that make me hard. And I got to roll with the Jackhammer today. I lost," he snorts, "I lost bad. But he makes getting choked out kinda fun."

"Choked?" I jolt in my seat and lean closer to study Cole's neck. "He *choked* you?"

"Sent me to sleep," he confirms, giddy. "But it was worth it, because we kinda bonded a little."

"You're not bonding when someone is choking you, Cole! You're wasting those brain cells you said you don't wanna lose."

Slowly, seductively, he glances across and smirks. "I bet I could put my hand on your throat right now and we'd be bonding pretty fuckin' well."

Geez. Why does my breath come faster and my heart pound harder when his words are a threat at best? *There's something wrong with me.* "I can't continue that discussion." Turning away, knowing my cheeks blaze red, I purse my lips when he chuckles. "So you had a good day at the gym? That's what this is all about?"

"Sure. Do I need to win the lottery before I get to be noisy?"

Pulling into a parking space on Main Street, Cole cuts the engine and shoots out of his door before I can even take a breath.

"I don't buy lottery tickets," he says the moment he opens my door. Then, because I haven't done it, he leans in and unclips my seatbelt. "So there's no chance I'm gonna win. But I stand a real chance of winning a future fight against the champ, and that makes me happy as fuck."

Standing tall, he holds my hand and gently pulls me out of the car. "I lost today and went to sleep, but Reilly said we'll roll again tomorrow, and the chick fighter said he's already coming around to liking me. I screwed up." He leans closer and presses a gentle, almost silent kiss to the corner of my lips. "But I say sorry when I do the wrong thing, then I work hard on making it better."

"So..." I step back, but I allow him to keep my hand in his. "You're making things better?"

"At the gym," he nods, turning to lead me onto the sidewalk. "And hopefully with you, too. And since I'm gonna be a famous UFC champion someday, I figure your fancy ass probably isn't slumming too low if I ask for us to be a thing, ya know?"

"Oh?"

He leads me through the front door of Franky's Diner and past the server with a wave. "I know I said all that shit about how you deserve better."

"You were pretty insistent," I cut in. "Often."

"Right. And it was true then, since being a car thief doesn't reek of good choices and sustainable income."

I stop beside a red and white booth and lower when Cole gently pushes me in. "Not the best career path."

"Exactly. But being a pro athlete." Instead of going to the opposite side of the table, Cole slips in on my side and keeps moving until we're hip to hip and I have no way to escape unless I climb onto his lap. "Going pro means money, Maya. It means consistency, and it means the cops won't throw me in jail every chance they get." He looks up when the beautiful, curvy server stops on his right and offers a coffee pot.

Cole flips his mug, then mine, and smirks as she pours. "You know the Rollers, don't you, Kat?"

"Well..." she finishes filling the first mug and goes to work next on mine. "Yes, I do. I figure I know them quite well. Why?"

"They're solid people." He stares deep into my eyes. "Solid people means a solid future. And a solid future means I don't feel bad about making Miss Blake slum to spend time with me."

"They're some of the best people I know." But sniggering, Kat leans around and meets my terrified gaze. "Your safe word is Lemon Zesty Burger. If you want to escape, you order that burger, and I'll get you out."

"She's got jokes." Cole rolls his eyes, and when Kat steps away, he reaches up and fingers strands of hair from my lashes. "You don't need a safe word, Maya, because I'm the guy who'll keep you safe forever." Coming closer, he presses a gentle kiss to the center of my lips, bewitching me, and like magic, has my mouth opening up to his. "You might even find slumming for me the best thing you've ever done in your life."

"I will?" My breath comes shorter. My pulse, faster. "Why?"

"Because I'll earn you," he answers easily. "Because I'll make fucking sure I'm worth it. Do you want something to eat? The pie here is good."

"S-sure." My brain, I'm quite certain, was left back in my apartment. But my loins and my libido, and that stupid hope in every little girl's romantic heart, followed me to this diner. "Pie sounds good."

He grins to show off a perfect smile that *has* to have come from genetics, considering the price tag attached otherwise. "If I go pro," he murmurs, "I mean, like, the real kind of pro, with cameras and reporters and all that shit Reilly gets, I think it'd be pretty cool if you were there with me."

His size and proximity cocoons me into the corner of the booth. But instead of feeling suffocated, I feel hugged, warm, desired. "I'm not saying shit has to move at a crazy speed between us. But it'd be cool if we were heading in the same general direction. You're working on your career, I'll work on mine. Sometimes we meet in the middle and hang out."

"You mean have sex?" I grumble. "You want a friends-with-benefits arrangement."

Instead of taking offense, his lips curl into a wolfish smile that makes my throat dry. "No, I just want *you*. All the fucking time. I want your loyalty, and I want your trust. I wanna know that we get to be together when it works for us both, and that you're not with someone else when we're apart."

"Y-you want us to be exclusive?" I stammer. "You're asking me to be your... possession?"

He shakes his head and chuckles. "I was thinking more like *girlfriend*. As in a mutually happy, rewarding, passionate exchange where we make each other smile a lot. Because you're no one's possession, Maya. And you're not something to be controlled."

"Cole—"

"There are four billion other chicks on this planet," he pushes on, "but you're the only one I wanna be good enough for." Leaning closer, he taps his tongue to my bottom lip, and grins when I open up. "You're the only one I wanna make proud. And I say that having never had proper sex with you."

"Ugh!" I smack his shoulder and shove him back when he barks out a laugh. "Why do you say the shit you say? I swear, Cole!"

"Pie." The server sets our plates on the table with a smirk that proves she hears every single thing he says. "Enjoy, and call out if you need anything else."

The bell above the diner door jingles, drawing her eyes to a teen boy, and beside him, a brunette girl about the same age.

Serious now, Kat brings her gaze back to Cole and purses her lips. "Mind the innuendo while my son is within earshot. He doesn't need to know more than he already does."

"I'll be good." Cole reaches up and does an odd, two-finger salute above his brow, then he turns to me and moves in to take up the space my smack pushed him out of.

"That girl," he whispers, tilting his head toward the teens, "she's a fighter, and so is her mom." Reaching out when I don't take my fork, he picks his up and scoops a corner of his pie. "I'm not too proud to admit she could beat my ass and clean the toilet with my head."

Impressed, I open my mouth and accept the bite he offers. "The mom could kick your ass?"

"Hell, the girl could, too." Taking more pie on his fork, he brings it to his own lips and draws my eyes down to the way his tongue cleans the fork of every morsel. "They were born and bred over there, Maya. Fighting machines, all the way down to the infants."

"I know," I counter easily. "I teach Jack's five-year-old, remember? He scares the crap out of me most days."

Laughing, Cole goes back to get more pie for me. "But they're all so fuckin' respectful. They teach the girls the way they teach the guys. There are no sex divisions in that gym, and age doesn't mean shit either. They spend more time and effort on her," he nods toward the teen girl, "than they do on me, despite me being twice her weight and ten years older."

I wrinkle my nose. "Probably means she's better than you."

"I know she is!" he barks out. "Like I said, born and bred fighters. They focus their time and attention on whoever wants it more. Which is why Reilly was always pissy at me."

"And of course," I counter dryly, "it wasn't because you tried to steal his car, right?"

"Well... that too," he concedes. "But cars are replaceable, and he has enough money to buy a million more. Mostly, he had a problem with the *stealing* portion of what I did, and figured I'd be lazy with training, too. Like, I didn't earn the car, and I wouldn't earn his time in the gym."

"But you've proved him wrong?"

"I'm starting to." He flashes a wide grin and takes more pie between his lips, while, somewhere in his pockets, his phone buzzes for attention. "I show up every single day and give them everything I've got. So I guess he's coming around."

"And the car stuff..." His phone, I swear, has created a negative association for me. Whenever it rings, chances are it's someone calling him to a world of theft and high-speed car chases. "Are you ever going back to that?"

"I have no reason to." Pushing up onto his hip, he fishes the still-vibrating device from his pocket and kills the call without so much as glancing at the screen. "I'm earning my keep over here with the gym. I'm even letting my apartment in the city go at the end of the month."

"What?" My brows shoot high in surprise. "What do you mean?"

"I pay month to month." He slices more pie away and offers it to me. "I haven't gone back since I got to town, and I can't say I miss much of anything in it. So I'm gonna head over in a week or so and pack up what needs to be moved. There's no reason for me to pay rent for two places when I don't have to."

"So you just..." My heart thunders faster. "You just give up your life that easily? You were living there, and now you're living here. It's that simple?" My voice breaks on nerves. "For a girl? Are you insane?"

Humored, his shoulders bouncing with gentle laughter, he taps my lip with the end of the fork. "For the gym, Maya. I'm moving for *them*, because they've committed time and money to me. It just so happens that I get to hang out with you when school's out."

"Oh, well..." Embarrassed, I sit back and firm my lips so he can't keep feeding me pie. "My mistake."

"But it's cute how you want to be my girlfriend, and you're trying really hard not to say it." He smacks a noisy kiss to my lips that melts away the ice I try so desperately to build around my heart.

Damn, damn, damn him for being so charming.

"I already showed you my cards, Maya Elizabeth. So it's totally cool if you do the same and stop making me feel unloved."

"No, I…" There's that word again. *Love.* "Cole, you—"

"Are devilishly handsome, good in bed," then he leans around to whisper in my ear, "and better with my tongue? I know."

"You're crude," I counter and shove him back, "persistent, and impulsive. You stole cars for a living and probably thought it was fun. And now you've moved town after just a couple of weeks inside a gym. I wasn't raised… I can't…"

"You were raised by stuck-up assholes who use the law to abuse the people they should protect. I doubt your parents have *ever* had sex, and I know it's gonna take you a minute to realize not everyone operates the same way they do."

"You were raised with negligence and a different kind of abuse, Cole. You thrill on impulsivity, because you've never known stability. And what if I'm just *this week's* impulse?"

Surprised, his eyes turn serious. "What?"

"You want me *now*." Desperation ekes into my voice as my fears come tumbling out. "Because I'm here, and you like my shorts. I've made this a fun challenge, and you enjoy competition as much as every other natural-born fighter. But what about when I give in? What about when I say *sure, let's bang every day and use the L word regularly*? Once I do that, the thrill goes away, and I become nothing more than a car you stole and took for a joyride around the city."

"Jesus." Cupping my face, he strokes my cheek with the rough pad of his thumb and hunches his shoulders to get down on my level. "You're so terrified of being hurt, you'd rather just stay cold? Seriously, Maya?"

"I'd rather stay cold, having never felt warmth, than to be comfortable for a while, and then freeze after."

"We're not a hell of a lot different, ya know?" Pushing the plate away and setting his elbow on the table, Cole moves closer so all I see is him. His perfect hazel eyes, and the long lashes that kiss his cheeks when he blinks. "Different tax brackets," he breathes. "Different neighborhoods. Different schools. You had two parents, and I basically had none. But we were both raised without affection. Neither of us had parents who tucked us in at night and whispered that they love us. You were controlled every damn day by yours, and the circumstances I was born into controlled me."

When I try to pull away, he places his fingers beneath my chin and tugs me closer. "The difference is, when you say those words to me, I wanna run toward you and grab on. Fuck, Maya Elizabeth, I love when you say *love*. Because I'm not sure I've ever felt something so good in my life. But when I say it," he strokes my cheek, "When I even hint at it, you're ready to bolt."

"I'd rather not be loved, if it's only gonna be snatched away later."

"Who said it's gonna be snatched away? Maybe I'm a thief, and maybe I've told lies, but I'm working on earning your trust. I'm working really fucking hard to prove to you I'm here and I'm sticking."

"But, Cole—"

"I'm not asking for us to move in together, Maya. Not yet," he lowers his voice. "I'm not asking for crazy, ridiculous commitment." Then he sets the pad of his thumb on the middle of my lips and waits for my eyes. "*Yet*. But I'm asking for you to trust. Or at least, *try* to trust. I'm asking you to give me the chance to earn this."

"And when you grow bored?" I know my eyes glitter with tears. I feel the sting, but I refuse to let them spring free. "When you get what you need and decide you're done?"

He shakes his head and presses a gentle kiss to my lips. "I'm not your parents, Maya. And I'll never weaponize your need for affection. If I love, I love freely and loudly. And if I'm thinking something, good or bad, I'm gonna voice those feelings so you know where I stand."

His phone vibrates again, making his jaw grind with frustration.

"You say such pretty things," I whisper. "But you have an entire life outside this town. You have twenty-five years of history, and it all belongs in the city with those people. It's not healthy, nor expected, that you just cut it all off."

"I don't have to cut my friends out to cut the illegal shit out."

Glancing across to his phone, he spies the screen and kills the call, then he brings his attention back to me. "My best friend lives in the city, Maya. And I love him. I'm gonna keep loving him, and when we can, we'll hang out. But I won't steal again. I won't risk the trust I'm trying to build with you. And I sure as shit won't risk the opportunity the Rollers have given me. Without them, I'm broke again, so although you're important to me, and a major reason I wanna do better, I'd be lying if I said they don't sit just as high on that list of reasons to improve."

It's crazy for me to feel insecure. Crazier yet to think I could be the one and only motivating factor in his life. But his loyalty to the gym helps add authenticity to his words. They're outside of us, completely removed from anything he and I have.

"If you get the urge to go back to that life, will you tell me first?" I drop my gaze and study his hands instead. "Say you wake up one day and just wanna steal a fast car—"

He chokes out a laugh that has my eyes swinging back up.

"Believe it or not, I've *never* woken with the urge to steal a car. I usually wake with an urge to earn money so I can eat later that day."

"And since you can earn money a different way..." I trail off.

"Exactly. Besides, my car is sexy enough on her own. She gets me where I've gotta go, and I have no desire to cheat on her with some other bitch."

"Comforting," I drawl. With a roll of my eyes, I press my hands to his chest and shove.

Or, well, I *try* to shove. But he's too heavy for me to move on my own. "Can you slide out? I want to get up."

"You're leaving?" He's too loud. Too attention-grabbing as he pushes up to stand. "I just poured my freakin' heart out to you, Maya Elizabeth, and you're *leaving*?"

"Shh!" I slam my hand over his mouth and blush when the teens look our way.

The boy, Kat's son, studies us with a slow flicker of his eyes before a sly grin has a couple of dimples popping above his chin.

"Stop announcing our business all over the place," I hiss and yank my hand away when he licks my palm. "Jesus."

"It's not *our* business," he protests at an annoying volume. "Because you're not my girlfriend yet, which means we're not an *us*. We're just a *you* and a *me*, so I'm announcing *my* business all over."

"Cole!" I wipe my palm on my shirt and hurriedly slip out of the booth. I grab my phone and keys, and though I take out cash for our pie, he snatches it up again and squeezes it into my back pocket before taking out his own and dropping it on the table.

"Won't you go steady with me, Maya Elizabeth?" He speaks too loudly, far too conspicuously, so even the cooks leave the kitchen and stare. "Please, beautiful! Love me back and make me an honorable man."

"You're a horrible human being." I dash away from the table, only to stumble when my eyes stop on Kat's, and a burning blush reddens my cheeks.

"Th-thank you for the pie," I stammer. "You can throw the rest in the trash. Put Cole out there too, while you're going."

"Oh!" He follows on fast feet and wraps me up with an arm around my hips. Smacking a noisy kiss to my cheek, he starts us across the diner so my feet drag on the floor. "She's got comebacks and sass, but she still blushes when people look at her."

Humiliation. Horror.

I hang like a rag doll and groan. "I'm begging you to stop."

"I'm begging you to love me!" He throws the door open—*throws it,* like a Disney princess greeting woodland creatures with a song. "Why won't you love me, Maya? Is it because I'm not good at reading and writing?"

"Oh my god." I close my eyes. If I can't see those on the street, maybe they can't see me. "You're insane."

"Just give me your heart," he hollers. "Share your life with me."

"Kiss him!" someone calls from somewhere along the street. "Don't break his heart."

"Yeah, don't break my heart." His laughter makes me bounce in his arm. "Just kiss me, Maya Elizabeth."

"You might be the single most high-maintenance person I've ever met." I get my feet beneath me and push up to stand straight, then I reach up to hold his face—not to kiss him, but to keep his could-be-undiagnosed-ADHD self still. "I've met a lot of divas, Cole, but none as exhausting as you."

"You were raised in a home where love was never a priority, nor freely given." Lowering his voice and bringing his lips just a breath away from mine, he adds, "If my desire for the opposite makes me high-maintenance, then I'll wear the label proudly. But while I wear it, I'll love you."

He kisses my lips and swallows down my startled sigh. "I'll *tell* you I love you." Another kiss. "I'll say it so fucking often, you'll think it's just another phrase that loses meaning." Then he shakes his head and follows my eyes so I can't escape. "But I'll mean it every single time."

Stay strong, Maya. Stay independent. Don't give in!

"Shit."

Smug, his lips pull up. "You can say it back, ya know. It's just a feeling.

An emotion you get to allocate to someone who makes you happy. It's *not* a lifetime commitment. Say it," he repeats. "I won't run away."

"I mean…" I pull a deep breath into my lungs and stop only when they threaten to burst. Then I exhale and grumble, "I guess I love you too. In a strange, terrifying, *you're a bit of a stalker, and you've-never-even-made-me-come-during-sex* kinda way. How do we even know you can deliver? And why are you so certain I won't be the one to break your heart, after I learn you don't know what you're doing?"

"Trust. We say the words now. We have sex later. By then, you've already committed to a relationship, and my inability to find your G-spot is no longer a valid reason to break up with me."

"It's cute you think that." I slide my fingers through his hair and grab on, purely because I can. Because it feels good. Better yet, the way his hips crush mine and his cock, hard and always ready, teases between us. "You wanna show me your new apartment? I've been curious."

"Hmm." He nibbles my bottom lip and slides his arm around my hip like a steel belt. "That was a nice segue, Blake. Tell me you love me again, and I promise to allocate ten entire minutes to sucking your clit."

Oh shit. I exhale on a gust, and though I don't consciously decide to move it, my head bobs in the affirmative. "I love you."

"Great!" He smacks a smiling kiss to my lips and pulls away so fast, I sway on my feet. Then he snags my hand and yanks me toward the car. "It's too late for lunch," he announces for the whole street to hear, opening the door for me to slide in. "Too early for dinner."

My heart thunders as he dashes to his side and slips in. Like he does every time, he starts the engine and has a moment with his one true love.

"Oh dear. And what do you suppose we should do with this odd in-between time, Cole?"

"We fuck." He backs out of our parking space and onto the road, then he drops the clutch and shifts into first. "Don't play innocent now, Maya Elizabeth." He places his hand in my lap and teases. Taunts with his fingertips at the hem of my shorts. "You want me to make you come. You practically said so in a diner full of teenagers."

"I did not." I cup my cheeks because I *know* I'm blushing. "You're exaggerating, and it's unattractive."

Snorting, he drives a little too fast to be legal. Speedy gear changes, and squealing tires as we round a corner. "Don't judge my apartment, okay? It's old as fuck, and I don't have much in the way of furniture."

My brows pinch tight as I consider his words, while in my mind, I imagine milk crates for chairs and paper plates for eating off. "I never judge."

"Really?" I feel the warmth of his stare on the side of my face. "Fancy-pants, rich-girl, lawyers daughter with her own law degree doesn't judge me... the thief?"

Pursing my lips, I glance across and meet his eyes, but what I'd intended as a serious expression turns to laughter when he grins.

"Fine!" I choke out. "I've been known to judge. But I left that life, remember? I'm working on a better me."

"Precisely." He abandons my thigh and twines our fingers together. But where I assume that's as far as he intends to take it—holding hands—I melt into my seat and groan when he slips my finger between his lips and nibbles. "We both lived lives we're not proud of, Maya. But now we're small-town folk, and getting a fresh new start."

"You're just looking for an out so I can't get mad about the stealing anymore."

And yet, a guttural moan rolls along my chest when he bites down.

"What you're doing is just so..." My heart thunders ridiculously faster. "Confusing! Sucking on someone's finger isn't sensual, Cole."

"No?" He steers the car with his knee and uses his free hand to shift gears. "Sucking on *anything* is sensual. It's so fucking taboo."

He pulls into a parking spot outside a broken-down building with trash cans overturned on the corner of the block, and a stray dog lifting its hind leg to pee against a tiny, dying shrub. Cutting the engine and releasing my hand, he pushes out his door and makes his way around to mine.

"It's no palace." He offers his palm and gently tugs me out. "It's not where I'm gonna grow old, but it's what a man can afford when he's paying two rents and hasn't got much in the way of savings."

"I'm not judging you."

But my eyes scour the parking lot. My mind searches for details to store away for later dissection. The old car on cinderblocks because it's missing wheels, and the guy sitting with his back against the wall, his knees up and his hands drooping between them.

"Don't ever come here looking for me, okay?" Serious now, Cole leads me through the building's front door and onto a staircase where the air carries a tang of constant moisture. "I'll come to you," he continues. "Don't come outside alone, not even to take out the trash. Don't talk to anyone except me, and if you hear screaming," he grabs me when I stumble, and sweeps me up into his arms, "you stay inside and mind your business."

Fear makes my hands shake, and nerves swarm in my belly. Not fear for myself, but for the fact he sleeps here at night. Alone.

"Cole—"

"I'll take care of you." He shifts his hold around my torso, so my legs wrap around his hips and my arms circle his neck. Then he dives in and nibbles on the warm skin behind my ear.

I have no clue if he can see past me, and if he trips, we're going to end up with broken necks, I'm sure of it. But he's so strong, so certain. So I hold on and trust, just like he said.

"I promise, Maya. I'm gonna keep you safe." Stopping in front of an apartment, he holds me high and works his keys with one hand. "I'll never let you get hurt for as long as I know you." Unlocking the door and swinging it wide, he pulls back and waits for my eyes. "There are four billion other chicks on this planet, but you're the only one I care about enough to keep safe."

With my heart in my throat and emotion building in my chest, I draw my arms back and cup his face. "You wanted to save me as soon as we met," I whisper. "You didn't even know me, but you knew what you had to do."

"Sometimes, the heart knows before the brain does."

Crossing his threshold and carrying me in, he kicks the door closed and stops because we're already in the middle of the room.

I straighten my back and look around to find a bed set up against the wall, and beside it, a loveseat that can't be all that comfortable. Across from the bed is a box television, and beside that is a tiny bistro table where I guess he eats his meals—though, personally, I'd sit on the bed.

"Maya." With strong fingers and fire in his eyes, he takes my jaw and drags me around. "I'm gonna end up somewhere nicer, I promise. This isn't—"

"I'm not judging." Unwrapping my legs and sliding down his body, I smile when my feet touch the floor and I'm reminded, yet again, just how tall he is compared to me. "I'm cataloging," I explain. "I'm learning my surroundings, just like I study gardens as I pass, or the lake when light shines off the water at sunset."

Pushing to my toes and purring when his arm wraps around my hip, my own personal safety belt, I take his free hand and slowly, but assertively, guide it down to the waistband of my shorts until his fingers slip inside. "I believe we had a deal. Something about you paying special attention to my clit."

"Fuck." He drops to his knees and undoes the button of my shorts, tugging them down until the fabric scratches my thighs and creates enough heat to make me hiss. "Let me make you come, Maya." He buries his face between my legs and bites, despite the fabric of my panties barring his way. "Let me make you scream until we both know you won't ever leave."

"I don't think I could leave even if I tried."

I cry out when he yanks my underwear down, then again when he spins me around and shoves me down so my chest presses to his bed.

My breath races at a dizzying speed, and my heart hammers against the soft fabric of Cole's bedspread. But whatever comfort I might've found in the cotton is thrown to the wall when he takes my ass cheeks in his hands and pushes them apart to reveal all of me.

So much of me.

"I'm gonna make you come." He bites the part of my leg where thigh turns to buttock. "I'm gonna make you cream. And I'm gonna claim all of you."

"Cole—"

"Because you love me." *Bite.* "And I love you." *Bite.* "And we're in this shitty-ass fucking apartment—the rich girl and the pauper—but you're not judging."

"Oh god," I whimper when the pulsing between my legs threatens to send me insane. "Cole."

"You're already dripping." He slides the tip of his finger through my folds, collecting and spreading, teasing, taunting, then he drags that finger up to my ass until I gasp. "Because you're a dirty girl who wants me to use you up."

"Cole—"

"Trust me to keep you safe." He slips his finger inside and growls when an involuntary scream rockets through my lips. "Trust me to be respectful, but to know what you need, even if you're a little scared at first."

"Oh god." My breath shudders out. Hell, I think my soul leaves my body. But I have absolutely no energy to give to the thought, because all of me is wrapped up in Cole. "Jesus."

"Trust me to put your wants and needs above my own." Slowly, he draws his finger back, while between my legs, moisture dribbles along my thigh. "I'm a selfish man, but that selfishness means I wanna see you completely strung out. For me." He leans in and slips his tongue between my folds, so his stubbled chin scrapes my clit, and my first release bursts free.

I make a mess of his floor. I make a mess of his jeans, since he's still dressed and kneeling between my legs. But I can't stop what's happening.

I don't have the strength, and I definitely don't have the desire.

"That's one," he rumbles arrogantly. "Easier than I expected, so I'll work harder for the rest."

"Oh god." My lungs clamor for air, but my hips jut back for more. For so, so much more. "Cole…"

"Look to your right."

Too weak to obey, I press my face to the cotton blankets and smother the panting breath I can't quite catch.

To demand my attention, Cole swings his arm back and smacks my ass hard enough to make me scream. And then I fill his hand a second time.

"I said," he rubs where he hit, soothing the burn that is both pleasure and torment. "Look to your right. See what I see."

"What? I… I don't…" Scared, I twist my head and rest on my shoulder, then I peek the way he instructs and find myself reflected in a mirror on the wall.

I see my flushed face, but my bright red cheeks. I see my ass in the air, and a fiery red handprint on my pale skin. I see Cole behind me, his eyes alight with hunger, and his cock standing at painful attention.

I see my shirt, still on. The black fabric, and the skeletal hand holding a flower.

"I'm gonna fuck you just like this." Commanding, exhilarating, Cole pushes up to stand so his cock rests between my ass cheeks, and his finger does magic, such pure, orgasmic magic that short-circuits my brain. "And you're gonna watch. And if at any point you obsess over how this looks instead of what you feel, I'm gonna smack you again."

My breath shudders from his delicious threat. My throat burns dry, but I'm not sure I have the wherewithal to do anything about it. "Okay."

"Don't look away," he orders.

Taking back his finger so I whimper at the loss, he unbuckles his belt and has steel clinking against steel.

Everything remains silent outside our bubble. Like nothing else exists, and it's quite possible we're the only two people alive on the planet.

After tugging the leather from the loops of his jeans, instead of tossing it to the floor and moving on with his zipper, he meets my eyes in the mirror so his stare burns. "You want me to bind your hands, Maya Elizabeth?" He snaps the leather, making me jump. "Maybe your ankles? So when I open you wide and fuck you, you can't do shit but lie there and take it."

I can hardly breathe, though my lungs try. I can barely think, and I'm certain my brain long ago left the building.

Pushing up to my hands, then balancing all my weight on one, I lift my top and struggle as I tug it up. I tangle myself up and work the fabric over my hair, then I free myself and cry when the tight material is gone. Finally, I reach back and unsnap my bra so my breasts fall free and I'm left bare. Naked in every way.

"Maya?" Cole's voice is sharp. "I asked you a question."

"You can bind my ankles." I place my feet together like a good girl and pant when he grins his approval. "I need my hands so I don't fall on my face."

Chuckling, he unsnaps his jeans and pushes them down just far enough to show off a defined V that disappears into his boxers. "So very logical of you, Maya Elizabeth. You have no clue how not to think."

Lowering into a crouch and tossing his shirt off in the same move, he wraps his belt around my ankles and nips the skin at the side of my thigh. "I never knew I had this naughty kindergarten teacher fantasy until I met you."

He tugs the belt impossibly tight and draws a sob from deep inside my chest.

"My kindergarten teacher was a mean, old bitch. But you..." He finishes with the belt and stands. Without pause, he lifts his arm back, swings it down again, and smacks my ass, sending bolts of electricity zinging through my blood. "You're the sexiest teacher I ever met, and if I could, I'd fuck you on your desk and make you cream yourself."

"Cole..." Tears burn my eyes, but I don't mind them. They don't scare me.

"But since I don't wanna be arrested for having sex in a school," he drags the tips of his fingers along my thigh, "I'm gonna fuck you here. In private." He reaches around to his back pocket and slips a condom from his wallet. "I'm gonna make you scream so the neighbors hear. But they don't give a fuck about you, Maya. None of 'em do, so they're not gonna come to help."

"Jesus," I breathe. "Cole..."

"Mmm. I like when you say my name."

He tears the condom open with his teeth and spits the trash to the bed, then unraveling the rubber and discarding the rest of the foil, he pushes his jeans down and slides it over his shaft.

For the first time since we met, I actually get to *see* his cock. Its length, and its terrifying girth. I see the thick veins feeding it blood, and his strong thighs that make it possible for him to move so powerfully.

"Are you ready for me?" He grabs my ass and slaps again, the very same spot, so fire turns to lava and a cry escapes my throat. "You don't want me to go slow, do you?" His eyes hold mine captive in the mirror, his jaw, grinding with barely restrained desire. "No way you want me to go slow."

"I like the way you do it."

My eyes flutter closed, but the sting of his palm on my backside brings them open again. I groan and know, just one thrust, and he'll fling me over the edge of oblivion.

"I like when you take me fast," I rasp past the dryness in my throat. "I like it when you take, without giving me time to adjust."

"Because you're a dirty girl who likes it when it hurts." He nudges me forward so my arms collapse and my weight rests on my chest and shoulder. "You're a sweet little kindergarten teacher who likes it when I fuck you until you cry."

"Yes," I whisper. My eyes close, but instinct has them opening again just in time to catch sight of his hand raised and ready.

"They're open," I rush out. "I'm looking."

"Good." He hits anyway, so the loud crack reverberates through the room. "I want you to watch, Maya Elizabeth. I want you to send us both crazy with your eyes."

"I'm watching."

The backs of my thighs burn, and my ass is on fire from his hand. But I don't fight it. I don't move.

"It's gonna be tighter than usual." He fists his cock and flicks the tip through my wet folds to collect lubrication. "Your legs are closed, babe, which means I'm gonna have to force it." Bending with a grin, he bites my ribs and chuckles. "And we'll both love it."

"God."

I want to cry, but not because I'm sad. I want to weep, but only because I've never felt so desired in my life. Never felt so free.

"Cole, I love you."

Sex aside, taunting and teasing and flirting aside, I know this is where my life is heading. He thinks a shitty, small apartment is something I judge, when really, it's his heart I care about.

I've met those who have nice things but bad intentions.

But he... he's everything they aren't.

"I do," I breathe. "I love you."

"Shit." He drapes his chest across my body and presses a gentle kiss between my shoulder blades. "I was going for this dark and dirty daddy dom thing, and you had to get all sweet on me."

I choke out a laugh and squirm beneath his weight. "Keep doing the dirty stuff," I snigger. "I like it."

"Can I call you Miss Blake?" One last kiss to the center of my spine, then he pushes up and shoves his cock between my folds until I scream. "I wanna pretend you're my kindergarten teacher."

"Oh god!" Tears spring from my eyes and track lines on my cheeks, but my body is on fire in all the best ways. "Cole. Shit."

"I love you too, Maya Elizabeth." He slaps my ass so hard that I explode in his arms, and spasm as my orgasm tears me apart.

He forces my knees to the bed, opening me wide while I cry out, then he thrusts forward with dizzying speed and brings us both to a peak.

It's like fire and ice wage war in my veins.

And all the while, his eyes hold mine captive in the mirror on the wall.

~

A knock at the door wakes me sometime later, when darkness envelops the room, and Cole's warm body cushions mine.

He sleeps with his lips on my brow and his hand on my hip. His after-shave in my lungs, and his warm breath feathering my forehead. It's like I lie in the world's most luxurious sauna.

But my comfort is short-lived when a second knock wakes him with a start.

"Cole!" A man's voice echoes from the hall, then another knock. "Dude!"

"Shit."

I guess he assumes I'm still asleep, because he takes care to slip out from beneath me without letting my head fall. He edges his chest away, and keeps his palm beneath my face until I'm resting on the pillow.

And I let him think I'm asleep because... well, I'm not sure.

"Cole!"

"Fuck. Shut up!" He bounds off the bed and lands on the floor with a thud.

I don't see him collect his clothes, but I feel his movements in the air. The rustle of fabric, and the wind that blows over me from his quick motions.

I lie still, my hands clasped between my naked breasts, and the mois-ture between my legs still sticky after lovemaking and cozying up under blankets. Though my heart pounds from my secrecy—*Why not tell him I'm awake?*—I study the darkness as he hurries to his door, then narrow my eyes when a bar of light from the hall shines across his face and chest.

"What the fuck, Pres?" Cole's voice is hard, unforgiving, as he snarls at his visitor. "It's the middle of the fucking night, dick!"

"It's not even eleven," the man rumbles.

Feet shuffle for a moment, then there's another thud as a hand hits the door as though to push through.

Tension bubbles in the air and grows more palpable after a moment of silence.

"Dude, let me in."

"No. I'm not alone, and you don't get to see her while she sleeps."

With a quick glance my way, though I know he can't see anything but my general shape in the darkness, Cole's throat bobs as he swallows. Then, with a sigh of defeat, he steps out into the hall.

The moment he's out of sight and the door closes all but an inch from locking, I shoot up in bed and tug the sheets up to cover my chest.

"What are you doing, Pres?" Cole's voice travels through the gap in the door. "And why are you here in the middle of the fucking night?"

"It's not the middle of the night!" *Pres* laughs. "The Cole I know is usually just beginning his day about this time. Why are you running banker's hours?"

"Because I'm working all fucking day like a normal, respectable human." Something gently hits the wall, then slowly slides down. In my head, I imagine Cole lowering to sit on the floor. "The Rollers have given me a real opportunity here, Pres. It's legit, and I'm gonna do what I can to make sure it works."

"And while you're off living your dreams," his friend rumbles, "you leave me out in the cold. You didn't stop to think about how our team stops operating once you bail? Jesus, Cole. You fucked me over and didn't even give me the benefit of a warning first."

"I'm not trying to fuck you over," he responds with an exasperated exhale. "I'm just trying not to steal cars anymore. Box is trouble, Pres. He'll throw either of us under the bus *any* night of the week, so why the hell should I stay there when I have something real offered to me over here?"

"Because I'm over there! Because you're my best friend, and you dropped me like last week's dinner. Now you're here, shacking up with a chick? You changed really fuckin' fast, man."

"I'm not shacking up."

His brush-off, his denial, makes my stomach jolt. I mean, he's not lying; we're not even close to living together. But I still exist. I'm still here.

"I'm exploring something that feels right. Something that feels really fucking important. I'm not walking away from that because of Box."

"What about for me?" his friend counters.

With a fresh new slice of panic turning my stomach, I push my sheets off and use the slim beam of hallway light to help me find a shirt to slip on.

"Won't you come back for me?" the other voice presses.

"You don't want me to be happy?"

Cole continues to have the right answers. He stands up for us every single time, and yet, insecurity rushes through my blood and makes my hands shake as I button one of his shirts over my bare torso.

"You would have me leave the gym, and Maya, all so we could go back to being car thieves? Pres! You're better than that, man. And I sure as hell know I am, too."

"I've still gotta pay *my* bills, Cole! *I* didn't get an offer to roll around on the ground all day. And I definitely don't have a beautiful woman in my bed right now that I make gaga faces for."

"Pres—"

"I'm happy for you. Really, I am. But I would've liked for you to still wanna hang out sometimes. And I definitely would've liked a little notice so I could figure out my business and not risk starvation."

"You need money?" Feet shuffle in the hall until my brows come together in a frown. "I'll lend you some to get through. You don't even have to pay me back."

"No, I don't want your fuckin' money." Those sounds of ruffling feet stop, and for a full minute, silence hangs heavy in the air. "I've got a job coming up. *Fifty*-thousand-dollar payday."

My heart stops in my throat and makes it impossible to breathe.

"That's a cool twenty-five for you to set up your life over here."

"Pres—"

"Don't say no yet," he cuts in. "Hear me out. Just one night. One run. It's a '69 Chevrolet Corvette. Four hundred and thirty horses. Sunflower yellow. Only two have *ever* been sold. She's kept in an airtight garage, with security up the wazoo and enough guards that the president's people probably ask them for tips. *But*," he rushes, as though maybe Cole opened his mouth to interject, "they have this thing going on. A big party, so the property will be opened up, and security will be run thin."

"No, stupid. Security will be *tightened*. They'll hire more to make it work. You have no chance of getting anywhere near that car, Pres."

"Keypad alarm system on the garage," he pushes on. "Keypad security on the estate gates. The property is approximately ten hectares with a winding driveway and three exits. Only two of them are secure. The third isn't documented, and no one outside the family knows it exists."

"Except you," Cole groans. "Of course you know."

"I pulled schematics from their private hard drives. This shit hasn't even been filed with state regulators, bruh. They're internal files only, and available only to those who have clearance."

"Except you," Cole repeats. "You got access."

"Fuck yes I did. I pulled those files as easily as we pull up the McDonald's app. I ordered me some blueprints and a side of fries all before I came here tonight."

Instead of being mad, Cole chuckles and softens toward his friend.

Which means, of course, that my pulse skitters in my chest.

He's going to say yes. He's going to join in on this adventure and break my heart.

"You're obsessed with junk food, man. Which is ridiculous, considering how small you are."

"I'm not small! You're just abnormally large, and I have a faster metabolism than you."

Then his tone turns serious, so I feel the change in the atmosphere from here.

"Come on this one last run with me. We drive in, we drive out. We do the job in under seven minutes if you follow the plan. Then we load her up in the truck, we take our fifty-k, and you sit pretty while you wait for your title belt and the money that comes with it."

I approach the door and set my hand on the knob.

Tell them I'm here. Tell them I can hear every word they say.

"You can't possibly have cash to throw around yet, Miller. No way are you rolling in it."

"I still have money left over from our last run," Cole mumbles. "And the Kincaids are paying me a little on the side to cover my bills. Once I go pro, that changes and I take winnings. Then we're talking millions. Lots of millions, once I reach the top."

"But until you get there, twenty-five thousand dollars will set you up. It'll get you from here to there, and you won't have to worry about making ends meet in the meantime."

Silence hangs for a beat. Then, "Come with me, Cole. It's easy money, and you know you could do with the cushion."

Clear your throat, Maya! Tell them you're here.

"No." Finality in his tone, Cole shuts everything down. "I made a promise, and I will not break it."

"A promise to a girl?" Pres laughs, like the thought is ridiculous.

"That's cute... until you can't afford to buy her dinner, then she dumps your broke ass and moves on to someone with more to spend."

"No, dickhead. I made a promise to the Kincaids. I made a commitment to *them* and to the career they've offered me. *They're* reason enough for me to say no. But I made a commitment to Maya too. I intend to keep it and become a better man."

"Maya..." Pres says my name so nerves ricochet in my stomach. "She's that important?"

"She's *everything*. She's where it all starts and ends. And maybe you don't understand it. Fuck knows I don't either. But I *feel* it, so I'm gonna grab on and hold tight."

"Even in the zombie apocalypse?"

I frown at Preston's odd, uncertain question.

But, "Yeah," Cole responds. "Especially then."

I can't stand in the dark any longer and pretend I can't hear them. I've become the sneak myself. So I open the door and blind myself with the harsh light in the hall.

My eyes hurt, and my brow wrinkles as I squint. Then slowly, as they adjust, I find the man clearly named Preston sitting on one side of the hall with his knees pulled up and a can of soda between his feet.

His gaze, bluer than the ocean and watchful enough to make the air stop in my lungs, lingers, inevitably dropping to my bare legs once he's done staring at my face.

"Maya," he breathes the word and brings his eyes back up. "I presume."

On my side of the hall, Cole's head wrenches around. He pops to his feet with frightening speed and pulls me into his arms, though I don't miss the way he turns us to shield me from his friend. "Babe?" He cups my face and looks down to catch my eyes. "What are you—"

"I was listening." I can't lie. When I demand honesty from him, I refuse to be the person with half-truths in return. "I was awake when you woke up," I rush out. "I saw you get up."

"It's okay—"

"I stayed silent while you answered the door, and then I listened to your entire conversation. I'm sorry, Cole."

I love how his hands hold me close. And better, how his arms wrap me up tight. I love that, despite my confession, his lips come to my forehead, and his chest presses close to mine.

"I was scared of what you would say to his question," I admit on a shudder, "so I stayed quiet and listened."

"It's fine, babe." He buzzes his lips along my forehead. "I promise, it's o—"

"Wow."

Pres' deep voice makes my stomach jump. His very presence makes me nervous for more reasons than just Cole's new direction in life.

"She's just a well of sinful confession, huh?" He tilts to the side, so when I look just a little to my right, I find him resting on his elbow and a taunting smirk crossing his face. "Ever considered just *not* incriminating yourself?"

"Preston..." Cole grumbles. "Stop it."

"What?" He straightens out with a laugh and presses his back against the brick wall. "No one was peeling her nails just now to get a confession."

"Being honest all the time isn't a—"

"Have you ever considered just not stealing cars?" I step back from Cole and come around to face his friend. I don't know why I notice the fraying on his shirt, or the hole on the knee of his jeans. The staining on his fingers that denotes hard work, but the glint in his eyes that promises brains behind his little thug act. "You could get a normal job instead. That way, there's nothing to confess when you're being questioned."

"Oh!" He coughs out a taunting laugh and shoves up to his feet. When his back is straight and his chest opens wide, I find he's taller than me by a long shot, and wears black all over.

It's only right now that a thought clicks in my mind: *They dress in black to make it easier to steal at night.*

"She's got sass, Miller. Good looks, yeah... you've always been into the beautiful types. But the talking back?" Preston teases. "I *never* would've picked that for you."

"Don't speak to her if you're gonna be disrespectful." Cole turns to stand in front of me again. Always protecting. Always the head of the spear. "Don't screw this up, man, because I really fucking want you and her to get along."

"But we'll *never* get along."

He says it so easily, so coldly, my heart trips in my chest.

Preston wanders to the right and stops only when our eyes meet. "You're never gonna like me, huh, Princess? Because I'm a bad influence." He tilts his head toward Cole. "He's a good boy with a brand-new athletic career laid out for him like a red carpet, and I'm that good-for-nothing runt everyone wishes would leave him alone."

"You're projecting." Swallowing my nerves, I stand taller under this man's stare.

He's intimidating and dark. His eyes are piercing, and his smile isn't friendly. All things that scare the crap out of me. But Cole is all of those things, too. He wears those same barriers to keep people away. But I know now, beneath the show he puts on, in Cole's case, is an incredibly sweet man. Rough around the edges, but selfless beyond compare.

"I don't even know you, Preston. I can't possibly know what you're good for. But I know Cole is extremely fond of you."

"Fond!" Insensitive to the late hour, Preston coughs out a booming laugh. "He's *fond* of me?"

"Pres—"

"We've been brothers a long fucking time, cutie. We've had each other's backs. I'd say I'm quite *fond* of him, too."

"Preston!" Cole steps between us when Preston starts forward, slamming a heavy fist to the center of his chest. "You need to chill the fuck out."

"I'm chill!" He slaps Cole's hand away and continues closer to watch me. Like a hunter and his prey. "I'm also *fond* of him. But you," he brings his attention to Cole, "aren't coming with me to collect that Corvette, are you?"

"No." Final, commanding, Cole shakes his head. "I'm not. Because I have too much to lose now if we fuck it up. But why don't you come in?" He reaches back to place a hand on my hip, still acting as my shield. My cover. "Have you eaten? Have you slept?"

"I'm fi—"

"Let me talk you out of taking that job." He grabs his friend by the collar and yanks him so hard, my breath catches in my throat.

But instead of getting mad when he's flung through the door, Preston only huffs and fixes his shirt.

Cole tells him, "I've got bologna in the fridge and a loaf of bread I bought just this morning."

Steering me through the door and shutting it at my back, he presses a gentle kiss to my temple. Warming. Soothing. Then a whispered, "Please stay."

Surprised, I pull back and look up at him.

"I want you to stay," he murmurs. "I want you to put some fucking pants on, then come spend time with my best friend. He's a good man, I swear."

My heart throbs in my throat, and nerves swish in my belly, but I can't say no, even if I wanted to venture out into this side of town at eleven at night.

I nod. "I'll stay."

Slipping out of his arms and making a beeline for my cutoffs that lay discarded on the floor—just two inches from Preston's scuffed boot, and when I look up, his questioning brow—I snag the denim and hurry back the way I came.

Stopping beside Cole before I move through the door to the bathroom, I place my palm on his stomach and give him a small smile.

His life is unconventional, and friends dropping by in the middle of the night is crazy. But he loves that man, and I love him. So we're going to make it work.

Stepping onto the tips of my toes, I press a kiss to his tense jaw, and smile. "Relax. I'll make him a sandwich so he loves me too."

He snorts. "Food will buy his love. I promise."

"So, this game is a little like Slap," Cole rumbles on the bed beside me.

He sits on one corner, cross-legged like a child, while Preston shoves the small circle table across the room and places it in front of us, then drags a chair closer and flops down on the other side.

Already, with a sandwich in his hand, he softens to my presence.

"But these cards have pictures on them," Cole continues—for my benefit, since Preston obviously knows the game already. "Every card has a bunch of different little ones. Our job is to find the matching pair. First person to snatch the card up and label the match wins that hand. Person with the most cards at the end wins the game."

"He cheats," Preston speaks around a mouthful of bread. "Like, he has no fuckin' shame about it. He would throw his mama in the trash if it meant he could win. So don't sit there all cute and shit and think he won't destroy you, too."

"First of all," Cole rolls his eyes. "I would throw my mama in the trash for the sake of hearing the thud when she hits the bottom. Second," he points to his friend, "stop calling Maya cute. First time was free. Second comes with a warning. Don't let there be a third. And finally," he turns to me and leans across to press a puckered kiss to my lips, "I don't cheat. He's a sore loser who makes up stories to feel better about it. He's also insecure about his height. His parents were short."

"Dude!" Preston shoves the table so the top smacks Cole's elbow and elicits a hiss of pain from him. "I'm not short! Five-eleven is entirely fucking adequate. You're just abnormally stupid."

He takes a hefty bite of his sandwich and looks to me with a wink. "I feel as though you've been misled, Maya. He can act like a decent dude when the stakes are high enough. But drop him in the middle of a game of cards, and you'll see him for who he really is." He flips the first on the stack and purses his lips. "It's not gonna be pretty."

"Just turn the next fucking card, dickhead." Instead of waiting, Cole reaches out and does it himself.

Before I even see the images revealed, he slams his hand down and shouts "CAT!" so loud, I jump.

He drags his winnings closer, while across from him, Preston flattens his lips as though to say '*See? I told you.*'

"Moon!" Cole screeches on the next card flip.

Knowing I have no chance at this game, I give up caring and instead watch the other two play.

"What do you do when you're not stealing cars?" I ask Preston.

"Door!" he shouts loud enough to wake the neighbors. Then he meets my eyes and grins. "I like your '*getting to know you*' segue, Maya. But it's not necessary."

"It is necessary." And because both men watch *me*, I'm the first to see the pairing on the next set of cards. "Hearts." Reaching across, I take my winnings and smirk when their eyes snap back to the pile. "You're Cole's best friend. Albeit a little short."

Preston shoots filthy daggers at Cole, who only giggles.

"So since I kinda like Cole, in that *my heart does weird things when he's around* kinda way, I feel inclined to know his friends."

"To know who to keep him away from?"

"So I know who we're having over for dinner on all the important occasions, dummy. Do you have a girlfriend?"

"Jesus." He glares across at Cole. "She doesn't fuck around, huh? Cat." He takes his cards and brings his gaze back to me. "I like to code. It's a skill that helps me steal the newer model computer-run cars. Cows." He slaps Cole's hand away before he loses his win. "But when I'm not doing that, I like to create software."

"What kind of software?" I press. "Games? Technical stuff that helps other people?"

"Anything I fuckin' want. Bicycle." He picks up his sandwich and takes a noisy bite. "Often, we're born, we go to school, and we learn shit that we can later use in adult life, right?" He tilts his head toward Cole. "He was born with a natural ability to drive and fight. Like, it's insane how he can walk into both careers and just *know* what to do."

"It's because I have such superb control of my body." Smug, Cole bounces his brows. "Makes me a monster in bed, too."

"Charming," I drawl. Then to Preston, I say, "He got choked out in training today. Like, went to actual sleep in another man's arms."

"Maya Elizabeth! *Cat!*"

Laughter rolls along my chest as Cole takes his cards and adds them to his pile.

"Well, the same way he can do that shit without formal training, it kinda turns out I was born with an ability with computers. Doll." Preston grabs his card before Cole can. "My brain knows shit I had no clue it knows." Then he stares deep into my eyes and grins. "Though, I want it on record that I'm equally skilled in the bedroom."

"No!" Cole reaches across and slaps his friend in the center of his forehead. "You don't look at her and say that." Then he turns to me. "You don't stare back and think about him in bed."

"I didn't do anything!" Giggling, I reach across to steal a half dozen cards while they're distracted with each other. "He was soliciting me."

"Then we have *No Solicitation* signs made up, and plaster them on your ass." He turns to Preston and points. "No."

"You slept with a man earlier today, asshole. It would seem your interests lie elsewhere."

"I won't tell you again," he snarls.

"So, this job." I speak louder than necessary. Awkward, when I don't really need to be. "A 1969 Chevrolet Corvette. Who does it belong to?"

More serious now, Preston brings his blue-eyed gaze my way. "His name is Rodrick Randal. Tycoon high-flying motherfucker. He's not a nice guy, so I don't feel bad about stealing from him."

"Pres—"

"Do you only steal from bad people?" I already know the answer— they tried to steal from Jack Reilly, after all—but I pose the question and wait to see what this man will look into my eyes and say. "Only the not-so-nice?"

"No." He claps his hand over the pile of cards. "Dogs. And I take from whoever has the car. I don't organize the jobs, Maya, I just deliver and use that money to eat. We could steal from an asshole this week, and the fuckin' pope next week. I'm gonna do the job no matter who it is."

"And you don't concern yourself with karma? Aren't you scared of what will happen to your future while you do these things?"

He barks out a laugh and slaps his hand over the card pile. "Palm trees. And no," he drags his hand back to take possession of his pair, "I don't worry myself about the future. Because if I don't steal today, I die of hunger tomorrow. I have no room in my life for cosmic clap backs."

"You sound like Cole." I bring my legs up and cross them on the bed. "The *I need to do it or starve* thing. There are other, safer jobs out there, ya know?"

"A moving speech from a rich girl who's never gone hungry." He looks me up and down, almost dismissive, but without the mean edge. "You clearly come from money. Tell me your story, Maya. Let me pick it apart the way you dissect mine."

"I don't—"

"Both of her folks are rich-ass lawyers," Cole supplies, throwing me under the bus. "They each have a firm of their own. Maya has a law degree, too."

"Undergraduate," I grumble. "And no desire to cling to my parent's purse strings."

"But you have parents," Preston inserts. "And they have purse strings. Must be nice."

"I don't—"

"*Dog*!" Cole slams his hand down hard enough to make the table rattle. And because I startle and growl, he looks my way with a sheepish smile. "Sorry, babe."

"I'm not dismissing the fact you had a tough upbringing." I look to Preston. "Either of you. But you're grown men now. It's time to make grown-up decisions so your future is brighter than '*might go to jail next week*'."

"Jail has a bed and three square meals a day," Preston quips. "Heating. Cooling. A gym with free membership."

"For God's sake," I roll my eyes. "You'll look for any excuse to keep doing what you're doing."

"And you have an inheritance from your grandmother," Cole counters.

When my head comes around and my eyes burn against his, he smirks. "How much money is in that trust fund, Maya Elizabeth?"

"I have no freakin' clue! I can't access it. But you know what I'm doing instead? Working a low-paying job I really like, and having the time of my life. What are *you* doing?"

"Sleeping in a man's arms, evidently. Cats." Preston snags his cards and smiles deviously as the main pile grows smaller. "Why don't you have access to your trust fund?"

"That's none—"

"Because her lawyer parents want to control her," Cole butts in... again. "They think she's wasting her talent and working a job that's below her." Then he flashes a wicked grin. "Kinda like the speech she's giving you right now. If she had something of yours, she would withhold it and bribe you for compliance to get it back."

"You're an ass." I push up from my spot on the bed and slap Cole's hand away when he reaches out. His fingertips brush my thigh, and Preston's eyes scan my legs with hungry intensity. "My parents wanting me to conform and work in law is not the same as me asking you idiots to work *within* the law. They're two entirely different things, and never have I emotionally manipulated you to get my way."

I head to Cole's mini fridge and bend to peruse the contents. I guess I was hoping for soda, but all I find is bottled water. So I take one out and crack the lid open, only to turn and find *both* men studying my ass.

"My parents are withholding my inheritance," I tell Preston dryly. "Money I'll never see, and belongings I'll never get back. It is what it is, and there's nothing anyone can do about it."

"There's always something to be done about it." Like I'm stupid, Preston scoffs and swings his gaze back toward Cole. "Want me to reroute the trust fund?"

"Wait—"

"You can do that?"

He makes the *psht* noise in the back of his throat. "Easier than winning this game against you. Airplanes!" He takes his cards and glances toward me. "All I need is your parents' names. Social security numbers, if you've got them, but I can dig and get those myself easy enough."

"No!" I set my bottle on the counter and scowl. "Don't search for my parents' information." Then I glare at Cole. "Don't steal from my parents!"

"But they're actually stealing from you," Preston argues, while across from him, Cole takes the last of the pile of cards and finishes the game. "It's not stealing to take back what belongs to you. It's... redirecting."

"It's grand larceny," I snap. "It's punishable by jail time, and you," I point at Cole, "do not have my blessing to touch any of this. I'm not asking for your help! I told you a story one time, and now you won't leave it alone."

"What can I say?" Collecting his pile and tidying them into a stack, he begins counting. "They've pissed me off. And I love you. So sue me for wanting to help you."

"I'm not asking for it." Then I turn my snarling attention to Preston. "Step away from my business and leave it alone. Count your damn cards and eat your sandwich."

"No one would have to know," he singsongs. "The account they're keeping your money in would simply..." he wiggles his fingers the way a magician might. "Vanish."

"I said no." Grabbing my water and heading back to the bed, I sit on the corner so the mattress bounces, then I pick up my measly few cards to count. "I'm asking the both of you to drop this topic forever. It annoys me to revisit it time and time again, and I'm tired of reducing my grandmother's existence to the presence—or lack—of money and a few diaries. She was far more important than that, so I'm done discussing it." Then I look to Preston. "And since we're on the topic, stop stealing cars! Jesus, man."

"Gotta buy my bread somehow, Cutie." He counts cards and finishes with a grin. "Twenty-six."

I frown. "I've got nine."

"Thirty-seven, bitches." Cole throws his pile into the middle, then turns to me. "I wasn't calling you a bitch, baby. It was just a phrase."

"You fuckin' cheated!" Preston shoves to his feet and leans across the table, then he slaps his palm to Cole's forehead and elicits a snarl from his lips. "No way you got thirty-seven wins, dick. And you cheated too," he brings his gaze my way. "I saw you win twice. Nine means you stole."

"I did not." *I absolutely did.* "Where are you sleeping tonight, Preston?" I cast a look toward the clock beside Cole's bed. "It's late and I'm exhausted."

"You inviting me in?" Straightening out, he smirks and wanders around the table to me. "One bed, plus me and you. Maybe I'll become a better man, too, if you shot me a little action."

"Hey!" Cole shoves to his feet. "Dude, watch it."

"So you're both crude and disgusting." I throw my nine measly cards to the middle of the table. "Color me surprised." Then I turn to my hands and knees and head back toward my pillow. "I'm going to sleep."

"And you're leaving." Cole rushes around to his friend and slams a hand to his chest before he can climb into bed beside me. "Don't test me, Pres. Friendship only stretches so far."

"You're grumpy." Scowling, he turns on his heels and heads across the room. "First you get possessive and won't let me drive your car. Now you get possessive and won't let me—"

"Don't even say the fucking words." He's angry, and yet, he chuckles. "Don't go there, man."

"It was nice to meet you, Maya." Preston picks up his car keys and his half-consumed soda. "I mean, except for the lectures on morality and whatnot."

"Uh-huh." A yawn stretches across my face and makes my eyes water. "It was nice meeting you, too. I mean, except for the objectification and mild sexual harassment."

"It's how I roll," he sniggers.

Stopping at the door and opening it a crack, he turns back to Cole and pulls him in for a hug as I watch on. "You're doing the right thing. You're a pussy, but she's cute enough to turn a man."

"Get the fuck outta here." Cole's words say *go*, but his hug says *stay*. "Don't do that job, Pres. Stay home and sleep instead. Randal's too protected for you to get in. And he doesn't count on cops for keeping the peace, so you won't be facing jail time on this one. You'll be looking down the barrel of a gun."

"Nah. I've got it worked out." He pulls back and claps Cole's shoulder. "Seven minutes, in and out. Fifty-thousand-dollar payday." I see his smile, but behind that, sad eyes that momentarily flicker across to me. "Box wants you on this one. He wants you bad, so if you change your mind—"

"I won't." He drags a deep breath in, then exhales on a sigh. "I can't. Tell Box I'm out for good. I have stuff happening for me here, and I'm not gonna mess that up."

"Fine." One last hug between friends. Between brothers. Then Preston steps back. "I'll see you around, Maya."

"Bye." I slide my hands under my cheek and pull my knees higher. "Stop stealing cars. Move here and hang with us more often. I'm kinda fond of you, too."

Chuckling, he makes his way through the door. "Uh-huh. I'm leaving before I sexually harass your girlfriend. But if you ever break up—"

"She doesn't have my blessing to come looking for you," Cole growls. "Call me tomorrow, okay? We'll get you away from Box too."

Soft laughter filters from the hall as Preston walks away. "I don't need to be saved, Miller. But I'll see you around. I'll visit more."

Slowly, as the sound of footsteps on the stairs echoes back to us, Cole closes the door and slides a chair beneath the handle to secure it locked. Then he flips the lights out and drapes the room in darkness.

I hold my breath for only a moment until I hear him.

"Babe?"

"Over here." I steer him with the sound of my voice. I beckon him with a whisper, and a thousand years of worry sitting heavy on my heart. "Come this way."

He moves to my side of the bed and hitches his leg over so he climbs across without crushing me. Then dropping down at my back, he hugs me to his chest and pulls me close to make me his little spoon.

"Are you okay?" He rests on one elbow and uses his free hand to stroke the ball of my shoulder. "I'm sorry we woke you up."

"It's okay." I turn to my back and hum with pleasure when his hand slides beneath my shirt. His palm is like fire on my ribs. His fingertips, like magic on the swell of my breast. "I enjoyed meeting your friend."

"He's a great guy." He leans closer, so I feel his breath on my tongue just a half a beat before his lips touch down. "Don't judge him because of the things he steals. His heart is good."

"Kinda reminds me of this other guy I know."

I open my legs, and groan when he climbs across. His cock is rock-hard, and his hands make quick work of flicking my jean shorts open.

"I love you." Tilting my head back, I whimper when his teeth feast on the warm skin of my neck. "I'm sorry for listening to your conversation earlier."

"I love you too." He nips my neck and works my shorts lower. "I have no conversations you can't listen to anymore. I'm in this, Maya." Growing impatient, he tugs my shorts down so the denim scrapes my skin. "I'm digging in and staying here with you forever."

"Good."

My pulse quickens and my breath comes faster. Then I whimper when my shorts are gone and I feel all of him pressed to my core.

"I want you," I whisper. "Now."

"Now?" He rolls his hips, teasing and tempting. "Right now?"

"Please." I slip my hands into his shorts and circle his cock so he can feel what I feel. So he can hurt and pant and want so much more. "Without the condom... if you want." Despite the darkness, I open my eyes and swallow down my nerves. "I'm on birth control. I swear."

"I trust you." Lowering, he presses his lips to mine and takes. Takes. Takes. "Forever, Maya Elizabeth. I've got you, and you've got me. It's the way it should be."

Cole

BROTHERHOOD

I work hard inside the Rollin On Gym. I turn up with the sun in the morning, and I go home with it in the evenings. I roll with every damn fighter in the gym, and I earn my keep so Jack can be proud, and Evie can know she chose right.

Aiden appoints himself my manager, and Jack assigns himself my very own personal ass-kicker. Because maybe I'm strong, and maybe I work my ass off to prove I belong. But he's the champion for a reason.

He's got skills I can only hope to someday achieve.

"I have your next fight lined up." At the end of another long day in the cage, Aiden snags a towel from the matted floor and brings it up to mop his sweaty brow.

He's not one of those '*do as I say, not as I do*' coaches who sits on the side and gets fat. He rolls too. He kicks my ass on the daily, and taps in after Jack is done with me.

"This one's bigger than the last." He lowers his towel and looks across to catch my eyes. "It's got a payday."

"Already?" My heart skips at the thought. It's one thing for them to pay me just enough to cover my bills. That already makes me feel legit as hell. But to compete in a fight that comes with a purse? "That's quick, Coach."

"You afraid?" He drops his towel and bends to collect his bottle of water. "Got cold feet?"

"No. I'm just..." I mirror Aiden's moves and pick up my own water. "Surprised, I guess."

"Evie's coming home in the winter, so I want you to have won a few by then. Show her what we've accomplished while she's gone. Luckily, being from this gym means you get to jump a few steps others can't."

"So... nepotism?" I tease. "Regular folks have to claw their way up every single inch of a mountain. But because I'm in with the Kincaids, I get to cruise the mountain a little easier?"

"It's not easier. It's still your face at risk in the fight. Still your reputation on the line. Either you'll walk away with two wins and no losses, or you'll limp away a loser. Me having industry contacts just means we get to walk through doors that others have no clue even exist. That's what *we*," he nods toward another dueling pair—Bobby and one of his students, "have worked so hard for. Either you want it or you don't."

"I do."

The second he turns away and starts walking, I dash from my spot and follow. "I want it, Coach. How much is the purse?"

"Twenty thousand dollars." He glances back before heading into the hall. "Winner takes fifteen, loser gets five. I take twenty percent of whatever you make."

"So I walk away with five grand no matter what?"

"No. You walk away with four grand no matter what. I stand to make a thousand if you lose, and three thousand if you win."

He moves into the kitchen and turns back when I stop in the doorway. "But I suggest you win, because if you do, you get another fight. Bigger purse. More opportunities."

"Fuck yes, I'll do it," I rush out. "When do we go to the big time?"

"We've got Ben running ahead of you." He reaches into the fridge and swaps his water for a Gatorade. "Maybe you don't like it, but he's family, he's younger, and he has years more experience on you. He'll get a chance at the title long before you. But that doesn't mean you can't make a damn good living on smaller gigs."

"Fifteen grand for my second fight?" I scoff. "Yeah, I think I'll make do. Ben can go on ahead, I don't mind. When's my fight?"

"A week from tomorrow." He closes the fridge and moves to the bench seat in the middle of the room. "It's short notice, I know. But the offer only came this morning; some team in the city wants to take a swing at the Rollers. I don't think you'll suffer for it, though. You work hard, and your consistency means you'll be ready. I think you've got it in the bag."

"I'll make sure of it." I wander closer with my water in one hand, and lifting a leg across the seat, I drop down across from him and rest my elbows on the table. "Where is it? What do I need to do?"

"You just keep being inside this gym every day until I say you can stop. We'll work until the day before, then you get to rest. Eat as much as you can, because the other guy is about ten pounds heavier than you. The fight's at a small stadium in the city, so we'll drive up the morning of, and you touch gloves at eight that night."

"Shitttttt." Nerves tickle my stomach and make my hands shake, but a long smile flits across my lips. "It's real."

"It's real." He picks up his Gatorade and waits for me to raise my bottle. "Your first payday's coming, Miller. You've worked for it."

"You're doing this for your daughter," I laugh. "You wouldn't fast-track shit or talk to contacts if not for her."

"Maybe not." He taps his drink to mine and brings it back for a sip. "But since I'm here doing it anyway, you may as well benefit. Change is coming to the fight circuit, Cole. The committee's ruffling feathers, and the younger generation of fighters isn't pleased. Something big has been brewing, so you better get in now while you can."

"I'm in. I'm here." It's already the end of the day, but I push to my feet and snatch up my water. "Fuck, Coach. I'm here. I'll be here every damn day so you know I've earned it." I turn toward the door. "You want me to roll with Reilly again today? I haven't made him tap yet."

Shaking his head, he rests on his elbows and chuckles. "Try again tomorrow. You can go home for now and get some rest."

"You sure? It's only six, so I can put in a few more and—"

"Ruin your tomorrow." His eyes shoot to the doorway and turn somewhat... *dopey* when a blonde woman with long, wavy locks and an hourglass body strides through.

Christina Kincaid. The wife he loves more than he loves air.

I become entirely redundant when she circles the table and makes a beeline for him. And that redundancy becomes voyeurism when she parks her ass on the table and sets her feet in his lap.

They're done with me, and I'm not all that interested in watching my coach make the *fuck me* eyes for his beautiful wife. So, having been dismissed, I turn on my heels and head toward the locker room just off the hallway.

I find mine and yank it open, then I snatch my phone and find it full.

Missed calls.

Messages from Pres.

Messages from Maya.

I open hers first and grin as she tells me a story of the Reilly kid who has become her class clown.

He's an attention-seeker. A peacock of the same ilk as the family he comes from. He's in lurrrrve with his Miss Blake, and according to her, was asking today why she was seen in town kissing his fighter.

His fighter.

I type a fast response that is basically what I would say to the grown Reilly if he asked the same question, but I tone it down for the five-year-old. Then I add a little something extra: *Come on a date with me? Tonight. Be ready in twenty minutes, and I'll swing by and get you. Wear something I can easily move aside. Panties optional. I feel bad every time I tear them, so it's best if you just go without.*

I love you.

Then I add a winky face and snicker as I hit send.

Navigating to Preston's messages, I read:

"Box is pissed. He's throwing his dick around and talking some shit, so stay over there in your tiny-ass town and ignore the noise from the city. I'll work on smoothing it over."

Frowning, I hit dial, then speaker, then I head to the showers and start undressing.

I have a date in twenty minutes, which means I multitask, or I ignore the Box issue altogether.

"Yeah?" Preston's voice echoes along the line as I push my shorts off and step under the hot stream of water. "You good, Miller?"

"I'm fine. I'm at the gym." I set my phone on the frame of the shower and pump soap into my palm. "You need to get away from Box, too. He's pissed at me, which means he'll come for you when he realizes I'm not bluffing about being out."

"I'm not leaving. I'm boosting the Corvette and getting my big payday. I was just warning you so you know to stay away and let things cool off for a while."

"He's not gonna tolerate me being gone." I bite out. "He wants his driver back, and I'm not willing. You can drive, Pres, but you're not getting that Corvette out on your own. This whole fucking job is doomed, so you gotta stop being a stubborn asshole and just walk."

"Uh-huh. I'll walk... *after* I get my fifty thousand dollars. What the hell are you doing?"

"Showering." I step back under the water and wash away the soap I've lathered all over. "I'm picking Maya up in twenty minutes and taking her out. I got some good news today, so I'm celebrating."

"Oh yeah?" His voice turns more chipper. "The golden boy got more good news. I'm so surprised. What's happening?"

I roll my eyes and know, beneath the teasing, is a guy who really thinks my life is blessed compared to his. "I got a fight. A paid one with a decent purse."

"No shit! When?"

"A week from tomorrow." I cup my hands and collect enough water to wash my face. "Twenty-thousand-dollar purse. Winner takes three-quarters, loser takes the other."

"That's the day after my job," he murmurs. Then, "Wait. So you get paid five thousand dollars *just* for turning up? Jesus, Cole! Do they have a division for guys like me?"

"You mean midget nerds?" I tease. "I'm sure they do... in the circus. Want me to call around and ask?"

"You're an asshole," he snickers. "I'm driving, and you're naked, so I'm not really digging this conversation. Is Maya busy tonight? I might wanna come on over and... come on over."

"I'm gonna kill you." Dropping my hands, I stare at my phone like it's nothing more than a steaming pile of shit. "I'm never letting you near her again."

He barks out a guffawing laugh. "You get jealous so quickly. You know she's into you. I'm hanging up, but I'm glad to hear you're taking her somewhere nice. Show her a good time. She's a good girl."

"*My* good girl," I snarl. "Stay away from Box. Start a new life. Go code something brilliant and sell it to Elon Musk. Life'll get good for you then."

"Yeah sure," he drawls. "I'm on it. I'll talk to you later. Enjoy your night of romance, bro. Think of me while you're slamming her."

"You're fuckin' sick!"

With wet hands and pent-up aggression, I kill the call and drop a puddle of water on my screen, then I go back to showering and finish up in less than a minute.

Switching off the taps and snatching a towel, I dry off and get dressed in fresh jeans and a shirt. I slip on a pair of socks, then my boots.

It feels odd wearing shoes in this gym, now that I'm accustomed to bare feet.

I stop by the mirror to make sure I'm dressed and decent, then I head back and snag my phone. Grabbing my wallet and keys from my locker, I loop my bag over my shoulder last and lope into the hall.

Passing the kitchen and finding Aiden's wife sitting in his lap, I smile and keep going, thinking it's lucky Evie's away at college and not here to see her parents fuck in public.

Could be traumatic.

I dash past the cage to find Jack rolling with someone—I have no clue who—while his overly pregnant wife watches on. Which probably means the five-year-old is here too, and if we cross paths, chances are he'll beat my ass because of the things I do to his beautiful Miss Blake when the lights are out.

With a giddy grin and that thought fresh in mind, I lope out of the gym and count cars until I reach mine.

The irony isn't lost on me that I'm parked right beside the Mustang I was once supposed to steal. It's still so shiny and perfect. So untouchable. And now it's the very symbol that marks my emancipation from a life I had no clue I wanted to be free of.

If it wasn't for Maya nagging at me to want better, I'm not sure I'd have thought to try something else. If it wasn't for meeting her, I fully expect I would be sitting with Pres right now, going over the plans to steal a rare Corvette from a dude whose bad attitude makes it easier for us to risk karma.

Beeping my Mustang open and turning away from Jack's, I slip into the front seat and check my phone when it chirps with a message from Maya.

"I'm ready. I'm starving. And I wore panties, because I'm not that easy."

Of course she did.

"See you in a minute." Hitting send, I toss my phone to the passenger seat and switch the engine on, then I'm on the move, pulling out of the parking space and slowly rambling through the gym parking lot.

Slowly, because there are kids in this place every day, dozens of them; most of whom have the same last name, while the rest are related to them, or go to the same school.

The owners of the Rollin On Gym might lead a life of pro fighting and ruthless training, but they're family men at heart. They spew obscenities between the hours of nine till three, they smash other grown men until they bleed, and I'm quite certain they fuck their wives wherever they can find privacy. But the second school lets out and the kids wander in, all that shit goes out the window, and we're suddenly running a G-rated establishment.

It's sick and twisted in a totally wholesome way.

I love it.

Exiting the parking lot and ambling onto the street, I cruise only a couple blocks over. My apartment is on the other side of town, but Maya's is close enough to throw rocks toward.

Music plays softly on my stereo, and my gas tank... runs a little low. But payday is coming up, which means soon, life will be good again.

I pull onto Maya's street, and grin when I find her standing on the curb. Indicating left and rolling to a stop, I lean across the passenger seat to catch sight of her tempting legs. "Sexiest woman I've ever picked up on a corner."

But when she crouches to look through my window with a scowl, I snicker. "You're the only woman I've picked up on a corner. But still."

"And I'm gonna remain the *only* woman you pick up. For the rest of your life." Opening the door and dropping into the passenger seat, she fishes my phone from beneath her ass and glances across with glossy pursed lips. "How does that feel, Miller?"

"You're trying to intimidate me with the commitment thing, when really," I loop my hand around the back of her neck and pull her in till our lips clash, "it turns me on. Hi." I kiss her again, and smile when she softens. "You look beautiful."

"Hi." She loses her icy demeanor and cups the back of my head to keep me close. "You're radiating good vibes. What happened?"

"You feel that?" One last kiss, then I release her and wait as she reaches for her seatbelt. "You can *feel* my mood?"

"I've felt it since the day I ran into you. Good day?"

"The *best* day." As soon as I hear the click of her seatbelt, I drive away from the curb and cast sneaking glances to her bare thighs. "Though I note you're wearing shorts and not a dress." I bite my bottom lip and lift my eyes till they meet hers. "How'm I supposed to fuck you with those on?"

"With a little finesse," she answers dryly. "And probably a bed, privacy, and a touch of romance. Is that so much to ask?"

"Tall order, considering I feel like fucking you in public today."

Happy on life, as her brows rise in question, I settle back to drive and drop my hand in her lap. "I got my next fight." I peek across to see her reaction. "A real fight, in a real stadium, with an actual payout whether I win or lose."

"Really?" Her spine shoots straight and she twists my way. "When?"

"In a little over a week."

"A week!" she explodes. "But that's... a week away! You can't fight in a week."

"I can. And I will. Aiden teed it up for me this morning. Apparently, the dude is a little heavier than I am, so I have room to eat this week. I'll train every day leading up, eight hours a pop. Day before the fight is rest day. Then day of the fight, we head into the city and take what's ours."

"You got a big fight," she breathes.

With a fun shimmer in her eyes, she studies the side of my face while I drive us toward a fast-food restaurant. She needs something in her belly, and then I want to take her someplace nice. Secluded. Quiet.

"I'm giddy for you, Cole." Exhaling, she sits back as her chest deflates. "I am, I promise."

"But?" I squeeze her thigh and pull her attention. "There's a 'but' attached to your sentence."

"But I feel like I'm going to puke. You're going to fight! What if you lose? What if he hurts you? What if you get hurt so badly, you can't train anymore?" Reaching up with shaking hands, she shoves hair off her face. "Will it be televised? Who will be there? Oh god," she groans. "I'm so freakin' nervous, and it's not even me fighting."

"If I lose, I shake it off and try again next time. But I won't lose."

I pull into a drive-thru and order enough to keep us content all the way into tomorrow. Then I look to Maya as the workers compile our meal. "You don't lose when you're trained by a Roller. Because no one works as hard as they do. No one trains the way they do. And they won't ever entertain a fight unless they know we've got it. Thank you."

When the girl on my left passes a paper bag through the window, I carefully hand it to Maya and watch as she settles it on the floor between her feet.

"I'm not gonna lose," I reiterate and pass her the drinks. "I won't be hurt, either. Bruises, sure. But that's it."

Pulling away from the window and back onto the street, I head toward Lookout Hill. They say it's where all the lovers go. Where the true, forever couples spend time. It's a place of magic, and hell, I can get on board with that.

"It's going to be livestreamed on the internet," I tell her, "I think. But not televised. There's not enough interest for that yet, but since I'm coming outta Kincaid's gym, fight fans will wanna stream it."

"So I can watch it on my phone?" Her voice trembles with nerves. "I won't miss it?"

"What?" I scoff and start up the winding road toward the hill. "You'll be *with* me, Maya. At the stadium."

"I will?" Nervous, she licks her dry lips. "You want me to come?"

"Of course I do!" I shake my head and reach across to hold her thigh. I need to touch, and she doesn't seem all that mad about it. "We're in this together, right? We're a fuckin' team, so that means where I go, I need you to be there. And wherever you go, I'll be there to have your back. You came to my first, and I won. I need you at my second. This is the most important one yet."

Anxious, I peer across to meet her eyes. "You'll come, right?"

She nods, slow and conscientious. "Yeah. I'll be there. I promise."

"And since we'll be in the city, you should take me home to meet your folks."

I'm joking, but the way she spasms beneath my touch is comical. "Are you insane?" Her voice booms through my car and makes me chuckle. "I'm not going to see them! Jesus, Cole."

"Ashamed to take the street bum home?"

"Projecting," she counters instead. "I'm mostly terrified you'll bolt to the other side of the country after you meet my mom and realize genetics mean I'll be like her when I'm older."

"Genetics is just one part of what makes us *us*." I lift my arm and wrap my palm around her neck.

One-handed, I drive us to the top of the hill and bring us to a stop near the edge so we get a view of the entire town, the small 'high-rise' apartments that top out at five stories, and the lake in the middle of town.

Slipping the car into park and switching the engine off, I turn in my seat and cup her jaw with my now-free hand. "If we let genetics rule us, then chances are, I'm gonna be a deadbeat dad with a hundred baby mommas and none that actually speak to me." Pulling her closer, careful of the drinks in her lap, I pucker my lips and wait until they touch down on hers. "I refuse to pigeonhole myself into that kinda bullshit future. That means I won't pigeonhole you either."

"Cole—"

"So if your mom's a total bitch, I'll infuriate her when she doesn't get a rise out of me. If your dad's a dick, I'll slap your ass when he's watching and let him know I'm your daddy now."

"Oh my god." She shoves me back and smacks her fist to my bouncing chest. "Why do you insist on ruining every moment?"

"Because you're so easy," I snigger.

Pulling her in again, I press a kiss to her cheek and steal a Coke from the tray in her lap. "Today was a good day, Maya." Then I sit back and look out at the city. "It was a really good fuckin' day. And my good days only started coming after I arrived in this town."

"You mean after you met me?" Sly, she glances across and grins. "That's correlation, no?"

"Technically, after I met Evie, the teenager with a big mouth. But yes."

I grab her hands when she winds up for another shot. "You too," I laugh. "I swear, baby. My good shit just kept growing after I met you."

I pull her hand across and kiss her knuckles. "One good thing led to another, then another, then another. And now here we are," I look out at the town that changed my life. "On the cusp of something that could be everything." Then I look across at her. "With you. I never believed in good luck before. But now…"

"That's called karma," she inserts with a soft smile. "You deserve good things, Cole. It just so happens your good things also get to be my good things."

"I did bad things," I tell her seriously. "I racked up a helluva lot of bad karma, so that probably means the shoe's gonna drop soon."

Curious, she frowns. "What?"

"This is probably all a lie." Relaxed, I rest my head back against the seat and turn her way with a smile. "I get good things now, to get a taste of what it could be like. Soon, though, it'll all be taken away, so the absence hurts even more." I flash a playful grin. "It's my lot in life."

"You're doomsdaying."

"I'm enjoying the moment," I counter. "Because tomorrow's never guaranteed. My moment, right now, has you in it, so I'm happy to stay here and chill the fuck out for a while."

Maya sets her soda in the cup tray in the middle console, then she unsnaps her belt and turns to shove her door open.

"Hey?" I push up straight and lean across the passenger seat as she escapes the car and leaves me with just a glimpse of her denim-clad ass. "Where the hell are you going?"

"To live in the moment."

She slams her door closed and dashes to the front of the Mustang.

Nerves swim in my belly because she's so close to the edge of a three-hundred-foot drop, but she doesn't linger, even with the sun going down behind her and the rays flickering through her beautiful, long locks.

Coming to my door and opening it with a seductive smile, she bends to take my soda. Her move surprises me—but not nearly as much as when she breaks *all* sorts of car rules and sets the cup on the roof.

If that was Preston corroding rings into my paint, I'd tear him apart and piss on his ashes. But with Maya... I can't find it in my heart to care.

When she offers her hand, and gently tugs when we connect, I unsnap my belt and climb out till I'm standing tall over her. Until our chests touch and my hands go to her hips.

She reaches back and takes her phone from her pocket, though already, we sway. While I hold her close and her tongue comes out to line her bottom lip, she scrolls and selects a song that settles deep in my heart. Then she drops the device beside the Coke—another rule broken, another chance for me to forgive the woman I'll someday marry—and brings her arms up to wrap them around my shoulders.

Finally, she sets her cheek on my chest and exhales. "Did you know Britt and Jack come up here every time they want to fall in love?"

We sway. We dance. Our hearts sync to beat together, and my future spreads out ahead of me.

I'll always hold Maya.

I'll always love her.

And when this *moment* is over, I'll create another just as safe and perfect to keep her in.

"She told me one day at school," Maya continues. "This is where they come when real life is hurting, when the gym is demanding, and being a mom has left her exhausted."

"I heard similar."

I take her hand in mine and place the other on the small of her back. Then I widen our steps so we dance further away from the car. So we stand at the top of Lookout Hill and own this beautiful new life we've been given.

"That's why I brought you up here tonight." I press a kiss to her temple. "The guys at the gym mentioned the lookout is where the real ballers take a woman to woo her."

Maya snickers. "Am I not already appropriately wooed?"

"Dunno." I bring my fingers to the bottom of her chin and pull her face up. "Can you tell me you love me yet without breaking out in a sweat?"

A furious blush warms her cheeks. Still, she says what I need to hear. "I love you, Cole Miller. And I'm so ridiculously excited for what our lives are gonna look like a year from now."

"A year?" I question. "Do we have an expiration date?"

She shakes her head. "Then I want to know what it looks like in five years. And again in ten."

"Twenty-five," I whisper and pull her in tighter. "Fifty."

"Then eighty," she sighs. "Maybe a hundred, if we're really lucky."

"I love you." I hold her face and pull her to the tips of her toes, just so I can taste. So I can have all of her, and she can know I'm never letting go. "Marry me someday."

Her body stiffens. But I knew it would, so I keep holding.

"Not now," I explain. "Not even this year. But someday." I drag my teeth along her bottom lip and swallow down her throaty sigh. "Let's make a promise to someday make a promise. When we're settled, and my karma levels out, and I'm not afraid anymore. When you've reached your career goals, and your independent '*I'm gonna live on my own like a cute badass*' stage has passed and you're willing to invite someone in. Let's make a vow that, wherever we go, and whatever decisions we make, it all leads toward *us*. Whatever that looks like, and whenever we get there."

"You just jump in with both feet." Two deep lines form between her brows and prove how stressed my words make her. "You go from zero to one-hundred in the blink of an eye, Cole, and I'm always left reeling."

"But I'll always be going a hundred miles an hour toward you." I pull her up again and study the wrinkle between her eyes. "Always. So I'm just hoping you'll do the same. You can move at five miles an hour, and I'll enjoy the ride. But I want you to be driving toward me."

"I only see you." Her eyes flicker between mine. "Everywhere I look, every time I dream, you're right there." Pausing, her lips slide up into a smile. "I don't know how to drive anywhere but toward you, Cole."

"Then I guess we're good." I lean in and kiss her, dragging her tongue closer as she opens up and welcomes me in. I swallow down her moan, and smirk when her nails dig into the back of my neck. "I'm so glad you stumbled into my life."

She pulls away, only to rest her cheek on my chest. "It's been a wild ride."

"Worth it?" I slide my fingers through her hair and pull long strands away from her face. "Do you wish you stayed clear of Club 188 that night I turned up?"

She considers long enough to make my heart pound faster. Long enough to make my stomach dip with nerves. But eventually, she shakes her head. "No. I'm glad for every step we took." Then she pulls back and catches my eyes. "Except the bit in the old warehouse where you dismissed me."

I groan.

"That sucked pretty bad," she continues. "Hurt my feelings."

"I'm sorry." I pull her bottom lip between my teeth and hope that someday, I can replace memories of that night with others that are much, much better. "I was in my head and stressing about other things, and you caught the blowback."

"Well..." The song changes and grows a little faster. A little more fun. Though, our slow steps remain exactly as they are. "Good reason to stay in the moment, I suppose." Reaching up, she circles her arms around my neck and holds on tight enough to signal she wants me to lift.

So I straighten my back and wrap my hands under her ass, and when her legs come around my hips, I growl because she's hot as Hades and pressed to my cock.

"Ever wanted to have sex on Lookout Hill?" Biting my bottom lip, she smirks when a long hiss works its way up my throat. "Ever wanted to have sex, *in your car*, on Lookout Hill?"

"Very specific parameters," I tease.

Turning, I press her to the side of the Mustang so her spine arches with the shape of the steel, then I dive in and bury my lips against the warm skin behind her ear.

"I've never had sex in my car. Ever. And I've only looked at you since I got to this town. So no." I bite down until she whimpers, and grind my cock against her core when her legs tighten. "But I'm here for it."

I nibble on the shell of her ear and love how she pants in mine. How her chest rises and falls, and her hands hold me in a viselike grip. How her legs demand I come closer, and her lips tremble every time she exhales.

"Fuck, I can't get enough of you, Maya. We're not suited for each other, but I can't walk away."

"We're suited," Her nails scratch my scalp, and her throat bobs with nervous breaths. "Screw everyone else and their rules of society. We're suited for as long as you love me and I love you."

"Maya—"

"We're suited for as long as you promise to have my best interests at the forefront of your decisions, and I promise to have yours at the forefront of mine."

"Fuck—"

"We're suited." Using her core muscles and pushing up, she slides her hand beneath my shirt and hums when her skin touches mine. "I love you, Cole."

"I love you too."

Somewhere in the distance, a car engine tickles the edge of my consciousness. But I don't truly hear it. I don't process it. Because I'm dancing with Maya, music plays in the air, and the sun quickly drops behind the horizon. Moonlight makes it so I still see her bewitching eyes, and love makes it so I feel her everywhere.

Her breath in my lungs, and her hair stroking my skin.

Slowly, I lean in again and take her lips with mine. A calm seduction, instead of the fast heat we're so used to. I move my tongue over her bottom lip, and swallow down her exhale when she can't keep it in.

I slip my hand along her thigh, beneath her shorts, so I hold her flesh in my palm. And when she wraps me up tighter, I cast all caution to the wind and soak in what she gives me.

"I wanted to dirty fuck you," I pant when our lips part. "But now I wanna try that finesse thing you were talking about."

She drops her head back, revealing her delicate throat, and laughs. "You're the epitome of delicacy, Cole. I've never met someone so gentle in my life."

"Mmhm." I hold her up with one hand and blindly reach out with the other to make sure my car door remains open. Then I roll her into my arms and pull her away so I can position myself and not smack her head.

Turning, I lower and slide onto the seat so she ends up in my lap. Tight spaces, careful work, but I hit the lever and get my seat back, then I pull my legs in and place my hand on her head to guide her.

"We don't need to have sex here." I bite her bottom lip and draw a long groan from deep in her throat. "But I wanna feel you grind on me for a bit."

She giggles. "Like I said," and still, she slides, "Finesse and delicacy."

"That's what they say." I cup her breast and draw her nipple to a peak, while she rides my lap and makes my cock hard as stone. "I'll make you come with my fingers. Then I'll take you home and let you ride my face."

"God." Arching her back, she presents her chest for my tasting.

The sound of a car engine grows louder, but the music coming from her phone makes it hard for me to care. The warmth of her breath on my brow gives me something else to focus on.

"You like riding my face, Maya?" I bite her nipple through her top, and wind my hand in her hair to give it a small tug. "Such a good girl when we first met. But beneath all that shine..."

"I like to ride your face." Her hips roll faster. Faster. Creating a delicious friction for us both to savor. "Jesus, Cole. I like it when you make me come."

"Happy coincidence."

I release her hair and bring my hand down to the gap between her thighs. The denim is tight, but I have room to explore.

To touch.

To tap her clit and make her cry.

"Cole!" Her body turns taut when I rotate my thumb around the peaked bundle of nerves. "Oh god."

Though she's drunk on desire and rigid from desire, something outside the Mustang draws her attention away from me and out to our surroundings.

I think nothing of it. I keep playing with her pussy and waiting for the inevitable explosion.

Mistake number one.

"Who are—*Agh!*"

Maya screams when a man's hand comes into sight and his fingers grab her by the hair. But this scream isn't the kind I'm used to hearing— it's something else entirely. Like the crack of a whip, that hand yanks her out of my car and throws her to the dirt outside.

That's all the time I allow myself to freeze. All the time my brain takes to process.

I shove out of my seat and spring toward one of the motherfuckers who surround my car. "Hey!"

With my heart in my throat and adrenaline zinging through my veins, I slam my fist to the side of the first guy's chin and send him to sleep with one fast jab. He's six-and-something feet of solid muscle and massive arms, but he drops like a tree in the woods, and hits the ground so a puff of dirt flings up, and rocks hit Maya's bloodied face.

Our eyes meet, hers and mine, as my whole fucking world flashes, and I realize that karma I said was coming has arrived.

A line of blood flows from her nose, and another from the corner of her lip. Her eye is already swelling, and her knees torrent crimson from when she hit the ground. Tears spring and dribble along her cheeks, while fear glistens in her stare when another asshole steps between us.

"Cole—"

"Maya!" I run toward her as soon as he leans in to grab her by the throat, but a fist comes around with a wide swing on my right.

I don't see the body it's attached to. I don't see his face. I just see his knuckles a mere second before they smash against my cheek and send my vision black.

"Cole!"

Maya grunts when her guard sinks a boot into her ribs. She cries out when he winds up and kicks a second time.

"Hey—"

The asshole on my right uses my preoccupation to wrap a meaty arm around my neck and cinch in. He cuts off my air, and my feet keep moving, but my body can't follow.

"Box has a message." The monster with size-fourteen feet slams his boot into Maya's chest, but he turns to me and winks. "He says come back to work. Or else."

"Stop!" I gasp out past the arm strangling me when the guy lifts his foot for another kick. "Fuckin' stop!"

"Can't."

When Maya's stomach rebels and hot vomit races out to splat on the dirt, Box's man crouches just out of range and sniggers. "Weak woman, huh?"

He cups her jaw and drags her face up until their eyes meet.

I want to watch. I want to close my eyes. More than anything else, I want to save the woman I love.

Though my brain stops working and my consciousness trickles away from lack of oxygen, my muscles come with memories of their own, just like the Rollers demanded. I raise my arm and cock my elbow, then I swing it back and knock my captor loose so he stumbles away and slams against the side of the Mustang.

Then I sprint toward Maya, only to skid to a stop when her attacker takes out a gun and presses it between her eyes.

"I wouldn't do that if I were you." His finger teases the trigger, and the end of the barrel warms the center of her forehead.

Tears spill from her eyes, torrenting over her cheeks, but she remains still. Completely and utterly still.

"I don't need to point this at you, Miller." He twists his head and glances at me over his shoulder. "Because I know she's the one you fight for."

Cocking the gun and eliciting a cry of despair from Maya, he turns back and studies her eyes. "Tell your boyfriend to get back to work, Miss Blake. You won't like what happens if he doesn't."

"Please go away," she sobs and sniffles back the line of blood dribbling from her nose. "Go away and never come here again."

"I've passed on my message." Straightening his legs, he lifts his chin and wordlessly commands his men to leave.

They sprint to a truck parked just twenty feet from my car and gun the engine when it starts. Their lights come on, blinding my good eye while the vision in the other remains damn near black. Then the wheels spin in the dirt as the truck rockets forward and stops just two feet from where Maya half-sprawls under the cruel watch of her guard.

"You need to stop worrying about her," the guy bites out. "Stop worrying about that gym. Forget this town even exists." Dropping his gun arm, he makes his way toward the passenger side of the truck and swings in. "Box is expecting your call, bitch."

Once more, the truck's wheels throw up dirt and rocks as they speed away, hitting Maya and creating a cloud of dust almost impossible to see through.

"Maya!" I dive through the mess and cover her, ensuring the brunt of the rocks pelt my back rather than hers. "Baby?"

I gather her in my arms when her stomach rebels and vomit splashes to the dirt. Then springing to my feet, I race toward my car.

My hands shake, and my legs feel like rubber. I want to toss her in. Move fast. Get her help. But I take my time, go carefully so as not to make her injuries worse.

"I'm so sorry." I fumble her seatbelt and struggle to see in the dark. "Baby, I'm so fucking sorry. Eyes open."

I cup her face when she drifts off, and shake her too hard. Too violently. "No sleeping, Maya Elizabeth! You're not allowed to sleep. Fuck," I choke out, "I'm sorry."

"S'okay," she slurs, allowing her eyes to slowly blink closed. But she opens them again before I demand she wake up. "My tummy hurts."

"I'm gonna get you help."

Pushing straight when her seatbelt is secure, I shove the door closed and sprint around to my side. I grab her phone from the roof and toss it into the back, then I slide into the front and start the engine with a roar.

"Maya?" I push the car into reverse and charge away from the edge of the cliff, then I pop it into gear and spin my wheels before we take off like a shot. "Maya Elizabeth?"

I can't look across. I can't speed down this fucking hill and study her too, and expect us both to live. "Talk to me, baby. I need to hear your voice."

"Slow down." Her voice is croaky, and a river of vomit follows to soak all down the front of her outfit.

My wheels skid against tar when we cross over from dirt to road, and streetlights outside illuminate the inside of the car.

That's when I find her vomit is red.

She's bleeding. Inside.

"Fuck." Tears burn my eyes and stop the oxygen in my throat, but I reach across and take her shaking hand while my engine screams too loud. Too conspicuously.

The moment we hit the bottom of the hill, I turn us toward the hospital and gun across town, giving no reaction when telltale red and blue lights pop up in my rearview mirror.

I've raced away from them a thousand times in my life, but this time, I have bigger concerns.

"Cole—"

"One minute. One minute," I chant, and drive twice as fast as the speed limit allows. "Baby, just stay with me for one more minute."

"Hurts," she cries.

Another river of vomit races along her throat so she chokes for breath. "Cole!"

"Half a minute," I cry out. "Just give me half a minute."

I catch sight of the bright lights of the hospital and desperately search for the emergency room driveway.

"Cole..."

"Ambulances!" I see a line of them parked, and arrow my car in their direction, then I fang my way into the driveway and under the massive steel awning that shades emergency arrivals from the weather.

My wheels skid against concrete, and security dash forward like they think they'll stop my car with their bodies alone. I slide to a stop just feet from the doors of the hospital and dive out of my seat without shutting off the engine. Then I duck the guards who want to stop me from doing what I need to do.

"I need doctors!" I sprint to Maya's side and tear the door open so the hinges groan.

On my right, the cops pull up with screeching tires, but I pay them no mind as I gently pull Maya into my arms.

She's covered in blood and bile, her arms too weak to hold onto me. But I push up straight and sidestep the cop I know is Ben's dad.

"I need a doctor." Then I keep going. "Help!" I push through when the glass doors slide open, almost stumbling when a couple of EMTs run toward me with a bed.

"She's vomiting blood," I tell them. "She was kicked in the stomach and ribs several times. Like, three or four times."

Carefully but quickly, I lay her flat and hate how the movement makes her sob.

"Dude kicked her a bunch of times," I repeat as our crowd grows larger. "Maybe she's bleeding internally or something. I don't..." I shake my head and hold her hand when they start wheeling her. "I don't know. He was massive, so he hit with a lot of force."

"Let's hook her up." A nurse joins our fray and pushes a blond EMT to the side. "When was the last time she ate?"

"I don't..." I don't release Maya. I can't. Even with the cops and the doctors and the nurses wanting access, I can't bring myself to peel her fingers away and leave her alone. "She said she was starving. We grabbed drive-thru, but we didn't get to eat it yet."

"Good." The nurse grabs an oxygen mask and slaps it over Maya's mouth. "How many times did she vomit?"

"Um... three?" I swallow down the anxiety in my throat and brush away the cop hands that try to pull me around. "Three times. All in the last five minutes. I don't know about the first time, but the next two had blood in it. And she's sleepy."

"Alright. We're gonna need you to step back now." The nurse—Kari Macchio, according to her nametag—stands over Maya and pulls a penlight from her breast pocket. "Hi there, Maya. You don't know me, but I know you, because my best friend in the whole wide world is Britt." She flickers the pen across one eye. "That means I'm gonna take care of you, okay?" Next eye. "Do you know where you are right now?"

"Hospital," Maya mutters. "H-hospital."

"Good." She puts the pen away and places the earpieces of the stethoscope in her ears, then moves the steel end to Maya's chest. "Do you know what has happened to you? Who hurt you?"

"Guys." Fresh tears spill over to roll along Maya's temples. She turns her head and pins me with a desperate stare. "Cole."

Freezing, Kari slowly looks my way. "Cole hurt you?"

The cop grabs me. He knows me, just like Kari knows Maya, but he chooses safety first and drags me toward the door.

"Take him out so she can talk," Kari instructs. Then she looks back to Maya. "Hey, you're safe, okay? No one will hurt you in here."

"Cole didn't..." Her voice is hoarse and pain-filled, but she shakes her head. "Cole didn't hurt me."

"Come on." The cop pulls me back, gently, like he knows this shit could escalate quickly. "You need to step out."

"I didn't hurt her." I tug my arms forward. "I didn't h—"

"I know you didn't. Kincaid vouches for you, so we're cool." He grabs me again. "But you need to come out and talk to me in the hall."

"Maya—"

"Is in good hands." He claps my arms behind my back and yanks me toward the door. "She needs help, and you're standing in the way."

"I love you, Maya." I fight his hold and stand my ground. "Maya Elizabeth! I love you, baby."

"I love you," she rasps. "Till the zombies take over."

"Babe..." Tears burn my eyes and spill onto my cheeks. "I'm gonna be right back, okay?" My boots squeak against the linoleum floor when the cop pulls me off balance. "I'll be right outside, so if you need me—"

"He needs to go," Kari snaps. Standing over Maya, she draws her eyes back. "We have to go for some scans, okay? We'll get you in for an abdominal x-ray and a CT. You could be bleeding internally, and your ribs might be broken, so we need to find out what's happening inside. Can you trust me to take care of you? Maya?" She snaps her fingers in Maya's face. "This is a small town, and everyone here is family. So I've got you, I promise."

"Come on." The cop drags me into the hall and shoves me against the wall when I turn to go back in.

His push is violent, but it doesn't elicit rage from deep in my heart like I expected. It brings me to tears, and with them comes a sense of defeat in my chest that weighs a ton and promises a lifetime of suffocation.

"It was my fault. The guys... I don't know who they were, but I know who they work for. I can—"

"Come and sit." He takes my arm and steers me toward a row of chairs. "My name's Deputy Franks. You can call me Oz. We've met before, do you remember?"

"No, I—"

"Hey!" He claps my cheek and grabs my chin until our eyes meet. "I'm gonna help get you through this, but I need you to sit before you fall. Your face is all messed up, okay? Whoever got her got you too."

"They shouldn't have touched her." I drop into a chair, thankful Oz led me this way. My legs were giving out no matter what. "I worked for this guy," I confess desperately. "I used to steal cars. You know that." I rat out my life of criminal activity as easily as one turns on a faucet.

Whatever Maya needs.

Whatever gets her help and retribution.

"I was a good driver," I explain, "and Box liked my work. So he's pissed I've left and committed to the gym."

"He wants you to come back?"

"Yes." I accept a cold compress from... somewhere. I don't even know. "He wants me back, and I'm saying no. So he sent a messenger to force my compliance."

"And in doing so, he roughed up our girl." Nodding, he looks across when a second cop walks through the hall.

I don't know where he's been. But he looks down at me now with chief bars on his shirt and a nasty scowl on his face.

"Vic's in trauma two," Oz tells his boss. "Beaten by some thugs and now she's bleeding internally. Kari's got her."

The chief's jaw clenches with rage. With venom. But he doesn't speak.

"So these guys... they got the drop on you?" Oz asks me. "How many of them?"

"Three? Four?" I shrug and realize the guy I knocked out is either still up on the hill, or his boys picked him up and took him with them. I didn't see either way. "I don't know how many, but they made it impossible for me to fight. One grabbed me from behind, while another was beating on Maya. They had guns—" I choke on the memory and hate my weakness. "He pointed a gun at Maya."

"You couldn't fight them with fists, Miller." Oz grabs the back of my hand and pushes up until the cold pack slaps my cheek. "Brawn is fun and all, even brawn trained by a Roller. But you can't stand up to a gun and hope to walk away."

"She wasn't supposed to be in the middle!" I roar. "She should've never crossed paths with these assholes." Pushing up to stand, I breathe through the dizziness and press a hand to Oz's shoulder to move him out of the way. "I'm gonna go to them." I step around him and pass the chief on my way. "I'm gonna take care of this."

"You're not." Jogging so his utility belt clanks with every step, Oz catches up before I leave the hall and swings me back around. "You need to stay here."

"I need to go make this right!"

"And Maya?" he asks coldly. "When she asks for you, do I tell her you left her here alone?"

"Fuck you, cop." I shove his hand off and keep going. "You tell her I went to fix what I broke. I went to avenge the pain they inflicted on her."

"And then Superman goes to jail."

He grabs me again and swings me around until my back hits the wall. Stepping closer, his breath hits my inflamed cheek, and his eyes bore deep into mine.

"I know what it's like to love someone, Miller. And I know the rage you feel when she's been hurt. But you're at a crossroads right now. You leave and go to them, you either come back in cuffs or in a body bag. But if you stay, you can be here to hold Maya when she's wheeled out of testing. You can be with her, and you *don't* lose everything you've worked so hard for."

"So I sit down and let that shit go?" I slam two palms to his chest and push him back. "I just let them hurt her and do nothing about it?"

"You tell me all about them," he snarls. "Give me faces, scars, tattoos, heights, weights, cars, tags, and weapons. Turner and I will find them, I'll lock them up, and then she'll sleep knowing she's safe."

"But—"

"*Beside* you," he growls. "She needs you here, not in a cage. So you need to use your brain. Think about your options, then choose right. If you get it wrong, you lose her, the Rollers, and the chance to fight professionally. You go to jail for a few years, then you come out again with nothing."

"I can't just—"

"Call Reilly." He takes a phone from his pocket and slaps it to my chest. "Call him and ask him to come here."

"Reilly?" My hand spasms as though the phone is made of electricity. "No way. He—"

"Will understand how you're feeling more than you know." He takes back the device and unlocks the screen, then he hits dial and hands it back to me. "Talk to him. Find your family, Miller. Because I promise you, they exist, and they're waiting for you to swallow your pride and ask for help."

"Hello?" Jack's voice echoes through the phone. "Pig? What's up?"

"Talk to him," Oz murmurs. Just like he lifted my hand to bring the ice pack up, he does the same with the phone. "Tell him you need your brother to come stand with you."

"Oz?" Jack's tone turns cutting. "What the fuck is going on?"

"Jack?" My voice breaks on that one word. That single syllable. "It's Cole."

"What's wrong?" He's already moving. Already running, as doors crash closed and feet stomp against hard earth. "Tell me what's wrong and I'll be there."

Maya

Beeps. Beeps. So many beeps, and cords, and bright lights burning my eyes.

The rhythmic sound coming from machines should stress me out, but it brings me calm. It helps me measure time, and slows my heart so I don't get myself worked up while strangers who are not actually strangers work around me.

They talk about CT scans, and fractured ribs.

Fractured?

They hook me up for fluids, but not for blood.

"We're going to roll you up to a room now and get you settled in for rest." Instead of walking beside my bed, the woman with mousy brown hair and a million freckles surrounding beautiful green eyes hops on, sits right next to me, and hitches a ride with a smile.

Her friendliness helps me relax. Her easy nature tells me things aren't as dire as I thought they were.

"You're being placed on the second floor in a trauma room, but you'll get the room to yourself and hopefully a decent night's rest."

"Cole?" my voice is raspy and dry. My throat is painful, so I swallow to lubricate it. "Where's Cole?"

"He's already there." Checking her nails as we roll into an elevator, she smirks when one of the guys pushing my bed winks for her. "We called down just as soon as the paperwork was filed."

Glancing my way, her eyes turn a little more serious. "He's been busy with Chief Turner making a statement, Maya. They're gonna work hard to find the people who hurt you."

"What's the time?" Moving just my head, I search the steel cube in search of a clock. "Time is it?"

"Just shy of midnight," she responds. "Testing takes a minute because we've gotta make sure we don't miss anything. But now you're being admitted to *Hotel de BadFood*, and Cole's been given special permission and an invisibility cloak."

"He can stay the night?" The machines monitoring my heart beep a little faster. Louder. "You won't kick him out?"

"If you *want* him to stay." Her eyes search mine, intense and probing. "If that's what you want, then I'll make it happen. And if you'd rather be alone, I can recite some stuff about hospital policy and get him ou—"

"I want him to stay." My monitors beep. Beep. *Beep!* "Yes please. I want him to stay."

"I think she wants him to stay," the guy at the foot of my bed chuckles. "She's keen, and she's kinder than some."

"Oh please." Kari rolls her eyes when the blond EMT's stare glitters with deviousness. "It's been years. You need to get over it."

Instead, he leans around and looks at me. "She kicked me out the first night we were together. Like, stomped my ass out the door and told me to never come back."

"It's a woman's prerogative to ask for time alone after a life-altering moment," she huffs. Then bringing her gaze back to me, she smiles. "He's sensitive. But your man can stay."

As the doors open on our floor, and the EMT prepares to push my bed, shouting voices in the hall make my stomach twist.

I shove up to sit, making my ribs crunch together and the wires tug my hands, and I gasp from the excruciating pain zinging through my blood. But none of it is as painful as hearing my mother's voice.

"You will remove him from this hospital!" she snarls in a policeman's face. "Have security escort him off the property *this moment!*"

"Lie down." Kari slips off my bed and presses a gentle hand to my shoulder. "Maya?" She stands over me and demands my attention. "You need to lie down."

"I don't want them to fight."

"Security will take care of it." Her feet move quickly, skillfully, considering the way men wheel my bed. "We'll move you in and close the door—"

"You're trash!" Mom shrieks. "Absolute filthy trash! And you think you can be here with my daughter?"

I know she's not talking to the cops now.

"Maya!" Her tone changes, and like a tidal wave, I feel her rush closer.

"Oh my gosh, sweetheart." She crashes to the side of my bed just as we move through the door of my room, and grabbing my hand, she squeezes and holds on hard enough to make it hurt. "Daddy and I are going to take care of this, okay? We'll get you moved first thing in the morning, then we'll have a new police department look into what's happened."

"Mom, I—"

"I don't want you spending any more time with that *person*." She spits out the word so I hear the P clearly enunciated. "If I'd known this is what you were doing here, honey..."

I look backwards, stretching my neck and torso, just in time to see Cole in the hall. Eyes red with worry, and a body slumped with weariness.

"If I'd known this was the source of your newfound loyalty for this crappy little town, I would've—"

"Where's Dad?" I bring my head back down as my bed is set in place and the locking mechanisms are engaged so I don't roll away, then I swing my gaze toward my frenzied mother. "Where is he?"

"He's making calls."

She sneers when Kari comes too close, like the poor nurse is beneath her. Though, Kari takes no offense. With a playful smile and a hip-bump that ends with a pithy '*Excuse me*', she shuffles my mother along and makes room to work.

"He's speaking to the hospital board, sweetheart. And he'll speak to the chief of police next. We'll get to the bottom of this."

Kari makes a silly face only I can see: wrinkled nose, squished-shut eyes. But the second she turns back to my mom, she schools her features. "Excuse me, ma'am. I need you to step out of this room. Visiting hours are long over, and my patient needs to rest."

"Your patient?" she screeches. "Your patient is my *daughter*."

"And your daughter is a grown woman, not a minor child." She moves along my bed, fiddling with my wires, so it looks like she's working, but in reality, she's creating space. "Maya needs rest and a follow-up with our doctors, so if you come back during visiting hours tomorrow, we can discuss what's next."

"I want to be here for the doctor," she growls. "I demand to be present."

"And yet," Kari takes Mom's hand and leads her toward the door, "that's not a demand you can make. I'll have my team escort you down to administration so you can provide insurance details if you have them. If not, that's fine too. Maya can take care of that tomorrow or the next day."

"I'm not leaving!"

"You are," Kari counters easily. "I suggest you go before security makes you do so. Each of my patients has a right to peace and quiet, Mrs. Blake. And right now, you're violating those rights and flirting with legal action. Please go quietly and allow everyone to rest."

"I will no—"

"Mom." I let my head drop to the side and wait for her eyes to come around to me.

For just a moment, relief flares in her stare, like I'm going to ask her to stay. But she's smart enough to know better, and after that moment passes, hope drops away to anger.

"You need to leave," I rasp out. "Go home. I'll call you tomorrow."

"I'm not leaving this town!" She hugs her purse close and stomps like a petulant child. "I'll be back the moment visiting hours begin." Then she spins and points at a shattered Cole. "You! You'll leave too. Visiting hours are over for us *all*."

"Mr. Miller needs to stay." Deputy Franks presses a hand to Cole's chest to keep him in place, then he turns a sugary sweet smile on my mother. "Until we're done collecting statements, he can't leave."

"You'll press charges, I'm certain."

"I'll run my case as I see fit." He lifts his chin toward the end of the hall in a silent, '*off you go.*'

"We'll bring him in just as soon as she leaves," Kari whispers just for me. She comes around to my IV and switches out the bag for another, then sneakily, she winks so her lips curl into a sly grin. "Take a breath and calm down."

"I can't." My heart races, leaving my stomach in painful knots. "She was so mean to him."

"And he feels awful." Fixing my blanket and grabbing a packet of wet wipes, she works the disposable fabric across my chest and neck. "He's going to need you to reinforce that you're okay. He'll need you to be strong, because only the men who are truly caring break apart. And that man," she raises a brow and peeks toward the hall, "he's hanging by his last thread. It's important you stay strong just a little longer."

"I'm okay." Tears back up in my eyes and spill onto my cheeks.

I'm overwhelmed. Emotional. In pain. But worst of all is the devastation I see in Cole's expression.

"Is he in trouble?" I look toward the cops in the hall. And Jack Reilly, who I know doesn't much like Cole. "Is he going to be arrested?"

"Should he be?" She folds her wet wipe to find a fresh side and continues wiping. "Did he do something wrong?"

"No. We were just..." Swallowing down the memory of what happened on the hill, I shake my head. "We were on a date. We were kissing and stuff, and these guys—"

My breath races again, faster, faster, along with my pulse.

Kari presses a calming hand to my shoulder. "If he did nothing wrong, then he won't be in trouble."

"Why's Jack here?"

Casually, she glances over her shoulder and studies the men in the hall. "Because family comes in all shapes and sizes." Coming back to me, she grins. "And of all the people in this town who have a connection with Cole, I imagine Jack's the one who could help best."

Finishing with her wipes, she moves back from my bed and throws the pile into a plastic bag. "He's been here before," she explains. "He's worried himself sick. And in the end," she glances across when Cole stops in the doorway, "he got the girl. Hey there, Mr. Miller."

Tossing the bag of wipes and peeling away her gloves, Kari approaches Cole and stops only when she's entirely crowding his space. "Has anyone looked at your eye yet?" She snags a fresh pair of gloves from the box on the wall, and after pulling them on, she reaches up and pinches his broken skin back together. "You're going to need a couple of stitches."

"I'm fine." He towers over Kari's head and holds me captive under a desperate stare. "Maya?"

"I'm okay." Vision blurry from tears, I extend the one arm that's not tied down, and cry when he circles our nurse and rushes in my direction.

He takes my hand and brings it up to cup his cheek.

"Everything's okay, Cole."

"You got hurt because of me." He's always so strong. So hard. So dark and unbending. But he crumbles tonight, folding his back and lowering his face to rest on my chest. "I'm so sorry, Maya."

"It wasn't your fault." I twine my fingers in his hair and scratch my nails along his scalp. "You didn't do that to me, Cole. They did."

"And they came looking for *me*." Lifting his head, he meets my eyes and shatters my heart with the defeat in his. "They would never have come near you if not for me."

"You can't be responsible for someone else's actions."

Over his shoulders, Kari wanders the room collecting tools and kits before dragging a chair across the floor so the feet *griiiiind* on the linoleum.

"Sit." She grabs Cole's shoulder and yanks him back till he lands with a thud, then she smiles for me and sets a tray on the bed beside my hip. "I'm stitching you up, because I'm still hours from my break, and my husband's looking to score in the supply closet. It's not that I don't wanna," she adds with a smirk, "but I enjoy making him wait. It's a thing we do."

"Who is..." Confused, and somewhat scandalized, Cole peels his eyes from mine and looks to Kari. "Why are you telling us this?"

"Because Maya and me," she tilts her chin my way, "we're friends, and girlfriends talk about that sort of stuff." Pulling on a third fresh pair of gloves and carefully opening the pack on my bed, she reveals a kit for sutures. Needle. Thread. Antiseptic. "Do you want something for numbing? Or should I just start?"

"Just start." Jack wanders into the room with Britt's hand clasped in his left.

Nerves jump in my stomach, and my palms turn sweaty as my colleague gets an eyeful of me laid up in a hospital bed.

Leading her around to my left where there's more room, Jack releases her hand and pulls up a chair to drop into. Then, with a taunting smile, he stares Cole down and pulls Britt gently into his lap. "You get yourself in these situations, Miller, you get the stitches without the numbing cream."

"Shut the fuck up," Cole grumbles, clearly in no mood for teasing. "I didn't get myself into—"

"But you were just crying about how this is all your fault, right? Either it's on you, or it's not. And before you answer," he cuts in with a sly look my way, "it wasn't. You didn't make them come here, and you sure as fuck didn't make them hurt her. You stood in front of a fuckin' gun for her, so stop being a sissy and start figuring out what you'll do to move past this point."

"Starting with putting your face back together," Kari grumbles. Slipping the first suture through Cole's brow, she bites her lips together when he hisses, and takes great pleasure in making a grown man hurt. "Jack, you need to get Britt her own chair."

"Oh, no, I'm—"

"What?" I turn her way and find what I was too preoccupied to see before now: her gritted teeth, and her clenching jaw. Her face, red from exertion, and then her hand, rubbing a stone-hard stomach.

"Oh my gosh!" I push up in bed and gasp when the movement takes my breath away. "You're having your baby!?"

"I'm having contractions." She rolls her eyes and slips onto the chair as Jack climbs off to give her room. "I've done this before. We have time."

"Holy crap!" For the first time in hours, I get to focus on someone else. On something else. "You're having a freakin' baby!"

"No. Not today." Hissing, she casts a look toward Kari. "What's going on inside Maya?"

"I'm just a nurse. I can't—"

"Yeah yeah, we'll act surprised tomorrow when the doctor comes through," she pushes. "Surgery?"

Cole's eyes burn hotter as he swings around to check her expression, which only messes with the stitches she's begun.

Cranky, she grabs his shoulder and pushes him back into place. "No surgery. Fractured ribs. CT came up clear. X-ray shows only those breaks. There are no punctures inside, no free air, no bleeds."

She looks to me. "You're gonna develop a helluva bruise along your ribs over the next week or two, but rest will take care of it. Doctor will prescribe you pain relief before discharge, so you can take the edge off with those. But other than that..." She ties a knot against Cole's face and starts a third suture. "You're gonna be just fine."

"And those guys?" he growls. "What about—"

"We find them." Deputy Franks steps through the doorway, having clearly listened to everything we've said. "We follow the line, up through that guy Box Bannin, we find his stooges, and we put them behind bars. They won't cross these town limits again. Literally," he presses. "We've got security and eyes on every road in, so you don't have to worry. Brittany," he studies her with a questioning brow, "I think you're having a baby, hon. You need to get your ass to Labor and Delivery."

"I'm not having a baby!" Yet, she crushes Jack's hand between her fingers. "We've got hours before I even have to consider it."

"X isn't coping," he laughs. "The chief's walking the halls and taking out anyone who looks at him wrong. So not only will he take care of your problem," he glances my way. "But he'll tear their nails up while he goes. This was a *bad* night for assholes to hurt a woman in his town."

"Though, of course," Kari mumbles, "*no* night is acceptable. Our local police would do the job even if their little sister wasn't in labor."

"I'm not in labor!" Britt grabs the rail of my bed and *heh-heh-heh*s her way through a contraction. "Talk about Cole again. That's way more fun."

"Not your fault." Jack shakes his hand to direct blood back into his fingers. "Which means you don't go looking for them."

"So what the fuck do I do?" he snarls. So much anger. So much fury. "Sit at home and be okay with what they did to her? Let it go?"

"You keep coming to work," he counters. "Every fucking day. You train for your fight, and next week, you win. You win in a really cool way so the bigwigs take notice, then you ride that shit all the way to the top. When you're standing beside me, we'll know you earned it. You can't do any of that if you're locked up behind bars."

"So I just let it go." Enraged, he almost—*almost*—slaps Kari away when she slides another suture through his skin. "Go back to life and pretend it never happened?"

"You take care of me," I rasp out. "You stay with me here until I'm discharged." Tilting my head, I peer at Kari. "Tomorrow?"

She hardly even has to think about it. "Yeah, I think so. He got you good, but you just need rest to get better. No surgery. No meds except pain relief. No infections. You can do all this on your own in the comfort of your home."

Nodding, though it makes my head hurt, I bring my gaze back to Cole. "You stay with me tonight. You help me with discharge tomorrow.

Then that's all your time off. You have to get back to work so you can win next week."

"You'll be off work, right?" He searches my eyes and brushes Kari's hand away, never mind the line of blood dribbling along his brow. "You're not teaching in your condition."

"Charlie's gonna go ballistic," Jack chuckles. "He's gonna rain hell down on this town the second he finds out Miss Blake got beat up."

"So don't tell him." *My sweet Charlie. Such a protective little boy.* "I'll take the week off," I tell Cole. "I'll rest, so you can focus. Do I need to lie down all day," I ask Kari. "Or just rest?"

"Whatever your body asks you to do," she responds. "Walk when you feel like it, sit when you need to. A week on the couch watching trashy TV wouldn't do you any harm."

"What about a week sitting inside a gym?" I look to Jack—Cole's boss, in a way. "Would it be okay if I come down to watch sometimes? Make sure he's focusing on that, and not on the fact he can't see me?"

"Doesn't bother me." He turns to Britt and wraps his arm around her hips to bring her to her feet. "A man knows what he needs to be at his best. So if you want to be there, and if *he* wants you there, then I have no room to say otherwise. Come on, Bambie." He guides her away from her chair, and strengthens his grip when she cries out. "Time to go have a baby."

"Oh lawd." Kari's hands shake with nerves above Cole's brow. "My baby's having a baby tonight."

"I won't." Britt *pants, pants, pants*, but she lets Jack lead her. "These will calm down soon, then we'll come back to see you," she assures me.

"You're gonna be fine." Jack stops behind Cole and presses a hand to his shoulder. Squeezing, he gives his friend that extra minute. "Everything will work out, I promise."

Cole lets his head droop between his shoulders. "Easy for you to say, Jackhammer. Your life is pretty fuckin' rosy."

"It hasn't always been. They had to rush my wife here once too—but her skull was fractured, and her life was at risk." Jack lifts a brow, then his blue eyes scan across and stop on mine. "You're gonna be just fine, Maya. Stay together, spend the night, and heal up. You're welcome at the gym any time."

"Oh god!" Britt cries out on a contraction and almost loses her footing. "I think I'm having a baby."

Laughing, her husband only resumes leading her into the hall. "Ya think? X, it's happening!"

"I'm done here." Kari forces Cole's head back and cleans up around the area she stitched. The lines of blood long ago dried, so she scrubs away the worst of it before peeling off her gloves and placing them on the tray the needles came from. Then she tells him, "Once I walk out of here, I won't be back for a few hours, so if you climb into her bed to hug her to sleep..." she grins. "I won't know about it."

Crossing my room and tossing her trash into the can, she glances my way. "If you need me at any time, for any reason, hit that button beside your bed. If you need to get up to pee, ask for help. Don't be a hero."

"I'll be good." I slide over in my bed and make room for Cole. "I promise."

"Then I guess we're done for now. I'm gonna go find my man. He's waited awhile, and if we don't hurry, he might get called out again, and we'll miss our shot."

"Have fun." I want to snigger, to enjoy this moment and tease. But my ribs ache, and my stomach is too tender to risk it. Simply breathing hurts enough.

"Cole." The moment my room door shuts, I say his name and draw his haunted eyes up to me. "Come up here."

"I'll stay where I am." His voice is hard. His anger, harder. "I don't want to take up your be—"

"Cole," I try again, sharper this time. "I want you to climb into my bed. If you don't, I'll get mad. So stop thinking of it as taking up my space, and start thinking of it as doing as you're damn told."

"Jesus." With a heavy exhalation and a groan of weariness as he pushes up to stand, he toes his boots off and studies my every inch, as though searching for where to place himself. "There's not enough room, Maya."

"We'll make room." I inch to the side and bite down my hiss when my ribs protest. But I stare into his eyes and wait. Wait. Wait. And refuse to give him room to weasel out.

"I'm so tired," I murmur as he goes to work emptying his pockets. His wallet. Keys. Phone. They all go on the table beside my bed, then he climbs up slowly, careful with every move he makes. "I need to sleep, but I feel like my mind won't stop."

"I'll help you." He gingerly moves to his side and turns toward me so his stitches don't touch the pillow, then he so very gently pulls me closer. "Lay your head on my heart," he murmurs. "Listen to it beat."

"Meditation." I place my ear over his pec and relax when the contact alone helps me calm.

My hands still shake, and my jaw still quivers, but being in his arms makes it so I can breathe again.

"I love you, Cole." I drape my arm across his chest and close my eyes. "I don't blame you for what happened."

"*I* blame me." He wraps me up close and kisses the top of my head. "I'll make it better, Maya Elizabeth. I won't let this go."

"But you won't leave me alone, either."

For as long as I remain in this bed, wrapped around this man, he's not out there, hunting down another and doing things that will end with prison bars.

"You're angry," I close my eyes and inhale the scent of Cole. His aftershave. His warm breath. Antiseptic lotions, and the tangy bite of blood in the air. "But of the four billion other women on the planet," I whisper, "I want you to stay with *me*."

"I'm here." He presses a kiss to my hair and exhales, finally, so his body releases an iota of tension. "I'm here with you, Maya Elizabeth. I won't leave. Now go to sleep." He strokes my arm and lulls me into relaxation. "I'll take you home tomorrow, and we'll keep on resting."

"I love you." I smack my lips and slowly drop toward sleep. "Forever."

"I love you too, baby. Goodnight."

Cole

WORD ON THE STREET

My phone trills somewhere around two. Could be three.

The nurse has come and gone a couple of times to check in, but she doesn't speak. She doesn't ask me questions, or scold me for the hate I so clearly wear in my expression.

For every minute I lie here holding Maya in my arms, and for every whimper she makes each time she moves in her sleep, my rage burns hotter.

My need for retribution sizzles. But I can't leave. I can't abandon her tonight and throw away all that she's asked me to hold tight. So I plot. And plan. I imagine what it would be like to end their lives and crush their fucking skulls.

And when the phone refuses to stop, I carefully reach out and grab it before it wakes her.

Checking the screen and finding Preston's name flashing at me, I slide to answer and bring the device to my ear. "Pres."

"What the fuck happened?" he booms.

Too loud. Too much. I quickly work to lower the volume before he wakes Maya.

"Cole!" he tries again. "Word's spreading that Box had you targeted."

"He sent some assholes to deliver a message," I bite out. "They put a fuckin' gun to Maya's head, Pres."

269

"What?"

"A gun! And he kicked the shit out of her till he busted some ribs and landed her in the hospital. She wants me here," I tell him. "But when I get clear—"

"You'll keep your ass there." Like everyone else in my life, he stomps out my need, my fucking *desire*, to come for them. "You stay there and take care of our girl. I'll see if I can find out who he sent."

"*My* girl," I rumble. Then, "You figure out who he sent, Pres, then *we'll* take care of it together. Whoever. Wherever. I don't give a fuck if it's fight night and I lose my contract with the Rollers, I'm not lying down on this."

"Yep." Serious, he clicks his tongue, and in my mind, I see him nod. "I've got you, man. I'll find what needs to be found, and then I'll let you know so we can plan it out. I've got that job coming up too."

"You're still doing it?" My heart jumps and threatens to wake Maya. "You'll still work for him after what he did?"

"No." His word comes out on a breathy exhale. "But I don't announce my business before it's time. So I'll act right until I get the information we require, then we'll take the next steps." He pauses for a moment, then asks, "She's okay?"

"She'll live," I grit out. "With broken ribs and a shiner that'll keep her face purple for a few weeks yet." My voice catches as the memory of a gun pressed to her forehead traipses to the forefront of my mind. "She could've been killed."

"But she wasn't," he cuts in. "She's okay, and so are you." He stops for a moment, and rubs a hand across his unshaven jaw. "I heard they popped you."

"What?"

"Dead," he snarls. "That's the word rolling along the airwaves. So you can understand my need to call you at three in the fucking morning to make sure you're okay."

"I appreciate you." I close my eyes and hold Maya tighter when she whimpers in her sleep. "I do, Pres. I know I left, and I know you didn't want me to. But brothers for life, okay? No matter what."

"No matter what," he sighs. "No limits to the things we'd do to protect each other."

"None. You let me know what you hear, then we'll make a plan to put it right."

"You got a deal."

An engine starts on his end of the call. A loud rumbling, and then music pipes through the radio.

"When is she being discharged? Can I come see her?"

Before I can answer, he adds, "I'm kind of in love with her, Miller. She's the hottest kindergarten teacher I've ever met, and she cheated when we were playing cards the other night. I saw her."

A soft chuckle rolls through my chest, though I tamp it down so I don't wake her. "I'm kinda in love with her too. She's like a little mushroom growing in the forest. I didn't plant her there, and I didn't intend to stay and watch her grow. But fuck if I can walk away now."

"Put that in your vows," he laughs. "The little mushroom you fell in love with. It works, in a creepy, weird-dude kinda way."

"Shut the fuck up." I roll my eyes and catch sight of the machines monitoring her pulse. Slow. Steady. Consistent. *Alive.* "When are you coming to visit?"

"As soon as I can." The sound of our call changes as he hooks his phone up to the stereo and my voice comes through car speakers. "Maybe tomorrow. Next day at the latest. I'll stay in Box's good books till we get what we need, then I'm out. Maybe I could do with a move too. Ya know, get away from the city, meet some new people. Find me a cute school-teacher to bang. Maya have a sister?"

"No. And probably don't steal anyone's cars while you're here, either. They take that shit personally."

"Noted," he snorts. "I'm heading somewhere now, so I'm gonna hang up. But I'll look for your guys, okay?"

"Yeah." My smile drops away. "Okay."

"You give a statement to the cops?" he asks. "They got a profile?"

"Yep. I gave them everything. They said they'll take care of it."

"We'll make it a competition, then. I'll pull the statement from their system and get the details, then I'll race them to the finish line and see who gets there first."

"But you won't make a move till you call me, right?"

"Right." He turns a corner, then the sound of his indicator flicks off. "I've got you, Miller. I promise."

"Alright. I love you, Pres. I'll see you when I see you."

"Take care of her," he adds softly. "I'll be in contact."

～

I can't be entirely sure I sleep.

I'll never truly know if I rested, or simply... zenned out. But morning comes, and Maya remains dozing in my arms. Her machines still beep; a sanity-saver for me, since I don't have to worry that she's slipped into some crazy coma.

The nurse comes and goes hourly, replacing bags of fluid and checking my forehead, though I'm not really her patient. The police wander in and out. They hang in the hall, and as the hours drag on, their numbers grow. But they don't watch me like they want to punish me. Mostly, I think, they just want to see Maya.

They want to know she's being taken care of.

No Reilly baby announcements ring out through the corridors, though I'm not sure they would. That's not our baby, not our family, and they probably figure we have enough on our minds. But while I stare at bland walls, I think of the tiny woman married to Jack 'The Jackhammer' Reilly, and sympathize with her for the things happening to her body overnight.

She'll likely be mad for the next little while, but she has every right.

The doctors start their rounds when the clock hits eight. A whole crew of them chatter in the halls, and as the time trudges on, Maya starts to stir.

She looks worse today than she did last night.

"Hey." I keep my voice low, my hands and body still, so I don't startle her as she comes out of her slumber. "Don't freak, okay? Don't sit up too quickly."

"It's okay." She slurs her words and smacks her lips in her half-awake daze. "I know where I am."

"Are you afraid?" I bring my hand closer and stroke her cheek. The nurse cleaned her up, but bloodstains remain to make my heart ache. "Do you need anything?"

She considers for a long beat, before finally settling on, "Water?"

"Of course."

I twist my torso, careful not to nudge her, and snag the cup of water Kari set down hours ago. Bringing it around and placing the straw between Maya's lips, I slip my other hand beneath her head and slowly push her higher.

"Careful, baby." I study her bruised face as she sips. The massive black eye she never asked for. The smudge on her brow that is shaped horrifyingly like the business end of a gun. "Don't hurt your ribs."

"I'm not as delicate as you think." But she hisses when her stomach contracts and her ribs crunch together. "Shit."

"I said be careful." Done with the water, I set it aside and slowly lower her back down. "How are you feeling?"

"Like someone kicked me in the stomach." Her lips curl into a teasing grin, but her eyes flicker closed as exhaustion beats her at her game. "More than once. Guess that makes me a fighter now too, huh? Do I get to compete next week?"

"No." I rest on my elbow and lean in to press a kiss to her brow, then another to her temple. "But you're a fighter, Maya Elizabeth. I always knew you were." With my free hand, I reach up and brush matted strands of hair from her cheek. "What a date, huh?" I want to cry. I want to break. But she's intent on smiling, and I refuse to take that away from her. "Not really what I had planned."

"I liked the bit where I was on your lap inside the car." Her voice grows rougher with every word. Licking her lips, she forces her eyes open. "I liked that."

"You didn't get to eat your nuggets."

She chokes out a laugh, but that turns to a gut-wrenching gasp as she clutches her ribs. "Ouch. Shit." Her eyes glitter with emotion, and a sob escapes her throat. "No laughing, Cole. Hurts."

"I'm so sorry this happened." Tears sit in my lashes and make my eyes itch. But I turn my face and use the pillow to wipe them away. Maya doesn't get to see them; I refuse to saddle her with worry about me. "I'm so sorry, baby. It was never—"

"Was the baby born?" She breathes through the pain radiating through her body and reaches up to comb her nails through my hair. Because she loves me. Because she knows I need the comfort, especially in the moments I won't allow myself to ask for it. "Is Britt okay?"

"I don't know." I lower my head to the pillow and close my eyes. "I haven't heard yet."

"She might still be going." She draws patterns against my scalp and lulls me into a sense of relaxation I haven't felt in twelve hours. "Sometimes these things take a while."

"Oh, you're awake!" Kari's chirpy voice echoes from the doorway at my back.

I don't turn over to look. I don't move a single muscle. But I feel her come closer.

"You're looking pretty good, Maya." Then she lowers her voice. "Is he asleep?"

"No. But he's tired. Did Britt have her baby?"

"She did!"

I open my eyes and watch the sweet nurse read reports coming from Maya's machines.

"She had another little boy, at two-thirty-five this morning. Mom and baby are thriving. Dad's breathing into a paper bag. Uncle Alex is happy again and back to work. And you..." She presses her fingers to my brow, eliciting an electric sting when she touches my stitches, "seem to be healing up just fine." Releasing me, she pulls back and smiles for Maya. "How do you feel?"

"Decent." She shrugs, but stops again when it hurts. "I haven't peed yet, and I'm getting a little desperate."

Kari sniggers. "We'll get you up in a second so you can do that. How's your head?" Making polite conversation, she checks Maya's eyes with a penlight, then adds more notes to her wad of reports. "Are you in pain?"

"A little headache," she rasps. "Nothing crazy." Then reaching up, she touches her bruised cheek. "My skin feels really tight."

"You're swelling, honey. It's gonna get worse before it gets better. How's your stomach? Do you feel sick?"

"Sore." Bringing her hand down again, she rests her palm on her hip. "But not sick. Can I get up on my own?"

"Wait," nerves rocket through my veins as I shoot up in bed. "What?"

"You can try." Kari starts unplugging Maya and setting things aside. She drops the rails on the bed, and pushes blankets down.

She doesn't give me time to think. No time to react. She simply leaves me flailing like a fish on the dock.

"You might feel dizzy," she coaches, dragging the IV line around so it doesn't get caught as they move. "Your legs might feel wobbly, so I need you to listen to your body and let me know if things start shaking."

"I'll be careful."

With a hiss of pain, Maya allows Kari to pull her up to sit.

"Just... wait. Fuck!" I drop over my side of the bed and slam to my feet hard enough to send pain ricocheting along my legs. But then I'm moving, my head swimming as I dash around the room. "Jesus, lady. You're like a bull at a gate with this shit."

"A girl's gotta pee." Kari chuckles. But she's kind enough to step to the left and allow me space to take Maya's arms.

"Two hands on each other at all times. Use him to stay up." Moving toward the bed, she places her hands on Maya's hips and slowly inches her off the edge. "If you start to feel dizzy, just say so. We'll get you into a chair faster than you can say *Britt's vagina exploded last night.*"

"Oh god." Maya laughs again, then whimpers from the pain. "Stop."

"I'm sorry." Kari keeps watch once Maya is on her feet. She checks her eyes, and studies her gait. Then when she's sure neither of us will fall, she nods and turns to grab the IV pole, since she can't disconnect that one. "Slow steps. Shuffle, shuffle, shuffle. Straight into the bathroom, then we turn her around and slowly lower her down."

"Then you leave," Maya says, staring deep into my eyes. "I'm not peeing in front of you yet."

"Aww." Kari shuffles with us. "New love is so cute. Do you fart in front of each other yet?"

"No!" With renewed energy, Maya scowls at her new friend. "Ladies don't fart."

"Okay. If you say so. The doctors will swing by your room soon, by the way. They intend to discharge you this morning, so long as you fart for Cole."

Pursing her lips, Maya twists and burns Kari with a glare. "I know you're joking."

"I totally am," she giggles. "Farting is not a requirement. I just wanted you to do it. Once they've come around and talked to you, we'll discuss how you take care of yourself at home. Then you'll promise to rest, and I'll go on with my life knowing you're safe. Ah, but you," she shoots a pointed look my way, "have a big fight coming up, huh? I heard all about it."

"I might postpone or something."

Positioning Maya in front of the toilet, I place her hands on the wall-mounted rail and drop to my knees to reach under her gown to lower her underwear. Her face burns red and her hands shake, but I long ago stopped giving a fuck.

"I can't train and leave her home alone," I tell Kari.

"I'll come to the gym," Maya pants, the walk from her bed to here exhausting her fragile body. "I already asked Jack, remember?"

"Babe." Staying on my knees, I reach up and take her hands. "You can barely fucking stand. You can't walk on your own. What are you gonna do? Chain yourself to the cage and hope you don't fall?"

"You're being exceptionally dramatic." With a roll of her eyes, she uses my arms for balance and slowly lowers to the toilet, then sighs when she's comfortable and able to pee.

She was full and ready to burst.

Her eyes flutter closed, like this is a holy moment for her, and her hands wrap around mine, like she needs the support. "I'll sit somewhere," she breathes out. "Betcha they have rolling office chairs in there somewhere."

"Or we could get you a wheelchair," Kari suggests. "Super easy to do. You won't want to sit all day, Maya—your ribs won't like it—but you'll get away with it for a while. Long enough to get our fighter in the octagon and training."

"So that's what we'll do."

She finishes, and simply sits as though to catch her breath, but her eyes snap open again when a shouted "*Where is she?*" booms from the hall.

"*I demand to know where she is!*"

"Jesus." On an exhale, Maya's chest caves a little with acceptance and sadness. "My mom's back."

"She has no rights here." Slowly, Kari places her hand under my arm to guide me up as I pull Maya. Then she kneels and pulls up Maya's under-wear. "If you don't want her here, security will escort her out." Finished, she pushes up to stand and steers the IV pole back toward the door. "You just say the word, and I become your bouncer."

"There you are!" Maya's mom storms into the room... and skids to a stop when she finds the three of us squeezing through the bathroom door.

She wears office attire: skirt, suit jacket, briefcase, and a fortune in gold wrapped around her neck and wrists. But when her glacial eyes stop on me, I could swear she vomits a little in her mouth. "Why is *he* still here?"

"Mom." Maya murmurs. "Stop."

"He doesn't need to be here," she growls.

Then she stupidly seals her fate.

Charging forward, she grabs Maya's arm, and in her attempt to take her daughter from me, yanks hard enough to pull her off balance. Maya stumbles forward, crying out from the excruciating pain of her broken ribs grinding together, and I just about lose my shit.

Already, I'm done tolerating her toxicity in Maya's life.

"Fuck off." I swing Maya into my arms, careful not to make her pain worse, then I stride by the woman and feel no remorse when Maya inadvertently kicks the bitch in the face. "You've just assaulted your daughter," I bite out. "She's in pain, she doesn't need you here screeching like a fucking banshee."

"And who are *you*?" The older Blake doesn't back down, not even when Kari slaps a call button and summons security rushing along the hall. "You're... what? A thug? A nobody."

"Mom," Maya whimpers. "Stop."

"She's not a target for you to take advantage of," the woman shrieks. "She's not a bank account for you to run dry. I assure you, her trust funds are tied up so tight, you'll be dead a hundred years before you get a cent."

"Her trust funds are tied up so tight, *she'll* be dead a hundred years before she gets a cent," I retort.

Placing Maya on the center of her bed and pulling her blankets up to cover her legs, I take her hand in mine, but turn to stare her mother down. "She's better off without your controlling bullshit in her life, so if you're here to make noise instead of ask how the fuck she's feeling, then maybe it's best if you let the door smack your ass on the way out."

"Excuse me?" Her voice turns icy cold. Kind of how Maya's does when I annoy her. "I don't know who you think you are, young man, but—"

"You didn't ask last night if she's okay." I shake my head and feel pity for them both. But especially for Maya. To have a mother who doesn't give a shit is worse than having my mother who was simply useless. "You haven't asked this morning either. You're more interested in making this about you. So if that's how it's gonna be, I suggest you see yourself out. Maya needs to rest, not host you and make sure you're receiving adequate attention."

"Let's go, ma'am." A security guard places his hand on Mrs. Blake's arm. "Time to leave."

"I will not leave!" She twists her torso, as though to shake herself free of his hold. "I refuse."

"If you bring Grammy's diaries," Maya murmurs, "this afternoon, I'll let you in to visit."

"Extortion?" Mrs. Blake blusters. "Seriously, Maya?"

"A request," she counters softly. "They're my diaries, Mom. And I'd like to read them today, since Grammy is who I would always go to when I was hurt."

"We'll discuss them another time." Throwing her shoulders back, prideful, she fights the guard who gently tugs her toward the door.

Behind her, a second guard steps in. Then a third.

"I'm keeping them safe for you, Maya. And until I'm satisfied that you're making responsible choices with your life, I can't in good conscience hand over that sentimental piece of my mother."

"So, control." Resigned, Maya casts her eyes toward the ceiling. "Nothing has changed."

"It would seem a *lot* has changed." The woman looks me dead in the eyes. "The situation has deteriorated greatly."

"It's time for you to leave now." Kari gestures for security to move the woman out of the room. Then when Maya's mother is gone, she comes closer and pulls her patient's tear-filled gaze. "You have balls of steel, baby girl. Moms are hard to stand up to."

"I have to, she's holding my grandmother's diaries hostage." The last word comes out on a defeated sob. "And she'll look for any reason to keep them from me."

With a soft hum in the back of her throat, Kari turns to reconnect the machines she unplugged before we went into the bathroom. "You should just go there and steal them."

I choke out a laugh and brush hair off Maya's forehead. "That's what I said, but she's got this moral code. Something about *karma* and being a goody-two-shoes."

"Shut up." Groaning, Maya reaches up and takes my hand from her forehead. But she links our fingers together and brings them to her lips. "I'm ready to go home," she rasps. "I'm done with this place."

"And that's my cue." Winking, Kari sets aside her chart and starts into the hall. "I'll get you outta here in time for Cole to cook you breakfast."

Maya

A LITTLE DISCOMFORT

Broken bones, like, right up in my abdomen, feel like a constant cramp that takes my breath away. Every time I move, it's as though they crunch together and chip a little more from what remains of me. Every time I yawn, it's like I'm inhaling fire, and every time I stretch...

Well... I try not to stretch.

But I get out of bed every day. I make damn sure I'm up and dressed and putting on a show that ensures Cole arrives at the gym without worrying about me. Because if I don't, he won't go. And if he doesn't go, he'll lose the one dream he's ever allowed himself to hope for.

"You look great. Stop poking at your face."

Preston walks beside me on the way into the stadium that Cole competes in tonight. He didn't steal that fancy '69 Corvette. He didn't go back to work for that repulsive man named Box. But even jobless, he's been noticeably absent from our lives all week.

Busy, he said. *Working.*

But tonight, fight night, he stands by my side and pretends not to notice how slowly I have to walk, or how desperately I fight for air as we make our way from the car into the venue.

"I have a massive bruise along the side of my face," I finally grumble in response.

This isn't like those fights Jack competes in. There are no cameras, no

EMILIA FINN

media, no paparazzi waiting to snap up something to sell to the news stations—which is a blessing for now, really. It means I can shuffle my way inside while I study my face in the camera of my phone.

"It's gone mustard yellow," I complain. "I look like I have gangrene or something."

"Literally not accurate." He loops an arm around mine and holds me closer so I can remain standing. "Cute dress by the way." Leaning back, he whistles obnoxiously. "Your ass looks fantastic."

"Thanks." I lock my phone screen and swallow down the nerves that make me want to puke. *We're approaching a frickin' stadium, and soon, Cole will be fighting for money. His dream!* "Now go tell your best friend you're checking out my ass."

Laughing, Preston only shakes his head. "He knows, babe. He absolutely knows. Have you heard from your parents this week? Or have they finally stopped bitching?"

"I hear from them daily. Hourly," I amend with a scoff. "They won't take a hint. However," I allow my voice to turn cheerful, "they don't knock on my door anymore. I'm pretty sure Cole scares them." I shrug.

"Cole scares a lot of people, cutie. It's his superpower."

He pulls me just a little closer as we step through the doors and find a crowd thick enough to make sweat bead on my forehead.

It could almost look intimate, the way he holds me, but it *feels* brotherly. Maybe he checks out my ass, and maybe he flirts and asks me out, but I got a brother the moment I met this man. A protector. A gentleman beneath the crass, and a guide when Cole can't be with me.

Like tonight.

Fight night.

"Geez." I press my free hand to my stomach and allow Preston to lead me through the crowd. "Do you think he's freaking out? Because I am."

"If he is, it's only because he's waiting for you to arrive." He wraps his arm across my shoulders and steers me through a group that take a minute too long to move.

They're caught up in their own business, excited to watch a fight and showing off to impress each other. So when Preston slams his boot to the back of a guy's legs and buckles his stance, he only grins and steers me around.

"He'll be fine the second he sees you."

282

"Have you heard anything about the guys who…" Nerves settle in my throat. "Ya know. The ones who hurt us? Cole doesn't tell me the details unless—"

"No one's snitching, and no one is giving us a name for the assholes on the hill that night. But Box is being watched."

He brings me past the octagon in the middle of the room, past a fight already underway, then into a hall filled with more people.

"They've got names on lockdown," he continues, "so until someone says something, I have no way of finding them. But I've got you."

He takes a turn into a new hall, like he somehow knows his way around, and passes a room overflowing with bodies and loud music.

"Dickheads in there would rather party than prepare," he mutters, shaking his head.

Finally, he brings us to a stop at the next door and looks down at me with a grin. "You ready for this?"

"What? What is…" Anxiety makes my lungs ache and my ribs smart. "Jesus, Pres. Why does this feel like a huge deal?"

"Because our boy gets to live his dreams tonight." Cinching me in tight and pressing a kiss to my temple, he releases me again with a laugh when I shove my elbow into his side.

Finally, he takes the handle and slowly pushes the door wide, revealing Cole on the other side of the room in black and purple shorts with a Rollin On Gym emblem on the thigh.

Pres and I make no noise. We hardly even move. But Cole's eyes zoom across the room and lock onto mine anyway.

"Fuck." Brushing past Aiden Kincaid and steamrolling across the space, Cole stops only when his arms come around my hips and his chest crashes to mine.

He hurts me, but I don't say so. I refuse to complain when I know he'll beat himself up more than his opponent will tonight.

"I've been waiting all day for you, Maya Elizabeth."

"I'm here now." Gingerly, I reach up and twine my arms around his neck. Resting my cheek on his chest and my ear over his heart, I finally catch my breath and release those nerves that wanted to choke me. "Preston wouldn't let us leave too early."

"I told her to rest," Preston grumbles. "Better she chill on the couch than stand in a fucking crowd."

"He made the right call." Pulling back, Cole presses a kiss to my cheek. Then a second to the other, bruised side. He kisses the line between my brows, and all the while, his hot breath bathes my skin. "Fuck, it felt like forever, waiting for you."

"When do you fight?" I don't pull away. I let him hold me up, gladly trading Preston's arms for Cole's. "How long have you got?"

"Probably twenty minutes." Jack hangs out across the room, a savage look in his eyes—a fierceness that comes with competitive fighting. But he stands close to Aiden, cradling a week-old baby in his arms, and smiles when our gazes meet. "Dude's name is Chester Daily. He's a douchebag with small cock syndrome."

"Which is an entirely appropriate sentence to speak in front of your infant," I tease. "Where's Britt?"

"Getting the girls." He flashes a sly grin and peeks to Cole. "Now you gotta get ready, Miller. Give her a kiss, send her out to find the ladies, then get your heart rate up again. I'm gonna be pissed if I worked this hard just for you to pull a hamstring in the first minute."

"I'm gonna hold her for *ten* minutes." He buries his face in the dip of my neck and inhales. Strong hands hold me up, loving palms stroke my back, and heaving breaths move his chest, like pulling me into his lungs somehow helps. "After that," he continues, "I'll walk her to her seat and make sure she's comfortable, *then* I'll get ready. How are you feeling, baby? How was the drive?"

"How are *you* feeling?" I pull back just far enough to see his face. "You're fighting *soon*. This is a big deal."

"It's not that big of a deal. He's just a guy," he rumbles. "He trains. I train. But he doesn't have the Rollers, so..."

"So he's gonna fuckin' lose," Jack inserts. "Because no one trains as hard as we do. But," he comes to stop in our space and smiles down at me when I glance up, "your boy's sixteen minutes out now, and he's gone soft. That's not gonna work for me."

"I said give me te—"

"I'll go." I take a step back, tweaking my ribs when Cole's hands remain fused to my body.

Reaching around and unclasping his fingers, I bring them between us and study the purple wraps covering his knuckles. I didn't even notice them before. "I'm going to go out there and settle in. I want to watch you win, okay?"

"Maya Elizabeth—"

"If you win, you get another contract. If you win," I push on when he reaches out for me, "you get fifteen thousand dollars. You've earned that money, Cole. Don't throw it away now."

"I want you on my corner." He stares deep into my eyes for a long beat, then twisting, he searches for Aiden's gaze. "I want her on my corner. I wanna be able to see her."

My heart thunders in my chest. "You need to focus on your—"

"I'll put her where she needs to be," Aiden assures him. Crossing the room, he nods over my shoulder. "Take her out," he says to Preston. "Keep her on the far side, closest to the exit. That's where Cole will be. The second he walks out, I'll clear a path, and you can bring her over."

"Alright." Preston extends his fist and waits for Cole to bump it. "I'm on duty, bro. I'll take care of her till you're there."

"Come on." I tug Preston backwards, because if I don't, Cole will never let me go. "Let's find our spot. Then you can mean-mug everyone who gets too close."

"My favorite hobby." He winks for his best friend and loops my arm around his. "I'll see you in fifteen minutes, Miller. Impress me."

"I'll impress *her*," he nods toward me. "She's who I'm looking out for."

"Look out for me," Preston counters, "'cuz I might find me a new town to live in. Ya know, since apparently all the cute girls live here."

"You have to go." Jack steps into the space between us and Cole, cutting off my view, and shepherds us toward the door. "Loverboy's gonna be fine. I had to fight for the world fucking title without Bambie there to support me. He's gonna survive."

"Maybe it's because she didn't like you very much," Preston taunts. Then peering around as though in search, he lifts a brow in question. "This Bambie cute?"

Aiden sprints between men and shoves Preston out the door. "Time to go, stupid."

He's gentler with me, but still pointed. "I'll come find you soon. He really needs you to go, though. He's running out of time."

"I'm going."

Stepping into the hall, I glance back in time to catch Cole's desperate stare. His pleading eyes. And then nothing, as Aiden closes the door and locks me out.

"Shit," I exhale until my ribs scream. "I'm so freakin' nervous."

"He's a scrapper." Preston takes my arm and leads me along the hall. "I haven't seen him lose a damn fight yet. It's gonna be okay."

He's gentle with me as we walk. Slow, because he knows I need it. But he does a good impression of a bobble-headed toy every time a female wanders by.

"Don't look at her," I murmur when his gaze locks on a beautiful blonde-haired woman.

Just two paces behind her, her man steps up and pulls her into his side. He's blind to Preston, but I see him.

"Her name is Laine," I inform my escort. "She works at my school, and she is absolutely *not* single."

"Shame," he mumbles as we continue on. "She's cute."

"There's two of them," I offer, since I guess I like to see him play with fire. "Identical twin sisters."

"Oh yeah?" He's like a lighthouse, the way his head spins. "The other one single? Because I'm ready to show her a good time."

"Not according to the rumors I've heard," I snigger.

My laughter turns to pain, but our discussion at least pulls my mind away from the reason we're here.

Cole.

Fighting.

Today.

Holy crap.

"I'm so ready for this day to be over," I groan.

Steering me left, Preston helps me through a gap of spectators. "This is the life you want, princess. And this is a tiny fight. If he's going pro, you better harden up before the media figures out who he is and what you are to him."

The music changes over the loudspeakers. Lights flicker throughout the stadium, and then heavy bass makes the floor thud beneath my feet.

"From the Rollin On Gym," a body-less voice thunders so my nervous system skitters with anxiety. "Trained by Aiden Kincaid, and the current UFC world champion, Jack Reilly—"

"Oh god." My breath races faster. Faster. Dizzyingly fast. "Oh god, it's time."

"Standing at six feet, two inches tall, and two hundred and forty-six pounds." The emcee's deep voice reverberates throughout the room and sends vibrations through the soles of my feet. "Here for his debut professional bout. In Roller purple, may I introduce to you, Cole Miller!"

The crowd roars so their cries turn my hearing tinny.

They don't scream for Cole, I don't think, but rather, for Jack, who comes out of the hall with him.

His baby is gone now, probably wherever Britt is, and he bounces on his toes like this is his fight, while right beside him, Cole trembles with adrenaline.

"Come on." Preston takes my elbow and gently tugs me toward our corner. "He wants you there when he arrives."

"He looks so good." I stare at Cole while Preston leads me. Bruising still marks his face, and his eye is still black. His stitches have come out, but a bandage covers the scar that'll so easily reopen tonight after the first jab. Despite that, Cole looks strong. Muscular and healthy. "He's going to win this, right?"

I stumble on someone's shoes, and hiss from the pain of overcorrecting my stance. "Shit."

"You need to focus on where you're walking." Grabbing me under my arms, Preston stops at one side of the octagon and lifts me to the platform to stand.

Once the fighting is underway, I doubt I'll be able to stand here. But for now, before the whistle rings out and gloves touch, I'm where Cole needs me. I'm exactly where he expects to find me.

Across a packed room and through several thousand bodies, his eyes find mine, and the tension in his jaw melts away to reveal a smile... though it's made silly because of the purple guard in his mouth.

Linking my fingers through the fence, a happy sigh escapes my throat when he makes a beeline through the crowd.

He looks at me. Only me. And though we're already *together*, already saying the L word, his stare has butterflies flapping in my stomach in the most magical way.

Aiden beats Cole to the octagon and opens the gate to allow him entrance, but before Cole can step in, he's stopped by an official who begins patting him down.

I suppose they're looking for weapons. Blades. Something crazy that'll piss me off once I find out what's happened in the past. But the inspection is over in the span of a single beat of my heart, then Cole's permitted inside the cage, and Jack is right on his heels.

Cole doesn't do that thing like on television, where fighters run laps of the cage and *hoorah* about how awesome they are. He comes to me instead.

He places his fingers through the holes of the cage and rests his forehead against mine. "You're gonna have to get down in a minute."

His musky aftershave and natural sweat fill my lungs and bring me *home.*

"Maya Elizabeth?" Placing a gentle finger beneath my chin, he draws my eyes up. "Thank you for being here for me."

"I said I would. Forever." For some insane reason, emotion clogs in my throat and makes my eyes itch. But instead of crying, I snigger. "I'm kinda fond of you."

He chokes out a laugh and presses a kiss to my lips through the chain-link. "I'm pretty fuckin' fond of you, too."

The music changes, letting us know his opponent is on his way, then the emcee's voice echoes ominously through the stadium.

"Standing at six feet, three and a half inches tall, weighing in at a cool two hundred and fifty pounds. With a five-and-oh record and aiming for his sixth victory, Chesterrrrr Daaaaaaaily."

Jack stands behind Cole, guarding him from whoever might think to approach while his back is turned, but that means I don't see Chester's arrival either.

I hear it. I feel it. And when he stops at the octagon and stomps his way in, I feel the vibrations in the floor.

"Hey. Maya." Cole says my name hard enough to bring my eyes back to him. "Focus on me, baby. Look at me."

"Aren't you afraid?" My voice quivers as I catch sight of Chester's back. The dragon tattoo that wraps all the way around, and his hair, short enough that I catch sight of a scar dug along his scalp. "I mean... He's pretty big, Cole."

"Not a great pep talk," Aiden grumbles from beside him. "Rein it in, Maya, or step down so he can focus."

"I-I'm sorry," I stammer. "I don't mean to—"

"This isn't your fight." Again, Cole drags my attention back to him. "It's not your war. In fact," his lips peel up into a beautiful smile. "It's not *anyone's* war. It's a fuckin' sport, babe. Someone wins, the other guy loses. We all go home at the end and plan for the next."

"I know." I shake my head and try to calm my heart. "I'm sorry. I know."

I glance over his shoulder, both to escape his close study and buy myself a moment to work the fear from my eyes, but instead, I'm caught in Chester Daily's nasty sneer. He watches me from his side of the cage and flashes a grin that says he's here to fuck shit up. But it's his eyes, his piercing stare, that makes my stomach drop to the floor.

"Oh god." My hands tremor with a violence I never could have expected. "Oh no."

"Focus on me," Cole gently coaches. "Baby," he reaches through the cage and grabs my chin to bring me back to him. "Eyes on me."

"No, Cole, I—"

"You're gonna freak me out too," he laughs. "You need to stop panicking."

"Cole."

My stomach rebels as Chester wanders closer. Because the face that stares now... matches the face that glared down at me a week ago. The hand that held a gun. And when I glance downward, the feet that broke my ribs and stole the oxygen from lungs.

"Cole!" I cry out. "Turn!"

"What?" He spins on his feet, confused at first, then incensed when their eyes meet. "*You!*"

"Jack!" I scream to get his attention. Then I scream some more because of the pain in my ribs and the fear in my heart. "That's him!" Tears stream along my cheeks. "That's the guy."

"Oh shit!"

Like in slow motion, he looks to Cole. But Cole breaks away from where he stands, drops his shoulders, and sprints toward Chester so they clash with the boom of a freight train hitting a brick wall.

"Miller!" Jack bolts toward the brawling duo.

"What the fuck?" Preston grabs me off the platform as the crowd swarms closer.

Like a tidal wave pulsing. Like a storm breaking open and destroying all it touches.

He holds me with an arm around my stomach, which sends icy shards of excruciating pain slicing through my abdomen, but he doesn't seem to care. He moves me away from the mess and tolerates my swinging fists to be set free.

"Let me go!" Tears torrent over my cheeks, but they're born of anger. Of fear. Of lust for violence. "Preston! Let me g—"

"Can't."

He carries me an easy twenty feet from the octagon and sets me on my feet, while everyone else rushes closer to the fighters. Jack wades between the two men, and Aiden does his best to pull them apart, while the referee skips out of the way like a coward.

"My job is to keep you safe," Preston reminds me. "That means we stay here."

"But he's over there!"

In the single second my guard glances back at the cage, taking his attention from me, I lower my shoulders and attempt to flee his grip. But my injured body is too slow, and his hands are much too fast.

"Preston!" I cry out and fight his hold. "He's with that guy who had a gu—"

"But he doesn't have a gun today." He wraps me in a bear hug and accepts my knee to his groin as payment. But he doesn't let me go. He doesn't let me rush away. "He's a competitive fighter. He's here, and he knew damn well who he was coming for today."

"Cole's in danger!" I growl. "How do you not care?"

"Because he's a *better* fighter."

He swings me back when I take an inch he wasn't willing to give. "If the cops found the dude before us, then he would've been dealt with in a wholly unsatisfying way. This way is better. This way, Cole gets to kick his ass."

"Did you know?" I slap his hands and try again to break free. "Did you know he was his opponent?"

"I didn't. *Fuck,*" he grabs me again when I try to run. "Just stop already. You're injured, woman. Jesus."

"*He* hurt me!" I shout. "He hurt Cole!"

"And Cole's about to beat his ass. Give the man a chance."

Officials and a dozen other fighters wade through the mess inside the octagon. With harsh shoves and loud shouts, they work to separate the men and drag them back to their own sides of the cage.

Jack wraps his arm around Cole's throat, angry and somehow sporting a goose egg beneath his left eye that wasn't there just minutes ago. He slams Cole to the fence with enough power to make the entire structure vibrate, but Cole remains infuriated, fighting for his freedom.

"Stop!" Jack practically plasters their chests together and forces his face into Cole's line of sight. "You stop!"

"I'm gonna kill him!" he roars. "I'm gonna fuckin' end him."

"Do it *after* the ref has started the fight. Hey!" He pushes Cole back again. "Do it now, and you're up for assault. Do it in two minutes, and you get fifteen thousand dollars for the pleasure."

"Let me go." I throw Preston's hand away and limp-shuffle my way through the pulsing crowd.

Their elbows hurt me, their bodies crash into mine. But I make a beeline for Cole's back, and cry out for him when I attempt to climb onto my platform and fail.

"Cole!"

He can't hear me.

"He hurt Maya," he snarls at Jack. "He was going to kill her!"

From struggling to flying, I gasp when hands lift me, and I look back to find Preston again.

He shakes his head, exasperated, but he helps me.

"Thank you." Then I spin and smack Cole's shoulder so the fence between us makes my palm sting. "Hey! I'm here."

"She's here." Jack's eyes scour mine while his body keeps Cole pinned. "Look." He speaks in a calming tone. Soothing. De-escalating. "Take a fuckin' breath, then look over your right shoulder."

"Cole!" A sob escapes my throat and leaves me breathless. "Hey?"

Slowly, he works on pulling himself under control and turning just his head my way.

His eyes are wild. Savage in a way I've never seen them. His chest heaves from the oxygen he sucks down, but he searches for me and studies my face when he twists far enough.

"He hurt you." He speaks around his mouth guard so the words are almost a slur. "Maya Elizabeth, I can't—"

"If you don't fight, you'll lose."

Help him compete? Or help him leave?

I don't know which way to go, but I do know he needs me wherever he is.

"If you walk away," I measure my words, "he wins."

"He. Hurt. You."

"So hurt him back." I grip the cage and come in closer to press a kiss to his cheek. "Do it in competition. It means you get to do whatever the hell you want, and not get arrested for it."

He pulls back and burns me with a glare. "This isn't a fucking game to me, Maya. He deserves death. He deserves to go to prison."

"So fight your fight!" I push on. "Make him pay. By the time you're done, the cops will be ready to take him away."

"Maya—"

"It's a double whammy." Slowly, a vicious smile stretches across my cheeks. Moral codes and karma and all that crazy stuff makes way for what is right. For what this man truly deserves. "Smash him up good, Cole. Then send him to jail. It's the best answer."

"And then you get a wad of cash," Jack inserts as the fighters push Chester against the fence on the other side.

Already, he bleeds. His brow dribbles, and his lip is split.

"You want that money, don't you?" Jack grabs Cole's face and drags him back around. "No way you want that asshole to have it."

"We'll use it to set us up," I add. "We can buy you new furniture and get rid of that shitty bed with a bullet hole in it."

Surprised, Jack's eyes swing to mine. "There's a bullet hole in your bed?"

"*His* bed." I push to my toes and bring myself closer to Cole's ear. "Fight, baby. Bring it home. Then *we* get to go home."

"Are you ready, Rollers?" The cowardly referee stands in the middle of the octagon, panting, like he was the one in the middle of an unsanctioned throwdown. "You have thirty seconds before we call it."

"You need to decide," Jack rumbles. "Don't let him take this from you, Miller. You've worked too fucking hard, and she deserves better."

"I don't... I can't—"

"I got to beat on the guy who hurt Britt." Smug, a long grin works across Jack's face until his eyes light with a vehemence that borders on crazy. "I got to be the reason he needed steel plates in his face and dentures in his mouth." He grabs Cole's jaw and drags him around. "He sucks guys off in prison with his gummy smile. He became somebody else's bitch, and I swear to you, man, it helps me sleep at night knowing I got that moment."

He smacks two heavy fists to Cole's chest so everyone inside this stadium can hear the thud. "Now I have babies with her. And a home. A life. I have the most beautiful fucking wife on the planet. But I wouldn't be happy like I am now if I left him to walk free."

"Cole." I stroke his shoulder and ignore the twang of pain in my ribs. "Compete, babe. Then take me home."

"She wants you to fight for her," Jack coaches. "She wants you to prove you've got this."

"Maybe I don't," he growls. "Maybe I won't be able to stop myself." Gulping in air so his chest grows, he shakes his head. "Maybe I'm not as good as you, Reilly. I won't be able to control myself once I start."

"You need to stop trying to be me! Stop comparing. You kept coming for me in the gym, kept stepping up and demanding that tapout. But half the fuckin' reason I gave you such a hard time these past few weeks was because you weren't living for you. You were so focused on proving you could beat me, you forgot to stop and breathe and be *you*."

He claps Cole's cheek, and smiles. "I already exist, Miller. And for the rest of my life, I'll always be the best version of me. Which means you can never be better than second-best. But if you stop for a second and start being the best version of *you*, then you get to be number one."

Glancing over his shoulder, Jack's blue eyes stop on me. "You're number one for her, and she and I both know you can do this. So get in there and kick his fuckin' ass. By the time you're done, we'll have the PD on site, and they'll have cuffs ready to snap around his wrists."

"Ten seconds!" the referee calls. "I'm calling it."

"Go fight for *you*," Jack presses. "Show him who the fuck you are. Maybe then, you'll figure out how to beat me."

"Shit." As though exhausted, Cole drops his head and exhales.

"Five. Four..."

"He's fighting!" Jack turns to the referee and gives him a thumbs-up. "We're competing."

Then he turns back to Cole and swings a fast jab to his jaw, snapping his head around and drawing a shocked gasp from deep in my throat.

"What the—"

"Getting his adrenaline up again." Chuckling, Jack taps Cole's fist and turns on his heels to swagger toward the cage door.

He pauses in front of Chester and winks. "When you wake up again, I have some things to say to you."

"Fuck off," Chester snarls. "Get the fuck out of my cage."

"Mmhm." The Jackhammer puckers his lips and blows an obnoxious air-kiss that has Chester's fury burning hot. Then he exits the cage and wanders around to where I stand, brushing hands off his body as spectators fight to get closer.

"You need to get down, Blake." He grabs me by the hips, careful of my ribs, and sets me on my feet on the floor. "You're in the splash zone," he warns. "I promise there'll be blood spray, so if you wanna get a little space—"

"I'm fine here." Nerves ball in my throat and make it difficult to breathe. But I remain standing. Strong. Capable.

"I want a clean fight," the referee commands. "I want you to defend yourselves at all times. I want you to listen to my instructions."

He rushes between the men again when Chester tries to push forward. "I *will* call this fight if I think you can't listen."

"I'm listening, old man!" He bounces on his toes and smacks his fists together. "I'm waiting to get started."

"Then go back to your corners and await my whistle. Touch gloves if you choose, but you will not begin your fight until I say so."

Smug, Chester extends his hand and waits for Cole. But Cole shakes his head and turns my way.

"Come back, pussy!" Chester laughs, maniacal and horrible, but Cole's eyes are for me.

His wild stare, while the fiery blood rushing through his veins makes his muscles larger. A deep line forms between his brows, and his jaw clenches so hard, he's at risk of breaking his teeth if not for the rubber guard between them.

"Ignore him," Jack says the second Cole's hands wrap around the cage fence. "Loudmouths are often shitty fighters. So let him run his mouth, and you fight your fight."

"I've got this." He slurs around the mouth guard and keeps his eyes on mine. Constant. Heady. Staring. "I love you."

"I love you." Emotion burns the backs of my eyes, but I can't decide if I'm sad, or happy, or something in between. I'm just... *emotional*. "You've got this?"

"Yeah. I promise."

"Turn around, fighter!" the referee watches Cole's back with exasperation in his glare. "We're starting."

"Turn around, babe." I bring my fingers up and press a kiss to the tips. Then I extend my hand and give that kiss to him. "Turn around. Be safe. Then maybe we'll get drive-thru and go home to rest."

"It's a date."

He kisses his fist and offers it back just as the whistle blows for his fight, then he spins at Chester's battle cry. The stomping feet, the charging run.

Readying his feet and squaring his shoulders, Cole cocks his arm back and swings just in time to catch Chester under the jaw. The momentum of his strike lifts the massive man clean off his feet, snapping his neck back with a crunch that makes my stomach twist, then Cole runs forward and slams Chester to the floor so the stadium rumbles beneath my feet.

The crowd roars as both men crash to the canvas and Cole's fists rain down on Chester's face. Then they boo when the referee dives in and tries to separate them.

"Well." Jack brings his hand up and rubs the stubble on his jaw. "That's one way to start your pro career, I guess."

He grabs my arm as the crowd pulses and shoves closer, then he and Preston lead me around the back of the cage while the door opens and the remaining Rollers storm in to stop Cole's one-sided fight.

They drag him off Chester's unconscious form and separate the two before a sanctioned bout turns back into an assault charge.

"Aiden will bring him to the locker room," Jack shouts above the noise. "Bobby will bring Bambie. Then we'll have milkshakes to celebrate." He looks down at me and grins. "It's tradition."

Epilogue

MAYA — 6 MONTHS LATER

"Sweetheart?" Mom pulls me aside in her much-too-expensive kitchen, while in the hall, Daddy leads Cole to the patio 'to talk'.

Everyone knows that's code for grilling a guy. And possible covert—or not—threats. Probably blackmail, too. And if my father is feeling frisky, there's a chance he'll pull out Cole's family history and say some hurtful things about his absent parents.

Despite all that, I still feel Cole gets the better end of this '*come to Maya's parents' house and act nice*' thing we're doing.

"I want you to talk to me, Maya." Mom begins loading the dishwasher after the world's most awkwardly silent meal.

Socialite parents rarely know what to say when their daughter brings home a 'bum' with bruised knuckles and a fresh black eye delivered by none other than the still-reigning world champion three days before.

That's my life now. A ridiculously gooey, constantly happy life.

But to my parents, it's a worst nightmare.

"Mom..." Sitting at the counter and resting my elbows on the stone top, I exhale and prepare for *another* monotonous discussion. "I'm not—"

"I spoke to my colleague, sweetheart. He specializes in domestic violence."

My back snaps ramrod-straight. "Excuse me?"

"He's a shark, honey. The best in his field, and he assures us he can get you out with minimal damage."

"Damage?"

My parents' home is quite warm, but the winter weather is harsh outside, which means I wore long sleeves that go all the way to my wrists. Folding my arms and slipping my hand into the sleeve opposite, I stare deep into my mother's eyes and growl. "Cole doesn't hurt me. He has never, *ever* hurt me."

"He's a violent man," she steamrolls over me. "And when you break up with him, he will react. He will try to restrain you physically, and when that doesn't work, he'll come for your inheritance."

"Oh, for god's sake!" I push up from the counter with shaking hands and a heart galloping from nerves. "I'm done."

Turning away, I leave her standing in place and head toward the living room. "I'm done with this constant argument," I call out. "I'm done with you judging my boyfriend. I'm done with your elitist attitude."

I snatch my coat from the rack and shove my arms in, while on the television, a news reporter speaks of a suspected homicide in the city. Maybe arson. Definite foul play. But no witnesses, no suspects, and no leads.

That kind of news piece in a city this size isn't unheard of. But the name of the victim gives me pause.

"Ethan 'Box' Bannin's remains were found earlier this morning. Police are investigating, but there are rumors he might've died in a warehouse fire that was started remotely."

"Maya!" Mom rushes into the living room, startling me out of my reverie and back into motion. "Honey. Don't you understand the abusive relationship you're in?"

"Actually," I drop one hand in my pocket while I use the other to reach for my purse, "I do, Mom. I know exactly the abusive relationship I'm in."

For just a moment, her face shows relief.

"And that's why I'm ending it." I turn on my heels and start toward the door. "Goodbye, Mom. I won't be calling."

"Maya!" She runs, knock-kneed and in heels, across expensive tile. "Honey!"

I shove through the door and surprise Cole and my father.

"Let's go," I tell Cole, then smile when he shoots to his feet without asking questions. "We're done here. Do you wanna get iced coffee on the way home?"

"Sure."

He moves across the porch in a heavy black coat and thick jeans. Grabbing my hand and pressing an obnoxious kiss to my temple, he skips down the patio steps beside me. "You doing okay, Maya Elizabeth?"

"Roderick!" Distraught, my mom cries out. "Stop them!"

"Don't stop," I murmur so only Cole hears me. With a bounce in my step and a grin I wasn't sure I would wear today, I stroll along my parents' yard and slow only when Cole beeps his car unlocked.

Opening the door and holding my hand, he lowers me in, his smile growing larger as my mother's voice turns louder.

"Roderick! Roderick, stop them!"

Closing my door and fixing my seatbelt, I watch Cole as he moves around the hood of his car. He opens his side and slides into his seat with a smirk. Then he closes the door and starts the engine so the deep rumble makes my stomach tug with happy nerves.

"I tried," I tell him as he pulls away from the curb. I lean across to turn down the stereo, then I twist in my seat and watch his face in profile. "I tried again to talk to her. I tried to make her see reason, but she was so focused on you and her potential loss of control, she didn't hear a word I said."

"I support your choices." Reaching across, he takes my hand and twines our fingers together. "Whatever you choose, whenever you choose it. And even if your choices change over time," he glances my way. "I support you."

"I won't be going back." I hold our hands in my lap and stroke his fingers. "She wants to control me. And I refuse to fold and be their pretty little puppet anymore."

"You won't ever see your inheritance." He pulls the car around a corner and heads away from suburbia. "You won't need it, baby. I'm gonna make sure we're doing just fine. But I want you to know what you're giving up."

"I'm more upset about the diaries," I lament. "But... it is what it is. Karma will take care of it all, and maybe I'll see Grammy again another day."

With my heart in my throat and nerves making my hands shake, I release Cole's for a moment and reach into my loose blouse sleeve to take out a tiny crystal saltshaker. Holding it between my fingers and turning it over so the glittering edges sparkle, I extend my hand and show off my prize. "I stole this."

"What?" A ridiculous bark of laughter escapes Cole's throat as he turns to examine my offering. "You stole?! Maya Elizabeth! Who are you?"

"I was rebelling." Tense laughter rolls along my throat. "She was going on and on and on about how you're a horrible human."

"Maybe I am."

"She was saying how I'm horrible too, because I wouldn't be who she wanted me to be."

He scowls now. "She's wrong, then, because you're definitely not horrible."

"She wouldn't shut the hell up." Nerves and heartache and grief coalesce in my mind until tears prick the backs of my eyes. "It's so stupid," I sniffle. "Because it's just a saltshaker. But she was being so mean. So freakin' judgmental and nasty. She talked and talked and talked just to hear her own voice, and before I knew what I was doing, I was stealing."

"Well..." he sniggers. "It happens. Sometimes, that shit just happens."

"I'm never going to see my Grammy again," I hiccup.

I'm having a mental *situation* in the front seat of my boyfriend's Mustang, but still, he steers us into a fast-food drive-thru.

"Iced coffee," he tells the box with a smile. "Extra-large."

My jaw quivers as reality smacks me. "Grammy intended for me to have those diaries, Cole. They hold *no* financial value. But my mother keeps them to hurt me."

He slowly rolls us toward the first window to pay. "That means she's not a very nice person." He takes out his wallet and taps a card to the machine. "She's just not very pleasant. But she's your mom, Maya. And sometimes we need our moms, even if we don't like them."

"I needed my grandma more. But whatever." Sniffling, I sit taller and push my shoulders back. "It's whatever. I can't fix it, so I live with it, knowing I give up her words and gain peace in exchange."

"That's a steep price to pay." He rolls to the second and final window to wait for my caffeine. "Your grandmother intended those diaries for you."

"Yeah, well..."

Wordlessly, he leans to the left and reaches into his heavy coat. Grunting as he works within the tight confines of his seatbelt and jacket, he yanks a thick book free and sets it on my lap with a wink.

"You don't pay that kind of price for as long as I'm here to save you. Thank you." He reaches out the window and accepts my coffee with a grin, while I look down, my eyes plastered to the diary in my lap.

"Sometimes, a person just steals." Setting the coffee in the center holder, he leans in to press a kiss to my cheek, then laughs when I remain stunned. Staring. "And," he adds arrogantly. "I'm really fucking good at it."

Read Preston's story in REGRET

Also by Emilia Finn

Sinful Promise

Lost Boys

MISTAKE

REGRET

Rollin On Novellas

(Do not read before finishing the Rollin On Series)

Begin Again – A Short Story

Written in the Stars – A Short Story

Full Circle – A Short Story

Worth Fighting For – A Bobby & Kit Novella

www.ingramcontent.com/pod-product-compliance
Lightning Source LLC
Chambersburg PA
CBHW021952010726
47494CB00003B/699